Designer
Genes

Designer Genes

EMMA HANNIGAN

POOLBEG

This novel is entirely a work of fiction. The names,
characters and incidents portrayed in it are the work of the
author's imagination. Any resemblance to actual persons,
living or dead, events or localities is entirely coincidental.

Published 2009
by Poolbeg Press Ltd
123 Grange Hill, Baldoyle
Dublin 13, Ireland
-mail: poolbeg@poolbeg.com
www.poolbeg.com

© EMMA HANNIGAN 2009

Copyright for typesetting, layout, design
© Poolbeg Press Ltd

The moral right of the author has been asserted.

1 3 5 7 9 10 8 6 4 2

A catalogue record for this book is available from the British Library.

ISBN 978 1 84223 369 6

Typeset by Type Design in Bembo 11/15 Goudy
Printed by Litografia Rosés, S.A., Spain

www.poolbeg.com

ABOUT THE AUTHOR

Emma Hannigan lives in Bray, County Wicklow, with her husband Cian and two children Sacha and Kim. She is a self-confessed chocoholic, with a flair and passion for shopping. This is her first novel and, although she has had similar surgery to one of the characters, she'd like to stress that this is most definitely not an autobiography. Apart from the part about the designer jeans, which is alarmingly close to the truth.

ACKNOWLEDGEMENTS

From the moment I knew my book was going to be published, I had a small demon lurking in the back of my mind: the "thank you" page. What if I leave someone out and they're so upset they never speak to me again? So knowing this could cause mortal offence, here I go . . .

Firstly, thank you to Poolbeg, especially Paula Campbell, Kieran Devlin, Niamh Fitzgerald and my wonderful editor Gaye Shortland. You've taken a chance on me and I hope I can make you all glad you did. Thanks to Tony Higgins for the photos and to Aisling Ayre for attempting to make me look decent, with your large black trolley of make-up. Am still wildly impressed and would secretly love to play with it all when you're not looking.

Thank you to Cathy Kelly. Not only are you the most amazing friend, confidante and a light in my life, but you have been the most encouraging, patient and brilliant teacher. Without you, I would never have turned my story into a novel. Thank you also to John Sheehan, for all your kindness and sharp advice.

I have dedicated this book to my husband Cian McGrath, and my parents Denise and Philip Hannigan. Cian, you have stood by me and paid more money in hospital car-park fees, coming to visit me, than a lot of people spend on a mortgage. Most men would have run a mile at this stage. Thank you for staying and for loving me, especially the bald and scarred version of me with a broken nose. Now that's dedication.

Mum and Dad, your steady, balanced and loving upbringing has given me the strength and determination to be the person I am today. I couldn't have been luckier. You can't choose your parents but, if I'd been allowed to, I would have picked you both.

I cannot express my gratitude to my two children, my son Sacha and my daughter Kim. Any time I have one of those can't-do-this-any-more moments, all I have to do is look at both of you. You inspire me, love me, humble me and give me the best reason in the world to keep fighting.

Thank you to my parents-in-law Orlaith and Seán McGrath. You are always there when I need you.

Thanks to Tim, AKA Mr Spring, for being my big brother, and to your partner Hilary. Thanks to my cousins Steffy and Robyn Macken for being my sisters! Thanks to Aideen Shepherd, Mitzi Seavers, Kristin O'Callaghan, Ruth Barker, Cathy Whelan, Anneliese O'Callaghan, Jackie and Neil O'Callaghan. To my cousin Fionn Seavers, I'm still sorry I cut off every strand of your hair when we were three. You are all a wonderful support.

Thanks to my sister-in-law Mary McGrath, my niece Molly O'Bric, and my brother-in-law Eanna McGrath, for your support.

Thanks to Paul Hannigan for always having "magic stars" for the kids! Thank you to our au pair Jana Volckova, for always being here to help out and keep the house going.

This is where it gets messy. I have so many wonderful, caring and awe-inspiring friends, I'm terrified of forgetting someone and leaving them mortally wounded for life. If that's you, I apologise.

My heartfelt gratitude to all the parents and teachers in St Gerard's School, Bray. With you I found an outreach and flurry of love and help which overwhelmed me. There are a few people I have to thank by name: the unpaid entertainers, who collected, fed, watered and played with my children, before driving them back home, at a time when I was on my knees and unable to be "fun mum". In alphabetical order, so don't scratch each other's eyes out (blame your parents for not calling you AA, otherwise you might have been first on the list): Amanda Cahill, Amanda Ferguson, Bernie Kinsella, Claire O'Donovan, Corina Tormey and Brigid Whitehead. All your names feature constantly in my diary, with a note, "Sacha and Kim going to play" beside them. You are all my unsung heroes. Words cannot thank you for all the times you went that extra mile. I will always appreciate you.

Thank you to my beloved Cork crew: Dervilla O'Flynn, Glena O'Reilly, Helen Eck, Nikki Walsh, Rachel Allen and Rowena Walsh.

Gratitude and love to my wonderful network of "girls", for the river of coffee and wine we must have consumed over the years – I can't believe the world still has any problems. Anne Lawlor, Elaine Flynn, Emer Shaw, Eva Durkan, Eve Keogh, Fiona Cullen, Fiona Costigan, Imelda Drumm, Jill Lyons, Josephine Power, Julie Magill, Kathryn Dicker, Marian Corson, Rufina Kissane, Sarah Gleeson, Siobhan Whelan, Suzanne Mackey, Patte O'Reilly and Tarja Owens.

Thank you to all the staff of Tallaght Hospital for getting me through the mastectomy surgery. Thank you most recently to Dr David Fennelly, Dr Francis Stafford, Dr Cal Condon, Dr Jenny Westrup and all the nurses, especially Mechelle, Lisa and all the staff in Blackrock Clinic. Without you all, I wouldn't be alive. No words can thank you all for what you do every single day.

To Regina Quinn, at Cunninghams' pharmacy in Bray: you go above and beyond the call of duty with me and all your customers. Thank you for always ringing to make sure I have my prescriptions. You are a shining star.

I hope that you, dear reader, have not died of boredom. Some people hate this page and skip over it. I, on the other hand, am very nosey and love to see if there's anyone I recognise.

Last, but by no means least, I want to thank anybody who is giving me a chance and buying this book. If one person enjoys reading it as much as I enjoyed writing it – then I'll have achieved something major personally.

I will leave a little space just here:

Just in case I've forgotten someone – yes, I am still paranoid about it – please fill in your name with black biro. Nobody will notice it wasn't there in the first place.

I dedicate this book to my husband Cian for meaning what he said on our wedding day. You have indeed loved me in sickness and in health.

And to my parents Denise and Philip Hannigan, who epitomise the practice of unconditional love.

Not a day goes by that I don't thank my lucky stars I have the three of you in my life.

PROLOGUE

Emily

Nobody likes to say goodbye. Especially when you're a mum saying goodbye to your two small children.

This occasion was no different. I knew I had to hold it together just long enough to make it outside. The lump in my throat felt like a basketball. But in the next five minutes I needed to appear positive, nonchalant and above all else, normal.

It was almost impossible.

My son Louis, daughter Tia, and my mum and dad were all in the sitting room of my parents' house. The fire was lit, the heating was on and the freezing sleet outside was obliterated. Cocooned by both the temperature and love, the children were relaxed. I had to make sure that everything was as run of the mill as possible for a Sunday afternoon. Disney movies, Sunday treats – all the things I normally did with them.

It had been my thirtieth birthday the day before. Under the circumstances, I'd chosen to have a small family party, with cake and plenty of sweets. My head was elsewhere, and if it hadn't been for the children, I would have gladly ignored the day entirely.

"Mum, will you come and sit here with us? A movie is starting and it's going to be great fun," Louis pleaded.

Louis was six, with big blue eyes, blond hair that falls endearingly over his eyes and a smile that cuts through to your heart.

"Please, Mum!" He patted a bit of couch between himself and Tia who was five and straight from Central Casting as a cherub, even if I say so myself.

They knew I was going, but young children forget things.

"Please, Mum?"

The pleading in my son's eyes hurt so much I had to grab hold of the back of a chair and steady myself. I closed my eyes and concentrated on blocking out the overwhelming fear, then swooped down on the couch.

"Big kiss for Mummy!" I launched myself at Louis. *Don't let me cry.*

"One from you too!" I grabbed Tia, fragile in one of her favourite outfits – a pink gaudy fairy dress with hard, itchy netting, purple patterned tights and an old gold-lamé evening top of my mother's, which Tia had sniffed out in a long-forgotten wardrobe upstairs. She had hideous dress sense, which I hoped would improve by the time she reached her teens. I felt winded at the thought of her teenage years: would I be around for them?

On the TV, some poor git was trying to present a report on penguins. His obvious struggle with the live creatures delighted the children and in an instant they were transfixed.

Thank God for the invention of children's programmes. In times of need, they can be a mother's best friend.

"Mum and Dad . . . bye."

Woodenly and hurriedly, I hugged and kissed my parents. We didn't speak. Us adults were trying to hold it all in.

"Bye," muttered Dad. For the first time in his life he looked beaten by a situation. He was always very controlled and upbeat. I could tell this was killing him.

Mum, who was my rock and knew what to say in any situation, was like a robot on automatic pilot. There was nothing she could say at that moment and she just stared at me.

Mum and I look very alike. She has European parentage, is very striking with sallow skin against white-blonde hair, and she seems to get more beautiful as the years go by. By contrast, Dad has dark hair and pale, almost translucent skin. I'm a mixture of the two of them with Mum's blonde hair and my father's milk-bottle complexion. My darling daughter Tia is sallow-skinned while my little Louis is almost blue he's so pale. The baby factory clicked on the skin-tone button and made him a shade lighter than me. His skin is flawless, like a porcelain doll's.

Both kids were engrossed in the television as I took a last look at them. They love their grandparents' house, which meant I was spared the trauma of them not wanting to stay while I walked out. I couldn't have coped with "Mummy, don't go!"

Holding back from running, I left the room.

Robbie was supposed to be waiting for me in the hall but he was busy trying to find the batteries for a radio he thought I might use.

Robbie is my ever-supportive husband. He has naturally spray-on-tan-coloured skin, caramel hair and a contagious smile. He runs his own public relations company, is chatty and sociable and yet always in control, which can be bloody irritating. The whole world can be on the verge of ending and Robbie will sit and remain annoyingly calm. Except for today.

I could hear him banging around in the kitchen, talking to the drawers as if they were going to suddenly change from inanimate objects into biddable working beings.

"I know you're hiding the batteries, I saw them the other day," I heard him growl. "So why don't you just make it easier for us all and spit them out?"

Normally when he's angry I sort it out. Right now, I could barely sort myself out.

I reckoned I had a space of about five minutes where I could let rip, so I stepped out the front door whereupon the wind whipped into my face and made my eyes water. Now nobody was watching me try to keep it all together, the way I had been since I'd heard the news.

"Me? I'm fine, totally fine. Honestly. Not a bit worried. I'll be fine."

I wasn't fine, though.

The sobs came from deep inside me. Frightened, grief-stricken, from-the-depths-of-my-soul sobs.

I wasn't feeling sorry for myself, really – I was just terrified that this was going to be the last time I would see my parents and my precious children. Louis and Tia, my babies. *Oh my God.*

Tears dripped down onto my pink fake-fur coat and I stroked the front of it for comfort. But the comfort dissolved instantly because Tia loved it. My baby, Tia. *"You look like a pink furry fairy, Mummy!"* I could hear her tinkling voice running through my head.

More tears streamed down my face.

As a parent, I wasn't ready to die. I wanted to be there to see my children grow up. I wanted to know how they turned out. What they looked like and who their friends were.

I wanted to bake their birthday cakes. Superman for Louis. Sparkles-to-the-Tonsils Barbie for Tia. I wanted to see them stretch and gain confidence and knowledge. I wanted to be there if they needed someone to talk to. I even wanted to be in the firing line when they became teenagers and hated me. I had a *right* to be the one they hated. I had given birth to them, wanting to and intending on being their mother for as much of their lives as possible, and more importantly for all of mine.

But the journey I was on might change all that. I might not be there.

Emily, get a grip, right? Hold it together. You're wasting your make-up. You can't look like you've been dragged through a bush backwards. What would the neighbours say? Think of . . . uh, think of the angels!

I had never been religious. At all. I'm three-quarters Catholic (well, in so far as I wore the dress with the veil when I made my First Communion and the day I got married) and one-quarter Jewish (I have a Star of David on my charm bracelet). I believed in Shopping and the Right to Earn as Much as a Man, but as for the God stuff . . . well, I wasn't so sure.

Yet in the past while – since what my friends were anxiously calling *"my news"* – a wide variety of people had raised my awareness of angels. And I was converted. I'd always been an admirer of all things pink, fluffy and sparkly, so this whole angel theory fitted into my world beautifully.

Laura, a friend I'd been to fashion-design college with, gave me a box set of CDs all about angels.

"We are surrounded by angels," she said earnestly that day as we sat in the coffee shop and she held my hand, snuffling back the tears.

She'd never had to hold my hand before. I was the more balanced and together one in our friendship. During our college days, Laura was always stoned in the corner talking about the colours of our auras.

"You call and they come," said Laura. "In times of need, we can call on specific angels to help us. If in doubt, Archangel Michael is the main man. He's Mr Fix It, Bob the Builder, Superman, James Bond, Mother Theresa, Luke Skywalker and every superhero rolled into one." She beamed at me. "You should try it, Emily."

She was so convincing that I totally believed her.

Standing outside my parents' house, waiting for my husband, having just said goodbye to my family, I realised that desperate times call for desperate measures. I yelled: "Archangel Michael, please help me to get through these next few hours without falling apart!"

Nobody answered.

The tears kept coming. Big, fat, hot blobs plopping down my cheeks, burning my skin against the freezing air. I kept telling myself to stop crying. But I couldn't.

I hadn't cried at all during this whole process so far. Now, it felt like I couldn't stop.

Think of Robbie – you don't want to let him see you crying. Come on, Emily, stop being a wuss. Get a grip for Christ's sake – now is not the time to fall apart.

"Mummy, are you going to get dead?" Tia had asked the day I'd told her I had to go into hospital. She had climbed onto my knee and started "fixing" my hair, while poking the mole on my neck.

I'd touched her soft cheek, wishing fiercely that this wasn't happening to us, because it was wrong for my little girl to have to even think about her mum being dead.

"No, darling, I'm not going to get dead," I said, in the voice I used for discussions on Barbie, Dora the Explorer and why we couldn't buy any more sparkly dust because the bedroom carpet was already full of it.

"Do you have an infection that makes you have a bad cough?" Her eyes were wide with wonder. "Will the doctor have to hide the cold thing and listen with his earphones while you do big breathing?"

I thought of our trips to the doctor where she'd learned how to be a big girl when the doctor used his stethoscope.

"Not quite, Tia. I'm not sick. I'm going to make sure that the doctors take away all the bad stuff before it has a chance to make me sick. Do you think you can understand that?"

She nodded her head, but her eyes were darting back and forth. It was about as clear as mud for her tiny mind. She was too young to absorb the facts and yet there was no doubt she had enough insight to know that there was something wrong.

It was the first time I realised that my heart could simultaneously break and continue to beat at the same time.

She trusted me to be all right and I didn't know if I would be. I didn't know what they were going to find. Nobody did. I had an 'altered gene' that had spelled a death sentence for two members of my family. A cancer gene. Would I ever be coming home to my babies again?

★ ★ ★

Susie

I could think of nothing but Emily that day. It took a gigantic effort to concentrate on work and actually listen to my clients. That was quite a problem: I'm a psychotherapist so listening is my job.

I was wishing with all my heart that I could be with her. Emily had been my best friend forever. She was much more than that, she was like my sister. I couldn't really remember my life before I knew her. But, despite all that, it was Robbie's place to be by her side today, not mine. That's marriage, isn't it?

I imagined them driving to the hospital. My bet was that he would be silent and she would be playing our special game in her head.

I should explain. As children, Emily and I invented this game and called it "Recipes Rule". We'd sort out our problems by putting them in a recipe and cooking them up, or boiling them down, depending on the mood. I suppose, when we started the game, we were using the cooking metaphor as a tool for venting our feelings. It was our own little way of telling each other how we felt and quelling our worries in the process. Years later, at university, I realised that we had unwittingly invented a very effective therapeutic tool.

The game was created when Emily wasn't allowed to wear a really gaudy Communion dress. After she'd told me all about it, she sat there brooding and then said she'd thought of a great way to punish her mean mummy. With her bottom lip protruding, she proclaimed: "Mean Mummy Mousse: Take one Mean Mummy. Steal her favourite shoes. Soak them in muddy water with worms and rotten leaves. Serve them to Mean Mummy covered in slugs!"

Clapping and thrilled, I'd finished with: "Watch as Mean Mummy says she's very sorry and won't be nasty ever again!"

We'd jumped up and down cheering, feeling that Mean Mummy had been sorted out. Even though Emily still had to wear the boring minimalist Communion dress, the slug-covered shoes had been a balm to soothe us when we felt we'd been wronged and in our heads we were the winners.

After that, "Recipes Rule" became our lifeline. We sautéed strict teachers, boiled bad boyfriends, massacred our poor mothers on many occasions. Suffice it to say, we sorted the world by cooking it and serving it up in a way that we felt was justified.

When Emily discovered her boyfriend was cheating on her at the age of fifteen, she'd cried with embarrassment and hurt pride until I came up with the Cheating Git Casserole.

"Take one boy called David. Add a stunning and clever girl called Emily. Remove David's brain. Make him think he needs to hang around with Sylvia the slut. Chop off David's bits. Put them in a big heavy pot with carrots, onions and gravy. Stew and make him eat said bits. Serve with a toss of the head and a look that tells him you didn't really like him anyway!"

"Thanks, Suze. I still feel like my heart is breaking, but I have to say I'll never be able to look at David again without imagining his bits floating around with chunks of carrot and onion!" Blowing her nose, Emily hugged me gratefully.

I wondered what recipe my poor brave friend was cooking up today.

I

SEVEN MONTHS EARLIER

Emily

Ice-lolly Sundae:
Take two small children, add sunshine, smiles and ice-lollies. Douse with water from garden sprinkler. Add mud. Allow kids to wallow. Hose down to remove muck. Dry and dress.

"Oh my God, that sun is hot. Not that I'm complaining, Emily. There's nothing like heat to unknot your shoulders, is there? I could do with a bit of relaxation after the week I've had with your father." My mother lay back on her sun-lounger with a big sigh.

We were in my parents' back garden letting the balmy sun heat our bones. Robbie and I had awful cheap old loungers in our house, so it was much nicer to visit Mum and Dad. I often came over on summer afternoons – if I went back to work, as I was thinking of doing, I wouldn't be able to suit myself as much.

The tweeting birds and smell of flowers would have created a beautiful and idyllic scene if it weren't for Tia and Louis chasing each other across the lawn naked, while yelling abuse and trying to maim each other.

"I've never heard anything like your father," Mum went on. "All I want to do is have the living room painted, and he's been backwards and forwards to the hardware store so many times buying bloody colour-match pots. He still hasn't decided what colour he wants. At this stage I don't care if it's luminous pink with orange spots, just as long as he stops telling me about it." Mum smiled in spite of her irritation, closing her eyes and drinking in the sun. "How is Robbie behaving? I hope he's not as annoying as his father-in-law."

"Robbie's fine. You know him. Once everything is ticking along and he's able to put each thing in its correct box, he's happy. He started going on about the kids' toy room again yesterday. He seems to think that they don't need any toys or DVDs or anything that makes a mess and takes up space. Let him try staying at home for the entire summer with no distractions! I'd say the toy-store vans would be delivering twice a day!"

Robbie and I argued constantly about toys. He thought a hoop and a stick between them was sufficient. I knew the children adored a variety of playthings. It was one of those subjects we should have avoided discussing. We'd never agree.

The roars from the other side of the garden got louder.

"Stop trying to kill each other, kids!" I screamed. "Can't you pretend you like each other for once?"

Of course they completely ignored me and continued to charge about like deranged, shrunken warriors.

"I'll turn on the sprinkler for them – it'll water the parched grass and keep them entertained at the same time," Mum suggested, peeling herself off her comfortable lounger. Within seconds, the fighting turned to delighted squeals and giggles. Tia and Louis leapt in and out of the chilly drops like little garden nymphs, twisting and cavorting, completely taken with their game.

"Was that the doorbell, Mum?"

"Didn't hear!" she yelled, over the noise of the children.

I got up lazily and meandered towards the house, avoiding being soaked by my two little demons. I had a nice slick of sweat across my face, which I tried to mop up with my T-shirt as I opened the door.

"Only me," said my Aunt Ellie. "You're looking ravishing, Emily." My aunt gave me a quick peck on the cheek as she floated past, looking elegant in a swirl of linen and silk, making me feel like a slob in my sweat-soaked outfit.

I cleaned up okay but just then my blonde hair was stuck to my head and I had no make-up on, a mistake when you've got fair lashes. Right at that second I was sporting the boiled ham look. My fair skin didn't exactly take the sun well. I never went brown – I just looked like I'd been fried.

"You can't come to this house smelling of cologne and wearing pretty floaty clothes," I said to Ellie. "You have to sit in greying underwear and smell like a rugby player's jock-strap to sit with us."

"Give me five minutes sitting in your mum's sun trap and I'll suit the description perfectly."

Outside, Ellie sat on one of the plastic garden chairs near the sun-loungers.

"Hi, Lucy! Hi, Monster Munches!"

"Hi, Ellie! Are you going to take off your clothes and jump in the water with us?" Louis begged hopefully.

Ellie was their all-time favourite auntie. She was always in a good mood and although she'd long since hit what she called "the dreaded forties" she could bounce on a trampoline as high as any six-year-old and play hide and seek for up to an hour, no problem.

"Not today, little man, but I'll watch you, if that's okay." She narrowly avoided being hugged by two dripping wet children, producing a bag with ice-lollies as a distraction just in time.

"Would anyone like a cold drink?" Mum asked, wriggling her toes into her flip-flops.

"I'd actually love a coffee, mad as it sounds," said Ellie. "I need a caffeine boost."

"I'll have a water, please, Mum."

By the time the ice-lollies had been opened and the children had fought over them, Mum was back with the coffee.

Then, as we were sipping our drinks, Ellie took a deep breath and said: "Girls, we need to talk. I have some news." She was looking from one of us to the other, and she wasn't smiling.

The children were darting around the garden, playing *Star Wars* by pretending their ice-lollies were light sabres.

Mum and I looked at each other, and I felt my heart sink. Ellie was one of life's happy, light-hearted people. Nothing got her down. Except one thing. I realised there could only be one type of news which could make Ellie look like this. Cancer.

She'd had breast cancer ten years before. Five of the girls from Mum's family had already had breast cancer, Ellie being one of them. Three survived. But Meg died at thirty-eight and Joanne died at forty-one. They left three devastated children in their wake.

"Just tell me you don't have . . . *it* again," Mum implored.

She could barely say the word "cancer". Being first-born in a family of seven girls, Mum was like everybody's big sister. Ellie was the youngest and, due to the fifteen-year age gap, looked up to my mother as her mini-mum.

"It's okay, Lucy," Ellie soothed her older sister, "but you're on the right track."

Mum looked instantly devastated. "Oh, God." The colour drained from her face.

Fear gripped me. I saw my children flash past, spitting sound effects from their tiny, pursed lips, as they swatted at an imaginary being with their ice-lollies. I remembered my aunts finding out they had cancer and I remembered how much pain and suffering they went through before they died.

To see someone you love being taken over by pain and suffering was awful. I was very close to Ellie and the thought of her going through that again was shocking.

"I had a test done recently, "Ellie said. "And it was positive. I am a carrier of a mutation of a gene called BRCA1."

We looked at her blankly.

"What does that mean?" Mum asked.

The two of us stared at Ellie – the kids, the heat and the sunny day forgotten.

"It basically means that I have an altered gene which makes me very likely to develop breast and ovarian cancer," she explained slowly.

"But you've already had breast cancer," I mumbled. My brain and mouth weren't connecting properly.

Ellie's shoulders slumped. "Well, that's why the hospital approached me. They know that we have a history of breast and ovarian cancer in the family, so they asked me if I would take this test." She paused, took a deep breath and went on. "The gene is called BRCA1 – which stands for Breast Cancer 1. They're trying to identify certain mutations of it in as many people as possible. Mutations of the gene are particularly prevalent in people of Ashkenazi Jewish descent, which as we know our grandmother was. I have inherited one of those mutations. If a woman carries the altered gene she has an eighty per cent chance of developing breast cancer."

We sat in a stunned silence.

"She also has a fifty per cent chance of developing ovarian cancer."

Mum's hands shot to her face.

The sounds of my children's happy voices faded in and out of my head. It was like having a bullet of ice shot through my chest. This had serious consequences for Mum and me. And Tia. Innocent and tiny, bounding around in the sunshine, could she be in serious danger in years to come?

As Ellie began to talk again, I managed to zone back in and listen to her.

"Nobody can say our family isn't aware of what cancer can do. Obviously, the more they can discover about this mutation, the closer they come to finding a cure. So I agreed to be tested."

"What did you have to do?" Mum's voice was faint.

"It was a simple blood test. They sent the sample to a lab in England and they searched for this specific mutation, which was present in all of us so far. The reason I'm telling you is that you may want to be tested yourselves."

Ellie dropped her gaze to the ground. I thought she might be about to cry.

"I'm so sorry to be the bearer of such bad tidings, but I had to tell you both."

At that moment I felt for her. It wasn't an easy bomb to drop.

"What about Heidi and Zara?" Mum wanted to know about her two other sisters, who'd both previously had breast cancer. "You said the mutation was present in 'all of us so far'. You mean they had the test too?"

Ellie nodded. "They've been tested and unfortunately they're both positive. I volunteered to come and deliver the bad news. But we didn't want to tell you we were doing it, not until we were sure . . ."

"Poor you, Ellie! Talk about being given a ticking parcel and told to run with it!" Mum's mothering instinct kicked in as she leaned forward and clasped Ellie's hand.

I loved my mum so much at that moment: even in the face of devastating news, she was thinking about someone else.

But Ellie was still concentrating on getting her message across as clearly as she could.

"So, Lucy, if you are a carrier, and only *if* you are, Emily also has a strong chance of testing positive. But you may not be, Lucy. And if you don't carry it, Emily cannot carry it either."

"Then Tia wouldn't have it," I whispered. It was a glimmer of hope for my baby.

Ellie squeezed my hand. "I'm sorry to have to tell you all this and ruin a lovely sunny day for you." She drank her coffee and waited for the news to sink in.

We remained quiet, deep in thought.

Ellie spoke again. "Two months ago, when I decided to go along and take the test, I assumed I wouldn't be a carrier – it's a bit like taking a pregnancy test and assuming you won't be pregnant. That kind of thing happens to other people, doesn't it? So I went back to the genetics lab last Friday, fully expecting to be told I was safe. But they told me I tested positive. I know I've had breast cancer already, but I really thought my test wouldn't come back positive."

Mum touched my hand, the concern for me written all over her face. I followed her gaze as she watched Tia stamping in the soggy, muddy patch they'd created with the garden hose.

"How are you coping with it, Ellie?" I asked.

"Well, I was really shocked when they told me, but when I gathered my thoughts and sat down and rationalised it all, it made perfect sense," she said matter of factly.

"Oh Jesus!" Mum said. She never cursed normally. Nothing was normal about today.

I just stared at Ellie. I wasn't sure what to think or say.

Ellie pressed on. "You need to decide whether or not you want to be tested. If you decide not, you should at least put yourself on a screening programme. The genetics lab sent me a letter following my diagnosis. It's kind of technical but it explains the whole gene thing very well. I've photocopied it and I'll leave it with you – one for each of you. I think it gives a –"

"Look at me, Mummy, I'm a chocolate girl!" Tia appeared beside me spattered from head to toe in thick, oozy mud.

"Oh Tia, what have you done to yourself?" I stood up and tried to grab her but she was too quick for me.

Squealing with delight, she dashed across the lawn towards the dancing sprinkler.

"Okay then, wash all that mud off with the clean water and stop turning the grass into a mud bath," I called, on automatic-mummy-pilot.

Tia had gone behind a tree, curling her arms and tucking her hands into her armpits, shouting, "Ooh, ooh, ooh, I'm a mucky monkey!"

Louis, similarly muddy, joined her and they began to leap about communicating to each other in monkey language.

"Leave them to it, Emily, at least they're happy!" Mum shouted over to me. "We'll hose them down before you have to put them in the car."

Why am I so anally retentive, I wondered silently? Here I am in utter shock, being told life-altering news, and all I'm worried about is my children being covered in mud. Who cares? I could imagine what my friend Susie the psychotherapist would say about my reaction – something to do with focussing on unimportant issues in order to avoid the horrible ones.

Ellie sat with us for about half an hour after that but we couldn't talk as the children kept running over and back to us. They didn't need to hear any of this.

My head was spinning by the time we waved Ellie off. The bright sun and the heat were suddenly too much for me. I woodenly grabbed the children, removed as much muck as I could with the sprinkler, dried them and dressed them.

"I don't want to go home – it's too hot to sit in the car!" Tia whined.

"We need to go now. Say goodbye to Oma now, like a good girl." The children had always called my mum "Oma", the German for grandmother. I'd had an Oma growing up, as my maternal grandmother is Austrian, and when they were born Mum hadn't felt like a Nana or a Grandma. So she'd opted to uphold tradition and become an Oma too.

"Don't forget your letter from Ellie." Mum stuffed one of the white envelopes into my handbag. "I'll ring you later on when we've both had a chance to digest all this."

She waved us off, looking drawn and pale. There was a darkness in her eyes I had never seen before. The sunny day and jovial atmosphere were well and truly ruined.

During the short car journey home, Ellie's words whizzed around in my head. She was so calm and steady about everything. I felt as far removed from calm as I could have been.

Glad to pull into our own driveway, I bundled the kids into the house. I needed to read the letter from the genetic lab and try to get my head around the news.

I closed the sitting-room curtains and turned the TV on to *Nick Junior*. Grabbing a packet of biscuits, I handed them to Louis, who looked delighted with the normally forbidden offering.

"Are these all for me to eat on my own?" he asked, astonished.

"No, share them with your sister. Mummy has to do some work for a few minutes, so you two can pretend we have a cinema and have a bikkie picnic, okay?"

I backed out of the room and shut the door. I desperately needed some space, even for a few minutes, to read the letter and let my brain compute what all of this meant to me.

Perched on one of the lower steps of the stairs, just inside the front door, I stared at the envelope in my hands.

An image of Robbie shot into my head. God, I wasn't ready to say goodbye to my family! Until that moment I'd never had to contemplate such a dreadful thing. It was like a smack in the face. A freezing cold shower, to douse the warmth out of my very existence.

2

Emily

Dawning Realisation Gazpacho:
Take one normal day, add a genetic defect, turn blood cold, stop heart temporarily. Raise hairs on back of neck, attempt to digest.

I ripped the white envelope open and pulled out the letter.

My heart thumped and I could feel my skin crawling at the thought of having to read it. But I knew that it could be a matter of life and death, so I needed to face this head on.

Head of Genetics
St Jude's Hospital
Dublin

Dear Ellie,
Further to our meeting last week, I would like to reaffirm the points we discussed then. About 1 in 12 women will develop breast cancer over their lifetime. Ovarian cancer is not quite as common. Only 1 in 100 women will

develop this. Uterine cancer is also rare, affecting only 1 in 100 women in the general population.

Some families are more prone to developing cancer than others. We recognise these families by the pattern of cancer within the family. The reason cancer is more prominent in these families is that individuals in the family carry a genetic alteration, which makes them more susceptible to developing cancer. Only 5% of all the breast cancer that occurs is due to hereditary predisposition.

As far as hereditary breast cancer is concerned, there are a number of genes which, when altered, predispose certain individuals to develop breast cancer.

The most important of these genes are called BRCA1 (for Breast Cancer 1) and BRCA2 (for Breast Cancer 2). BRCA1 and BRCA2, when altered, predispose individuals to develop both breast and ovarian cancer.

We inherit one set of genes from our mothers and the other from our fathers. Your maternal grandmother had an altered gene, carrying breast and ovarian cancer. This means that each of her children would have a chance of inheriting the cancer-predisposing gene.

Not everyone who carries the altered gene will develop breast or ovarian cancer. But the odds are high. Approximately 80% of those carrying the altered BRCA will develop breast cancer. 40–50% will develop ovarian cancer. Men have very little breast tissue and obviously no ovaries, so by nature they may carry the gene and not develop any symptoms. But this means that a man could have this gene and pass it on to his daughters.

The type of mutation that is present in your family is known as an Ashkenazi Jewish mutation called BRCA1 187 delAG. Your grandmother was of Ashkenazi Jewish descent and within the Ashkenazi Jewish population there are common founder breast-cancer mutations, known as BRCA1 187 delAG, BRCA1 5385 insC and BRCA2 6174 delT. So when someone is of this origin, their blood sample is automatically tested for these mutations.

The options when BRCA1 187 delAG is present are either screening or surgery.

Screening means we watch and wait to see if cancer develops. For the breasts it involves monthly self-examinations, six-monthly clinical examinations and regular mammograms. The ovaries are screened using regular trans-vaginal ultrasounds.

The surgical option is a bi-lateral prophylactic mastectomy with reconstruction. In English: a double mastectomy with replacement surgery. Plus removal of the ovaries before cancer appears, known as a bi-lateral prophylactic oophorectomy.

As we discussed during your visit, there is a specialised family genetic assessment clinic in St Theresa's Hospital here in Dublin, should you wish to take this matter further.

I wish you luck with your future decisions and remind you I am here any time if I can be of assistance.

Yours sincerely

Dr Cleary

"Well, fuck-a-doodle-doo," I exhaled.

I certainly hadn't woken up that morning expecting this one. I rubbed my eyes and sat motionless at the bottom of the stairs.

Numbly, I reread the letter. Certain phrases stood out. *"Should you wish to take this matter further"* . . . *"the options are screening or surgery"* . . . *"a double mastectomy with replacement surgery"* . . . I shuddered at the thought.

I had a sudden flashback of Joanne, my beloved auntie. She had started off as a beautiful and courageous and vivacious woman. The cancer had spread and slowly the combination of drugs and the cancer had changed her completely. She became bloated, her hair fell out, her skin took on a pale deathly tone. Her eyes sank backwards and the spark went out of them. It was like a light was quenched in her soul. We'd all had to watch her battle and ultimately lose her fight for life.

I hoped I would never encounter such raw human suffering ever again. The mere thought of cancer freaked me out. Some people are afraid of spiders, some are freaked by mice. My biggest fear above all else in this world, hands down, has got to be cancer.

Not knowing what else to do, I walked to my computer which was housed in the little downstairs box-room Robbie and I called the study, and typed the words 'BRCA1' into Google. Immediately it responded with 586,000,000 sites. Okay. So that proved that lots of people had heard of this gene and no doubt its mutations. We weren't the first people on the planet to know about this.

The phone rang. It was Mum. "Did you read the letter?" she asked, her voice quavering.

"Yep, just finished it. I was looking on the internet. Apparently millions of other people know about this thing, so it's not just us idiots." I always joked when I was upset.

"Right, I don't know if that helps me right at this moment." Mum sighed heavily. "Well, I suppose there's no point in jumping to conclusions until we know the stark facts."

And then I asked the million-dollar question: "Are you going to have the test?"

I willed her to say yes. Although the consequences could be awful for her, I needed to know if I could be a carrier. If I could have given it to Tia.

"I suppose I'd better really. It has implications for you too. Do you want me to find out or what way are you feeling about it?"

"I want to know. There's no point in sticking our heads in the sand. If we are predisposed to cancer, and we can find out for sure, at least we can do something positive about it. I think you should go for it. If we find out you are a carrier, I want to be tested too."

The dull ache of fear was rising through me as the full implications of what we might be told were starting to hit home. This was serious – life-threatening serious.

With that, Tia and Louis came charging into the hallway. Fuelled by the sugar of most of a packet of biscuits, they were extra-hysterical.

"There's a huge furry bee trying to sting us!" Tia was yelling, jumping up and down with excitement, tugging on my wrist. "It's big and mean and stripy – come and see it, Mum!"

"I'll ring you in the morning, Mum. I'd better deal with the children."

"Okay, darling, I'll talk to you in the morning. I'm going to give Heidi and Zara a call as well. I know Ellie said they're very upset, but I'll just check in with them and let them know Ellie has spoken to us."

"All right, talk to you then."

I was dragged into the sitting room to observe the killer bee, which turned out to be a bluebottle.

"Look at it, Mum – it's gi-normous, isn't it?" Louis was half-scared and half-impressed with the bug.

"Okay, stand back, both of you. I'm taking control of the killer bluebottle. Using my magic magazine, I'm going to slay the enemy." With two swift swats of the glossy, the bluebottle was toast.

"Well done, Mummy! You're the winner!" Louis looked impressed.

Tia was standing at the door, not quite sure if she should be happy or sad about the bug's demise. "Did the bluebottle go to heaven?" she asked.

"He sure did. In fact, he's having a party with all the other flying things right now." I grabbed her and hugged her. She giggled and wriggled down to the floor and scurried away. At least she wasn't planning on dwelling on the recent death. I fleetingly thought what a pity it was that I couldn't squash the cancer gene with a magazine. If only everything nasty in life could be removed with a swift flick of a wrist.

I knew I had to cook dinner but, suddenly, all the normal stuff was totally irrelevant. Luckily Robbie was away for the night so he didn't have to be catered for. I quickly dialled the local pizza-delivery service and ordered a family-sized pizza, salads and drinks. Knowing it would give me a few minutes' grace, I ran the bath and chucked in a huge dollop of bubble bath, about three times more than I usually put in.

"Come on, you two, you can make bubble pies!"

I undressed the children and they hopped into the suds, flailing about delightedly at the excess bubbles. I sat on the bathroom floor, staring at my two children. What was all this going to mean to us? What if I found out I had it? What was I going to do about it? The surgical options were pretty scary. A double mastectomy and my ovaries removed. Would I go that far? As tears misted my eyes, I looked at my children. They were only four and five. They were *babies*. They needed me.

"Look at me, Mummy, I'm Santa Claus! *Ho, ho, ho!*" Louis had made a beard out of the bubbles from the bath.

Would I have my breasts and my ovaries removed so I could stay alive and be their mother? There was no question. I would have my limbs removed to protect my children. I didn't want to die. I was certain of that.

I had a sudden flash of my Aunt Joanne, twelve years before, lying in a hospital bed, her body wasted, her face puffed and swollen beyond recognition by the cancer treatment, a silk scarf tied around her bald emaciated skull to afford her a last shred of dignity.

"Would you like me to paint your nails for you, Joanne?" I'd asked her.

"That'd be nice, honey." Her voice was raspy and weak. "While you're doing that, can you promise me something?" She looked at me intently.

"Sure. What?" I busied myself with the pink nail varnish.

"When I'm gone, will you be there for my girls? They look up to you. You've always been a role model for them because you're the oldest. If they need a shoulder to cry on, an opinion or just a hug, can you do that for me?' Her eyes were haunted and yet she was pleading with me to let her know her girls would be okay.

She had fought with her body, mind and soul to beat cancer, but she didn't win. Cancer won. At five o'clock in the morning, she slipped away. Free from the pain and suffering, but also removed from her children forever. That could be me if I had this altered gene.

"Mummy, does Santa Claus ever have parties with the Tooth Fairy or the Easter Bunny?" Louis asked.

"Sure he does. They have lollipops and chocolate and drink rainbow juice out of glittery goblets." I rubbed my tummy and licked my lips to illustrate how delicious it all was. I smiled at them and widened my eyes.

Louis and Tia laughed loudly, delighted with the fantasy.

"You're funny, Mummy." Louis was staring at me with sheer little-person's glee in his eyes.

I surveyed the frothy madness of my children's bath time and vowed I would do everything in my power to stay alive and be with them. Forever was a bloody long time.

If I was being offered a chance to beat cancer before it beat me, I was going to take that chance.

3

Susie

Breakfast on the Go:
*Open one portion of shop-bought fruit salad, add a cup of black coffee,
scrape out already empty sugar bowl. Curse loudly and promise to go
and buy milk and real food. Apply make-up while trying to eat fruit
which oddly tastes like chunks of chilled turnip instead of melon. Vow
to improve diet, some day soon.*

The alarm clock burst into my dreams, cheerfully belting out a
George Michael hit. Groaning, I whacked the snooze button,
knowing the time was ten minutes fast and I was allowed two snoozes
before I had to peel myself out of bed. I could hear the rain tapping on
the window. It was still dark outside. I didn't need five years of training
in psychology to understand my hatred of the cold. As a child, I'd
loathed having to dance around on an icy floor in the dark, being able
to see my breath as I dressed myself as quickly as possible. Mum never
had money to pay heating bills, not that most of the places we lived in
had heating.

My heating was on a timer and I made sure the place resembled a sauna every morning. I loved my apartment. It was a modern, two-bed in a yuppie-ish suburb. Minimalist with the right amount of girly touches. I'd bought it four years before, and I was still waiting to take it for granted. And yes, it was a far cry from the higgledy-piggledy-hippy-type places Mum and I had lived in when I was a child.

Being a psychologist is so annoying, because you have to analyse yourself endlessly, right? It doesn't take a first class psychology degree (I was first in my class, naturally) to work out that having been raised by a single mother on benefits had made me somewhat driven in the home-owning stakes.

I love being a psychotherapist. I get a serious sense of achievement with almost all my patients. Just the fact that they've made that call and come to look for help fills me with admiration. I believe every person has the ability to achieve – sometimes they just need a nudge in the right direction.

I had a happy childhood, by the way, despite the no money. But understanding pain helps. Hilariously, patients never think their therapist has gone through anything. If I had a euro for every time a patient shrugged anxiously after pouring their heart out and said, "That must sound mad to you, I'm sure you have none of these worries," I'd have been living in a beach hut in the Caribbean on my early retirement money, with a nicely oiled black man mixing me mango and coconut cocktails.

I stayed single, by choice. I was engaged once to a guy called Kevin but I called it all off – much to my mother's distress. Kevin wasn't exactly my soul mate as it turned out, but that was almost irrelevant to my decision. I just knew it wasn't the right move for me at the time. Marriage, the whole thing.

You see, my father wasn't around when I was growing up and so I didn't want to do the whole conventional family thing. Kevin did. It might sound callous to you, but I also found Kevin's assumption that I would want to turn into a baby machine a bit hard to deal with. I felt I hadn't spent years of hard graft, research, attending conferences and busting my ass to sit at home like a beached whale, waiting to produce a small, eating, shitting, screaming thing.

I did feel appalling, calling off the wedding. I never wanted to hurt Kevin. But it would have been crueller to go through with it. Take Emily for instance. Herself and Robbie had their ups and downs like any other couple but she was pretty damn sure she didn't want to live her life without him. I, on the other hand, felt an overwhelming sense of relief when my engagement to Kevin was over.

He took it all very badly. I try not to think about that episode really.

"Do you realise what a cold callous bitch you sound?" he'd yelled, crying. "Did you ever love me? In fact, don't even answer that. Leave me with some dignity at least!"

Poor Kevin. I hope he's managed to find happiness.

Just as I walked into the clinic my mobile phone rang.

"*Happy birthday to you, squashed tomatoes and stew, you look like a monkey and you smell like one too!*"

"Thanks for remembering, honey, but keep your voice down. You know what I'm like about birthdays and other pointless celebrations. The last thing I want is Fiona shuffling in with a Black Forest Gateau!" I hissed.

I waved to my secretary and cradled my mobile between my shoulder and ear as I grabbed my patient list and kicked my office door open. The smell of my favourite Jo Malone oil was burning. The coffee percolator was spitting out a freshly brewed caffeine fix. My secretary knew just how I liked to find things in the morning. I shared a suite of offices with two other therapists and we shared the same secretary, Fiona.

"Ah lighten up, you old bag!"

Emily was trying to sound upbeat but I could tell she had something on her mind. She was attempting to act all perky but I'd known her too long.

"So, Em," I continued, "what's up?"

"I'm fine, Susie, honestly."

Her slight hesitation was enough to set off alarm bells for me.

"It's me you're talking to – spit it out!" I instructed.

"Are you sure it's not a bad time for you?" Emily definitely sounded odd.

"No, not at all. I've got twenty-five minutes before my first patient.

Talk away." I settled myself at my desk and switched on the socket at the wall, breathing electricity into my computer system.

"Okay, listen, I've a bit of news which might shock you."

"Don't tell me you're up the pole again?"

"Not quite up the pole. Up the creek, more like." Emily's voice sounded a bit tight. "I've just been told that I may be a carrier of a certain mutation of a gene called BRCA1. Have you ever heard of it?"

I stopped moving at that moment. "Yes," I said slowly. I sat down on my cream leather chair and began to fix my jar of pens, trying to calm myself. Displacement activity. "When did all this happen? Christ, are you okay?"

"I found out yesterday. Ellie called over. She was approached to have a genetic test because of all the cancer in our family and she tested positive for the mutation. She told Mum and me about it. We're just trying to get used to it all at this stage. Look, I know it's a bit of a bomb to drop, but I wanted to tell you as soon as possible and I thought you might have a colleague in the clinic who might have some information on the whole gene thing . . ." Emily trailed off. "I've been on the internet but I never know whether to believe half of what's on the health sites there. So you've heard of this altered-gene thing before?"

"Yes, of course, but I've never had cause to delve into the whole subject too much. What do you want me to do? Do you want names of specialists?" I was back on familiar ground, sorting the problem out. That's what I was good at, not this emotion, this fear thing.

"Maybe you could ask around with some of your colleagues? Maybe they know something which could be useful . . ."

My head was spinning with possibilities. I needed to take the time to figure this out. I felt the hair on the back of my neck rising. Christ, this was really scary. I wasn't great on cancer, but I'd damn well find someone who was. "All right, straight off I'm going to call an old college friend – she works in a cancer clinic in the States. Leave it with me. Are you sure you're okay?"

"Yeah, I'm still trying to take it all in." She sounded deflated.

"Listen, I've got a full clinic this morning, but I'll drop over later on this afternoon." I knew I needed to remain in control for both our sakes.

"Okay, Suze. The kids have a birthday cake for you too, so we can kill two birds with one stone. Talk to you later and don't worry, okay?" She was gone.

I put the phone down and sat staring at the large picture to the right of my desk. It was one of those abstract-shapes-on-pale-canvas pictures.

Emily and I had met in school, although it's all a bit woolly at this stage, as we were only three at the time. I'm an only child, or 'a lonely child' as Emily always thought it was called. She became the sibling I never had and I became her sister. "Boys are dumb," was our mantra when we were six, although we got over that when we were thirteen. We even used to tell people we were sisters – impossible, in fact, as we are too close in age. It was pretty doubtful whether they actually believed us, as I've always been much taller than Emily, with auburn wavy hair and remarkably dark skin. Emily is a small blonde person, with tiny everything and skin the colour of milk. I'm now almost a clear foot taller than her and I take size eight shoes, which was fantastic when we were going through our Doc Marten boots stage, but the rest of the time I've had to stalk the shops for anything at all that fits. If it's actually attractive, it's a bonus.

Cancer. I was stunned by what she'd told me. She sounded so calm too, with the background noise of Louis and Tia rip-roaring through the house like wild fire as usual. How could she have such calm in her voice delivering such earth-shattering news?

I'm the controlled one. I can sit and listen to situations from brutal rape to attempted suicide and deal with it. I can rationalise heinous and awful events. I can break them down and help to heal the damage. But not today. This was too close to the bone. This was Emily.

I could feel my eyes began to pepper with tears. *Pull yourself together*, I berated myself. I was not going to cry. I didn't do crying. It didn't solve anything and it certainly wouldn't help Emily. What I needed now was to get some information and some relevant help.

I stared at the receiver and sat in the cushioned silence of my neutrally decorated consulting rooms – earthy tones are better for my patients. It was still only nine thirty, the wrong time to phone the States, to talk to Sheila, the girl I trained with, who was working in a cancer-treatment centre in Florida. She was the head of psychology there and would be perfectly equipped to deal with patients who were presenting with a terminal or treatable cancer. As soon as my morning clinic was over, I'd call her for some advice.

I went and got a coffee and sat back at my desk, thinking back to my childhood. Emily featured in all the scenes in my mind.

Oddly, personality-wise she was more in tune with my mum, Pauline, than I was.

For a lot of my childhood, Mum was in her second-hand (or vintage, as they like to call it now) wedding-dress phase. She still is.

"I wish *my* mum had a rail of wedding dresses. Your mum is like a princess-minder, isn't she?" Emily's eyes would shine with delight. "We're so lucky to have Pauline – she sees the magic and shares it with us." Mum insisted that Emily call her Pauline, not like the other mums who were all Mrs whoever. But Mum had to be different.

Emily made me see Mum in a more positive light than I might have, left to my own devices. I was more of the opinion that Mum lived in a land of marshmallows, candyfloss and bluebirds, which simply couldn't and didn't exist, but if Emily accepted and loved the way Mum behaved, then I figured it must be mildly tolerable.

Of course I hadn't always felt so impatient about my mum's obsession with weddings. It was fabulous when I was a tiny girl. I always knew when the Children's Allowance came through because she would take me to Oxfam and we would root through the rails of prom dresses and wedding gowns. We'd buy full-length veils and headdresses too. I wasn't so cynical that I didn't enjoy those mornings. I loved the adventure, and I knew Emily would be waiting with bated breath to find out what we'd found.

"Now we have to go to the coffee shop and buy a drink and a cake and sit and imagine what kind of wedding this dress was the Star of the Show at." Mum's eyes would shine and we'd skip together to the nearby café and begin our little fantasy.

Mum was twenty-five years older than me but we might have been the same age the way she acted. She had a wonderful imagination and a vivid and magical way of describing the dress's wedding day.

I remember one day in particular – the day we bought the Claudia dress.

"The sun was just breaking through the clouds when Claudia woke up on the morning of her wedding," Mum began as she cut the sticky chocolate slice into smaller pieces. "Claudia had been dreaming of this day for her whole life. She tip-toed over to her wardrobe and carefully opened the door. Waiting patiently behind the clear plastic was her dress."

I remember watching Mum peel the dress out of the bag and spread it across our two laps. Taking my small hand, she placed my fingers on the beads around the bodice.

"Claudia stroked the beautiful seed pearls lovingly as a flutter danced across her heart. She knew that her husband to be . . . *what's his name?*" she whispered to me, including me in the story.

"Bert!" I shouted, thrilled.

"Bert was just stirring in his bed upstairs in his mummy's house. As he opened his eyes, he tried to imagine what Claudia was going to look like when she floated up the aisle of the church to marry him . . ." Mum took a sip of coffee.

"His eyes opened *this* wide," I shouted excitedly, pulling my eyelids apart. "'You are the most beautiful bride in the whole world. You are as pretty as Barbie and I am going to take you away to the Land of Lollipops on my white horse!'"

Mum squealed, delighted with the whole scene, and lovingly folded Claudia's dress and put it into the plastic bag.

"When we get home, you can call over to Emily and tell her that we have a new dress for her to see. Seeing as the sun is shining, maybe we can have a little wedding breakfast in the garden this afternoon – what do you think?"

Mum was just as excited as me.

"Did you ever have a wedding, Mum?" I asked her, not for the first time.

"No, darling. Your daddy died in a terrible car crash, before you were born. We never had a chance to get married." Mum looked wistful.

"Poor Daddy. Is he watching over us now?" I'd heard this story so often, it was almost like a fairytale in itself.

"Yes, of course he is. He's your special angel in the sky, minding you from heaven."

I always loved that conversation. It was the only link I had with my father. I always thought I was special because I had my very own angel daddy.

I remember racing home that day and ringing Emily's doorbell. She lived less than five minutes from our rented flat. At the time, Mum and I were living in a ground-floor flat of a semi-detached Victorian house. It had a sizable back garden, which was fairly overgrown and neglected-looking, but it had lots of daisies and dandelions and we thought it was beautiful.

Knocking on Emily's door, I was dancing a jig of excitement as I heard her footsteps trotting up her wooden hall floor.

"Hi, Susie!" Emily pulled me into her hallway by the hand. "Where have you been? I called for you but there was nobody there."

"It's Children's Allowance day! Mum and I went to get another dress. Wait till you see it! It has a veil and headdress and everything. Ask your mum if you can come to my house. We're going to have a wedding-breakfast-dinner in the garden!" I could hardly get the words out I was so excited.

"Can we make invitations as well?" Emily asked over her shoulder as we ran to find her mum.

"Oh yes. It's Claudia and Bert's wedding today."

"Oh, I love Claudia and Bert! They're so in love, aren't they?" Emily immediately immersed herself in the game. "*Muuumm?* Where are you?"

"In the garden!" she answered.

"Hi, Mrs Cusack," I gasped in excitement. "Can Emily come my house for dinner – we got a new dress and my mum said we can have a wedding in the garden? We'll walk her home later on when the wedding's over. Can she?"

"Okay, no problem. Say hello to your mum from me, Susie." Lucy smiled as she watched us skip out holding hands.

That day we cut and pasted invitations and 'posted' them. We dressed ourselves up in wedding dresses, and with teddy-bear grooms and Pauline as the priest, Claudia and Bert (there were two of each) tied the knot.

We then sat on an old picnic rug in our revolting lace ensembles and ate sausages, beans and chips, washed down with orange squash. At the time, I thought the whole world revolved around white dresses and flowers and frills.

Mum worked in the library and I only realised when I was bit older that she was always broke. She had looked the same forever. Home-dyed frizzy hair. Could be henna-coloured or dark brown depending on her mood or the time of year. She was definitely more flower child than designer chick. She was never fat, nor was she a stick insect. She didn't bother with faddy diets, up-to-the-minute fashion or pretty much anything dictated by the outside world. I suppose you could say she's always been her own woman, which is probably the only thing we have in common. She's much smaller than me and certainly doesn't share my love of order. In fact if she was any more laid back, she'd be dead.

By the time we made our First Holy Communion, Mum was beside herself with excitement. It was her first ever real white-dress event. All the God stuff went totally out the window in our house. It was all about the outfit. I was the only girl in my class with a choice of four dresses on the day. We'd been doing our Oxfam shopping for a good year beforehand. With Mum's encouragement, I managed to wear three of them during the course of the day. "I think you've got a little bit of chocolate on the sleeve of that one. Let's change you!" Mum was ready with a new replacement. I was allowed to have a parasol, hard glittery laced gloves, a handbag, full-length veil and clumpy-high-heeled shoes with bows on the front. My veil was actually a wedding one, so Mum had to walk behind me for most of the day holding it like a bridesmaid. But of course she didn't mind.

Emily and her mum, on the other hand, almost came to blows about the whole Communion issue. Emily wanted to have the full ensemble like me, but Lucy was holding fast: "I've made your dress, it will be simple and tasteful, you are not going around looking like a child bride and that's final."

Emily's dress was made from cream Egyptian cotton with an Empire line detail. She had a headband of cream rosebuds and her shoes were demure Mary-Janes.

"Never mind, Emily!" my mum said. "You can come and dress up tomorrow in my house!"

Mum hugged Emily and understood her sadness. Amazingly, she never took offence at Lucy's attitude. She had her way of doing things and Lucy had hers, and that was that as far as Mum was concerned.

"We're all different, Susie," she mused. "That doesn't mean one person is right and the other is wrong. We just need to learn to tolerate each other and accept one another for who we are."

I thought I looked like a princess and poor Emily looked like a sad deflated little ghost in comparison.

"Look, Emily," Lucy had finally snapped, "Pauline is sadly deluded and if she wants to take Susie along with her that's her business. But I am not allowing you to look like a Barbie doll and that's final. End of story."

While Emily had a bit of a tantrum, I felt the whole world come to a halt in the kitchen that day. I remember being a bit shocked that Lucy was saying something negative about my mum. I had no idea what deluded meant, but it kind of worried me.

Did this mean that Emily and me couldn't be friends?

But we got over the mother row, over school, college and me being a bridesmaid when Emily got married. We were friends for life, it was that simple. I couldn't imagine my life without Emily in it.

So sitting here, at the age of thirty, in a very expensive suit, with my own practice, with keys of a convertible and a modern apartment to my name, I felt like I'd been hit with a sledgehammer. One phone call and it had all been put into perspective for me. All my achievements were hard-earned and appreciated, but none of it mattered as much as Emily. How would I be able to get through my morning?

I specialise in OCD, or Obsessive Compulsive Disorders, on a Monday, so I had to focus and give my patients my all.

I had a sudden image of Emily dragging me to parties when I was in college. I had started to do work experience with a renowned psychologist, Mr Breen, and Emily thought this was fantastic news. At smoky house parties she introduced me to all her pissed friends who were having boyfriend problems.

"This is Susie, my friend I was telling you about. She's studying to be a psychologist, so she can figure out all the madness in your head and tell you what to do. Can't you, Suze?"

And I'd be left standing in front of a deranged person who would proceed to tell me about her on-off relationship with a guy who refused to commit to her.

"Well, he sounds like he just wants to have fun," I'd say. "If he really cared about you, he would commit. I would suggest moving on and trying a bit of what he's doing. Have fun and meet new people. It will broaden your horizons and who knows? Maybe you'll find Mr Wonderful on the way."

Then I'd grin and hope to God they'd go away and leave me alone.

"Emily, you spanner!" I'd say later. "Stop introducing me as 'a psychologist' and telling people I can fix their lives. I'm not a bloody magician. There's more to my job than being able to wave a wand and make virile randy alcohol-fuelled men become doting monogamists. If I can ever do that, I'll be a fecking millionaire!"

"Ah, Suze, you love it really. It's going to be fantastic. Almost everyone we know is fucked up in some way. You're going to make a fortune!" And Emily would link my arm and drag me across the room to find beer.

The phone on my desk rang and Fiona told me my first client was in reception. I tried to calm myself down. I had to get through my morning before I started making phone calls on Emily's behalf. I felt sick to my stomach at the thought of her being linked in any way to cancer. I knew it had killed two of her aunts, had haunted her family. It couldn't take her too. What would I do without her? She was my family.

4

Emily

Hold it Together Trifle:
Take one crisis, melt into brain. Mix with oblivious innocent children.
As the information is assimilated into your mind, add one unsuspecting
husband. Ice a smile onto your face and pretend you are fine. Serve
with temporary denial.

Even though it felt like two weeks had passed since the afternoon
when Ellie had delivered her bombshell, it was only teatime the
next day. The early evening sun was still warm enough to allow the kids
to eat outside. We have a lovely sunny spot, just outside the back door,
which is perfect for summer dining.

"Hi guys, anybody home?"

Just as I had settled the children at their miniature garden table
outside the kitchen door with some left over pizza from the previous day,
I heard Robbie in the hallway.

"Hi, Robbie, we're all out here!" I sounded a hell of a lot more jovial
than I felt. How was I going to tell him?

"Hi, darling, hope you had a great night away – by the way, I might have a gene which predisposes me to both breast and ovarian cancer – would you like a slice of pizza and some coleslaw?"

He stepped through the patio doors into the garden.

"Hello," he said. "Eating *al fresco*? Very nice."

I smiled at him and greeted him with a kiss. I inhaled and drew in the familiar scent of him. It made me want to throw my arms around his neck and sob with fear. Instead, I smiled and played the game of pretending everything was normal.

"Hi, Daddy! Come and sit with us!" Louis patted the tiny green plastic chair beside him.

Robbie scrunched his long legs up towards his chin and manoeuvred himself onto the chair, grabbing a slice of pizza.

"Was Mummy being lazy refusing to cook our dinner again?" he joked to the children.

I stood against the jamb of the patio door, surveying the scene. I felt like the Wicked Fairy at Sleeping Beauty's christening. I knew I had a shocking bomb to drop on Robbie, but suddenly I wasn't sure if I should tell him yet. Maybe I would wait until I knew for certain whether or not I tested positive. What was the point of worrying him for no reason? This might all be a storm in a teacup. It might all amount to nothing. If Mum didn't have it, I was in the clear.

"Are you on a diet, Emily?" Robbie looked up at me from his scrunched position.

"No, I've had a slice already, I'm not that hungry, must be the heat. I think I sat in the sun for too long this afternoon."

I rushed upstairs. I could hear the children's happy babbling through our open bedroom window and the feelings of dread became all-encompassing. I would have to tell Robbie what was going on. I'd said nothing when he phoned the night before from Cork but this was too big to keep inside. He had a right to know and anyway I was going to need his support.

By the time the children were in bed asleep, I looked like I'd been beaten up. I had bags under my eyes the size of suitcases and the stress of Ellie's news was stamped all over my face.

I needed to talk to Robbie.

"You look cheerful – what's the matter?" Robbie plonked down on the sofa beside me, pulling me towards him. For once I didn't feel safe in his embrace. Right at that moment, I wasn't sure if I'd ever feel truly safe again.

"My Aunt Ellie called over to Mum's house yesterday afternoon."

"How was Ellie?" he asked idly, grabbing the remote control and turning on the motor channel.

"She's okay. She found out last week that she has an altered gene which predisposes her to breast and ovarian cancer." I looked sideways at him to gauge his reaction.

He nodded and tried to look concerned, but I knew he wasn't registering the impact yet.

"This altered gene is in Mum's family, inherited from our grandmother. Both Mum and I could possibly be carriers too." I could see the realisation slowly hit home.

"What do you mean?" His brow furrowed and he pressed the mute button on the remote control.

"We haven't found out yet but there's a strong possibility Mum is carrying this altered gene. If she is, I could be a carrier."

"Who told her all this?"

"A geneticist, in one of the Dublin hospitals. She sent Ellie a letter explaining it all. Do you want to read it?"

"Sure."

I found the letter and gave it to him. He scanned the pages. His face gave very little away. He read the letter a second time.

"There's nothing you can do until your mum is tested. Is she going to go for it?" He threw the letter onto the coffee table and sat back.

"I think so. I'll call her in the morning and find out what she has decided. She's still thinking about it."

Robbie didn't say much for a while.

"There's nothing you can do at the moment then," he repeated. "We'll take each stage as it comes. There's no point in getting too het up about it until we know the facts." He patted my feet and turned the volume back up on the television.

Astounded, I sat beside him feeling like I was from another planet. I know about all this stuff about women being from Venus and men being from Mars, but this was taking the theory to the extreme. Was he honestly that calm and matter-of-fact about the whole idea? Either he was or he was a fantastic actor.

An hour passed as Robbie drank a beer and watched his plasma screen TV. He really was able to put all this to the back of his brain until it had to be dealt with. I was beginning to get annoyed. The letter sat on the table, freaking me out and being totally ignored by him.

"Robbie," I said at last, "does it not worry you at all that I may be predisposed to cancer?"

He turned down the volume again and sighed. "Emily, the whole thing is insane at this moment in time. There's absolutely no point in driving yourself around the bend and back again. None of it may be relevant to you. Speak to your mum tomorrow, find out what she's going to do and take it from there. If you have to take the test, we can discuss it further then. But right now, it's all a bit pie in the sky, don't you think?"

"Not really, no," I said furiously. "In fact, I find the whole thing a bit bloody scary. This could have implications for Tia too." I hoped to shock him into reality.

"I understand that. And if and when we have to delve into all this, I'll be prepared to go and see these people and discuss it at length. But right now I think we should keep it to ourselves and try to remain calm. There's no point in being hysterical about it. I'm not trying to sound callous or unfeeling, but I just don't think we should get too excited until we know for sure that any of it relates to you. Do you understand how I'm thinking?"

Robbie had always been very black and white about things but it had never annoyed me as much as right now. I simply didn't understand his reaction.

I stomped off to bed and when he came up later I pretended to be asleep. Secretly I wanted him to hug me, tell me he was worried but that it was all going to be okay. He didn't. He took my pretend-sleep at face value. Within minutes, he was asleep, satisfied that he was taking this news one step at a time, man-style. And I was wide awake, glaring at him. The fear and uncertainty of what might lay ahead for me was like a double espresso at bedtime. I was exhausted by the revelations of the day, but there was no way I could go to sleep.

Finally, I got up to surf the internet again, delving into medical websites and reading other women's stories detailing their experiences.

Far from making me feel better, of course this made me feel worse and freaked me out more than I could ever have thought possible.

It was two in the morning before I crawled back into bed beside my slumbering husband. As I tried to stop my brain from buzzing, I wished I could be a bit more from Mars. I had to try and get a hold of my emotions. Maybe Robbie was right. I gently patted his sleeping form.

Mum phoned me first thing the next morning.

"Emily, I've made a decision. I am going ahead with the test as soon as possible. I think it would be wise to know the truth. How are you feeling about it today?"

"I really want to know too. I need to find out if I could be a carrier too."

"How did Robbie take it all?"

"Strangely really. He doesn't seem to want to get too worried about the whole thing until I know for certain. I know he's very pragmatic so he really only deals with fact." I didn't want to tell Mum about last night and how I'd felt like putting a pillow over his face when he fell fast asleep without a care in the world, leaving me tossing and turning, with my mind doing overtime.

"How's Dad?" I asked, diverting from Robbie.

"He's shocked and wants us to be tested. He agrees we should avail of the information if it's there. He's gone the other way from Robbie – he wants the test to be done yesterday and is like a cat on a hot tin roof. He's phoned me twice already to see if I've made an appointment with the geneticist. I'll phone the hospital and let you know what they say."

After Mum had hung up, I sat and thought about the whole dilemma. It would be much easier to pretend nothing had changed and just carry on as before. But I knew it would eat me up if I didn't find out where I stood. I just didn't understand Robbie's attitude. When had he become so rational and contained? Surely he hadn't always been like that?

I sat and let my mind slide back to the beginning. To the beginning of Robbie and me.

5

SEVEN YEARS EARLIER

Emily

The Perfect Hangover Cocktail:
Mix wine, beer and spirits, remove all food. Melt make-up under disco lights and bake brain to a mush while leaping around in dangerously high heels. Pour into bed in daylight, with birds singing. Do not, under any circumstances, drink a pint of water before bed as this might actually help.

There had been eight of us that night, all twenty-somethings dolled up to the nines, with lots of Prosecco inside us and very little food which meant we were loud and squeally. As it was my birthday I'd brought along sparkly, plastic Barbie tiaras which we had all rammed onto our heads. None of us were married, two of us had boyfriends, there were no children at home. The world was our oyster.

I was twenty-three, with a waist the size of a polo mint, blonde hair down to my pert bottom, a face as smooth as porcelain and not a care in world.

We'd stormed into the bar, oblivious to anyone else. Wrapped up in our girly conversations, intent on having a night together, with no men to spoil the fun.

"Here's to the girls, men are far too much trouble!" Belinda raised a glass and swayed slightly. "The only man you can trust is your daddy!"

"I can't even do that! So I guess I'm fucked," Susie grinned. Her father had been killed in a car crash before she was born.

"He would have been fab, though, Suze, if he was alive." I put my arms around her and we hugged.

"Ah yeah, he'd have been mega all right," she sighed. "Maybe even normal, unlike my mental mum!"

I grinned back. Susie's mum, though wonderful, could *never* have been called normal.

The smell of sweat and smoke and the dull thud of the music filled our senses.

"Let's do tequila slammers," I suggested to a response of cheers.

Always a great idea at the time, they were a head-melting reality the following morning – but we didn't care. We could stay in bed all day if we chose.

We downed the shots, I paid the barman and Susie waved a note at him to do the same again. "Okay, last shot and we'll move to G & Ts," we all agreed. Gin and tonic being the sensible option after nine bottles of sparkling wine altogether and two shots apiece.

Spotting a table being vacated, we scuttled across the bar to claim it, then myself and Belinda went back to the bar to get the second round of shots along with a round of G & Ts.

As I was shuffling back, trying not to spill any of the drinks up my own sleeve, I bumped straight into a guy with light brown wavy hair, dressed in red jeans and a tight black T-shirt.

"Oh sorry, I wasn't looking where I was going," I apologised.

"No worries. Can I help you carry them?"

We regarded each other.

"Did you go to Irish college in Galway about ten years ago?" he asked me.

Irish college is when teenagers go to Gaelic-speaking areas and live with a family for a month to learn the language. Theoretically it was a language-learning experience; realistically, it was a month of fun.

A memory of this guy's handsome face returned through the fuzz of years and alcohol. "You're Robbie Cusack?"

"And you're Emily, aren't you?"

I nodded. He carefully took some of the shot glasses from my hands and followed me back to our table. Without being asked, he sat down.

"So what have you been doing with yourself since I saw you last, apart from becoming incredibly beautiful?"

"Is that the best you can come up with?" I laughed. He was utterly beguiling and he actually got away with being Mr Cheese. "Well, I went to fashion design college and had a few jobs, none of which made any money, so I did the sensible thing and made myself do a computer course. So I work in IT. I can't say it rocks my world, but it pays the bills and the hours are fairly sociable. What about you?"

I drank him in, trying not to look him up and down in a completely obvious way.

"I set up my own PR company some years ago, and so far so good," he said. "I employ fourteen people and I suppose because it's my baby I get a buzz out of it."

"*Everybody clap your hands, let's see all the hands in the air!*" The DJ was revving the already frenzied crowd into a state of hysteria.

The music pumped into my head, the lights flashed, the smoke was rising and the atmosphere was electric.

"Come and dance with me," I said.

I grabbed his hand and dragged him behind me as I bounced towards the throbbing dance floor. Robbie didn't seem to mind. In fact, he was smiling as if this was exactly where he wanted to be: dancing with me.

"Where did you find this one?" Susie wanted to know when we bounded back to our table.

"We just bumped into each other, literally, and recognised each other from Irish college years ago," I yelled into her ear as she desperately tried to focus on my face, which was no doubt looking, like everyone else's: like a fibre-optic Christmas tree, changing colour constantly with the disco lights.

"Lucky you!" she sighed.

We both looked over at Robbie.

Lucky me, I agreed.

Robbie and I danced all night till we were wet with sweat and high on having fun. After that, we ended up at a party in a city-centre apartment with all the girls in tow.

"You don't mind us landing on top of you, mate?" crowed Robbie over the pulsating music to the flat-owner, Matt. "But I have Snow White and her seven beautiful sisters with me!" He was looking like the cat that got the cream.

Matt thumped Robbie on the back. "I could do without your ugly mug, but the Princess Posse can certainly stay! Stunning birds laden down with bottles of booze! You're all very welcome, ladies!"

By now the music had been turned up to window-smashing level and us girls were happily leaping about, clapping and stamping our feet. I'd say the neighbours must have been cursing us. But it wasn't our flat and we didn't give a toss. Life was all about having fun and living the moment, fuelled by as much alcohol, make-up and loud music as possible.

In the middle of all the uproar, Robbie came over and put his arms around my waist from behind and we swayed together. I leaned against him, thinking that it was lovely to have someone choose me out of the whole group of girls. The sense of being wanted and fancied made me feel warm from within. After a few minutes, I turned to face him.

Instinctively we kissed. His lips were soft and full. I felt comfortable and yet alive.

Robbie smiled down at me. He was a lot taller than me, and although he wasn't what I would call a large man, he was stocky and made me feel safe in his embrace.

"I knew there was a reason my mother sent me to the middle of nowhere all those years ago, to learn my native tongue," he said and kissed me again.

The world didn't stop turning, actually. It was quite the opposite. I felt like my whole life had been put on fast forward. I felt elated and incredibly happy.

Deciding to quit while I was ahead, I ushered him over to the kitchen counter where we glugged more booze into chipped mugs. In that state, we would have drunk the stuff out of a twenty-year-old shoe, just as long as it didn't have a hole in it.

"This is the best fun I've had in ages!" I said, leaning against him comfortably. "You're a good laugh, Robbie Cusack. Has anyone ever told you that?"

"Sure. I have girls following me around day and night trying to compliment me. It becomes a bit of a drag after a while." He grinned as I punched him in the arm.

He joked with everyone and made all the girls giggle repeatedly, but I was the only one he put his arms around or kissed. I felt special.

We stayed there until it was bright, by which time hangovers had set in and make-up was beginning to fade.

"Emily, I'm going to die and my liver is hardening as I stand here – are you coming?" Susie was looking a great deal less sparkly than she had a couple of hours earlier.

"Okay, I'm coming, give me a minute. I need to find my stuff."

Having to actually move and get my head together was not easy. Reluctantly I staggered around, gathered up my belongings, shrugged into my coat and stuffed my swollen feet into my hard, sparkly way-too-high shoes, wincing with pain and barely able to walk.

Robbie approached.

"Why are you running away, Princess?" he grinned.

"The girls are heading off. I think I should go with them." I shrugged my shoulders, suddenly feeling a bit shy and awkward.

"Can I have your phone number?" he asked, looking uncomfortable.

I felt for him. It was hard for the guys to always have to make the moves. But had he really thought I wouldn't give it to him, after the evening we'd spent together? I pulled an old receipt from my bag and scribbled out my number and address, just to be sure.

"Ah, it's 01 – so you live in Dublin then?" He held my gaze.

"Yeah, I have an apartment in that new complex on John's Road. I bought it six months ago. Number 66 – almost hell, but not quite. The girls call it 'the devil's kitchen'."

We kissed again. Robbie stroked my hair and traced my face gently with his fingers. I felt the intensity of our connection again. The electricity was definitely flowing.

"Come on, Emily, you soppy cow! Peel yourself away!" said a voice. "I need my bed. I'm going to turn into a pumpkin or something much less attractive."

It was Susie, standing with her shoulders hunched, her hair in a mess and a ladder in her black tights.

"Stunning look, Susie," I said.

I waved over my shoulder at Robbie and linked Susie's arm. Like Cinderella I fled the scene. I would have loved to have stayed with him but I'd been dumped on by so many worthless men in the past, I wasn't going to let it happen again.

I finally knew the right way to play my cards. I had to leave and put the ball in his court. If he didn't call, then I'd know that he wasn't all that interested in me, that he was just looking for a snog and a couple of hours of fun. I hoped it was more than that.

As I walked away, I stole a glance behind me. Our eyes met. Robbie was looking confused.

It's up to you, Robbie, I thought.

It took a lot of will power to walk out the door. But something in my head was overruling my heart and making me put this guy to the test. If he was really The One, then he'd come to me, wouldn't he?

I woke the next morning with a filthy hangover. I turned my head to look at the alarm clock and realised that sudden movements, especially involving the head, were a bad idea. My eyes felt like they were full of glue. Groaning, I realised I had fallen into bed without removing my make-up.

While trying to pick the dried-in mascara out of my eyelashes, I remembered Robbie. Robbie who'd kissed me, who'd asked for my number, who'd made me laugh till I snorted. What more could a girl ask for?

I just hoped I hadn't blown it all by leaving. Maybe I should have stayed.

Just as I was staggering into the bathroom to assess the damage to my face from last night's unremoved make-up, the buzzer to my apartment rang.

"Oh shit, who's that?" I muttered.

Thinking it was one of the girls arriving for the low-down on the previous night, I tottered to the door and flung it open.

There stood Robbie with a huge grin on his face and a convenience-store bag full of breakfast ingredients.

"Hey, Cinderella, you look like you've been *hit* with a ball!"

He burst out laughing and, dropping the bag, put his hands on my hips and turned me around to face the hall mirror. The image that met me made my heart stop. I had wiggly streaks of glitter and black splodges of mascara all down my cheeks. My remaining lipstick was smudged around my mouth, giving me the just-punched-with-a-cricket-bat look. My right cheek and forehead had the imprint of the magazine I'd fallen asleep on emblazoned all over it. My hair was like a bird's nest, I was wearing a "*Frankie says Relax*" T-shirt, a pair of comfortable knickers – Virgin Mary blue – and bubble-gum-pink bed-socks with teddies on them.

I tried to work out what was the quickest way to kill myself.

"Not that you don't look highly gorgeous and all that," Robbie said calmly, "but why don't you go and have a shower and do whatever it is you girls do and I'll make us some breakfast?"

He seemed oblivious to my inner pain and embarrassment, so I pretended I didn't feel like banging my head off the wall.

Using what dignity I had left, I casually bolted to the safety of the bathroom. Within minutes, I was back in my bedroom rummaging through my wardrobe. The waft of toast and frying sausages encouraged me, and I somehow managed to dress myself in a crisp white linen shirt and a pair of tight black jeans. Not the most comfortable thing I owned, but very slimming.

As I stepped into my kitchen, I suddenly felt very shy. Robbie was flying around with a fish slice in one hand and a large knife in the other. The worktops looked like they'd just witnessed an explosion. There were bacon and sausage packets strewn on the floor, tomato seeds and mushroom stalks all over the table, and burnt toast floating in a bowl of murky water in the sink. Somehow, it all smelled good, despite the carnage.

"Hi. Sit. I'm nearly ready. Everything is under control," said Robbie. He was very flushed with his hair stuck to his head but he still looked kind of cute, and I was immeasurably impressed by the effort he was going to.

Within minutes he produced a mouth-watering plate of food. Then he sat opposite me at the kitchen table and stared. He was motionless for so long that it began to unnerve me.

"What?" I asked through a mouth full of bacon – crispy, just the way I liked it. How did he know?

"You look a lot prettier without the glittery tar all over your face but the knickers were damn attractive," he teased.

I almost choked on my rasher. "Do you always make such a disgusting mess when you cook?" I countered, to cover my embarrassment.

"To be honest, I've never cooked a breakfast like that before. Must be the effect you have on me."

He tucked my hair behind my ear and planted a quick kiss on my lips, then wandered into the small living room of my apartment and switched on the television.

"Make yourself at home, why don't you?" I shouted in.

"Hey, you don't begrudge me a little unwinding time, do you, after all that effort? In fact, I cleaned up the apartment after you and your messy minx friends, so you owe me one!"

I ran to the doorway, threw a damp teacloth across the room and hit him right in the chops. Within a split second, he'd jumped up and run into the kitchen to get me. Before I had a chance to escape, he'd turned on the tap and starting splashing great handfuls of freezing water all over me.

"Get off!" I shrieked.

He pulled me towards him and at that moment, I didn't care that I was wet or hung-over. His mouth found mine, we kissed and nuzzled each other – in between trying to maim each other.

After a further scuffle, we settled down and watched the television, the dirty kitchen and the rest of the world forgotten.

When Susie phoned for the juicy details and I told her the details were sitting right beside me on the couch, I had to muffle the phone so he wouldn't hear the screams.

"Go, girl!" she shrieked into my ear. "Ring me ASAP. I *need* to know everything!" And she was gone.

How would I describe life with Robbie? Let me put it this way: there were no games. None. None of that *'can't phone 'cos I called last time'*. To be honest, I found it all a bit unnerving. What was wrong with this relationship? Where was the shit part?

"The weird thing about Robbie is he says he'll call me later, and then he does," I explained to Susie.

"And the problem is what?" She sounded amused.

"Well, it's all supposed to be a guessing game, isn't it? It's running into weeks at this stage and he's still calling when he says he will and turning up when we arrange to meet. I can't get my head around it." I was genuinely puzzled. None of my previous bozo boyfriends had done this. "Come on, you're a psychologist. Pretend I'm a client. I'm asking you, what do I do?"

Susie's voice changed into work mode. "Okay then. Accept that maybe you have defied all probability and found a nice guy. Enjoy it and, Em, don't fuck it up purely because it's too good. Maybe Robbie's going to restore our faith in men."

Susie was right, as usual. She was so brilliant at sorting my head for me. I had to just accept that maybe Robbie was, possibly, dare I even think it – The One.

"Hi, baby," he'd say when he phoned me first thing in the morning, just after I'd had my third coffee.

"Hi, yourself," I'd reply, pleased.

It was as if he'd always been a part of my life. Any time I needed to talk to him, he was there.

It helped that we fancied each other madly. He was utterly gorgeous in a young George Clooney kind of way. He wore suits to work, but managed to put his own twist on things with a quirky tie or a really cool belt. His eyelashes were to die for. Why do men always have amazing eyelashes? His pale grey-blue eyes had a sexiness mixed with mirth, and every time he looked at me it made my heart skip a beat. His skin was the type that tans easily, and although he could do the afternoon-shadow stubble look, he didn't look like an ape. I dated a guy once who was a nice enough looking guy first thing in the morning, but by lunch-time turned into a cloud of black hair with eyes. Robbie was serious eye candy. Every one of my friends who met him did the sideways glance at me and gave the nod of approval.

Of course, we didn't always agree with each other and had some fairly heated discussions. Eventually I realised that me disagreeing with Robbie was almost his favourite thing. He loved a good old-fashioned argument and adored teasing me. He had a knack of being able to rile me like no other man I'd ever met.

He was modest too. Only for the fact that I had seen photos of him in cap and gown, I wouldn't have known about his degree and it wasn't until I met two of his colleagues for an after-work drink one night that I realised just how dynamic he was.

"Cheers, guys, and thanks for today – we nailed that account. Those Japanese businessmen were bowled over by the presentation – I didn't think they'd hire us on the spot." Robbie lifted his pint of the black stuff and smiled at his employees.

"I think most of the praise goes to you. When this guy clicks into sales mode, Emily, he's something else," said John, who was clearly Robbie's right-hand man. "I've never met a man who compels silence and inspires confidence in his business the way Robbie does. Those Japanese people are difficult to impress, but they fell under Robbie's spell today and that was it. Signed, sealed and delivered."

I stared at him, misty-eyed. My man.

I know it all sounds a bit vomit-pie, and we should drag out the violins and dress in *Little House on the Prairie* outfits, but that was the way it all happened. Quite quickly, I couldn't imagine myself without him.

Within weeks he had moved into "the devil's kitchen". Then one night, about four months after we'd met, we were sitting on the living-room floor, eating Chinese takeaway out of the foil containers to save on the washing up, when Robbie coughed awkwardly and looked at me.

"What?" I asked with my mouth full of noodles. I looked down at my sweatshirt to check if it was on fire or covered in sauce.

Robbie stared at me intently. "Will you marry me?"

How I didn't choke on the noodles is a mystery.

"Have you gone fucking insane?" I asked.

"Yes, probably. I hadn't planned on saying that. But now that I have, will you for Christ's sake give me an answer?"

He looked slightly vulnerable for the first time since I'd known him. He was always the strong one, joking and messing when it suited him. This time, I knew he was wearing his heart on his sleeve.

"Oh fuck!" I screeched at the top of my voice. "I'd love to!" I threw my arms around his neck and kissed him all over his face.

"Not exactly the words we can repeat to our grandchildren, but what the hell!" He jumped up and pulled me to my feet, then swung me around, kissing me. "I love you, you crazy chick!"

"When will we get married?" I asked a few minutes later.

"Well, I'm not into long engagements. If we're going to do it, let's get cracking. I'll suss out some venues on Monday and we'll try to agree on something soon."

He began kissing me again. Soon, right, we'd get married soon. Soon turned out to be three months.

I had a blast organising the whole thing. People talk about the stress of organising weddings but I don't get it. Mum and I used the opportunity to push the boat out and have great fun.

Susie was my bridesmaid, of course, so we made her come and do stuff with us though she was very black and white and quite allergic to the whole wedding thing.

"You'll think differently when you meet the right person. You need to be more open-minded about it all," I told her as we stood in Madame Felipe's – the poshest bridal shop around – and I teased her by producing a lurid orange meringue-type bridesmaid dress.

"Emily, I'm thrilled you've found Robbie but this whole rigmarole is just not me. I'll wear the dress and hold the flowers and I'm sure we'll all have a fantastic day, but I don't ever see myself being the one in the white dress." She was firm. "Or this orange one, for that matter!" she added, prodding the hideous thing I was pretending she had to wear.

Susie was worried about her mother as well. The only way to describe her mum, Pauline, is to say that she believed utterly in alternative medicine, thought antibiotics were evil, and still dressed in hippy clothes like it was 1970. I loved her and thought she was funny, but then I didn't have to grow up with her.

"Your wedding is black tie, Em. She's going to turn up in one of her mental outfits and make a show of me," Susie groaned. "Knowing her, she'll have a patchwork quilt draped over her or, God forbid, one of her charity-shop wedding dresses on."

It was amazing how different Susie and her mother were. When we were kids, Susie's bedroom was always perfect, with her clothes folded and the bed expertly made. Pauline's idea of a wardrobe was an ancient basket-weave chair, which sagged under the bundle of mess she flung there. Her bed was never made, just pulled up with the cat still sleeping in it.

Pauline's one motherly skill was cooking – she was a marvellous cook and was always boiling vats of jam with various berries she'd picked from the hedgerows. With her hair tied back with an old pair of knickers, she'd hum to herself, totally lost in her task. The place would be a mess, though, and I could tell that Susie was almost sitting on her hands to stop from cleaning.

Now Susie's kitchen was used for heating up take-out food and most of the cupboards were filled with psychology books rather than tins of tomatoes. The oven still housed the instruction booklet and the shelves were still in the clear plastic packaging.

"Susie, how can you eat like this? Don't you ever crave a home-cooked meal?" I asked her one night when she was proudly showing me the unused oven.

"It gives me a warped sense of satisfaction. I keep thinking of the bombsite kitchen when I lived at home." She shuddered at the thought of the disarray.

"But don't you think she had the right idea?" I said. "She was happy. Isn't that what it's all about?"

"I'm not disputing the fact she was happy. I just couldn't bear the disorder. I would have to wipe the scattering of crunchy sugar off the counter, soak the sticky pot and wash the hundred and one utensils she'd used to test the jam for setting. I wasn't able to walk on a crunchy floor, so I'd have to sweep and mop it. By the time I'd sit down to join Mum, who would be absent-mindedly babbling away about jam-making with her grandmother and getting stung by a wasp as a child, I felt like killing her."

"I loved going to your house! *And* your mum! But I suppose I didn't have to live with her. "

Now, in the wedding-dress shop, I remembered Pauline's dottiness with affection. Who cared what she wore to the wedding?

"Don't worry about what your mother wears to the wedding," I insisted. "She'll look great and she'll be in seventh heaven. She loves nothing in the world more than a good wedding."

The day finally dawned and it was picture perfect. The sun split the stones, and the grounds of the country house where we were staying looked like a picture from a fairy-tale book.

Dad and I had a misty moment when I walked down the stairs to greet him in my dress.

"Oh darling, you look so beautiful. I'm so proud."

He hugged me to him and we stood in that embrace, fighting back emotion. It was a moment I will never forget, accepting a warm hug from my dad, with the knowledge that I was about to be a married woman.

Susie appeared at the top of the stairs, looking stunning in the pale blue simple gown we'd chosen for her. Her auburn hair sat in luxurious waves, like licks of flames against the cool-coloured fabric. She hesitated, not wanting to break up our moment.

"Come and have a group hug, Suze – you look stunning," Dad held out his arm to her and we all embraced.

Inwardly, I thanked my lucky stars that I had my dad. Maybe that was one of the reasons Susie was kind of anti-weddings. She knew she wouldn't have her dad to give her away.

The ceremony was quick – I didn't want to have one of those weddings where people end up staggering out of the church with numb bums, gagging for a drink, delighted the "boring bit" is over.

"Love you," whispered Robbie as we posed outside the church.

I squeezed his hand tightly back. "Love you too."

The rest of our wonderful day passed in a flash, then we danced the evening away, finally ending up in the residents' bar where a good old-fashioned sing-song ensued.

At seven o'clock the next morning the poor barman was gratefully relieved by the morning staff.

"I think we've dragged the arse out of our wedding day, Mrs Cusack," Robbie grinned with one eye open.

"Yeah, we're really married," I said dreamily as I tried to focus on my ring finger. I knew there was a wedding ring there – it was just a bit blurred. "And they all lived happily ever after," I sighed, trying not to slur.

And we did live happily ever after. For the next six years. Until Ellie dropped her bombshell and things began to come apart.

6

Emily

Life Parfait:
Take one happy mum and two energetic little children, sprinkle with
sunshine, ice-lollies, buckets and spades, coat liberally with sand. Turn
up the heat to a divinely relaxing temperature. Serve with a fixed smile
and a liberal seasoning of fear of what's to come.

That summer was glorious. It was like the summers I remembered as a child: blue skies, sunhats, ice-creams and trips to the beach. The sun shone endlessly and it made things so much easier with the children. We went to the local beach, where they got more mileage out of cheap buckets and spades than any of the expensive toys at home. We went for more picnics than the teddy bears and drank more lemonade than the Famous Five. We tried to catch butterflies with nets. Tia wanted to pet them, Louis wanted to pull their wings off and trap them in a jam-jar. We ate salt and vinegary chips while sitting on damp towels on the promenade and rode the ghost train, with sandy feet and delighted screams.

And all the time Mum and I waited for an appointment with the geneticist. We were living on a knife's edge. I tried not to become obsessive and frantic but the waiting was killing me. To pour salt on my wounds, Robbie was as cool as a cucumber about the whole thing. In fact he was blissfully going about his business as if nothing was happening.

Finally, four weeks after Ellie had dropped her bombshell, Mum and I got a cancellation appointment with the geneticist. She had agreed to see both of us together, so she could talk to us about the implications and help us to make a decision about being tested.

We were happy to go together. Dad was finding the whole thing too painful and Robbie was acting like a small child – all he was short of doing was sitting in the corner with his fingers in his ears, with his eyes firmly shut and humming. It was almost as if he'd decided if he ignored the whole situation, it might just go away.

On the day of our appointment, we arrived at the hospital and were shown into a small stuffy waiting-room. The walls were painted in magnolia and there was one print of a Van Gough painting in a cheap black frame, hanging crookedly in the middle of one wall. Other than that, the room was bare.

I felt sick to the pit of my stomach.

"Dr Cleary will see you now, ladies, please follow me," said the secretary.

We entered a bright, spotless and sparsely furnished room where a small, kind-looking, rotund lady held out her hand to greet us.

"Hello, it's lovely to meet you. I'm Dr Cleary, the Head of Genetics at this hospital. Thanks for coming in and agreeing to speak with us. We need families like you to come forward and agree to be tested. The more information we can accumulate, the closer we get to finding causes and cures for the different types of cancer. So I congratulate you both for taking this step today." She smiled encouragingly.

She was the only one smiling in the room. Mum and I stood rooted to the spot, looking back at her like startled chickens. I tried to maintain a calm demeanour, but inside I was quaking in my boots. I felt like having a tantrum like Tia – running around the room, swiping papers off the desk and lying on the floor kicking and screaming. Yelling that I didn't like this whole conversation, that it was yukkie and scary. Instead, I sat down with Mum and listened politely and tried to nod and murmur at the right moments.

She went through the whole genetic babble again, explaining about the mutated gene. We had a fifty per cent chance of testing positive. Fifty per cent sounds like bad odds if you were betting on a horse but surprisingly scary ones when it's about a cancer gene.

"It's just a blood test – very straightforward," she went on. "What is a hell of a lot more difficult is knowing if you are ready for the answer. We must be as sure as we possibly can be that you can cope with your results if those results are positive. Are you both with me?"

I answered first, glancing sideways at Mum. "I certainly want to know if I have the altered gene." I knew they wouldn't test me unless Mum's results were positive. It was part of the whole genetic therapy protocol.

"Yes, I would like to know too," said Mum. "Mostly for Emily's sake, but I would of course like to make sure that I am safe myself." Mum looked decidedly uneasy. A forced fleeting smile flickered over her lips and left.

I felt a pang of guilt inside. Was I forcing her to have this test done because she knew how much I wanted to know?

"Mum, try to take me out of the equation. Would you still do this if I wasn't gently nudging you?"

There was silence in the room as we all waited for Mum to answer.

"Look, Emily, if I'm very honest, I wouldn't do the test if it only concerned me, but I *have* to take you into consideration. That's what happens when you have children, as you well know. I don't feel a burning need to find out. If I get cancer, I get it. But you *do* need to know and if I can be the stepping-stone to help you achieve that, then of course I'll do it."

I felt a torrent of emotions flood through me. Usually I would have told Mum not to do anything she didn't want to just to please me. But this time was different. Our lives could depend on it. I just couldn't let it drop. I had to know.

"I'm sorry, Mum. I know I should say that I don't want to put you through all this, but I can't. The feeling is too strong. Something is telling me to keep going with this. Are you okay about carrying on with the test?"

"Of course I am. There is a part of me that wants to know too. By all means we will go for it. Absolutely."

We reached across the small gap between our chairs and held hands. We were in this together.

When Robbie came home that night, I filled him in on the day's news.

"Right." He exhaled loudly and rubbed his eyes. "Glass of wine?" He didn't look at me, just busied himself with opening the bottle.

I was immediately irritated with him. Why was he being so dismissive about all this? "Did you hear what I said?"

"Yes, Emily, I heard every word. I understand the plot. But we have no solid evidence to go by right at this moment in time, so if it's still allowed, I'm having a glass of wine." He rubbed my arm for a second and continued to open the wine.

Dr Cleary insisted we attend counselling sessions to prepare us in case of a positive result. This involved attending the same hospital and speaking with a man named Simon who looked very like he might have been a bumblebee in a former existence. He had a round body and wore a yellow, hand-knit jumper and black cords. His hair and spiky beard were black and he balanced tiny round glasses on the end of his bulbous nose.

"Hi, girls, you're great to come and talk with me. Let's get started. Moving directly to 'go' I need you both to try and express, in your own words, how you might be feeling about this genetic test idea." He rubbed his feelers together and looked at each of us in turn.

"Mum, why don't you use your own words first and then I'll do the same." I grinned at my mother.

She shot me a don't-be-a-cheeky-cow look and I tried to quash a giggle.

"Well, I would like to find out, both for myself and my daughter. It would be very useful to be armed with this knowledge so we could then choose what we would like to do about it."

"I'd like to have the test done because I'm still young," I said, "and I have small children and a husband and I was kind of planning on living for a good while longer." The giggle was gone from inside me as I spoke. "I've watched family members battle with cancer and I'd rather not go down that road, if I have a way of avoiding it."

"Mmm, yes, dear, that's a very good way of looking at it. I suppose it could be taken as a very positive step in a way, couldn't it?" Mr Bumblebee held his furry head to one side and squinted at me through his toy glasses.

"I think it's enormously positive," I said enthusiastically. "I think it's bloody miraculous to be able to find out if I could get cancer and knock it on the head before it knocks me out."

I noticed Mum's face changing. Her eyes filled with tears. She struggled for control and then said firmly, "Now that I hear Emily speaking so frankly, I am with her one hundred per cent. She's right, we have to take this and use it in a positive way."

We agreed to meet Mr Bumblebee again in a week. As we shook hands I resisted the urge to pat his fuzzy head. I wondered momentarily if he slept in a honeycomb.

"Are you okay?" I asked Mum as we left.

"Yes, love," she said and held my hand all the way back to the car. "It's a bit early in the day for drinking straight vodka," she said then, "so will we opt for a coffee?"

"Sure." I tried to gauge what Mum was thinking.

We drove to the nearest café and ordered two cappuccinos.

"Do you want a scone or something?" I mouthed over to Mum who'd grabbed a table. She shook her head and waved her hand to motion no. I couldn't stomach anything either.

When I reached the table, Mum stood up and hugged me.

"Whoa, you'll spill the coffee!"

We sat down and I pulled my chair in close to her.

"Are you okay?" I asked.

"Not really, Emily. What if I've given you this bloody damaged gene? I don't care about myself, but I can't bear the thought of you having it too. Christ, if they say you have it, I don't know if I'll be able to bear the guilt." Her eyes were mirroring her pain.

I felt a rush of love for her. I pulled her to me and we hugged for the longest time. With damp eyes I placed my two hands on her lovely face.

"Mum, all you've ever given me is love and understanding. You are the best mum in the world. If I have it, so be it. We'll have to deal with it. This is totally out of our control and if it weren't for the amazing technology they have to identify this thing, we'd never have known in the first place. I want you to promise me that you will banish all negative thoughts. We'll cope, we always have. As long as we've got each other, nothing can harm us."

As we hugged and picked up our coffee with wobbly hands, I swallowed the same icy fear I guessed Mum was harbouring. An image of my little pixie, Tia, flashed through my mind. If I had this gene, Tia could have it too. I would have to take my own advice and banish the nasty gremlin voices in my head. We would get through this. Of course we would.

The week flew. Mum and I chatted about the test on and off, but she had definitely relaxed about the process.

"You're so definite about things, Emily, but I have so much pent-up emotion about the whole cancer subject," she sighed. "Of course I wonder if I'm going to be next. I'm the only girl in my family who hasn't had cancer – it might just be waiting around the corner for me. But I can't live like that. I've had to put those thoughts out of my head. I'd managed to do that quite successfully and it's hard to dig all that up again and deal with it." She was struggling to even talk about this. She'd cared for Meg and Joanne as they'd died, washed them, fed them, held their frail hands. "But I'm now certain that I can face this head-on and deal with the result. It'll be better to know either way. There is also the chance that I don't have the altered gene. Then the matter will end there, right?"

"Right," I answered.

We went back into the hospital a week later to have our final meeting with Mr Bumblebee.

After a short discussion he said, "Okay, ladies, I am satisfied that you have both come to a conscious decision and I am happy to recommend to Dr Cleary that you go forward for the test."

Mr Bumblebee buzzed his signature on a form and we were ushered back to Dr Cleary's offices.

"Hi, Lucy and Emily! Come in and tell me what you've decided."

I handed her the form and she placed it in her file.

"We're ready to do this." Mum was now in control and sounding confident.

"I'm glad. Well, no time like the present – do you want to come with me now and I'll get a nurse to take the blood?"

We followed her to the out-patients department, where she spoke to a nurse and handed her some forms.

"I'll be in touch," she said then to us. "It takes six weeks to get the results and I would like you to come back in so I can give them to you in person. That way we can discuss what happens next – depending on the result." She squeezed the top of Mum's arm and was gone.

After a short wait in the corridor, Mum was called into an examination room.

"You can come too, if you're not squeamish about needles," the nurse said, nodding cheerfully at me.

We sat and the nurse tied a tight elasticised band around the top of Mum's arm. The vein protruded on the inside of her elbow. A needle drew the blood into a phial. It took seconds. Those seconds would produce information which could change our lives.

7

Emily

Psychotherapist Flambé:
Take one psychotherapist, dip into a shocking conversation first thing in the morning. Marinade brain for weeks, while simultaneously fixing other warped brains. Serve frazzled.

It was my four o'clock session, the one where I always felt the day's exhaustion hit. The client in front of me was fucking mad, and no, that's not a professional term. She was one of those patients I had to struggle to move forward with. She was argumentative and unreasonable and seemed to think she knew more than I did about my job. I'd been seeing her for four years. Sometimes I found her intriguing as she was such a challenge. Today I wanted to strangle her.

I knew I wasn't giving her my full attention, a fact which was so unprofessional that it was annoying me. I was never unprofessional. Nothing got in the way of my work. But she was my last client of the day and I was just willing the hands of the clock to tick a little bit faster.

This had become a fixed pattern in recent weeks. Earlier in the day

I could force myself to concentrate on my work but, when my energy slumped in the late afternoon, my mind would inevitably slide back to my friend and her situation.

I had tried to get Emily to open up to me about her feelings on the matter, thinking it might help her to talk, but she hadn't fallen for my therapist's wiles.

"I'm fine, Susie, honestly," she'd say. "All I can do is take this thing one step at a time."

My mother always worried that I spent too much time analysing things. She never analysed anything. I often wondered if I had inherited this tendency from my father. But, of course, I knew nothing about him. He never even knew Mum was pregnant. She only found out a few weeks after his funeral. They were engaged, but not yet married. Then he went out on a very wet night in January and his car skidded and hit a wall. He died instantly.

She'd never really expanded on the story. She'd get that faraway pained look in her eyes and I always felt an invisible boundary stopping me from pushing her further about him. Mum had a sense of fragility about her, as if her state of mind was delicate, and even as a child I knew not to push her when she didn't want to talk about something.

The older I got, the less I felt able to approach Mum about him.

Once, when I asked about my paternal grandparents, she shuddered and told me how they had shunned her.

"They didn't think I was good enough for him to begin with, and when they realised I was pregnant they totally rejected me and my unborn child." Her voice rose and began to shake, her face went all blotchy and I knew the tears would come soon.

"And you just accepted it?" Even though I knew it was upsetting her, I kept going, I so wanted to know. "Did they ever see me even? Didn't you want to march to their front door and say here is your granddaughter? She's your dead son's flesh and blood, a last remaining part of him. Had you no compulsion to stand up and be counted?"

I spun around to find Mum sitting with her hands up to her face, looking like a cowering puppy expecting to be beaten with a rolled-up newspaper. I felt terrible. I'd pushed her too far.

"Mum, should we not talk about this?" I begged. "I'd just love to know about him. Places you used to go? Did you have a special song? Was he funny? Was he quiet?"

"It's too painful right now, Susie. You'll have to give me a bit of time. I can't dredge up all that anguish at the moment. We don't need to have this conversation right this second." She inhaled deeply, closed her eyes and exhaled, stretching her palms out in front of her.

Subject closed. That was it as far as she was concerned.

A part of me wanted to yell and scream that she'd had fourteen years to come to terms with her anguish and that *I* wanted to have that conversation. But in her own way Mum was as stubborn as a mule and once she'd switched off and decided she was finished, I might as well bang my head off a brick wall as try to sway her.

Another part of me agreed with her: the past should be left in the past.

She spent that entire evening reading her Mills and Boon novels. That was her way of escaping. She'd wrap herself in a revolting self-created patchwork quilt and immerse herself in a world of romance and fluff, her legs curled under her, with cups of sweet tea. She was almost childlike when she got into that mode. But that had always been the problem: she was supposed to be the adult, not the child.

The morning after I'd tried to make her talk all those years ago, I woke to find her making pancakes, in one of her Empire line floaty dresses, with Tom Jones droning on in the background.

"Good morning, darling. I thought we'd have a pancake party. That'll be lovely, won't it?"

As usual the entire kitchen was dusted with flour, the sugar was everywhere and dribbles of cracked egg and a pool of milk coated the small Formica kitchen counter.

I found myself having to grit my teeth not to go over and swipe all the mess onto the floor and yell at her to stop living in La-la Land and get in touch with reality. But as I watched her ladle the batter into the frying pan, her head bobbing to the music, I knew she just wasn't going to let me break her fantasy. I sat seething at the kitchen table and marvelled at how she could genuinely take an unpleasant or upsetting issue and just bury it. Sweep it under the carpet and make it go away. There! Gone! Let's make pancakes.

I gave her the silent treatment for almost a week that time. I just couldn't forgive her for being so secretive and passive. I needn't have bothered, mind you – she simply carried on skipping and pottering and twittering just as she always did.

I'd never even seen a photograph of my father, but I assumed I must look like him. Mum was almost five foot tall and I towered over her. She was also dark-haired and brown-eyed. I share her sallow skin, but that's where our similarities end.

His name was Jim. In my mind's eye, since I was a child, I'd created an image of a tall, stocky, well-built man, with auburn hair like mine, dressed in a smart suit with shiny black shoes. He was always smiling in the image, which was nice, but for all I knew he might have been a grumpy old sod who never cracked a smile in his life.

I would have loved to have another relative in my life. I had an awkward and stilted relationship with Mum's parents, Granny and Granddad Rosedale. They'd played very little part in my life growing up. Mum was their only child and she was a sore disappointment to them when she arrived home with the news of her pregnancy. She was a disgrace to them.

She had managed while I was a baby but they'd never forgiven her, nor had they helped her. We saw Granny and Granddad Rosedale about three times a year. Their house was dark and cold, even in the middle of the summer, and it smelled.

"Say hello to Granny and Granddad!" Mum would kind of push me forward into their little dank hallway. We always brought a cake and a couple of bottles of orange with us.

"Don't, whatever you do, drink out of their cups," Mum would warn. "And wash your hands if you have to use the bathroom." Mum was never what would be classed as house-proud but our home was never a health hazard. Granny and Granddad's house was neglected and their poor eyesight hindered by the lack of natural light ensured every surface was kind of greasy and sticky, with dust coating everything.

I'd drink my bottle of orange (by the neck) and eat a slice of cake (off my own hand). We'd have the same conversation each time.

"You're getting bigger by the minute," Granny would sniff and look down her thin bony nose at me.

"How are your studies going?" Granddad would ask, shouting, "What?" before I could even answer. He was as deaf as a post and had a huge honker of a nose, and ears which stuck out so much I could see the small amount of light which managed to claw its way through the manky windows shining through them, making them look kind of purply and veiny. For years, I would run to the mirror when I got home and hold up my hair to see if my ears looked like his. Thankfully, they never did. It's something I always keep a close eye on all the same.

So it was always Mum and me against the world. I suppose she made it that way. She allowed Jim's parents to shun me and didn't push the limits with her own parents. She seemed content for us to be together as a little unit of two.

On several occasions I rooted through Mum's two shoeboxes which she kept under her bed. They contained letters and postcards from friends, photos and other meaningless-to-me bits and pieces. There were no love letters from Jim, or photos of him. I had no links to him.

But since Emily had phoned with her news involving genetics, it had raised a question for me. I knew nothing about my father's side of the family. I knew nothing about him. What if they had a history of cancer or heart disease? Even more importantly for a woman who worked with minds, what was he like, who was he, really, inside? What characteristics had I inherited from him?

Maybe I should try to find out about this Jim person. I would have to think it through before I broached the subject with Mum. I was a grown woman now and we could have a grown-up chat about him. Or so I told myself.

Our previous conversation was still a source of pain for me though. I could still see Mum's quivering hands covering her face, trying to protect herself from the trauma of her past. It would be a tough call to push her to tell me what I wanted to know. I would work out the best approach.

But not right now. First and foremost, I needed to help Emily.

I had eventually managed to talk to my friend Sheila in Florida – as bad luck would have it, she'd been away on a month's holiday when I first tried to contact her – and she had given me the benefit of her knowledge and expertise. She had also put me in touch with some clinics in the States which specialised in genetic cancers.

I now wanted to talk to Emily and Robbie, armed with the information I had collected to date.

I wrote up my notes for the day and then phoned Emily.

Robbie answered. Emily wasn't home yet but he expected her any minute, so I asked him if I could come by to discuss my findings on the gene.

"I'd like to come right now," I said, "but if that doesn't suit I'll come any evening you wish."

His response astonished me.

"There's no point in getting on your high horse until we have some solid facts, Susie. Emily's not dying of terminal cancer. Let's get the whole thing in perspective here. She probably doesn't even have this problem. In two months' time, we'll probably all have forgotten about this whole thing. Probably just a storm in a teacup if you ask me."

And he chuckled.

Who was he trying to convince? Bloody typical male. Sticking his head in the sand and refusing to deal with it until it came up and bit him on the arse.

"Okay, Robbie, have it your way, but I'm going to do as much as I can to research this gene, just in case Emily gets a positive result. You can do nothing if that suits you, but I'm on a mission here!" I hung up feeling furious with Robbie.

So far, I wasn't too happy about the prognosis with this mutated gene. All the medics in the States were saying that surgery was the way to go. But surely there was a less barbaric way of dealing with this? The thought of Emily having to chop her body to bits seemed hideous to me. There had to be another way. If there was, I was going to find it.

8

Emily

Suspense Stroganoff:
Take three relations, place them in a hospital office, fill to the brim with trepidation. Add two cups of anticipation, one cup of apprehension and half a cup of anxiety. Let the fear drip from every pore. Hold breath and sit awkwardly on the edge of uncomfortable grey chairs.

Mum, Ellie and I all sat in the familiar surrounds of Dr Cleary's offices. It was six weeks since we'd taken the test, six horrendous weeks when I couldn't look at the kids without my heart jumping into my mouth with fear.

The only amusing element so far was Ellie insisting the three of us go in together.

"Girl power," she muttered.

Our own little support network definitely made it somewhat easier.

Mum was first to be called in.

"I'd like Ellie and Emily with me," she told Dr Cleary.

"No problem. Hi, girls." The doctor smiled warmly. "I won't string this out for you, Lucy." She walked us all into her office and we sat down on hard chairs.

The doctor held Mum's gaze. "I'm afraid to say your test results are positive. You carry the BRCA1 gene mutation. I'm sorry."

I cannot describe what I felt in that moment.

Dr Cleary took Mum's hand gently and held it, kindly asking: "Are you okay, Lucy?"

"I'm okay," said Mum shakily. "I'm just a bit shocked."

Her eyes filled with tears and she looked to Ellie and me, trying to control her emotions. We all hugged. No one spoke for a few minutes. We all needed to take this information on board. The silence in the room that day spoke volumes.

"At least we know now. It's good to know, isn't it?" Mum said.

"Yes, it is," Dr Cleary encouraged. "I have an information pack here for you. It outlines the options open to you now. There's nothing new here. Just the surgical and non-surgical options and where to attend next, should you want to. Obviously, there are now implications for you, Emily." She turned towards me. "I don't want to have that discussion today, if that's all right with you. What needs to happen now is for you all to go away and digest this information, before deciding what to do next. Okay?"

"Sure." I managed a smile. I already knew what I was going to do. I wanted that test done, as soon as possible. I also knew if it was positive, I wanted the surgery. Immediately. I wanted all the dangerous bits ripped out. If it meant having my arms and legs chopped off along with my breasts and ovaries, I'd do it. Never in my life had I felt so passionate and determined about anything.

But perhaps now was not the time to express that opinion. Today was about Mum. I needed to make sure she was able to cope with what she'd been told.

"It's amazing in light of this result that I haven't developed cancer before now," Mum said quietly.

"Well, this doesn't mean you will definitely develop cancer, Lucy. It just tells us you are predisposed to it. It tells us that you should keep a close eye on yourself. Do you understand?" Dr Cleary waited for Mum to answer.

"Yes, I understand." Mum sighed and stood up. "Let's go," she said to us. "Thank you, Dr Cleary, you've been very sympathetic. I don't envy you your job. You handle it marvellously."

Mum was right, this woman was doing a very serious and difficult job every day, and she was brilliant at it.

We drove to a nearby small city park and sat on a patch of grass together. If we'd gone there under normal circumstances it would have been gorgeous. A pond with low iron railings surrounding it was filled with happily quacking ducks and flowering lily-pads. To a stranger, we represented a lovely scene. Three women chatting in the sunshine, surrounded by wide-open green space, on a warm and bright afternoon.

"So where do you go from here, Lucy?" Ellie was stretched out on the grass.

"Well, Mark and I have spoken about the options. We both agree that surgery isn't the road I would like to take. I've already had a hysterectomy and I really don't want to go for a mastectomy."

"And Dad agrees?"

"Yes, he does. For women of my age, the latter half of fifty, mammograms are very successful."

I had very mixed emotions about her initial decision. In one way, I was glad she was happy and certain about how she wanted to handle this. If she didn't want to go under the knife, that was fine. But another part of me wanted her to have any breast tissue that existed removed, so she would be safe.

"We have each other and there's a great system in the hospital that you can tap into, Lucy, so you're going to be just fine." Ellie was as strong and positive as ever.

"I'm behind you all the way, Mum," I said, "whatever way you want to handle this."

I hugged her. All I could think was how much I loved her. All my life she'd been my night and day, she'd taught me how to be the woman I was.

As we hugged, I closed my eyes and begged the angels not to take my mummy away. I couldn't bear it. My life would be so cold without her. I suddenly had one of those moments when I felt like a child again. I'd forgotten for one brief second that I was now married and a mother of two. Just for that nanosecond, I was a vulnerable child once more, and all I wanted was my mummy.

Next, I had to tell Robbie. I had turned my phone off while we were with Dr Cleary. Now I purposely left it off until I got home. I didn't feel it was right to tell him over the phone.

He was there when I finally got home. The house was quiet apart from the television. The children were in bed, which I was thankful for. I needed the space to talk to him.

He looked at me when I walked into the living room. "Well? How did it go?"

"Not great. Shite, in fact. Mum has the altered gene." I could feel my eyes welling up. Saying it out loud to someone else for the first time made it real.

"Okay. Fine. So Lucy has this gene. What are they going to do about it?" He got up and began pacing up and down. "She can have medication or have the tissue removed, can't she?" He was rubbing his chin and doing his I-am-a-robot impression.

"There is an option of surgery but Mum doesn't want that. She's going to phone St Theresa's Hospital and take it from there. They have a special unit for families at risk of cancer. She'll know more when she sees them."

"I need a drink," he muttered and headed for the kitchen.

As Robbie opened a bottle of wine, I could see his agitation growing. He missed the bottle seal with the knife and nicked his finger.

"Fuck it!"

"Robbie, take it easy." I went over and put my arms around his waist.

He carried on struggling with the wine bottle. "When is Lucy seeing these St Theresa's people?"

"She hasn't phoned them yet. I'm sure she'll get in touch with them over the next couple of days." I sat at the kitchen table, appreciating the silence. The only sound was a glugging noise as the wine filled the glasses.

Robbie didn't say cheers and clink glasses with me, which he always did without thinking.

"When are you having the test done?" Robbie's face was like stone and he didn't meet my gaze.

"As soon as possible," I answered quietly. His demeanour was unnerving me slightly. "Robbie, are you okay with this? Hadn't you considered a positive result over the last six weeks?"

He ran his fingers through his hair and drained the substantial glass of red wine. "Obviously not, Emily. Obviously not." He refilled his glass and wandered into the living room.

His reaction was astonishing. Why was he so upset and angry about this? But I couldn't deal with what he thought right now: I needed to sort out what I thought.

The next evening I found Robbie sitting at his computer late at night, insisting he had to do some research for an annual fundraiser which he organised in aid of an animal welfare group.

He was tense and irritable. "I need something different this year. They do such amazing work and I know this fun day is vitally important for them."

"You're a good man, Robbie, to put so much into that for them. I hope they appreciate you doing all this work free of charge every year." I hugged him and left him to it.

Robbie had always vowed when he went into PR that he wasn't going to turn into a social climber. He hated the fickle end of the business, the air-kissing and the only-speaking-to-the-people-who-mattered end of it. When his business was a year old he decided to start doing a couple of charity functions, offering his services for free. Now one of his biggest events of the year was the one for the animal rescue people. It was always a great family day out and generated much-needed funds for the charity.

I knew he was upset but I had learned in the past to leave him alone when he was mulling things over. He would come to me when he was ready.

The previous day Dad had been pretty rocked to the core by the news too. He'd gone through the information pack which Dr Cleary had given us.

"You'll need to get in touch with St Theresa's Hospital tomorrow morning, Lucy, and tell them that you need an urgent appointment." He was thumbing his way through the pages, underlining parts as he went.

"Yes, dear," was Mum's reply. I think she said "*yes, dear*" in her sleep. It was an automatic-pilot response, which worked very well for them both. Dad felt he was being taken seriously and Mum felt she had shut him up. Perfect.

Mum had phoned St Theresa's Hospital and arranged an appointment with the family risk and assessment clinic. She had taken the first step towards being monitored and looked after. I was glad.

Mum and Dad attended the clinic at St Theresa's the following week. They phoned me as they left after their visit.

"Hi, Emily, you're on speakerphone in the car. Dad and I have just left the hospital. Mr Green is extremely nice and has put me on a screening programme." Mum sounded more relaxed than I'd heard her in a long time.

"He was good all right," said Dad. "Seems to know his arse from his elbow which is always useful."

If even Dad was impressed with him, he must be a magician as well as a good doctor.

Two weeks later I returned to the genetic testing lab, along with Robbie, to have my test done. Dr Cleary was there once again to greet us. For Robbie's benefit, she went through all the technical information again. I signed a form stating that I had requested the test of my own free will, and was prepared for whatever the results showed.

Robbie was more himself and asked a few questions.

"How accurate is this test then?" he wanted to know.

"It's very accurate, Robbie," Dr Cleary answered calmly. "The gene mutation is found at a specific point along the line when we look at a gene. So it will either be present or not. It's very cut and dried."

Satisfied that Robbie had finished, she led us to the out-patients clinic once more.

"Okay, Emily, I'll leave you now. You know the drill from here. I'll call you as soon as we have your results and you can come in and see me." Dr Cleary shook both our hands and walked away.

"Do you want to come in with me?" I asked Robbie.

"Not unless you particularly want me to. I don't really do the whole blood thing as you might remember from our children's births." He smirked and we exchanged a smile. Robbie hadn't handled the whole birthing process too well. He'd found it all a bit gory and graphic. He wasn't one of those fathers avidly videoing his wife giving birth. In fact, he'd passed out.

Within minutes, the nurse had filled the phials with blood and sent me on my way. I tried not to think how important those little phials were to my future.

"Well, that's it all done for now," I stated in the car on the way home.

"Yep, no point in getting too het up about it until we know the results."

Robbie drove home like a bat out of hell and cursed at the other drivers. Nothing unusual about that.

Somehow I got through the next six weeks. Life went on as usual. The children played, went to school and fought. Susie phoned frequently, gently providing support, and we met occasionally. I shopped for groceries, cooked, cleaned and tried to be calm. It wasn't easy.

Meanwhile, somewhere in a laboratory, there was a small phial of my blood floating around waiting to be tested. The results of that test could change my life forever.

9

Susie

Accepting the Past Bombe:
Have your mother drop a large bomb. Take information and place in gullet and try not to choke. Run through all emotions known to woman. Place in a large mixing bowl covered with bone and hair, commonly known as the brain. Toss about violently until all reason and sensibility are lost. Chew over in one's mind a little more, causing as much anguish as possible to self. Finish off by wanting to crawl into the oven and gas oneself.

I left my mum's little cottage and broke the habit of a lifetime. Ever since I'd owned my car, I'd either spend my driving time talking on the phone or blasting music. It was a little quirk I had, that I couldn't drive in silence. That night I needed and welcomed the quietness. I inhaled deeply and the smell of the soft cream leather filled my nostrils. As I drove back to Blackrock, the rain started to fall. It was gentle and rhythmic at first, but by the time I pulled into the underground car park at my apartment block it was lashing. That sideways, right-in-your-ear-hole, bounce-off-your-cheeks type of rain.

I remembered all the conversations Emily and I'd had about my dad when we were kids.

"He could be an Arabian Prince who my mum had an affair with, and she had to flee the scene and never tell anyone about my existence," I said.

Emily had been doubtful. "Nah, I don't think Arabian Princes have wavy red hair, do they? And he'd have given Pauline something surely, a little palace or even a few gold bars. None of her tiaras are even real. I don't think so."

How different our conversations would have been if we'd known his name was Jim Lynch and he worked in a supermarket.

Because that was what my outrageous mother had told me that very evening. After a lifetime of silence on the subject. No, not silence – a lifetime of *lying* on the subject. He hadn't died in a car crash before I was born. He hadn't died at all as far as she knew. They had met stacking shelves in a supermarket in Bray. It had been a one-night stand – actually more like a five-minute stand – and she had simply never told him about me. The final insult was that I had been conceived on top of a freezer cabinet of frozen veg. She might have spared me that bit.

I had gone to see her, fully intending to probe gently at first and then to insist gently but firmly. The last thing I had expected was for the floodgates to open with hardly a nudge from me. Well, that didn't describe it very accurately – there hadn't exactly been a great flood of information and it was all delivered quite casually as if we were having an everyday conversation.

My head was throbbing and I knew my forehead looked like a ploughed field, it was so wrinkled with tension. I was glad at that moment that there was no one waiting to talk to me at home. I cast my mind back to Kevin. He could have been sitting there with my dinner ready and a bottle of wine opened, waiting to greet me with a kiss . . .

Sometimes I had fleeting moments of regret, but most of the time I knew I'd done the right thing, ending my engagement to Kevin. We'd been together for two years when he proposed. For me, it was totally out of the blue. I'd been happy with our relationship before the engagement. We'd done a lot together. I'd even gone on my first sun holiday with Kevin.

I was nineteen and in my second year of college. I'd got the points I needed in school and got into UCD on the first round of offers to do psychology. I did really well in my exams – in fact, I got the highest in my class, so I won a cash prize, much to my delight.

"Let's blow the money on a nice couple of weeks in the sun," Kevin had suggested.

"No, I need that money for next year, and besides I'm starting work in the bank for the summer. It's a nice idea, but it's just not feasible for me, sorry, Kevin."

"Susie, when are you going to learn to live a little? Most normal young people go away on holidays. Can't you tell the bank you'll start two weeks later? We all know that you're going to become an amazing psychotherapist, that's bloody obvious. You've more brainpower and determination than anyone else in the class. But what use will you be to anyone if you're miserable and alone? Don't miss out on all the fun stuff. Don't let life pass you by and spend your later life regretting the fact that you never let yourself live."

"You make me sound like a fucking hermit! Things are just different for me, Kevin. I don't live in a nice four-bed semi, with two parents with high-paying jobs. I have to pay my own way. If I want to get through college, it's down to me all the way. That's the way it is. That might seem very boring to you and I apologise if you don't like it, but I'm not going to jeopardise my future just to suit you."

I knew after I'd said it that it all sounded a bit dramatic. Maybe Kevin was right. Maybe I should use a little of the money to pay for a holiday. The bank would hold my job for two weeks, I was pretty sure of that. It took me two days to admit to Kevin that I'd actually like to go on a holiday. My stubborn pride was one of my bad points, and it was damn hard to admit I agreed with him.

"That's fantastic, Suze. We'll have a great time! I'll grab some brochures today and we'll book a last-minute deal. All you need to do is get a passport sorted and we can get going!"

His delight was endearing. He really did want to see me enjoy myself. Mum was delighted too.

"Oh, that sounds like a super idea! The money for the fees will turn up anyway. You take life far too seriously at times. You're young, you need to experience life. It'll be fabulous!" And she clapped with joy.

If only I had known how "fabulous" it was going to be . . .

Three weeks later we arrived in Tenerife and took the bus to our hotel.

The only seats left were beside a couple with a small screaming baby. It kept looking at me and screaming more.

"Babies hate me. I don't do anything to them but they just seem to sense my unease and scream," I whispered to Kevin.

"Ah, you'll get used to them when we have our own," he smiled and patted me on the leg as he looked out the window.

An alarm bell went off in my head. What did he mean when we have our own? I had no intention of having babies or getting married for quite a long time – if ever. I had a plan mapped out in my head. I was going to be a successful career woman. I was going to make it. None of that involved mopping up baby sick or sitting on holiday buses in the middle of the night juggling small yelling creatures.

I let Kevin's comment go. We'd only arrived in Tenerife and I didn't want to cause a row and end up spending the next two weeks with someone who wasn't talking to me.

The apartment was right from the seventies, with cracked terracotta floor tiles, a pair of battered divan single beds, a shabby chipped dressing table, two white plastic chairs and a round wobbly white plastic garden table.

"It's basic, but it'll do," said Kevin.

He was cheerful. I felt like crying. Some of the flats Mum and I had ended up in when I was growing up had been dingy, but none of them were a patch on this dump.

"We won't care about the place anyway – we didn't come for the décor. Let's go and get pissed!" Kevin was already opening the door to leave.

And that was the theme of the entire holiday.

"Let's go to the main night-club area and find the Irish bar," he said when we exited the hotel.

The sign for Paddy O'Grady's Pub flashed in neon Kelly green up ahead.

"Here we go – home for the next two weeks, I reckon." Kevin rubbed his hands together and dashed in ahead of me.

I felt as if I didn't know this person. I felt that even more as he yawned and burped his way back up the road after consuming multiple pints of Guinness in Paddy O'Grady's with a group of pissed louts, talking about Gaelic football. And even more when, back at the apartment, he collapsed across the middle of one of the beds, in his clothes, making noises that resembled a choking walrus.

After that, I did my own thing: swimming, sunbathing, reading, studying, getting pedicures and manicures. And he did his: getting pissed.

I knew that I should have broken up with Kevin as soon as we returned home, but somehow the time seemed to march on. The summer passed and I got into my work in the bank. He wasn't the focal point of my life, we weren't living together and I really wasn't that bothered by him either way. I know it sounds a bit cold of me, but he was someone to go to parties with and he was nice enough to me, so I kept up the charade.

By the time I was ready to graduate from college, I knew we had outgrown each other.

I was honestly planning on telling him that we needed to go our separate ways, when he proposed.

It hit me like a ton of bricks. I'm sure I must have looked like one of the fish from Sea World when he got down on one knee and offered me the small felt box. It was the furthest thing from my mind. I had no intention of ever marrying anyone, let alone Kevin.

"I love you so much, Susie. We're great together and I know we're quite young by modern standards, but you'll be out of college and into work next month. You'll be working with the best. Things are on the up for you. With my engineering degree, I'm going to have my pick of jobs. Why wait? We know we work well together. We can think about buying a house together. With our combined wages and your links with the bank, we'll secure a mortgage no bother. What do you say?" He looked so sure I was going to say yes, I just couldn't say no.

"Erm . . . yes, then."

I know this sounds shallow and dim of me, but the whole thing just ran away with itself after that. I had thought we could have a long engagement, as in ten years or more. But Mum was like she'd won the lotto. All her dreams had come true. A real wedding to organise!

I told both Kevin and Mum that I didn't want a huge hoo-ha. That I just wasn't that sort of girl. It wasn't going to be a huge event, sixty people max. But before I knew it, the church was booked and a venue was secured. Kevin paid the deposit and I found myself spending every spare Saturday and late-night shopping evening in bridal boutiques with Mum.

"We can always have one of these dresses copied if you really love it. My friend Margaret in the library is a talented seamstress and I know she'd be delighted to help out." Mum still hadn't lost the thrift shopper in herself.

"These are a shocking price, Mum. Why on earth would anyone spend two thousand euros on a dress that they're planning on wearing for a few hours?"

"I never understood that but I suppose it's a very important day, isn't it?" Mum was away in dreamland.

I thought, looking at her, she couldn't have been made to feel any more euphoric. A gram of crack cocaine wouldn't have had such an uplifting effect on her.

Eight weeks before the wedding, Kevin and I were in the car on the way to the stationer's to organise the invitations. We had applied to the bank for a mortgage. Everything was moving forward. I felt like I was in a coma. It was like I wanted to shout out, "No, everybody stop, this isn't what I want!" but my voice wasn't working. My life was like the car of a roller-coaster, building momentum, dipping and diving away. Everyone else was enjoying the ride so much I felt stunned into silence.

We were sitting in a traffic jam. It was December and the weather was unseasonably warm and calm. Some enthusiastic people had already put up their Christmas trees, and I could see the twinkling lights peeping through the window into the dusky early evening light.

"Just imagine this time next year, we'll be married," Kevin smiled across at me.

"No, we won't. Kevin, I can't. It's not going to work. I'm sorry, it's all wrong, it has to be stopped, I'm so sorry!" I blurted it all out, making a total mess of the whole thing. Although I'm not sure if there's a more eloquent way of telling someone you don't want to marry them.

"What are you talking about, Susie?" Poor Kevin looked sideways as the lights turned green. "You're having me on, aren't you?"

"No, I wish I was. I'm sorry. We need to pull over. I can't do this any more. I never meant to let all this go on as long as it has. You and Mum have been so excited and everything just seemed to take off. I kept thinking there'd be a right moment to tell you, but it never came and now it's just all come tumbling out. Oh, God, Kevin, I'm so sorry! I can't marry you. I don't want to marry anyone. Not now, and to be honest, not ever. I'm just not that way inclined. I want to build my career, I want to be in control of my life." I felt like such a bitch as I saw the hurt in his eyes.

"But you can build your career," said Kevin desperately. "You're doing brilliantly with Dr Breen. You're making your mark really quickly. You're going to have loads of your own patients. I'm never going to stop you from doing what you love. We'll just have each other as well. You're just suffering pre-wedding jitters. You'll be fine, Susie, it happens to loads of people."

"No, I'm not. I know this is going to sound so cruel and mean of me, but I never wanted to marry you. I'm sorry. But that's the truth." I couldn't look at him.

"Thanks, Susie. What a lovely thing to say! Jesus, you really know how to throw punches, don't you? So is that it then?"

I could hear the anger building in his voice. I didn't blame him. I knew it was a lousy thing to do, but I couldn't help how I felt. I knew I'd been a coward letting it all get this far, but I had honestly never meant it all to happen.

"Maybe you should take a couple of weeks. We won't contact each other, you can think things through, and we could discuss it then. What do you think? This is all a bit highly charged now and rash. Let's just take stock of the situation and talk in a week or so? What do you say?" Poor Kevin was sitting on the hard shoulder of the dual carriageway, with his hands gripping the steering wheel for dear life.

"No, Kevin. I'm sorry, but it's not going to change the way I feel. It's not a rash decision – I've felt like this for a very long time. From the moment we got engaged in fact. I'd only be dragging the inevitable out further. I'm sorry. I have a whole different idea in my head of what I want. I want to do a Master's which means another two years studying and I don't want to be married at the moment."

"Well, thanks for finally letting me in on the secret. How kind of you. Do you realise what a cold callous bitch you sound? Did you ever love me? In fact, don't even answer that. Leave me with some dignity at least!" He thumped the steering wheel.

"I'm sorry, Kevin. I really am." I removed my ruby and diamond engagement ring and placed it in the little cubby-hole between the front seats of the car. I opened the car door to get out.

"What the hell are you doing? You can't get out of the car on the side of a motorway! Don't be bloody ridiculous, Susie. I'll take you home." He was shaking his head and looking at me as if I was insane.

"I'll be fine. I'd rather be on my own. Good-bye, Kevin." I slammed the door and walked back down the motorway. I felt like such a mean cow to hurt Kevin like that. But the relief was overwhelming. Grinding my hands into my coat pockets, I walked on. I bit back the tears. At least I was free. I was me again. I didn't look back, I didn't regret telling Kevin the truth. I did feel rotten to the core for hurting him and leading him on. I knew it was wrong of me and I also knew the poor git would probably spend rather a long time in some other psychologist's office trying to come to terms with what I'd done to him. I had handled myself really badly, and I knew I had to make sure I didn't do that again. I had to take control of myself and my own life. I couldn't afford to keep leaving waves of devastation behind me like that. I had enough skeletons in my closet without creating more.

Now, I was still on my own. I was happy with it that way. I finished my Master's and I'd been able to work and focus on my goals. Men came and went and that was just fine with me. I was not looking for any long-haul commitments, I didn't feel the need for a constant man in my life. I had worked my way up the ladder in lots of ways. I had my own home and car. I had my own practice. I went for pedicures every six weeks like clockwork. That still made me feel good. I knew it was silly, especially in Ireland, where my feet spent most of the year cocooned in boots, but I knew my trotters looked good. It was like wearing expensive underwear. Nobody knows whether your knickers came from a chain store or a lingerie shop, but they feel so different.

I realised I was still sitting in my car. It was getting late and I needed to get ready for work in the morning. As I made my way over to the elevator which would bring me up to my apartment, I thought about Jim Lynch. I wondered where he was. Was he even alive still?

I couldn't wait to tell Emily about my mother's confession.

10

Emily

A Recipe for Disaster:
Take one married couple who've been marinating for several weeks.
Sift into a small stuffy room. Rub salt on an open wound. Feel the pain
and try desperately to hold it all together. Assume delicate relationship
is ready for a battering.

My results came back two months later. Robbie came with me to see Dr Cleary. It felt like a strange case of déjà vu – I'd been here before.

"Emily, we have your results here," Dr Cleary said. "I'm afraid the result is also positive. I'm so sorry." She looked gravely at us both.

"It's not your fault, Dr Cleary," I said immediately.

"How do you feel?" she asked.

How did I feel?

"I'm relieved to know and I'm not surprised," I replied. "In fact if you'd told me it was not positive, I don't think I would have believed you." My heart was beating like a drum. I could feel my hands shaking. My throat was tightening and I found it hard to speak.

"Are you okay, Robbie?" she asked.

"I think so," he replied, looking a little shell-shocked.

The conversation which followed was stilted and I wasn't really paying much attention.

We didn't hang around for long. We stood outside the main hospital door and I tried to feed coins into the parking machine to pay for our ticket.

"Here, Robbie, you do it. I can't make them fit." I stuffed the coins into his hands because mine were shaking so much.

We drove out of the car park in silence.

"Well, it's good to know," Robbie said finally. "Now we can go home and talk this over and decide what way you want to run with this. You have plenty of options."

But I knew already what I wanted to do. I wanted the surgery.

"I've already made up my mind, Robbie. I want the surgery. I want all the dangerous stuff cut out of my body. There is no question about it."

Robbie didn't answer.

We drove home with the radio doing all the talking. For me, there was no decision to make. I didn't feel I had an option. I felt as if these people were telling me, "We have a riddle for you, but we also have the answer." I knew what the answer was, so I was going for that option. I wanted to ensure my safety.

I could have been knocked down by a bus any day crossing the road. There are a million and one ways to die. I didn't want to die of cancer and leave my small children motherless. The surgery could stop me getting breast cancer or ovarian cancer. I had to do it. I wanted to do it.

"But it's so drastic," Robbie stated, "having a mastectomy and your ovaries removed."

"I know, but believe me, it's necessary."

He'd never known anyone with cancer. He'd never seen anyone he loved being eaten away by this malignant parasite. If he had, he'd have known exactly why I was so adamant about my decision. I had to paint the picture for him. I had to recapture the hospital vigil at the bedside of a young and beautiful woman, whose body was eaten up from the inside by this evil and despicable disease. A woman who was someone's daughter, and someone's mother, a sister, a partner, an auntie and a friend.

"It's kind of barbaric," he added.

"Robbie, it could be the easy option when compared with the alternative. Barbaric it may seem, but death is very fucking final. There's no arguing with that. Bringing the kids to visit Mummy's grave would be even less fun."

The radio droned on again.

Why couldn't he get this? The doctors knew how cancer could hurtle out of control. They couldn't guarantee a successful outcome should the bastard strike me. Tia and Louis could easily be visiting Mummy's grave.

"I'll support whatever decision you make, Emily, but you should take some more time to look at the options," Robbie begged. "There has to be an alternative – let's talk to some doctors in the States or other countries. Let's find out what they are doing."

"The surgery would reduce my risk by 95%. That's huge. Robbie, I think it's time we called Susie and got her to come over with the info she's gathered. You know she's been wanting to."

"Okay, ask Susie to call over maybe tomorrow night if she's free. I'd value her opinion." He was still staring straight ahead. At last he was willing to listen to her and read the information she'd collected.

Through all our years of marriage and being together, Susie and Robbie had always got along. I knew I was lucky. If they'd hated each other, it would have put me in a really difficult situation.

Susie did as I'd asked and spent the following evening talking Robbie and me through her findings.

"I've been in contact with clinics in the States and more recently in Holland. They're a lot more familiar with the gene and have thousands of patients who have tested positive. Their advice is to operate, and do it quickly. They don't agree with waiting around for cancer to strike." Susie showed him a bunch of letters she'd printed off. All on headed paper, from physicians with letters after their names.

She was great at dealing with men. Maybe because of her profession, or maybe because she was quite male in her thinking a lot of the time. Suze was a real no-bullshit type of girl. She was astute and always to the point. Her direct nature was just what I needed at that time. Robbie responded to her too, which was a godsend.

"I know why you want to do this, Emily," he said, "but it's not easy to sit by and let this happen to you either. I'm not trying to be difficult, honestly I'm not. It all sounds so horrific. Why did this have to happen to you?"

My heart went out to him. He was so torn between his need to protect me and what he knew was the right choice.

"This is the way to go, Robbie. You've got to trust me on this one. I have never been so sure of anything in my life." When I felt his arms lock around me, I knew he was on my side.

We made an appointment with Mr Green in St Theresa's. We met his team: Lillian the co-ordinator and family genetics lady, Hayley his specialist cancer nurse, and Nora his secretary. They sat us down and explained what the surgery entailed.

"This is major surgery and you must be very sure this is what you want," said Hayley. "You are different from a cancer patient. They have no choice. They present themselves to me for this chat and they have to go for surgery. Their life depends on it. They don't have time to mull it over. You do. Make fully sure you are happy to put yourself through this."

"I understand why you're saying all this," I answered. "I know you're also covering yourselves so I don't come back and say 'I've made a mistake, I've changed my mind'. I know I am young and I don't have cancer, but I have something just as bad. And mentally it's eating me up almost as much as any cancer might."

I knew it was my job to convince this woman and the surgeon that I felt like a ticking time bomb and I wanted to defuse it. I was not going to turn around in six months' time and say 'Sorry but I changed my mind! Scoop all the breast tissue out of the bin and put it back in!'. I was utterly certain of what I wanted. I just had to get that opinion across to these medical people and convince them to help me.

"Okay, Emily, if I do this surgery on you, there are a number of ways of going about it." Mr Green seemed to be taking me seriously. "You may have to have one breast done at a time. You may lose your nipples. Have you considered that?" He regarded me closely. "I have a book of photographs here, illustrating women who have undergone similar surgery. Would you like to see it?"

He handed me a black folder which had laminated pages of photographs.

"Do you want to see this, Robbie?" I turned towards him and tried to gauge his reaction.

"I suppose I'd better go for it," he muttered.

I felt desperately sorry for Robbie at that moment. I was looking at this book with interest and to see what might happen to my body after the surgery. Robbie was having to face, head-on, what could be his new view of me for the rest of our lives. His young wife would be a scarred version of herself forever.

We saw photographs of women who'd had the different types of surgery. It was a book designed to show what type of results to expect. We dubbed it the *Book of Horrors*. It wasn't as distressing as I'd expected. But certainly for Robbie it was a harsh view of what was to come.

"This is a very serious decision," Hayley warned me again. "Please be sure that you are doing the right thing."

Hayley was obviously Devil's Advocate in the hospital and I knew she was supposed to probe reactions, push buttons and evoke emotions. But there was no doubt in my mind. I didn't find the decision difficult, at all. Not for even a millisecond. I knew in my heart and soul that this was the right thing to do. All I had to do now was convince everyone else.

I left the hospital feeling even better about the whole thing. The more information I received the calmer and more empowered I felt about the whole process. Just like anything in life, it's always easier to face your demons or angels with a little bit of knowledge. I was slowly piecing the jigsaw puzzle together.

If I opted to have the bi-lateral mastectomy, Mr Green would remove as much of my breast tissue as he could. There was a possibility I might lose my nipples. This was hard to come to terms with. Then they would reconstruct my breast.

For the two days following our meeting, I thought about this possibility endlessly. How would I feel in a changing room at the gym? Would I feel comfortable changing in front of the children? Would my appearance scare them? Would it make Robbie see me as a freak?

All those questions whizzed around in my mind. Three days after the meeting, I dropped the children to school and decided to go for a walk to think. It was the beginning of November and the wind was whistling. I drove to the local beach. The promenade was almost deserted, apart from a handful of hardy walkers wrapped up against the elements, battling with dogs on leads.

The sea was grey, choppy and frothy. The sky reflected the wintry pallor. Pulling on a pink and purple felt My Little Pony hat that I'd found on the floor of the car, I zipped my puffa coat up to the neck and braced myself. The salty smell and crashing waves jostled with the howling wind. The fronts of my thighs were numbed with the cold as I battled into the force of the wind. I hadn't planned ending up here, so I was badly equipped for the elements. Stuffing my stinging cold hands into my pockets, I struggled forwards. My eyes and nose began to seep, but the air was strangely cleansing. I reached the end of the promenade and stood looking out to sea.

I tried to imagine how I would feel if I was standing here knowing I had terminal cancer. How would I face saying goodbye to all the people and places I knew so well and took for granted? Watching the power of the ocean, writhing back and forth, it reminded me so poignantly how fragile life is.

Turning around, with the wind behind me, pushing me along, doubling my speed back to the car, I felt empowered and had an enormous sense of personal calm. I was being given a second chance here. I was allowed to choose. I wanted to choose life.

II

Susie

How to Easicook a Soap Opera:
Take one batty mother, have her live a fabricated life involving several tons of denial. Mix truth and deception in a haphazard way with only child. Simmer for too many years. Take out of bag, only when overcooked and almost beyond redemption.

I finished writing up the file from my last patient of the day. I felt very pleased with myself. A patient I'd been seeing for the last three months was really starting to respond. We had just had a great brainstorming session.

"Thanks so much," she said as she left. "I feel like my life is slowly coming back together. I'll always feel indebted to you."

Patients like that made my job worthwhile.

I picked up the phone now and dialled Emily's number.

"How are you today?" I asked her.

"Fine, and you?" Emily sounded tired.

"Look, I know you have a lot going on right now but how do you fancy meeting me for a cup of coffee? I've got gossip. If nothing else it'll take your mind off things for a bit. *EastEnders* has nothing on what I've got to tell you!"

"I'm there. See you in ten minutes in *Café-au-lait*," Emily hung up.

Packing a few files into my brief-case, I left the office. I shoved 'Take That' into the CD player and let the music wash over me as I sped down the motorway.

Emily was at the top of the queue when I arrived. The constantly busy, out-of-town coffee shop served the best coffee and scones for miles around.

"Grab a table and I'll be over in a second," Emily mouthed over to me.

Within minutes, we were busily cutting and buttering our scones.

"So? Spit it out? What's going on?" Emily was dying to know my news.

"Well, all this genetic stuff you're going through at the moment made me think a lot about my father," I began.

"Right." Emily was leaning forward.

"So I decided to call out to Mum in Bray the other day and ask her about him." I shoved a piece of scone in my mouth.

"Bloody hell, how did Pauline take that? She's never been very forthcoming about him. His whole death has always been kind of sketchy, hasn't it?"

"Well, that's just it. He might not be dead."

I watched Emily's eyes open wide as she nearly choked on her cappuccino.

"Fuck off!" she spat.

"Yep. His name is Jim Lynch and they met stacking shelves in a supermarket in Bray." I sat back looking triumphant.

"Oh-my-God! This is fucking brilliant! Tell me everything. Don't leave out a single detail!"

I filled her in on all of what Mum had told me, including the fact I had been conceived on top of a frozen-veg cabinet, which made her laugh herself sick. As I was telling her, even I found it all a bit surreal.

"Wow! So are you going to try and track him down?"

"I'm not sure at the moment. I'm trying to get my head around the whole thing, to be honest. It's just so weird. For years we invented this man, his personality, his likes and dislikes. But he was always dapper and young and a bit like Action Man. Now, he's in a brown shop-coat and is called Jim Lynch. It's not really the same thing, is it?" I stared at Emily.

"Don't you want to try and find him and meet him? Even to let him know you exist? Aren't you curious about who he is, or where he's ended up? Jesus, I'd want to know if it was my dad!" Emily was enthralled by the thought of this mystery dad.

"Maybe I will try and look him up, but not right this minute. I need time to sort through the new circumstances in my brain. Does that sound weird to you?"

"Frankly, yes, it does. Can I find him instead? It'd drive me insane. I'd have to know."

"But maybe that's because you've always had a dad? I don't miss mine because he was never there. I need to catch my breath and think about the consequences if I decide to try and find him."

"You're being a bit Dr Susie about it, you know. This could be a fantastic change in your life. Maybe you have half-siblings, imagine that? More flame-headed bean-poles for you to hang around with!" Emily teased.

"It's a lot to think about. Maybe they don't want me butting into their lives. Maybe he's married and this could ruin his marriage. Maybe he'll hate me and all the turmoil I could stir up for him. It's a big step, Em. I can't just barge into this man's life without thinking this through properly. If I find him, it could be a huge mistake. I might regret it for the rest of my life."

"If you don't at least try, give it a shot, you might regret that for the rest of your life too!" Emily wasn't giving up.

12

·

Emily

Bull by the Horns Ragout:
Accept gene positive result. Douse husband with wine, hold breath,
close eyes, stick fingers in ear and hum. Serve with the hope that things
will work out in the end.

Robbie sat opposite me in Danielle's Bistro with a glass of wine and
some ciabatta doused in olive oil. Danielle's was the local cheap
and cheerful, mid-week-meal type place. It would never hold a Michelin
star for excellence, but it served a purpose. Robbie and I enjoyed the
relaxed atmosphere and the basic décor. The small square tables could
be pushed together depending on how many you booked for. There was
years-old red candle-wax dripped on most surfaces. Candles provided
most of the light in the place, so it was intimate in its own way. I also
loved the fact that I could go there wearing the same clothes I'd put on
that morning. The flickery dim lighting meant that even if I was caked
in the kids' food and looking like death warmed up, it didn't show in
Danielle's.

Tonight I was a woman on a mission. I talked to Robbie again to make sure he was definitely going to be with me all the way.

"I'm going to go for this like a bat-out-of-hell now, you do realise that, don't you?" I held his gaze.

"When have you ever been any different? I'd be more surprised if you sat back and did nothing. The day that you become silent and retiring, I'll begin to worry." He put his hand out across the table for me to take. "We'll get through this thing, Emily. But right now, I want us to enjoy our dinner, have a few glasses of wine, and take each day as it comes." He squeezed my hand.

After two further meetings with Mr Green and his team, they had realised I was not going to let this one slide. I wanted the surgery done – yesterday.

"I am well aware of the fact that I am still young. But, turning that fact on its head, I'm also too young to die. I am also not a twelve-year-old. I am fully in control of my senses and am capable of making a conscious decision about my own body and my own destiny. Please, all I'm asking is that you grant me the intelligence and cop-on to make my own choice here."

It was my final pitch with Mr Green. A couple of months had passed since our first meeting. It was three weeks before Christmas and I needed him to agree to operate.

I had undergone all the relevant examinations. I'd even had a mammogram.

I felt each day that passed the clock was ticking loudly in my subconscious. Tick, tick, boom, boom! It was getting louder as the days went by. I felt a sensation of panic and a palpable lack of control setting in. I hated the feeling of flailing, terrified limbo. I felt as if I was literally floating between one road of destiny and another. I wanted to be allowed to choose the road I travelled. I was so certain in my own head that the other one was going to lead to destruction. I wanted to be afforded the opportunity to change direction, to take the new road that was almost within my grasp.

The children were getting excited about Christmas and I was glad they were oblivious to the whole agenda about me and my body.

The TV ads and radio hype pushing all the latest toys were beginning to send them into a total frenzy. We put up the advent calendars and they fought each morning to make it to the kitchen first to see if the elves had left them a sweet. I had one of those wooden calendars with a little door and compartment for each day.

"Mummy, the elvzes have been during the night again! Look, they left us both a sweetie!" Tia was booting up the stairs with Louis in hot pursuit.

"I want the green one! Tia, don't you dare eat that! I'm not eating a pink one!" Louis launched himself at her, wrestling the sweet from her grasp.

"Okay, the elves are watching you and so is Santa Claus. If you behave this badly, he won't let the elves come here any more, and he won't bring you any presents on Christmas Eve." I warned them about this approximately sixty times a day. They didn't give a toss. In fact, they were both already gone off into their separate rooms to play.

I love Christmas. I would have a tree in every room of the house if I thought I could get away with it. But right at this moment in time, I had a niggling worry in the back of my mind which was preventing me from being as enthusiastic as usual. If I could just get a date from Mr Green, a definite timescale for when I could have this surgery, I would be able to concentrate better.

I sat the children down on Sunday evening with a pen and paper. We spread out four catalogues on the coffee table and I told them to search for the five things they wanted Santa Claus to bring the most. I had already finished most of the shopping but I just had to make sure there were no 'new' ideas they might come up with. I hated the thought of a disappointed little face on Christmas morning.

Dear God, what a chore! I suppose it was utterly unreasonable of me to expect small children to narrow a thousand pages of toys down to five items. Mental note: Do not forget that children have a limited capacity. They are not adults, they do not have the ability to condense information and sort it in order of descending importance. They want everything. Nothing is reasonable or rational. On the positive side, a bottle of 50c bubbles has the same value as a remote-control Formula One car. They are not able to distinguish.

"Okay, okay, you two. I think Santa Claus will know what you want on Christmas morning. He's magic after all, so we won't try and do a list."

There, all fixed.

"But we want to do a list!" They both promptly burst into open-mouthed-screwed-up-faced tears.

Oh Jesus. Why did I do these things when Robbie was out at work?

Robbie had a big golf function that day and night and wouldn't be home until the wee hours of the morning. I had stupidly had an image of myself and the children and the lit fire, with the wind (snow would have added to the fantasy nicely) making a list for Father Christmas in a cosy, loving way.

To calm the situation I gave them each a bar of chocolate, even though it was nearly bedtime, and poured myself a large gin and tonic. Well, a gin with a dash of tonic. The phone rang. It was Laura, my mad angel friend from college.

"Hey, Em, how are things?"

"Fine, I've hit the booze and the children are eating chocolate."

"Sounds like a good plan. Listen, my cat has had a litter of kittens and I was wondering if you'd like to take one? It'd be great for the kids and besides I really need to get them homed – they're shitting all over my flat." Laura was always very straight, I had to give her that.

"Let me talk to Robbie about it. I'd love one and I'm sure the kids would adore it. I'll get back to you tomorrow. What flavour are they?"

"I've a black one and white one with tabby patches on it. Don't ask me what sex they are. I'm not very good at that stuff. They both have pink bums, that's about the height of my knowledge."

"Okay, Laura. I'll give you a buzz tomorrow when I have a chance to talk to Robbie."

I hung up and thought about how nice it would be for the kids to have a kitten around. Especially over the next few months. It would be a good distraction for them.

Robbie got home very late so I didn't broach the kitten subject until we were on the phone mid-morning the next day.

"Oh, Laura rang last night. She has kittens she's looking for homes for . . ."

"Well, tell her to look somewhere else. I hate cats and anything that's been born in her care is bound to be completely insane. It probably has an extra head and barks."

"Robbie, that's not nice. Besides, I think a kitten would be a good thing for the kids to have over the next while."

"No. No. No and no. Can I be any clearer?"

In fairness Robbie had never liked cats, but I wasn't about to give up. I rang him every half hour for the next three hours.

"Please can we get the kitten?"

"No. Fuck off, Emily, and stop phoning me in work."

"Please can we get the kitten?"

By now he was getting seriously irritated.

"Emily, get your bloody kitten, but believe me, if it pees or craps near me or any of my belongings, I will skin it."

"Thanks, darling, and it won't. Cats are very clean creatures. I'll ring Laura now and tell her the good news."

"Fabulous. Make sure she isn't in the kitchen with her magic wand when I get home from work."

The last time Laura had called over, she had been in the kitchen doing my angel cards when Robbie walked in. She unfortunately tried to convince him that he needed his cards done and his aura read. Let's just say they will never see eye to eye on this issue.

That afternoon the kitten arrived. He was the cutest little fuzzball I'd ever seen. The kids were so thrilled with him.

"Ooh Mum, look, he's like a teddy!" Tia jumped up and down in glee.

"Can I hold him?" Louis held his hands out to take the little bundle.

Luckily the kitten was used to being handled so he didn't try to scratch or bite the children. He was an instant hit.

"What'll we call him?" I was thinking along the lines of Fuzzy or Fluffy.

"Rasher," said Louis firmly.

"Oh, that's a good idea," Tia agreed.

So Rasher it was. Who was I to argue?

"Let's ring Daddy and tell him Rasher has arrived." This was my gentle way of letting Robbie know that the kitten was now ensconced and here to stay.

"He's so cute and he purrs when you pet him," Tia told Robbie. "He can move his head and walk all by himself!"

"I thought of his name and he loves it!" Louis had snatched the phone and was shouting into Robbie's ear.

Smiling, I decided not to talk to Robbie, just in case he told me to give Rasher back to Laura. By the time Robbie got home that night, Rasher had discovered the Christmas tree. He had already smashed two decorations and the kids, screaming with delight, were egging him on.

13

Emily

Baking up a Storm:

Take two adults with too much on their minds, mix with two small people with a man in a red suit solely on their minds. Boil with innocent wide-eyed excitement and a large dollop of hopping from one foot to the other. Force feelings of foreboding through a mangle. Try to swallow fear until New Year. Then set New Year alight by preparing for dissection.

It was six days before Christmas. My final appointment before the holiday with Mr Green gave me a last-ditch effort to make my pitch for surgery.

And at last I heard the words I had been longing to hear.

"Okay Emily, you win!" he said with an exaggerated sigh. "I will operate on you. Both Hayley and I agree that you are as certain as you can be about this surgery. In fact, if it will stop you phoning and making appointments to harass me, I'll do anything!" He held his hands up in mock desperation.

Well, he was probably ready to murder me for real. I was so intent on moving this procedure along, it had become my main objective in life. The poor man was probably at his wit's end with me badgering him into submission. In fact, if he hadn't agreed, I might have had to follow him home and started calling in to him three times a week.

"Go away and enjoy your Christmas with your family and I'll organise a date with the theatre staff and write to you in the New Year. How is that?" Mr Green looked at me hopefully.

"Thank you. I'll look forward to that letter."

Robbie and I left the hospital and I felt less panicky inside. At least the ball was rolling.

I would start the New Year with a plan of action in place. I could earmark the next year in my mind for sorting this gene once and for all.

Robbie was quiet in the car going home.

"That's good news, isn't it?" I ventured.

"Well, it's not up there with the best news I've had in my life. But I know what you mean. At least you have a time frame to work from now."

"You're still with me on all this, aren't you Robbie?"

His expression was blank but he answered, "Yep. I'm still with you. It's just not a very Christmassy subject. Let's drop this thing, enjoy the holidays and deal with it in the New Year."

We arrived home and the children were like little rubber balls bouncing around the house with excitement. Santa was almost on his way.

But Robbie was still unusually quiet.

"Are you sure you feel okay about all this?" I asked.

"I'll be fine, Emily, don't worry about me. It's just kind of hard to take in at times. Only a few months ago we hadn't even heard of BRCA1. Now look at us. We're planning a full year pretty much dedicated to its cause. We really never know what's around the next corner, do we?"

"No, we don't."

"Look, I'm just feeling a bit pensive that's all. Christmas can do that, can't it? Makes us all think about the year just gone and the new one on the way. We'll get through it. We'll be fine." He kissed me on the nose and went to flick on the Christmas-tree lights.

I began to plan. I interviewed and subsequently hired a live-in Polish au pair called Maisy to help with housework and the children. I was going to be completely incapacitated for a few months after the surgery. Mr Green had suggested that we hire some help if we possibly could.

"Robbie, I can't believe I'm actually going to have 'live-in help'! It's going to be so exciting."

"You've gone to serious extremes to achieve that. If I'd known it was so important to you, we could have discussed it before." He was looking at me as if I'd lost my marbles.

"Well, I never felt justified in having someone full-time. It's going to be a real treat. Do you really think we'll be able to afford it?"

"I think it's a case of having to make provisions for it at this stage," he said. "I can't take too much time off work. Being self-employed has its drawbacks. But on the positive side, the business is going well, so we should be able to afford it. For a while anyway."

Spurred on by the thought of 'home help', I organised Tia's fifth birthday party. I'd always felt it was slightly unfortunate for her, being born so close to Christmas. She found it confusing, not knowing which thing she should be more excited about.

Her party was all set for the Saturday before Christmas, with Fi-fi the Fairy coming to entertain fifteen small bundles of tulle and glitter.

"Can all my friends come as princesses or fairies? Can we also have no chairs or tables in the house? Instead get Daddy to put a castle with mossy rocks and little mushrooms for us all to sit on!" Her face was aglow with the idea of it all.

"We can't quite remove everything in the house, Tia, but we'll get pink fluffy lights and all your tea-party things will have sparkles, how's that?" I smiled.

The party was a roaring success. As it turned out, Robbie and the other fathers probably paid more attention to Fi-Fi the Fairy than the children. She was more porn-star than pink fluffy person, with a rather risqué tu-tu which left very little to the imagination. Her saving grace was that she was fantastic at face painting.

"Can I have her for my birthday?" Robbie grinned.

"Shut up, you dirty old man! She'd better be good with the kids or you'll have a mini riot on your hands shortly."

"Ah leave her alone, Emily! She's a great girl!" Robbie raised his eyebrows and grinned as Fi-Fi jumped up and down to the pop music, while blowing bubbles for the fairy disco.

Needless to say, Robbie was sent into the kitchen to fry sausages, while I made sure the small children were having fun.

As Mr Green promised, a letter arrived from the hospital during the first week in January. The operation was scheduled for Monday, February the 13th. I was to go into hospital on Sunday the 12th.

Mr Green called me in for the final consultation. Once again Robbie and I met in the hospital car park.

"Okay, Emily, this is the last time we'll meet before your surgery. Are you definitely sure this is what you want?"

"I've never been more sure of anything in my whole life. The sooner we get this done the better. I feel like a ticking time bomb. I'm even imagining pains now and every morning in the shower, I'm almost afraid to wash myself, in case I find a lump. If it's possible to give yourself cancer, I reckon I will have a positive diagnosis pretty soon."

"I've never had a patient who has beaten me down so belligerently as you have. I must congratulate both you and Robbie."

"What do you mean?" Robbie looked confused.

"You're a tough man to be able to live with this one!" Mr Green was smiling. "Emily, you have incredible determination and courage. I hope your operation will be successful. I have no doubt in my mind that it will be. I wish you both luck with the journey you are about to undertake. I'll see you on Monday the 13th, please God." He stood up and shook Robbie's hand.

Instinctively I hugged him. "Thank you," I said happily. I had never felt so grateful towards another human being. It was like he held the key to a prison. He was opening the door and beckoning to me to walk through. The next time we'd meet, I'd be unconscious, and he'd be dressed in green with scrubbed hands.

Robbie and I walked out of the hospital hand in hand. Our journey was about to begin.

I was elated.

14

Susie

Indecision Fricassee:
Take some vital information, ferment in head until you can't ignore it any longer. Mix with two ounces of trepidation and four ounces of hesitation. Find yourself in a quandary. Take every ounce of courage you possess and try to put it to good use.

Weeks had passed since I'd found out my father's identity and we were now in the New Year. I had hardly noticed Christmas and New Year passing, I was still so blown away by my mother's revelation. I didn't know what, if anything, I should do with the information.

I began to think about the man who had become my surrogate father in my student years, the kind and wise Dr Breen. I needed to talk to him. Mum was so tetchy about the whole subject I couldn't bring her in on my feelings. Emily would always support me, I knew that. But the person who could really advise me was Dr David Breen.

I had worked with Dr Breen during my placement in my final two years of study while I was taking my Master's. He worked two days a week in one of the large hospitals and the rest of the time in his own private clinic in Ringsend, just outside the city centre in Dublin.

He had approached me just before my finals and offered me a job in the clinic.

"I need some young blood," he said. "I have a lot of patients and I know they would respond better to you. You're the opposite to me, being both young and a woman. I think you'd be a great asset. It would be a good opportunity for you to break into the whole field too. Will you think about it?"

You could have knocked me over with a feather. I needed to pinch myself to believe this. "Do you honestly think I need to go away and mull this over?" I was shocked and delighted. It was a golden opportunity and one very few graduates were ever offered. "When do you want me to start?"

"Get your exams and we're in business," he chuckled.

I'd always had the drive and motivation but this was the final push I needed to keep my effort going. I buried myself in my books, gave the exams my all and achieved a first in my Master's.

"Look at the brain on you!" Emily had teased me as she hugged me. "My God, Suze, you're obviously not as thick as you look!"

"Less of that, or I'll have you taken away by the men in white coats and placed in a squashy room for the rest of your life," I warned.

"Sounds bloody marvellous to me, right now," Emily had joked. She was pregnant with Louis at the time, and finding the whole expanding-body thing hard to cope with.

Several months later, I started my job at Dr Breen's clinic, and although it was exhausting and I was nervous at first, I loved every minute of it.

"It's your job to help, not to judge. The stories your patients tell you are not yours to pass on or keep. You are simply being allowed to dip in and help for a spell. Never forget that if people can't trust you, you will never make it as a good therapist."

I could still picture his kind face as he spoke. He was a tall, straight man, in both stature and personality. He had lectured all over the world in psychology. He was incredibly clever and learned, but most of all he was very in tune with human nature and how to make the most out of his patients.

After I had worked with him for two years he called me into his office one day.

"Susie, you've come on in leaps and bounds. You're a very fine analyst. I've noticed how many clients you've gained in your own right. An opportunity has arisen which is going to help us both, I think." He removed his glasses and sat back in his chair. His smile always put me at ease. He was one of those people who could calm a storm just by looking at it.

"I'm intrigued," I answered.

"I'm not getting any younger. Mrs Breen is always telling me I'm going to end up as the richest man in the graveyard. She wants me to retire. I suppose she has a point. I'm seventy-one next birthday, there are no pockets in a shroud, so the time is probably right." He shrugged his shoulders.

"I never really thought about your age, all I see is a great doctor, but when you put it like that, I suppose it makes sense." I was feeling a bit nervous. What was I going to do if he closed the clinic?

"Flattery will get you everywhere," he chuckled. "The thing is, I've been approached by a crowd who are setting up this new, swanky, all-whistles-and-bells private clinic in Blackrock. It's going to be called the Rochestown Clinic and it's going to be a major success. No two ways about it. The board of management has asked my advice with regards to the psychology department. I would like to recommend you for your own rooms. How would you feel about it?" He raised his eyebrows.

"Oh Jesus Christ! Are you serious?" I was stunned.

"I kind of am, yes," he grinned.

"Do you think I'd be any good, well, good enough?"

"Yes and yes. It will mean a lot of hours and a lot of work, but you have the ability if that's what you're asking. You have the knowledge and although you may not have as many years experience under your belt as some of the others I'm recommending, you've intuition that no number of years can ever make up for. I think you can do it with your eyes shut. The question is whether you want it or not."

"Do I *want* it? Are you insane?" I laughed loudly. "This is a dream come true. In fact, never in my wildest dreams would I ever have seen myself having my own practice so soon – and in a private clinic! David, if you recommend me for this, I promise I won't let you down. I'll give it my all." I ran around his desk and hugged him.

"I know you will. You're a great girl, Susie. I'm very proud of you." He patted my arm affectionately.

Without warning, tears streamed down my cheeks. Dr Breen was the first and only man I'd ever had in my life who'd really cared about me and wanted me to succeed. To have him tell me he was proud of me was a moment that would remain with me forever.

"No man has ever told me he's proud of me before. That means so much to me. I would have loved to have had a dad like you growing up. I hope your sons appreciate you." I whipped my forefingers across my eyes, removing the dark streaks of mascara which I knew were pooling there.

"Well, if Nora and I had been blessed with a daughter and she'd turned out like you I would be beaming with pride. You're a fantastic girl and I know you'll continue to do me and yourself proud. I saw something in you the very first day I met you. I'm very rarely wrong, and you have proven yourself in bucket-loads. You've rejuvenated me over the last two years. You've breathed life into my practice too. But I think it's time Nora and I find out if we still like each other after all this time." He looked reflective.

"So I won't be the only nervous one over the next while then?" I sat on his desk and he patted my hand.

"No, you won't. Sometimes knowing when to stop can be harder than starting off or progressing," he said wryly.

Time seemed to move like a cyclone after that day. I got my practice. I got my room, Suite 7 in the Rochestown Clinic, with my name inscribed on a brass plate on my door.

I knew I was going to miss this dear and clever man. I made a mental note to stay in contact with him and keep him informed on all the progress I hoped to make. I also knew he would always be a wonderful sounding board if I ever needed one.

Dr Breen and Nora were off on a cruise soon. He always complained that he hated being retired and that he only went on holidays to keep her company, but I was pretty sure he was secretly happy to go. He was never a pushover. I still called him whenever I needed advice, either on a patient or on business matters. We met for lunch at least once every three months and it was like finding a dear old childhood teddy bear every time I saw him. Familiar and comforting.

Now, in my present dilemma, I knew he was the man I needed to talk to.

I phoned him and arranged to meet for lunch. We were alone as Nora was in the shopping centre buying the last few things for the cruise.

"How can women need so much stuff? We'll be on a boat in the middle of the ocean, we'll probably never see those people again, so what does it matter if she wears one of her dresses twice?" His eyes crinkled at the corners, indicating that he was actually quite pleased with Nora's excited last-minute spending.

"Well, you said you don't want to be the richest man in the graveyard, so Nora's very kindly helping you out with that. You're a man who knows plenty about the psyche – you should have worked out by now that wearing the same outfit twice on a luxury liner can lead to severe mental anguish. Cop on to yourself!"

He chuckled and patted my hand, with his head over to one side, enjoying the banter.

"I do miss you still, you know that?" I smiled at him.

"And I you, but life is good for us both, isn't it?" he smiled. "Nora says I'm not to ask you but have you met any nice young man yet?"

"No one worth talking about, no. I don't feel the need though. I'm too busy in work and I have my social life going the way I want it. I can go out when it suits me or stay in if that's how I feel. I don't need a man to make my life whole."

"Just as long as you're happy, pet, that's the main thing."

"Well, there is just one thing disturbing my calm at the moment . . ."

He listened intently while I told him all about Jim Lynch and pondered a while before speaking.

"I think locating this man would bridge a large gap in your life. Even if you didn't ever form a relationship with him or decided not to even meet him, knowing who he is and having some solid facts about him would only benefit you. Even if it was all difficult in the beginning and, worst case scenario, if he was either dead or didn't want to know you, at least you would know who he is. You need to know that. It's a large piece of the jigsaw puzzle of your life that has always been missing. I'm glad you're on the road to finding that link."

That was enough for me. With David's blessing and confirmation, I knew I would go ahead and locate my father. Yet I still hesitated, as if I was waiting for the right moment.

Then the right moment arrived.

I was sitting in my office one Friday morning, putting the finishing touches to a letter to a patient, when I had a sudden compulsion to speak to my father. It was like an invisible force from within was willing me to pick up the telephone.

I dialled Directory Enquiries.

"Hello, Directory Enquiries, John speaking. How may I help you?"

"Hi, John. I'm looking for the number of some private detectives in the Dublin area, please."

I heard John typing the information into his computer. I almost expected him to ask me what I wanted a detective for, but of course John didn't give a toss about me or anyone else who called him.

"I have three in the Dublin area, do you want them all?" John stifled a yawn.

I felt like shouting, "Stop sounding so bored, you ignorant fucker! I'm trying to find my father!" but I didn't.

"Yes, please." I scribbled them down and hung up.

With trepidation, I dialled the first number.

"Hello?" a small child answered the phone.

"Oh . . . hello? Is your mummy or daddy there, please?" I really hadn't been expecting that.

"Yes, Mummy's on the toilet, I'll go and find her. Wait there. Who is it?" the little gremlin voice shrilled.

"No one, it's a wrong number, sorry. Bye-bye!" I clicked the button on my phone, cutting the call dead.

I drew a line through the number and tried the next one. After two rings, it was answered by an adult, and a professional-sounding one at that.

"Good morning, Complete Investigation Services, Mairéad speaking, how may I direct your call?"

"Hi, Mairéad, my name is Susie Rosedale and I am looking for some help locating my father. Do you deal with that sort of thing at all?" I would consider myself quite intelligent but right at that moment I felt bloody stupid.

"Yes, we deal with all sorts of missing-person cases. Thomas is the man you need to speak with. Can you hold the line and I'll check if he's free?"

After a short rendition of "Greensleeves" courtesy of the hold button, the line clicked and I heard a man's voice.

"Hello. Susie, isn't it? Thomas Richards here. How may I help you?"

Thomas Richards sounded quite normal but I couldn't help visualising him as an Inspector Gadget figure. In my mind's eye he looked a bit batty and wore a trench-coat and one of those hats with the sheepskin-lined flaps which sat on his side burns, and tiny round spectacles. My imaginary detective even ate his sandwiches with a magnifying glass in one hand, in case there were any stolen diamonds hiding in his egg mayonnaise.

"Hello, Thomas, now this probably sounds a bit strange to you but I'm kind of searching for my father." I knew I sounded embarrassed.

"No, that doesn't sound the least bit strange, Susie. That's what we do here, find missing people, among other things." He sounded firm but not in an aggressive way.

"Why don't you give me a quick outline of what you know and I can take it from there?"

"Oh . . . right . . . well, I don't actually have very much information for you to go by, I'm afraid. All I do know is that he worked in a supermarket, in Bray, with my mother, Pauline Rosedale, thirty-one years ago. They had a brief flirtation, well, bonk to be exact . . ." I heard him coughing gently. "My mother had no contact with him after that and before she knew it she was pregnant with me. She never told him about me, and she hasn't seen or heard from him since. All I know is that his name is Jim Lynch . . ." I trailed off, nervous about his reaction to this sparseness of information.

"Okay, Susie. Do you have an email address?"

"Yes, I'll just give you my hotmail address, rather than the work one. It's Susiesue@hotmail.com."

"I'm going to forward you a brief questionnaire, which I would like you to fill in as best you can. Can you come into my office and meet me?"

"Yes, but what kind of money are we talking here?" Although I was earning good money, I had never managed to shed the money-conscious attitude Mum had drummed into me.

"All cases differ. But our fees start at five hundred euros. That will include your consultation and our preliminary investigations. It really depends on what leads we get and how far we have to go to find your father. If you can fill out the form I'm mailing to you, and come in and see me, I'll have more of an idea. We won't proceed at any stage until we've discussed the cost involved. How does that sound?"

"That's fine." I pulled out my diary. "I can meet you on either Tuesday or Friday afternoon if either of those are available next week?"

"Let's go with Tuesday then, and try to get this show on the road for you. I'm sure, now you've made the decision to find your father, you would like as quick a result as possible."

"Yes, that would be great. Thanks, Thomas. I'll see you then."

I hung up, feeling oddly excited. Good God, what was I doing? I felt a little bit hysterical almost. I poured myself a cup of coffee from my percolator in the corner. I decided there and then to keep the whole thing to myself until I knew more. I was good at keeping secrets. My job had made me that way. My patient confidentiality had taught me over the years to keep my mouth shut. This was different though, because this concerned me.

The following Monday, checking my email, I realised Thomas Richards had sent me the form to fill out. I added all my details and sent it back to him. As I pressed the send button on the computer, I felt butterflies awaken in my tummy. What on earth was this man going to find? Imagine, by next Tuesday, he might have some information on my father. I was filled with mixed emotions: excitement, fear, trepidation, nerves. You name it, I felt it at that moment.

15

Emily

Birthday Anticipation Cake:
*Take one boy of five and seven-eights. Allow him to remove kitchen
calendar and place under his bed. Tick off the days until "my birthday".
Mix with possessed excitement and total obsession. Add ten pints of
oblivion to the rest of the world and everyone in it. Thank your lucky
stars for children and their innocent glee.*

It was coming to the end of January. The weather was seasonally vile
– grey skies with the odd attempt by the sun to poke its nose through
the thick grey mass of clouds. Delighted to have a positive focus, I
planned my son's sixth birthday party, two weeks before the surgery.

"Mummy, can I have a mud and worms cake instead of an ordinary
birthday cake? I'm sick of *Star Wars* and I'd like to have something
different." Louis was consumed with what type of cake he was going to
feed his friends. I was decidedly relieved that he had gone off *Star Wars*.
Trying to recreate Darth Vader with sponge and mixing black icing had
been a bit of a chore last year. His cake had ended up looking like a cross

between Nelson Mandela and a deranged doll. My fingernails had been stained with black icing paste for weeks afterwards too.

Mud and worms I could do, no hassle. Chocolate icing with a stream of runny chocolate sauce squirted around it, topped off with jelly worms would do the trick. It sounded vile, but I suppose it's always good to remember that children have hideous taste.

I always had my birthday parties at home and wanted the children to have memories of their parties as they grew up too. When I was little, we played traditional games like musical statues, three-legged-races, egg and spoon races, blind man's buff and all the old favourites. I didn't quite have the head-space to organise an afternoon of games, so I phoned a magician instead. I nearly fell off the chair when he told me how much he charged.

"Jesus, you'd want to be bloody good for that price!"

"Well, I've been doing this job for a long time and will definitely be able to control even the most lively children. I'll arrive fifteen minutes before the guests and will do everything apart from the food. I provide party bags and will take the burden off you." He sounded very confident and I decided to believe him.

The week running up to Louis' birthday was frenzied. He was almost sick with excitement. Tia was not happy.

"Why does it have to be only Louis' birthday? Why can't I have a birthday too? 'Snot fair. Not even a little bit. I hate it when it's not my birthday." She stuck her bottom lip out and folded her arms tightly across her chest.

"But you've just had your birthday, Tia. Everybody has a birthday, every year. It's just Louis' turn right now," I tried to explain calmly.

"But haven't I had much more birthdays than Tia?" Louis was brilliant at stirring things up and specialised in riling his sister like no one else on earth could.

"Mummy, that's not fair!" Tia took the bait and burst out crying.

"Louis, please stop trying to annoy her. If you're not nice to her, she won't get you a present." I winked at Tia, who managed to suddenly switch off the tears.

"Am I getting a present too?" She was suddenly very interested. She climbed onto my knee. "I love you so much, Mummy. You're my favourite Mummy in the whole world!" She cocked her head to the side and stared at me.

"You'll have to ask Louis about the present situation. What do you think, Louis? Would it be a nice idea for your sister to have a little present too, so she's not sad?"

Louis thought about it for a few seconds.

"No, I think I should have all the pressies and Tia should have none." Louis raised his eyebrows in delight as Tia burst out crying.

"I'll tell you what. Both of you had better be very good and stop fighting and we'll see who gets presents on Saturday, how's that?"

They both looked a little unsure of how it had come to this. They would have to try and behave in order to get gifts. It was annoying, but they understood it clearly.

I was delighted to have a distraction and a cheerful event to throw my heart and soul into. I know the magic-man had said he would provide party bags, but I decided no one could do going-home bags like I could. So I trawled the pound shops and collected everything from bottles of bubbles to fairy crowns with glitter and fluff on them. Knowing I would probably be hated, I found water bombs and whoopee cushions.

"Cool, Mum! All my friends are going to love the farting cushions. That's the best pressie we could give them."

I produced the little plastic party bags, soldiers for the boys and Bratz for the girls.

"How about you fill up the boy bags and Tia can fill the girl ones?"

"That's fine because I can't touch those girls' things – I might get a disease." Louis was shaking his hands violently as if the pink stuff might contaminate him. It was amazing how at the tender age of almost six he was already becoming aware of the gender divide. Even if it was only to do with party bags.

Louis fired the stuff in as quickly as he could. "I'm finished first! That's it. All done. Bye-bye." He was gone, off out to run around like a lunatic.

Meanwhile Tia was savouring every second of the ritual.

"Hi, Lady. Welcome to my shop. Now, what would you like to buy?" She had her superior expression firmly fixed on her face.

"I would like twenty girls' party bags, please."

"Okay and what kind of thing would you like in the bags, Lady?" She was standing with her hands on her hips, demanding an answer.

"Well, do you have any lollipops? I'd also like something pink and sparkly if you have anything like that?"

"I can offer you these crowns, but they're very expensive. How much money do you have?" She was a serious businesswoman. She wasn't going to do any deals, even for family.

"Well, I have five euros if that's enough." I smiled, thinking she was so grown up in some ways and yet still a baby in other ways.

"You'll have to pay me now, or else I won't be able to give you the things." She had her little hand out and her lips pursed. I rooted in my bag and found some change to give her. Taking the money, she scribbled on a piece of paper. "Here's your receipt. You can come back and collect them in a while. Good-bye, Lady." Then she whispered, suddenly worried in case I didn't know it was only a game. *"Now you have to go away, Mummy!"*

I beat a retreat with a smile on my face.

At a quarter to two on Saturday, the magician arrived. He was young and vivacious and the two children instantly warmed to him.

"Which of you is the boy and which is the girl?" He scratched his chin in pretend confusion.

"I'm the girl, that's why I'm wearing a pink dress!" Tia shouted jumping up and down.

"I'm a boy and it's my birthday! I'm six today, my name is Louis."

"I can't believe you're six! You're so big, aren't you? What's that stuck in your ear?" The magician pulled a coin from behind Louis' ear. Both children stood and stared in amazement.

"Now, my name is Silly Sam and I'm going to do lots of tricks and magic for you and your friends." Louis and Tia sat cross-legged on the floor as Silly Sam set up his things. He was full-on, with his own Madonna microphones and PA system. The doorbell began to ring and the possessed-with-excitement children bounced in through the door.

Silly Sam was amazing with them. He managed to involve them all, while still keeping control.

The throng was then moved into the kitchen where they ate their own bodyweight in junk food laced with E numbers. I produced the mud and worms cake, which made the girls scream and the boys nod in approval. The party finished with a disco, involving ear-splitting music, a bubble machine and flashing lights. Not for the faint-hearted or epileptic. The walls and leather sofa would be covered in burst bubble spots forever more. But right at that moment, I'd have agreed to let them try heroin if it kept them from crying, fighting or trying to hurt themselves. Being in charge of lots of other people's children is not all it's cracked up to be. I knew Louis had a ball, and I would do it again for him, but I couldn't imagine I'd ever have an urge to open a crèche or childcare service. My nerves wouldn't stand it.

Eventually, all the parents came to reclaim their little darlings. Quiet descended on the house. We were left with a lot of stepped-on cakes, burst balloons, bedraggled streamers and enough presents to fill a toy store.

As I tucked Louis into bed that night, I lay down beside him for a little chat.

"Did you enjoy your party?" I asked him, stroking his hair.

"It was so brilliant, Mum. I wish I could have a party every Saturday. It's so much fun. Is Silly Sam coming back tomorrow?"

"No, darling, you'll have to wait until next year to see him again."

I was just about to give him a hug and kiss and get up when he sighed heavily.

"What's all that sighing for?" I smiled at him in the dimly lit room.

"Will you be alive next year when Silly Sam comes?"

I could see his eyes shining in the dark. My heart stopped. "Of course I will, Louis. Why would I not be here, sweetheart?" The panic was rising in my throat.

"But you're going in the hospital and Steve in school said that lots of people who go in the hospital get dead." He exhaled loudly.

"No, Louis, I am going to the hospital for a very different reason. I am not sick. I'm going to hospital to get the doctors to make sure that I don't get sick. I also really, really want to be here for your party next year and that's why I need the doctors to fix me. Do you understand?" I hoped to God that he believed me.

"I think so. I just don't want you to be put in a box and put in a hole in the garden."

Sweet Jesus, who the hell had told him all this? In a way it would probably be a better idea not to find out. I would end up not seeing him on his birthday next year, because I'd be in prison for murder.

"I'm not going anywhere, Louis. I'm staying here to mind you and look after you, okay?" I held his shoulders and his gaze.

"Okay, Mum. I love you." He snuggled into his bear and settled down, for what I hoped would be a sweet dream.

16

Susie

How to Give your Life a True Roasting:
Take your previously dead father's name and give to a stranger. Pay said stranger to try and find him. Chew nails to the quick, eat enough to feed a mouse and douse with enough wine to stock a brewery, while you wait. Try not to go insane.

I felt unbelievably nervous as I walked out of the lift and found the Complete Investigation Services office. It was in a purpose-built block and was clean and bright.

Inside, I met Mairéad who I had spoken to on the phone and sat while she went to check if Thomas Richards was ready for me. I was flicking nervously through a glossy interiors magazine when I heard him greet me.

"Hi, Susie, I'm Thomas Richards. It's nice to put a face to a name."

Thomas looked like a regular type of guy. He wore a pinstriped suit, with a blue shirt and a revolting patterned tie. No sign of trench coats or crazy hats, no magnifying glasses on display. He didn't look remotely like Inspector Gadget. So far, so good.

"Come on through this way." He motioned towards a small corridor which led to a surprisingly spacious, dimly lit office. The walls were painted a dull yellow colour, and there was a desk with two visitors' chairs, a sideboard and several filing cabinets, all in blonde wood.

"Would you like a cup of tea or coffee?" he asked.

"No, thank you, I've just had a cup." I smiled fleetingly.

"Okay, Susie, further to your email I have followed a fairly straight line of investigation. This is a very easy case as it happens. I have already managed to locate a man I believe is your father." Looking triumphant, he leaned forward and smiled. His two front teeth were crooked and yellow. Why did none of his friends tell him to have them seen to? They really spoiled his whole face.

"Are you serious? Already? How do you know it's him? Have you spoken to him? Did you ask him if he knew my mother?" I felt my mouth getting dry.

"Gosh no, nothing like that. I haven't approached him. I simply found him and took some pictures of him, which I have here." He rooted in a drawer and took out an envelope. "He is managing a supermarket in the Midlands. Hence the reason he was so easy to locate. I approached the supermarket where himself and your mother used to work. As you informed me, he'd moved from that store the year you were born. But he stayed working for that particular chain. He has been manager of the same store for the last twenty-odd years. Here are the photos. Would you like to see a picture of your father?" He looked understandably delighted with himself.

"Damn right I want to see him!" My heart was thumping so loudly it was almost drowning out the sound of his voice. With shaking hands I took the A4 envelope from him. Sliding the shiny photos out, I saw the back of a man in a suit, walking towards the door of a shop. Quickly flicking through shots from various angles, I came across one of the same man taken from the front.

I could hardly breathe. He was tall and angularly thin, with a tight haircut, smart navy suit, very shiny shoes and a bright red tie. He wasn't conventionally good looking, but he was definitely attractive. He was carrying a clipboard. His plastic name badge on his right lapel read: "Mr James Lynch. Manager."

"I have all the other details written here. The address of the supermarket etcetera." Thomas handed me a sheet of paper.

"Thanks." I was in a trance. I couldn't take my eyes off the photo. I was in complete disbelief that he'd been so easy to find. How had Mum never had the urge to find him? If she'd tried, even a little bit, she would have found him. A mixture of feelings spread through me. If Mum had bothered, would I have had a dad growing up? They needn't have had to be together or married or anything like that, but maybe he would have helped out.

I remembered playing with kids in the park near our flat. Their dads would turn up and call them in for their dinner, or to tell them it was bedtime. There were always screams of "Daddy, look at me!"

The Christmas play in school was always a hard one for me. I remember huddling behind the scenes with my classmates as they peeped through the curtain for their parents.

"There's my mum and dad!" they'd say, bouncing about excitedly.

There was never a proud-looking man sitting with his camera poised, waiting for me to say my one line.

Mum never said, "Just wait until your father gets home."

The fathers' race at sports day was another one. Times have changed now, so many couples split up and there are plenty of single-parent families, but back then it was less normal. Whether or not it was noticeable to others, it was to me.

Mum did her best and I know she did what she felt was right, but look at how easy it had been to find Jim. Why hadn't she done so?

As I stared at the photograph of this man, my own physical self finally made more sense. He was taller than average, thin and had auburn hair. My auburn hair. With bitter-sweet regret I realised that, had he been around when I was a child, everyone would have said, "My God, aren't you the image of your daddy?" But nobody had ever had the chance to say that, and now it was too late.

I felt sorry for Jim Lynch too. Maybe he might have wanted to know me too.

I suddenly felt nervous and unsure. Maybe he had two or three other daughters and he wouldn't want to know about me. If I looked so like him, maybe I had a sister who looked and acted just like me.

Zoning back into Thomas Richard's office, I shoved the pictures back into the brown envelope.

"Thank you for your quick and efficient work. How much do I owe you?" I was hassled and my head was hurting.

"Seeing as it was all so straightforward, we'll leave it at five hundred euro, okay?" He handed me a printed bill.

I rooted in my bag and produced a chequebook. Signing the cheque, I tore out the slip and passed it to Thomas.

"A pleasure doing business with you. Next time I have a missing father, I'll call you immediately." I shook his hand.

By the time I reached my car, I was furious. How could Mum have been so bloody flippant about all of this? She really lived in cloud-cuckoo-land.

I drove home and flicked on the kettle. Actually, I'd open a bottle of wine instead. I needed a glass of wine to steady both my nerves and my temper.

As I drank my wine I studied the photos some more. I couldn't see his hands so I wasn't sure if he was married or not. Although a lot of men didn't wear a ring, so that was no guarantee. I wondered if he was well off financially. How much would he earn being a supermarket manager? Was his house big? Had he bought before the property boom? Did he drive an expensive car? Was he keen on travel? Did he drink or go out much?

Maybe he married late in life and had small children. Maybe I had half brothers and sisters who were only Louis' and Tia's age.

I picked up the phone and called Emily.

She was thrilled. "Wow! I'm dying to see the photos. What are you going to do? Are you going to contact him?"

"I just don't know the best way to approach him. I think I do want to make some kind of contact. But I'm going to have to prepare myself for rejection. I'll have to consider the worst-case scenario. I will probably be an unwelcome shock in his life. I know that sounds harsh, but it's the reality. I can't imagine there are many men who would take kindly to a thirty-year-old woman turning up on the doorstep and announcing herself as the illegitimate daughter."

"I think you're being too negative about this, Susie. Maybe he has four sons and has always longed for a daughter. Or maybe himself and his wife couldn't have children and he's always yearned for a child of his own."

"Yeah, and now his wife will know for certain their childless state is definitely her fault, and leave him," I concluded.

"Maybe he's single and lives in a bed-sit with a small mongrel with a collar made of string, and wishes every night that he had someone in his life!"

"He's a manager, Emily! Not a mongrel-with-a-bit-of-string type." I looked at the photo again. "Maybe the most unobtrusive way of going about it would be to send a letter. That way, if he doesn't want me in his life or if he needs time to think about it, I won't be standing there putting pressure on him."

"You could always jump out at him from behind a cauliflower in the supermarket? Or get the customer service desk to make an announcement? '*Could Jim Lynch please come to the information desk, his illegitimate, secret daughter is standing here waiting to frighten the living shit out of him. Thank you for your attention.*'"

"I'm glad you're finding this all so entertaining, you old bat! How are you, by the way?"

"Sick to the back teeth of talking about me. Your soap opera life is far more interesting." Emily was so into the whole thing.

"It is pretty good, isn't it?" I found myself smiling. Emily always had the ability to make me smile, even in the face of adversity.

"I'm going to have to call over to Mum now too and tell her I've found him. I hope she doesn't get too upset, yet at the same time I've an awful urge to strangle her. Can you believe he's lived less than two hours away from me all my life and I never knew?" I could feel my blood pressure rising again.

"Pauline meant well, Susie. I know you get cross with her but she did her best and always acted in your best interest, as she saw it."

"Her own best interest more like it. Emily, she lives on Planet Zog and always has. I know it's utterly futile getting annoyed with her and I can't change the past, but it's all so frustrating. I do honestly think she needs to shoulder some blame in all this."

"I understand what you're saying, Susie, but Pauline will never be any different. She's more of a floater than a face-them-head-on type of person. What you need to do now is decide what *you* want to do, regardless of her. Would you like to meet your father?

"Yes," I said. There it was. My answer.

I finished a second glass of wine and went to bed. I had a fitful night with images of Jim Lynch zoning in and out of my thoughts. I woke early the next morning feeling muzzy and exhausted. I knew I had a very busy clinic that day. But it was only six fifteen now so I knew if I got up and went into the office I would have some quiet time to begin writing *that* letter.

Within half an hour, I was sitting at my desk, with a strong cup of coffee.

Dear Dad . . . no.
Dear Jim . . . no.

Dear Mr Lynch

You don't know me and I've just found out about you. You might remember a girl called Pauline Rosedale. You worked together packing shelves in a supermarket in Bray, in 1979.

You had a brief union and parted ways. That union resulted in me. I am writing to ask if you are interested in any further correspondence. If you are not, I will understand, and I won't bother you again. I don't want to infringe on your life or make things difficult for you in any way.

In case you are interested, I will give you a brief outline of who I am. I am thirty years of age, 5ft 8ins tall, with auburn hair. I am a psychologist.

I am not married and have no children. I am currently single.

My mother spoke very little of you when I was growing up. In fact I was told as a child that you were dead. I employed a private detective to find you. I am curious to find out about you, and would be very grateful if you could take the time to reply to my letter. Even if it is to say that you are not interested in taking our relationship any further.

I hope my announcement is not going to cause you any heartache or trouble.
Yours sincerely
Susie Rosedale

I read it over and over. I knew it sounded a bit stilted and odd, but what the hell was I supposed to write to a man I'd never met, who also happened to be my father? Sadly, there weren't any information booklets on this subject. There was no established protocol to follow.

I sealed the letter into an envelope and attached a stamp. I walked the short distance to the nearest post box and posted it before I could change my mind. All I could do now was wait. The ball was firmly in Jim Lynch's court.

17

Emily

Recipe for Distraction:
Take one pre-surgery victim, add as many friends and cups of coffee as humanly possible. Steam in a sauna and float in a pool. Don't allow to sit alone for too long. Add one pair of designer jeans mixed with drool and a coveting desire beyond all previous experience.

I planned the week running up to the operation down to the last second. I filled my diary with coffee dates, swimming sessions and every distraction known to woman. I shopped till I dropped. This operation was the be all and end all of my life at that time. It was all I thought about day and night. Sure, I was managing to function and continue with the day-to-day chores. I had to, there was no choice there. But I was living for the time when I could go into hospital and diffuse the time bomb.

Hayley phoned from St Theresa's to see if I had any last-minute questions.

"Don't forget to bring plenty of pairs of button-through pyjamas with you. Remember you won't have the full use of your arms post surgery, so you won't be able to get into T-shirts or any over-the-head tops."

Fantastic. I had a valid reason to go shopping again. I shrugged into my coat as Hayley was still talking. In my mind I was halfway to Dunmahon shopping centre, already planning which shops I would visit on the pyjama trail. I searched every shop, from chain stores to lingerie departments.

There were stunning pyjamas, sexy pyjamas, pretty pyjamas, cosy pyjamas, ugly pyjamas and children's pyjamas. But no button-through pyjamas. Whoever designs these things has never heard of the word mastectomy – never mind bi-lateral mastectomies. I was becoming desperate until I walked into a large, cheap chain store. There like a mountain of gold, resting under a beam of light, with "halleluiah" music booming out, was a pile of button-through pyjamas.

They came in two colours, Virgin Mary blue and knickers pink. But I didn't care if they were luminous green with orange frogs on: they had buttons. I went completely mad and bought five pairs of each colour. I celebrated with a strong cup of Americano coffee. It was like molten tar and mouse-trotter style. Fuelled by the caffeine boost and a general sense of exhilaration, I skipped into Harvey Nichols. I always went in there thinking it was good to know what the designers were doing, what the season's must-have styles and shapes were. That way I could build up a similar wardrobe using high-street stores. I was drawn to the back of the shop where all the designer jeans were housed.

It was there, like a shining Mecca-type figure beckoning to me from the glass display box, that I saw them. *The* jeans. I had read about them and heard all the kerfuffle about them, celebrities and Jo Public alike were all raving about them, but until I laid eyes on them it didn't make sense to me. The Victoria Beckham Rock & Republic Jeans. I know lots of people disapprove of her, and that she's the wrong side of skinny according to many. But I happen to find her fascinating and have to admit I will always buy magazines with stories about her inside.

Like her or loathe her, those jeans were a work of art. I must have been standing with a rabbit-in-the-headlights look on my face as the assistant approached.

"Nice, aren't they? They're selling really well. In fact, we only have two pairs left, those ones and a smaller size. Hard to believe how quickly they flew out considering how pricey they are."

"Why, how much are they?" I actually didn't give a flying fuck what they cost. I wanted them.

"They're €560, but they're stunning on. Would you like to try them?"

My mind was screaming no, but my heart obviously won the battle with my brain.

"Yes, please," said a voice that sounded alarmingly like mine.

She reverently removed the jeans from the glass box and gently placed them over my arm. My mouth was dry and I felt a bit dizzy as I shut the changing-room door. Oh dear Jesus, what was I doing? €560 would educate an African village. This was insane. Okay. I would just try them on, they'd probably make me look deformed and that would be that. I could go home with my cheap button-through pyjamas and forget the whole thing, and never tell anyone. Especially Robbie.

But I knew as I was pulling them up my thighs that they were going to be fabulous. I zipped and buttoned them and turned around. I had heard they did wonders for ladies' bottoms. Well, all the rumours were true. I stepped out of the changing room to look in the full-length mirror.

"Oh wow! They really suit you. You have to get those!" The assistant sidled up to me and whispered, "I've seen them on a couple of people but they didn't look as good as that."

I know, I know, I thought. *She's on commission, she's probably lying. But I don't care.*

I bounced into the fitting room and removed the precious Rock & Republic jeans. Rushing to the counter I thrust them at the assistant.

"Wrap them up quickly before I change my mind."

It was a race against time. I had to do the dastardly deed before my brain caught up with my wallet. I rooted violently in my bag and fished out my purse.

There was €150 in cash there, probably to buy the week's food, but things like that couldn't be taken into consideration at that moment. It would work to my advantage – the borrowed cash would reduce the amount on my credit card.

"Can I pay you €150 in cash and put the rest on my credit card?"

"Sure, whatever way you'd like to do it."

"That way they'll only be €410 and that sounds so much better, doesn't it?" I knew I was clutching at straws.

"Hmm . . . yeah . . ." The assistant now looked as if she wanted to get away from me.

With my designer jeans in the Harvey Nichols bag – a nice big glossy bag with ribbon handles at that – I left the shop. I know I had such a guilty face I must have looked like I'd been shoplifting. With my head down I made a beeline for the car park and found the safe haven of my car. Exhaling deeply I quickly rustled the jeans out of the tissue paper. The pale blue crown with gorgeous diamante detail twinkled and winked at me. I was in love.

I took them home and removed the labels. Carefully I chopped them into tiny pieces, so even if Robbie took all the pieces out of the bin and tried to stick them together (which I know was highly unlikely) he would never find out how much they'd cost. Even if we won the lottery Robbie would never understand spending that amount of money on a single item of clothing. He was missing that gene. No pun intended.

I folded them and hid them under a pile of sweaters in my chest of drawers.

Then grabbing my bundle of cheap pyjamas, I shoved them in the washing machine hoping to soften them so I didn't look like I was folded when I put them on. The creases were moulded into them, giving the impression they could never be peeled apart and actually worn.

Satisfied that they were boiling nicely, I set about packing my bag for hospital. I'd got a Christmas pressie of a pretty wash-bag about the size of a supermarket bag, which I now proceeded to stuff with every product from mouthwash to nail varnish. You never know what you might need while in hospital.

It was Thursday. Three days before Hospital Day. A group of the mums from Louis' class in school were taking me out for dinner. The unconditional support they were giving me was amazing. I had only known these women two years, since my son had started school, but they were so compassionate and helpful.

They bought me beautiful gifts and cards with heartfelt messages. I felt so special and so loved, and from a source I would never have dreamed possible the first day I walked my baby through the doors of his classroom. Yet again, I felt lucky.

We had a howl that evening. We christened it a "hen night" for my boobs to the horror of the other diners in the restaurant and flirted outrageously with the waiter despite the fact he was clearly "one of the girls" himself.

As we toasted womanhood and the fight I was going to win over the next few months, my mobile rang. It was Susie.

Excusing myself from the girls, I went outside.

"Hi, it's only me. How are you doing?"

"Good. I'm at dinner with the school mums."

"Oh, the night of the mummies!" Susie was a bit beyond understanding how people who had nothing in common but children could go out together on the piss.

"It's fab – we're having a great laugh." It was bloody freezing, so I had to jump from one foot to the other to keep warm. "Hey, did he call?"

"No, not yet."

Suze sounded so deflated that I realised she had probably called me to buck her up.

"Oh, it's early days, Suze! Give the man a chance to get his bearings! He will ring, believe you me."

"Do you really think so?"

"Yes, I do," I said firmly. "By the way, have you spoken to Pauline about that yet?" By now I was shivering so much I could barely speak. The copious amounts of wine were not helping my speech much either.

"No, I haven't. Listen, you sound like you're about to die of hypothermia there. You'd better get back to the mummies."

"Tell you what, I'll call you tomorrow and we can have a big chat. What's your clinic like in the morning? Can you do a quick coffee?"

"I'm free from ten thirty to twelve, if that's any use to you?"

"Perfect. I'm going for a quick swim and I'll meet you in Blackrock at around quarter to eleven."

"Great, enjoy your night, babes. See you in the morning!" She sounded more cheerful.

"See you then!" I hung up and returned to the madness inside the restaurant.

The following morning the wine and flaming sambuccas, which had been a marvellous idea the night before, had produced a brass band in my skull. I needed sugar. I made myself go for my swim and met up with Susie for strong, frothy cappuccinos and home-baked cake with cream.

We were only just tucking in when my phone rang.

"Emily, it's Hayley, from the Breast Clinic in St Theresa's Hospital." She sounded subdued. "I have bad news for you I'm afraid."

"Okay, Hayley, what's wrong?"

"Emily, the hospital is backed up. Casualty is overrun with patients and we've had to give up our surgical beds today. There won't be a bed for you this week. I'm afraid your operation won't be going ahead."

I was stunned. I conducted the rest of the telephone conversation like a robot.

"But how can they just postpone my surgery like that? Don't they realise the mental preparation and organisation I've been through working up to this?"

"Emily, I understand how upsetting and shocking this is for you but it's out of my hands. If I could sort this out, I would. I'm sorry my hands are tied. There is no alternative at the moment."

She was definite, she wasn't joking. This was real.

"But when will the operation be then?" I was trying not to cry.

"We don't actually know yet. As soon as you can be rescheduled, we will do so. I'll call you first thing on Monday morning and hopefully I'll have more information for you then. Are you okay?" She sounded genuinely concerned.

"No, Hayley, I'm far from okay, I haven't been less okay for a long time." I could feel the tears burning my eyes.

"I'm sorry, Emily, but there's nothing I can say or do to help at this moment."

She was struggling, it wasn't her fault, I shouldn't make her feel bad. I knew that, yet I wanted to scream at her and make her feel awful.

"It's okay, Hayley," I said insincerely.

"I'll talk to you on Monday, Emily."

She was gone.

"My operation isn't happening," I whispered incredulously to Susie and promptly burst into tears.

This was the first time I had cried in public since I was a child. I had never felt the need to cry like this before. But since the floodgates had been opened, my God did I cry!

Susie was so astonished and shocked she started to cry too.

"I'm sorry, Susie," I gulped, "it's just such a shock."

"I'm sorry too. I should be supporting you instead of snuffling along with you. I'm no use at all." Susie looked as shell-shocked as I felt.

I drove home and phoned everyone I had a number for in connection with my surgery. I wanted reasons and answers. I wanted a new date. I wanted to grab someone and shake them.

I had geared myself up, both physically and physiologically, to do this and now it had been taken out of my hands. I resented the lack of control I felt. The disappointment choked me.

It may sound absurd to say I was disappointed, but I was. This operation had become a milestone. Although not pleasant, like any impending event, be it Christmas, a birthday or surgery, you build up to that moment in your mind. This news was devastating.

18

Emily

Best Before Date:
Psychologically accept impending surgery. Write four million lists for the au pair and husband. Say farewell to all friends and congratulate self on being "together". Have hospital cancel surgery. Spin with shock, shake up until you feel like the rug has been pulled from under you. Serve with lashings of waiting.

I was totally numb after my phone call from Hayley. It was like something inside me kind of snapped.

Time seemed to have stopped. The weekend was the longest one in the history of the world. It was torture. I found the waiting almost unbearable. I felt like an outsider sitting in my own body. Functioning and existing, only barely.

I waited until the following Tuesday to hear from the hospital.

"Emily, it's Hayley, how are you?" she asked tentatively.

"I'm okay now, Hayley, how are you?" I asked back.

"Not too bad. I cannot tell you how distressing and upsetting I found it, having to make that phone call to you last week. I hope you appreciate that it was out of our control and we would have done anything in our power to facilitate you. It just wasn't possible. No one else had surgery yesterday, if that helps at all?"

"Well, it does help a little, but what can I say? What's done is done, or rather what's not done," I said, trying to make light of the situation.

Hayley continued to apologise on behalf of her team, Mr Green's team and Mr Green himself. They were as upset as I was. I believed that. The surgeon was very sorry. I believed him. The state of the medical system in Ireland was a disgrace. We all agreed it was not their fault. But I had become the victim.

"Now, the good news I do have for you is that your surgery has been rescheduled for two weeks' time. You will come in on Sunday the 26th of February, and your operation will be on Monday the 27th. Does that suit you?"

"Of course. I'm hardly going to be doing anything more important, now am I?" I said sarcastically.

"No, of course not."

I felt sorry for Hayley. She was such an amazing woman – sympathetic, knowledgeable and just trying to do her job. She had all the skills, brainpower and organisation. All that was letting her down was the inept hospital system. That was certainly out of her hands.

"That's great, Hayley, and I don't blame you for one second. It's all just very frustrating and emotional. I hope you realise that none of my anger is directed at you personally. You're doing a wonderful job and I wouldn't want you to feel bad for one second."

"I understand perfectly, Emily. Thanks for saying that."

I could hear her smiling down the phone.

"Before I go, Emily, please do be aware that we will do our best to get you in, but that the same thing could happen again. We don't anticipate a situation like before, but you will have to keep the possibility of a reschedule in the back of your mind. Nothing with the hospital is set in stone these days."

I resigned myself to the fact that the operation might not happen on the proposed day. I was to phone on the morning of Sunday the 26th to confirm that there would be a bed available.

It was a blessing in disguise as my children were on a week's mid-term break from school. So, once I calmed down, I was happy to be able to spend time with them. Their routine was upset anyway, so it was great to be able to do some fun things together. Luckily they were at the age where they were too young to understand the concept of time. They knew I was going to hospital, but they didn't know when. So I didn't discuss it with them.

I planned a fun-filled week with the children, vowing I would enjoy the borrowed week with them. But by the middle of that week, I'd had enough of Louis' behaviour. He is a normal, six-year-old boy. Not an angel by any stretch of the imagination, but he's not a nasty or particularly naughty child. But overnight he had grown three sixes on his forehead and turned into Damien.

He was cheeky beyond belief. My gorgeous, usually sunny-natured child had turned into a mini-teenager. He hated everything and everyone. Nothing was good enough for him.

"I'm so bored, Mum, nothing good ever happens to me," he sighed. "There's nothing to do. Why can't we go bowling?"

"I will bring you bowling, no problem, but not if you carry on like that. I need to see a bit of happy, cheerful behaviour first."

Although I was driven demented by him and felt like throttling him, I knew he was in turmoil. Since the night of his birthday, he hadn't mentioned my trip to hospital at all. But now I wondered if he needed to know more. I sat him down and asked him why he was behaving so badly.

I tried to talk to him like an adult. "Louis, what's going on, why are you being so grumpy and nasty to Mummy all the time?"

"It's not me, Mum it's Yoda from *Star Wars*, he's making me do it." He looked at me with wide innocent eyes.

"Louis, nobody likes liars." I was rubbing my forehead with stress.

"Okay, it's the aliens – they climb in my ear at night-time and make my head all fuzzy and then the bold and naughty stuff comes out during the day." He looked so sincere.

I had to hand it to him, he had a great imagination, and if I wasn't so fed up and stressed, I might have let him away with it, but I knew we needed to have a chat, so I couldn't let it go.

"Louis?" I was stern.

"All right then, it was Pudding."

An alarm bell went off in my head. Pudding was his imaginary friend, who only came out when he felt threatened or upset. We hadn't heard from Pudding for quite a while.

Louis sighed from the bottom of his toes and slumped his shoulders forward, wide-eyed.

"You're getting dead, aren't you, Mummy?"

It wasn't really a question, it was a statement. Remembering I was supposed to be the grown-up one in the conversation, I battled to keep it together. If I wavered, I would have started blubbing, loudly, and I don't think I would have been able to stop. Thankfully, I didn't.

"No, darling, I told you about that before. Remember? Pudding is wrong about that. I am not going to die. Quite the opposite. I have some blue beads all across my chest, well, in here in my boobs," I pointed to my breasts. "These beads could turn red. If they are allowed to turn red, they will make Mummy sick – so the doctor is going to take them all out."

He listened intently, hardly breathing. "But that's going to hurt you and I don't want anyone to hurt you!" he wailed.

His little body crumbled and he let it all go. He cried until his throat hurt. All I could do was hold him and rock him. I stroked his tiny blond curls and insisted over and over again that it was not going to hurt me.

"The doctors will give me lots of medicine to take the pain away. I will have a big long sleep while the doctors take the bad beads away. It will be great. I even got new pyjamas and slippers and a dressing gown to bring with me, isn't that lucky?" I tried to remain positive.

"But what if you have a nightmare while you are asleep?" he implored.

"There's no way that's going to happen," I informed him firmly.

"Why not, Mum?" he asked.

"Because I will be dreaming about you," I stated simply. "The only reason Mummy is going to hospital to have this operation, is so she can be well and live for a very long time. Do you believe me, Louis?" I looked into his eyes and held his gaze.

He nodded slowly with tears in his eyes.

Children are like little sponges, they soak up all the emotions around them. I needed to realise Louis was fully aware of my fears. I made a mental note to keep him more in the picture with what was happening.

The time dragged until the 26th. It was like being overdue with a baby. I kept meeting people who looked surprised to see me. I knew they were trying to work out whether I had made a miraculous recovery or if I'd had surgery at all. I was glad I told everyone and was open from the start about the surgery, but at that time it became a drag for everyone. I felt like we were all holding our breath until it happened. I know I was.

All the while my inner time bomb was ticking away. Tick, tick, tick! It was louder each day. Every morning in the shower I would avoid touching my breasts too much, terrified I would find a lump and I was still imagining I felt some pain in my left breast. To me, this constant fear was torture.

I had to wait until eleven thirty on the morning of the 26th to phone admissions. I'd been up, had breakfast, showered, dressed and played with most things in the playroom with Louis and Tia, and it was still only nine thirty. So I went to the supermarket. I pushed my daughter around in the trolley and bought about ten things in the space of an hour. Eventually, what seemed like twenty-five years later, it was time to make that call.

"Hello, St Theresa's Hospital, Gillian speaking, how may I help you?"

"Hi, Gillian, this is Emily Cusack. I'm ringing to confirm that you have a bed for me today. I am due to have surgery tomorrow." I held my breath.

"Yes, that's fine, Emily, your bed is ready. You won't get a private room unfortunately, but we will move you to a room when one becomes available. Is that okay?"

"Perfect, see you later." I said goodbye and put the phone down.

They had a bed. It was happening. I was delighted and nervous and scared and calm all at the same time. At least the show was on the road, as they say. The journey was at last beginning.

19

Emily

Surgery Spring Roll:
Take one woman, wrap in a starched hospital sheet, add pyjamas and hospital bed. Douse with sleeping tablets. Wake at the crack of dawn, loudly. Bake in strip lighting. Place in shower and leave to sweat.

I was woken from a drug-induced sleep at 5.45 a.m. My body felt stiff as a board.

"Good morning, Emily, rise and shine! You've plenty of time but you might like to trot into the shower." The nurse was looking bright-eyed and bushy-tailed, as if it was mid-morning.

I peeled myself out of bed and had a shower and hair wash. I savoured the ease with which I could do these things, while thinking about the fact that washing my hair could prove impossible next time.

I donned my delicious hospital gown. For those who haven't experienced them, they are a bit like a posh version of a strait-jacket. White, with coloured writing all over, and ties at the back. Luckily I had my dressing gown in the bathroom with me so I didn't have to walk back down the ward baring my bum to all. I struggled to tie the fastenings behind me, wondering if I was the only patient who ended up nearly falling into the toilet while trying to reverse myself around the small bathroom, tying ribbons backwards.

I had a "nil by mouth" sign above my bed, so I sat and listened to the clattering of breakfast as the ward sprang into life.

Suddenly a very camp voice came from behind me. I turned to see a big, eager-looking teddy bear blinking at me. His badge read: *"Father Peter."*

"Would you like a blessing with my special oil?"

He'd already taken it out of the inside pocket of his jacket before I could explain that I didn't do the God stuff. Unable to crush his enthusiasm, I heard myself saying, "That would be lovely."

Just what I needed at a time like this. Not.

He was beside himself with excitement, fumbling with his little jar of oil. Before I could move, I had an oil-slicked sign of the cross dribbling down my nose and making greasy pools in my eyebrows. He lisped, "In the name of the Father, and of the Son and of the Holy Spirit . . ." and nodded at me to finish the sentence.

God forgive me, I had such an urge to shout "Bollox!" But I controlled it and piously said, "Amen."

Father Peter then did a big long mutter, while rolling his semi-shut eyes. When he was finished, he opened his eyes, making them all round and wide. A sheepish grin crept across his face and he willed me to share his joy. For fear of offending him, I did the first thing that came into my head. I started to clap.

A look of utter shock froze his smile for a split second. Jesus, I was never good at the whole religious thing and this was more proof of the fact.

"That was fabulous, Father Peter, good man yourself!" I said heartily. I felt I had to say something to try and crawl my way out of the large hole I'd dug myself into.

"Erm . . . thanks . . ." He looked at me with genuine confusion in his eyes and scurried off, almost tripping over a drip-stand on the way.

I kind of figured that would be the last of my encounters with the religious folk of the hospital.

Soon all the curtains were whipped back, to reveal all the other patients who seemed to find the early start normal.

"Good morning!" Betsy the farmer's wife waved cheerfully at me, while readying herself for her breakfast. She was recovering after major surgery to remove a kidney. "I find it such a treat to have my food handed up to me. I'm sure you think I'm a bit of an old fool, but it's the nearest to a hotel I've ever experienced!" She giggled, genuinely excited by the prospect of her impending meal.

"Well, your husband should pull out all the stops when you get out of here. A five-star hotel in the Bahamas for three weeks if you ask me," sniffed Delia across the way.

Delia was the tanned polished one, who was not-here-for-a-hard-time.

"Sounds lovely, dear, but I can't see my Johnny wanting all that in a month of Sundays," Betsy chuckled, while shaking her head. The image of her husband in shorts on a beach, and staying in fancy hotels, was enough to make her laugh out loud.

"I think you're mad," snorted Delia. "You've been through a huge ordeal, Betsy. You should demand to be taken somewhere comfortable. It's his duty as a husband to look after you and cherish you. You shouldn't let him away with it, darling. Men are slow on the uptake at times, you need to train them, like monkeys. He won't come up with the idea on his own. You need to help him. Take my Derrick, for example. A darling man, no doubt about it. But, he needed to be helped along at the beginning of our marriage. I had to tell him what side his bread was buttered. He still slips up from time to time, but I haul him back in. These men need to realise how lucky they are to have such wonderful women in their lives. I look after Derrick, I am a good wife, and I deserve my rewards," she sniffed. She sounded like the shampoo ad – *"Because I'm worth it."*

Betsy listened with her warm face alight with a smile. Her leathery, weather-beaten skin crinkled as she grinned. "Yes, dear, I understand what you mean, but Johnny and I have a different way about us. We weren't reared to fancy hotels and a posh life the way you were. I feel we have what we need. It's an alternative to the life you love, but it works for us. I get my jollies from a bed of crocus opening out. I love the berries appearing on the holly bushes. I enjoy a calf arriving healthily into the field. A loaf of bread rising in my oven gives me joy. They are things which may not interest you, but they are my world. I'm glad you are happy and your man makes you feel good. You deserve that, of course you do. My husband Johnny is so busy with the farm. My son JJ, or Johnny Junior, has just opened a new dairy section and it's going well, but leaves little time for gallivanting up to Dublin hospitals to look at someone sitting in a chair. They have enough to do without having to come to a place like this."

"But don't you feel like you'd enjoy seeing them even for a few minutes?" I was shocked by the way she was being neglected while she was so ill.

"Not at all, child! Sure how could they explain to a herd of cows that they'd be back to connect them up to the milkers later on? Animals don't care if you've got a dodgy kidney. A farm won't run itself and you can't send a fax or a text message or turn on an answering machine to organise the animals."

I'd never thought about it that way. I suppose farm life made you very practical.

"I was never a woman for reading many books but it's nice to have the time to sit in the armchair and do a bit of knitting." The clickity-clack of her needles gently drummed away, as she waited for her breakfast. I don't know if she was knitting coats for the cows or what the hell she was doing, because yards and yards of yarn were knotted into a variety of coloured blankets. I had images of her Johnny and JJ draping hand-made rugs over each cow, complete with matching leg warmers, as they stood and mooed in the field, the brightly coloured wools stunning against their black and white, and brown and white coats.

"My Johnny will be waiting for me when I get home, and we will continue, please God, with our life. Pure and simple. That will be my reward," Betsy chuckled and smiled easily at Delia.

I thought Delia was going to cough up a lung.

"But Betsy, you deserve more than a cow giving birth or having to make your own bread. You should be pampered and have someone else to cook for you. Not the other way around. I'm sure if you were looked after properly for a while you would see what I mean," she spluttered.

It was amazing to see how one woman's quiet confidence and happiness was almost a threat to the other. I'd say she was more worried about Betsy telling hen-pecked Derrick her thoughts. If the poor bastard realised what a raw deal he was getting, the gravy train might grind to a halt for Delia. I had no doubt that Delia was happy to be a pampered fat cat. In fact, after being in her company for less than 24 hours, it was already obvious that she wouldn't survive a day in Betsy's world. But I quietly wondered which woman was the happier. Betsy had a sense of ease about her. She was comfortable in her own skin. There was no aggression or tension emanating from her. She didn't feel the need to impress anyone, nor did she want to be impressed. She was fully content in her own world, with the people she loved.

She made Delia appear spoilt, brash and almost forceful about her happiness. Not that Delia would have noticed for a second. She was too busy putting on her designer dressing gown and flapping about with her matching luggage and wash-bag set. I suppose the difference between the two women was that Betsy's world revolved around her husband and her family, whereas Delia's world revolved around herself.

Robbie arrived shortly after nine. The kids were in school and I hoped were oblivious to what was happening. I thanked my lucky stars that they were both at school-going age. Their routine could be kept, so at least some normality would prevail for them.

"Hi, how was your night?" Robbie sat beside the bed.

"Fine, I slept thanks to the sleeping pills," I answered.

"Get me one next time, will you?" He looked exhausted.

"How are the kids?" I felt a stab of longing hit me in the chest.

"They're fine. They fought all the way to school and then ran in the door delighted with themselves."

Robbie and I made small talk. We didn't ask each other how we felt. There was both nothing to say and yet so much.

"You look divine in your gown and stockings. You shall go to the ball, Cinderella," he laughed.

I had gained a pair of skin-tight, thick, white, thigh-high stockings. They weren't socks, they were stockings. They were utterly vile. They were also itchy beyond belief.

"I'd say I'll have the legs scratched off myself by the time I get out of here," I mumbled, while trying to get at a part at the back of my knee.

"They're attractive." He stared at the stockings like they were going to bite him.

At nine thirty the "Undertaker", as I called him, or the porter as everyone else called him, came to collect me. Robbie hurriedly said goodbye and I was off. As they wheeled the bed away with me in it, I had an incredible urge to cry, loudly, like a child. But I didn't.

The Undertaker swivelled the bed so I could see Robbie. He stood motionless in the spot where my bed had been. I waved as we entered the lift. He waved back, looking forlorn and beaten. I hated having to put him through all of this. I hoped he didn't hate me at that moment.

The Undertaker picked his nails and looked at his hair in the mirror. "I'm off for a cup of tea when I drop you. I'm parched, it's very hot in here, with all that running up and down the stairs," he yawned.

"Yes, I suppose it is." I felt like kicking him in the shins and saying, "At least you're not going to have your gonads removed, you stupid arsehole!". Instead, I smiled like a good girl.

My bed was parked in a holding pen where my details were taken and I was left to wait for what seemed like a decade until my slot.

I counted the curtain rails which circled my bed, then the squares on the ceiling. They were white square tiles, which covered the ceiling in every room. Basically I did anything I could, to pretend I wasn't there. I was very aware of my spine while lying on the trolley which was rock hard and rigid.

"Do the beds have to be so uncomfortable?" I asked the nurse.

"Well, it's not a bed, dear, it's an operating trolley you're lying on there. It has to be inflexible or you'd flop all over the place when Mr Green is conducting surgery," she answered matter-of-factly.

I felt a shudder run down my spine. I would be still on this horrible contraption, out cold, being chopped up shortly. I banished the thought from my head and tried to think nice thoughts.

That worked quite well and then I was moved into a little cell with two doors on either end. One end was the corridor from which I'd come and the other led to the operating theatre.

"Hi, Emily, we meet again. I came around to you last night," the anaesthetist greeted me. I must have looked like a startled chicken, because he immediately offered me something to calm me down.

"I recommend the fuzzy juice, it's always a good vintage and has the desired affect," he encouraged.

I gratefully accepted. I got a shot of some magic liquid and almost instantly didn't give a shit if they cut my leg off with a spoon.

The poor man then had the job of entertaining me while we waited to go to theatre. This guy should be on the stage. He held up his hand and, counting on his fingers, went through his usual topics of conversation with women.

"What'll we chat about – kids?" He regarded me with his head to the side.

"No, too emotional," I slurred.

"Husband? Is he a bollox or do you like him?"

"Not a bollox, no, yet again too emotional a topic."

"Okay, shoes and bags? Or is that even more emotional?"

We agreed that shoes and bags are an entity that only women understand. He explained how he owns only two pairs of shoes. I commiserated with him and promised him I'd buy him some shoes and bags as soon as I got out of the operating theatre. He'd obviously learned not to point out that all his patients talked drivel. He just nodded enthusiastically. He even managed to look interested when I started to tell him how he should be using Crème de la Mer face products. I told him where to buy it and explained that even though it's a ferocious price, it's worth it in the end. We only get one face, so we should look after it. I'd say he was ecstatic when he could finally knock me out.

Ten seconds later I was awake and covered in tubes. The surgery had taken seven hours. Much longer than anticipated. I was blissfully ignorant of the whole thing. My poor husband had spent the day sitting, pacing and tearing his hair out. Waiting, waiting and more waiting. My family and friends were all worried, and longing for Robbie's call to say

I was out, that it was all over. Eventually, at around seven o'clock, I was wheeled back to the ward. I remember being woken up in recovery.

I couldn't talk much due to the sedation and the oxygen mask.

A muzzy face leaned over me. "Hi, Emily, it's all over."

"A gin and tonic, please," I answered.

"Everything went very well, you're doing brilliantly," said the fuzzy image.

"That's just amazing, isn't it?" I answered.

What the hell were they all talking about? I would just have a quick snooze for a year or so, and then I'd feel right as rain. I'd be able to get up and make the dinner in a minute.

I was aware of being in the lift and when I approached the ward I knew Robbie was there. I recognised his footsteps and could clearly hear him talking to the Undertaker who was returning me.

"She's completely out of it," he scoffed to Robbie.

Like I've heard coma patients describe, I tried with all my might to speak or move or do something to let them know that I could hear. That I wasn't "completely out of it". But nothing happened. Nothing worked. I was shouting and yelling, but no one could hear me. What was wrong with them?

"Hey, Em, you've been gone for a long time, but it's all over now." Robbie kissed my forehead and stood back.

What the hell was he on about? I hadn't gone anywhere. I'd been in a lift for half an hour and now I was back. They were all behaving like deaf, deranged zoo creatures.

If I could just get my voice to work I could explain myself. It was too difficult though, so I went to sleep.

"Emily, can you listen to me for a minute?" The nurse was insisting I open my eyes.

"I am putting a black button into your hand." She guided the small remote control into my palm. "Whenever the pain gets bad, I want you to push the button. It will release a shot of morphine. There are no medals for being in pain – in fact you will impede your recovery if your body is tense and sore. Do you understand?"

"Yes, ma'am." I smiled, feeling my eyes wanting to shut.

20

Emily

How to Create a Human Cabbage:
Take one human, anaesthetise and chop off breasts. Add a morphine drip and pour into bed. Leave to fully bake.

The rest of that first night after my surgery was a blur. By 3.00 a.m. the morphine pump was starting to really do its worst. I must have been coming through a barrier, because instead of using the pump and it taking the pain away, I was now hallucinating. There were orange, gelatinous hands with long claws coming through the curtains.

I recognised the hands from one of Louis' toys at home. They were waving and grabbing at the curtains. They'd also started to make a noise. I was trying to rationalise it in my head. I knew I was on drugs and that the hands weren't real. But that was a turning point. I thought, *Sod this, I'm not into having growling hands visiting me while I'm awake. Never mind nightmares while asleep.*

"You are not real, I am on drugs," I kept saying under my breath. I thought it would be better to regain a little control, so I stopped pressing the button and therefore stopped releasing the morphine.

The next thing I knew, there were two nurses there talking to me, as if they knew me.

"Good morning, Emily, how are you feeling now?" one girl asked me. What did she mean *now*? I'd never seen her before.

"That was a long night for you, but you've managed the morphine pump well. How are you today?" She smiled and waited for an answer.

I looked down at my body. I had four drains coming out of the wounds on the sides of my breasts, a drip in one arm, a morphine pump in the other arm and a catheter coming from my bladder. The nurse was still waiting for a reply.

"Well, I wouldn't mind going into the Four Seasons for a few drinks. Are you coming?" I replied.

"I'd be there in a flash if I thought we'd get away with it," she chuckled.

I looked like a bag of spaghetti and I could either laugh or cry. I was not very into crying, so I thought the best way would be to try and see the funny side of the whole situation.

I made an effort to look on the bright side:

★ I didn't have to get up and go to work.
★ I didn't have to make breakfast or dress the children.
★ I wouldn't have to drag the children to school while they fought.
★ For the first time in my life, I was supposed to lie there like a cabbage, and I didn't have to feel guilty.
★ I didn't have to put on make-up or wash my hair.
★ I didn't have to decide what to wear.

All things considered, I was planning on having a fairly easy day.

But first I had to get rid of the morphine and the orange claws. I called the nurse back.

By nine the pain specialists came round to visit.

"Now, Emily, Nurse O'Shea tells us you are not using the morphine pump any more and that you want it removed. Is this true?" The white-coated person was standing there looking oddly cross.

"Oh yes, that's all true. I am not interested in growling, orange claws flailing through the curtains at me. Would you mind removing the morphine, digging a large hole in the grounds and burying the pump at least twenty foot under, in case it comes near me again?"

There was silence as the white-coat brigade all stared at me like I was insane.

"You see, I can't say that I'm fully enjoying the hands and sound effects coming through the curtains while I'm awake. I know it's a bit boring of me, but that's just how I feel." I looked at the crew staring back at me.

One of them, a power-suit-clad woman with a clipboard, devoid of sense of humour and personality, took centre stage.

"I don't think you fully understand all the positive properties of morphine. It's the most effective painkiller in the universe and, to be honest," she gave a little dry laugh, "you're a very lucky lady to have it on tap. You'd have to change to suppositories and oral pain relief in its place." It was almost a threat.

"Look, lady, at this stage, I don't care if you want to rip my head off and shove painkillers down my dismembered neck. I just want this evil bastard pump and its poisonous twin morphine taken as far away from me as possible. Apart from anything else, this spike you have shoved into my vein to feed me this poison is hurting me." I was knackered after my outburst.

She looked at me as if I was a petulant child. She raised her eyebrows, I assume to say something condescending in reply. I beat her to it.

"How often do *you* use morphine, Mrs Clip Board?" I asked.

"Well, I've never actually used it, but I am fully aware of its properties medically. It's a very effective source of pain relief." She had the cheek to look smug.

"Okay, so we've established you have never used it. Well, guess what? Funnily enough I have, just last night in fact. And guess what else? It's not my friend, medical properties and all that. It's sending me off my rocker, making me want to crawl through the curtains and to top it all off it's not even killing the pain that much. I just feel sick."

She wrote in my chart that I was to have alternative pain relief and stomped off, quite annoyed. Thoughts like *"Fuck her"* sprang to mind.

One of the nurses bounded through the curtain.

"Hi, Emily, I believe you want rid of the morphine pump," she said. "It doesn't suit everyone. If it's not helping you, you're dead right to try something else. Sure, you might as well have a go of some other stuff while you're in here."

"I was just made to feel like a leper for not becoming semi-addicted to the stuff. Mrs Clip Board was furious with me that I wasn't asking for phials of it to be sent to my family and friends."

"Ah, don't take too much heed of her, she's good at what she does, until someone questions her or wants to change something. She takes it as a personal offence. She'll get over herself in a minute." The nurse rolled her eyes to heaven and began to peel off the plasters which held the morphine drip into my vein.

I got quite excited when the pump was removed. It was the first piece of spaghetti to go.

"One down, six to go." I was delighted. "You'd better not take it all out in one go. If I drink a glass of water I'll spout in every direction like a garden sprinkler."

Shortly afterwards, they removed the catheter. I was then faced with the challenge of having to get out of bed to use a commode. My God, how life and situations can change a person. I never thought I'd be excited about using a commode, but I was utterly ecstatic at the thought of it. Two nurses came to help me into a chair first of all, so my bed could be made.

"Okay, we're going to catch you under your arms and try to move you forward on the count of three. Are you ready, Emily?"

"Let's do it." I was determined to make this move. As I tried to sit up, my head began to spin. I felt like I'd drunk two bottles of Blue Label Vodka and danced in six-inch high heels for twelve hours on the trot without eating. This was a hangover with a difference though. They gathered my drains and drips and together whooshed me into a chair. I was so pleased with myself. It was great to be upright so I could look around the ward instead of at the ceiling tiles and the curtain hooks.

"Good one, Emily. That's a big milestone for you. Just rest easy for a minute and we'll change your bed."

My bed was changed with precision and left crisp and ship-shape, ready for me to be folded back in. The trainee nurses came to do this. I sat like a little doggy and watched from my throne.

"How long does it take to learn how to make those corners?" I asked.

"It's surprisingly quick when you have to make over fifty beds a day," one of the young nurses replied.

"Here's a remote control, Emily. We'll leave you to sit for a few minutes. If no one comes back and you're tired, press the red button and someone will be along to help you back into bed." The nurse handed me the control panel.

I managed to sit in the chair for about half an hour. Suddenly I felt like I'd done a round with Mike Tyson, so I pressed the red button on my remote control and a nurse came and helped me. I found it astonishing how the nurses could deal with all these wires and drains and the fact that I was about as mobile and pliable as a corpse, with total ease.

I knew it was their job, I knew they had training in all this sort of thing and they saw it all the time. But that was not the point. How could they be so cheerful and relaxed? They were a different breed of person to me. I would balk at all of it.

I decided to try and use the commode while I was out, figuring that it would be far less painful than having to do the whole getting up thing again from scratch.

"I think I need to go to the toilet before I lie back down." I told the nurse.

"No problem, the sooner you can get your waterworks going, the better. It can be a little difficult to gauge when you need the loo, due to the medication, but we'll pop you on to the commode and see how you go." She skipped off to find one.

So the commode was wheeled in. Whoever thought of the idea of a chair on wheels that you can wee into was a genius. I needed to go but when I sat on it, I got stage fright.

So I had to sit for what felt like three hours, waiting and trying to coax something out.

"Anything there?" the nurse encouraged.

"I feel like a two-and-a-half-year-old on a potty. Will I get a sweetie if I do a wee?"

"I'm out of treats at the moment, but would a round of applause do instead?"

Eventually I managed to perform. I was helped back into bed, a lid was put on the pee-chair and the nurse began to wheel it away.

"I do apologise that you have to clean the commode," I said.

"Don't even think about it, darling, it's all part of a day's work." She shrugged and carried on.

Bloody hell. How did they do it?

By that night I was knackered. I felt like I'd done a triathlon in less than two hours. I'd managed to sit out a couple more times and wee in the chair a few more times too.

I even ate a rubber omelette with grilled tomato and drank a pot of herbal tea.

When I explained that I didn't drink tea and that I had herbal tea bags with me and only required hot water in a pot, that caused a major malfunction.

"What do you mean you don't drink tea?" I was asked by the flabbergasted tea lady.

I took a deep breath and tried to explain. "I hate the smell and couldn't possibly drink it."

"That may be, but you haven't tasted my tea, now have you?" She tried to convince me that her tea was better than anyone else's tea and that it would make me feel better. So I had to compare tea to the contents of the commode. She backed off and left me a pot of water suspiciously. I made my hippy tea and sipped it, feeling like I was almost doing something illegal, like smoking a joint in the bed. I have to confess, it made the tea taste better.

I took everything else they offered me.

"Do you want a sleeping tablet?"

"Yes, please."

"Do you need more pain relief?"

"Yes, please."

After having one baby with an epidural and one without – not by choice, my daughter appeared in sixteen minutes, from the first contraction to the birth – I knew there are no medals. Pain relief and drugs were invented for this exact situation. So I took them all – except the morphine.

The drains were torture. They had been installed to remove any excess fluid from the cavity where the breast tissue had been removed. They were metal-tipped tubes, with small expandable bags attached to them. The bags grew heavy as they filled with bloodstained liquid, produced by the wound. They were uncomfortable and caused a lot of pain when I tried to move. Any time I moved, I had to remember to grab the drains first, so they wouldn't tug and cause pain.

Sleep that night was difficult. Firstly I had five others in my room, all of whom had their own way of breathing, snoring, mooching and tossing about. Secondly, I had my blood pressure and temperature taken constantly. Thirdly, the lights were on – dimly but they were still there. Fourthly, I always sleep either on my side or my tummy – now I had to sleep on my back which was an alien position to me. Fifthly, due to the drains and the pain I was tense and hunched up. I kept thinking of Pilates, shoulders away from ears. Relax, breath deeply in and out. But quite honestly, when you have throbbing pain and are trying to relax on a rock-hard bed, it's all a bit futile.

Then the pain started in my left side. It was a sharp, burning pain. It felt like something was touching off a nerve. The general pain across my chest was different – it was more of the dull, thudding type. This pain in my side was shocking, sharp and raw, like a blade was being twisted inside me. I wriggled endlessly to try and alleviate it. When I found a position where I could feel it less, I held that position until exhaustion took over and I slept.

When I woke to have my blood pressure and temperature taken, I knew I literally hadn't moved a muscle. It was like my body knew it was such a chore to find a comfort zone, so it didn't want to spoil it.

21

Susie

Freak Yourself Out Stew:
Send letter to long-lost father. Fry brain with all possible anticipated and speculated reactions. Become totally paranoid and negative. Leave for many weeks stewing until tender and vulnerable.

It had been weeks since I'd sent the letter to Jim Lynch. I had become obsessed with the post-box in the lobby of my apartment block. I'd given him my home address, just in case my secretary opened a letter from him. That had been when I'd assumed he'd reply.

I called in to see Mum. I still hadn't told her that Thomas had found my father. But seeing as he wasn't bothering to reply, I figured I would show her the photos and fill her in on what I'd done.

I guess I had been playing a stupid eye-for-an-eye game with her. She hadn't told me about him for years, so I didn't tell her for weeks. Not quite the same thing and totally childish and stupid, I know, but that was what I did.

"Mum, I need to talk to you about something." I sat on one of her kitchen chairs, as she buzzed around the small kitchenette.

"Oh, have you met a nice man and fallen in love?" She stopped and lurched her head forward hopefully. Standing in her Disney Princess pose, with her hands clasped and a hopeful smile on her face, her long eyelashes fluttering in anticipation of the longed-for news.

"No, Mum." I tried to remain patient.

"Are you pregnant? Because that's all right, you'll manage, you know. It's not the end of the world, Susie." She was off on a tangent.

"Mum, hello? Mum? I'm not pregnant."

"You're not, you know . . . gay? Are you? Not, that it matters, look at that lovely Elton John and his partner, they had a fantastic wedding and everything. Just imagine, I could look for two wedding dresses instead of one . . ." She was off on her own planet again.

"Mum, stop it. Sit down and stop babbling, please." I knew I was shouting and sounding like a headmistress, but she was so bloody difficult to communicate with.

"Oh sorry, love. I'll sit quietly now."

She looked all sad and hurt, which annoyed me even more. She had a brilliant talent for making herself look like a freshly beaten puppy dog.

"Mum, ever since we had the chat about Jim Lynch, it made me very curious to know more about him. So I hired a private detective."

"You did not. A real one?" She looked astonished and very impressed.

"Yes, a real one. The thing is, they found him. He lives in the Midlands about two hours drive away from here. I have some photographs of him. Would you like to see them?" I tried to gauge her reaction.

"Oh, how exciting! Give me a look and I'll tell you if it's him!" She didn't seem overly upset at least.

I handed her the envelope and she pulled the pictures out.

"Yes, it's him all right. Jeekers, he hasn't changed much, you know. The years have been kind to him. Although he's more attractive than I remember. But, having said that, I only met him the once, like I said, so don't go by me." She put the pictures back in the envelope.

"Is that it?" I was astonished.

"What?" Mum looked at me with slight confusion in her eyes.

"After all this time, does it not evoke any kind of emotion for you at all?" I found her flippant attitude astonishing.

"I don't know what you want me to do, love. I hope he writes back to you, if that's what you want. But he was never a part of my life." She shrugged her shoulders.

"Yes, I'm bloody well aware of that. I was here too, you know? Don't you feel even slightly guilty that you deprived both of us a relationship, me and him? Do you never question yourself? Or think that maybe you were wrong to hold your silence for so long?"

"Not really, no. As I've said to you before, Susie, I'm not an analyser. I don't do things and spend the rest of my life wondering if it was right or wrong. I genuinely thought it was the right thing to do at the time. What's done is done. The past can't be changed. What do you want me to do? Berate myself and hate myself over something none of us can change? You'll have to put the past to rest. If you want things to change in the future. There's a possibility you can control that. I'll help you in any way I can, but you can't expect me to change the past. It's just not possible, love. You're a clever girl. Surely you can see that for yourself."

Although I felt like strangling Mum, I knew she was right. There was no point in hating her for doing what she felt was right.

I refused tea and cake and stayed with her for as long as I could stomach her. She buzzed about and babbled away in her usual manner, the whole conversation of Jim done and dusted in her head. She genuinely had this built-in mechanism which enabled her to sweep things under the carpet if it suited her. The whole issue of my father wasn't pleasant and fairytale, so she just boxed it and carried on.

Fucking astonishing. I watched her – really watched her. I didn't listen to her. It was as if I tuned her voice out with an invisible remote control and was left with just the picture. Her face was animated, she was making plenty of hand gestures, she had a bounce in her step. She wouldn't lie awake all night tonight and think about Jim. She wouldn't let any of this affect her, in any way. How the hell did she do it? Her oblivion to my frustration and pain became too much and I had to make my excuses and leave.

"Bye-bye, dear. It was so lovely to see you. Come again soon, won't you? Or maybe we could organise a girls' lunch soon. Emily might come too. What do you think?"

She was waving like a moron and smiling as if she hadn't a care in the world. Well, I suppose she didn't.

Feeling utterly frustrated, dejected and alone, I arrived at my apartment and opened my metal letter-box. I stood dumbfounded for a few seconds, unable to touch what was inside. There was a handwritten envelope lying there. I immediately knew what it was. Looking around to see if anyone was watching I reached in gingerly and took the letter. My heart thumped as I ran up the stairs, taking them two at a time to get there quickly. Fumbling with the lock, I burst in, dropping my brief-case on the hall floor. The heavy door clicked shut behind me, as I perched on the sofa. I examined the envelope, turning it over in my hand again and again. My hands were sweating. My mouth was dry. I had to take a deep breath and calm myself. What I was about to read could swing either way. I could be about to face the biggest rejection of my life. On the other side of the coin, I could be on the cusp of a whole new dimension in my life.

For the first time in my life, I wished I had a boyfriend, husband or partner beside me. I just wasn't sure if I could do this on my own. I could ring Emily. She'd come over in a heartbeat. But she was in hospital waging her own bloody battle. I was alone. I had to face this by myself. A frightened and strangled noise rose from my throat.

"Get a grip on yourself, Susie. You can deal with whatever lies ahead. You are a strong, intelligent and sound-minded woman, who can cope with this letter," I said slowly and clearly to myself.

I tore the envelope open and revealed a single sheet of writing paper. White with a handwritten letter, in blue biro, covering both sides of the page. The writing was neat and small and quite precise. Not unlike my own writing, I realised. Mum was, of course prone to big, curly penmanship, with tiny circles instead of dots. This was more like me.

16 River View
Lanestown
Co Offaly

Dear Susie

Thank you for your letter. As you might have guessed, I was very shocked to learn of your existence. I had no idea Pauline was pregnant.

It has taken me a long time to reply, as I simply wasn't sure what to say, or where to go from here. Having thought about you a lot, I have come to the conclusion I would like to know more about you. Since receiving your letter, I have thought of very little else, if I'm honest. It has taken me until now to reply, as I am not a brash or spur of the moment character and I wanted to be sure I was making the right decision.

I am not married, but have a long-term partner. We've been together for over twenty-eight years now, and we have no children. So you are my only child. I'm sorry if you were expecting siblings.

After many lengthy discussions with Jean, we came to the conclusion that I should pursue a further line of enquiry with you. I am sorry if I sound formal. I have written and re-written – letter after letter, – none of them seem to hit the mark.

I have so many questions, as I'm sure you do too. I would love to correspond with you and maybe get to know you. Perhaps we could even speak on the phone or eventually meet up?

I was understandably shocked to hear about you at first, but now that I've got used to the idea, I am very excited. Once again, I apologise if this is a very mundane letter, but I am so conscious of making a right or wrong impression.

I hope this finds you well. Bye for now.

Jim

Okay, it was positive really. I was amazed he hadn't any other children. I hoped my letter hadn't caused a big row between himself and Jean. But, he'd hardly have written back if Jean hadn't approved, would he?

I opened a bottle of wine and sat and read and re-read the letter until I almost knew it off by heart. I tried to picture himself and Jean sitting and discussing me. His daughter. Had they gone through a bad patch because of it? Had I been the cause of a huge row? Had I made Jean cry for days on end? Were they angry at Mum? Did they feel sorry for me? If they had no children, was it because they didn't ever want any or were they not able to have them?

After the first glass and a half of wine, I was quite glad there was no phone number on the letter, or I know I would have phoned him, built up by my Dutch courage and boosted by the positive elements which I had highlighted in yellow pen. (I know I am a tool, but I did try to psychoanalyse the letter.)

Instead, I took the safer option and decided to begin drafting my second letter to Jim. I wanted to keep up the correspondence. I didn't want this to become dead in the water. It was different to meeting a new boyfriend. I didn't want to play hard to get. I didn't want him to think for one second that I wasn't interested, so I immediately flicked on my computer.

Dear Jim

Thank you so much for replying to my letter. I know it must have been a bolt out of the blue for you. I too have thought of very little else since I found out about your existence. I have been watching the post-box like a hawk, hoping every day that a letter might appear. Thank you for putting me out of my misery!

I understand your discomfort with writing your letter. There aren't many guide books with information on writing to a long-lost family member, are there? For the record, your letter was perfect.

I would love to keep in contact and perhaps meet up, as you suggested. If we both remember we are in the same boat here, not knowing what is the right or wrong way to approach each other, maybe it could make things easier? There are no rules with this as far as I can see, so let's try and take it slowly and hopefully find our feet.

The reason I suddenly made contact is due to my best friend, Emily. She recently found out she carries a gene which predisposes her to cancer, and it made me think about the fact that I knew nothing about my real father.

But don't think I contacted you purely to find out if your family has any known defective genes, although this information wouldn't go astray!

I would love to speak with you on the phone or even arrange a meeting. My e-mail address is Susiesue@hotmail.com if you would like to contact me there. My phone number is 01 2223457 and I am here most evenings. I will post this letter tomorrow, so maybe you would call me next Thursday evening, after seven?

Thank you for replying, it means a lot to me.

Yours sincerely

Susie

22

Susie

Carvery Lunch:
Take one best friend and put her on the butcher's block and chop.
Arrive with large suitcase of magazines, toiletries, cuddly toys,
chocolates and other useless gifts. Take deep breath and march towards
maimed friend while trying to hold it together.

I arrived in the ground of St Theresa's. Christ, huge public hospitals
gave me the willies. Emily kept saying what a great place it was. All
bright and modern. It still looked bloody scary to me. I had been at the
Rochestown Clinic for so long now I had become utterly removed from
public hospitals. The whole hugeness, the smell, the vast shiny spaces,
the sheer volume of people.

Robbie had told me what ward and floor Emily was on, so I went
straight for the lift and travelled to the second floor. Although I'd
worked for two years, during my placement, in a hospital, this was
different. Mental health didn't involve chopped-up people with drips
and scary stuff. (Unless the patients were into self-harming.)

As I walked the length of the corridor, I spotted the *"Yellow Ward"* sign. Emily was apparently in the last bed on the right near the window. The curtains were drawn around the bed, so I flagged down a nurse.

"I'm here to see Emily Cusack. The curtain is pulled around her bed, what should I do?" I felt like I was going to pass out. I really wasn't good at the hospital stuff, when it involved someone I knew and loved. I was beginning to panic. What if Emily looked all blue and wasn't able to speak? How would I pretend she looked normal? I could feel my armpits wetting my clothes. My throat was tight and I really wanted to run back to my car and drive as fast as I could away from this place and this awful situation.

"It's okay, I was just emptying her drains – you can go on ahead and see her. She's very weak, so don't stay too long, if you don't mind." The nurse buzzed off speedily.

With a thumping heart I walked towards the curtained-off area. Gingerly, I poked my head around the curtain.

Emily was lying with her eyes closed, with big, scary-looking plastic things attached to her sides. Her hair was stuck to her forehead and she looked like a corpse. As I drew a breath, her eyes opened.

"Susie, hi, sweetie, thanks for coming in!" She tried to move a little to sit, but winced and stayed in the same position.

"Don't move. Fucking hell, Emily, you look like shit. What the hell have they done to you?"

"It's okay. It's not as bad as it obviously looks. The drains are going in a couple of days, just try to ignore them. Pull over a chair and sit down and try to calm yourself, you useless cow!"

"Oh, Jesus, I'm sorry. I should be shot. I'm not good at this at all. In fact, I didn't realise how bad I am at this until I got here. It's fucking scary in here. There's a real air of sickness and death about the place, isn't there?"

"It's a bloody hospital, what did you expect? The Ritz? Enough of the death shit. I'm trying, quite successfully, to do the exact opposite, if you don't mind!" Emily was smiling. "It's good to see you, you mad old bitch! How's the Jim thing? 'Dear Jim, can you be my daddy?'" Emily tried to laugh, but something caused her to twist in pain.

"Fuck, what happened? Will I run and get a nurse?" I was already on my feet, ready to sprint and rugby-tackle the first nurse I saw.

"No, sit down, you spanner, I'm fine. Just pretend from now on that I'm perfect. Tell me about Jim, spill the beans." Emily shut her eyes. "Go on!"

"He wrote back, I've got the letter here, I'll read it to you. It's handwritten too, which is kind of nice." I tried hard to read the letter in an upbeat and normal voice but it was quite impossible.

I only stayed for about twenty minutes, before kissing Emily on the forehead and leaving. She held my hand and with her eyes mostly shut, she spoke.

"This is the worst bit. I know you, Mrs Psychologist-I'm-in-control-freak. Don't you dare go out of here feeling sorry for me. I'm going to beat this. All the bits attached are just for show, to make it all look more dramatic." She smiled with her eyes closed. "I'll be out of here and back to annoy you before you know it."

"I know you will, darling. You're brilliant and I love you so much. You just rest and make sure they take these telephone wires out as soon as possible. They don't match the surgical gown – they're ruining your image."

Gulping in the cold air outside, I felt like I was going to vomit. How could Emily be so upbeat and in control? With all those drains and drips hanging out of her and the horrible smell of dinners mixed with illness hanging in the air?

She'd even said how lovely the nurses were and that it wasn't too bad being in there. Fuck. Had she lost her marbles altogether? For the first time in our friendship, I saw Emily in a very different way.

I had always thought Emily was the softer one of the two of us. I'd always assumed that because she'd taken the marriage and kids route she'd taken the easier road in a way.

I'd studied so hard and worked so hard on my career; in my own slightly smug way, I'd always felt I'd done the stronger thing. It hit me like a sledgehammer at that moment, how I'd misjudged Emily's strength. There was no way in hell I could do what Emily had just done. I certainly wouldn't be chatting and cracking jokes if I had.

I had always loved Emily, like a sister, and thought I knew her inside out, but today a line had been crossed. I saw her in a new light. Her courage was astounding. Mine was flailing. It was time I realised I was not a machine. Nor was I able to control every element of my life. Between Emily and Jim, the rug had been firmly pulled from under my steel exterior in the last while. I had some serious soul-searching to do.

23

Emily

Pure Shower Indulgence:
Have surgery and add drains, clamps, dried blood, greasy hair and a general feeling of mankiness. Ferment in itchy bed for two days. Add two angelic nurses and the promise of fresh water and shower gel. Serve with a smile and a feeling of unabashed sheer delight.

It was seven in the morning, two days after my surgery. It was still dark outside and most normal people were probably trying to peel themselves out of bed. As usual, the hospital had come alive just after six. As I was a little bit less like a corpse, I was told I would be allowed to have a shower. Two of the nurses, Maria and Zoë, were there to aid me. Luckily I'd been through the experience of having a baby, and also having a shower with a nurse's help, so I wasn't bothered about being naked and helpless.

"Okay, Emily, we're going to try and walk you down to the bathroom," said Zoe. "We are not in a hurry – take all the time in the world and you'll be fine. We will go on each side of you. Don't worry about falling, we won't let that happen. Are you ready to make a move?"

"I reckon so," I answered feeling much the same as a climber must feel at the foot of Everest.

"Okay, on the count of three, we will stand you up. One, two, three!"

I was like a newborn foal, staggering to find my footing. Slowly we moved off, my slippers shuffling across the shiny floor.

When we reached the confines of the bathroom, Maria removed the hospital gown. I looked down at my breasts, or rather where they had been.

I was totally nonplussed by the look of my chest. I had never been nervous of how I would look afterwards. My surgeon had promised he would try to preserve the nipples, and he had done so.

The only difference was that they looked a bit deflated and sad. They looked about twice as droopy as they did after a full breastfeed. The only cuts were on the sides, near my armpits, so it wasn't barbaric or scary looking.

"How do you feel?" Maria asked gently.

"Fine. I thought it would all look more scarred and interfered with. They just look like someone let the air out of them." I smiled. I was delighted with the result. There was no blood and guts. Nothing gooey and awful-looking.

I did have my drains in tow, so they had to be attached by Velcro to my legs. I sat in a white plastic outdoor stackable garden chair.

"Are you ready to have a shower?" Zoë turned the shower on and detached the hose from the wall so she could position it over me.

"Go for it!" I braced myself, wondering if it would sting or hurt. It didn't. Instead the water felt soft and warm and wonderful. "Girls, I'm sorry I'm such a nuisance sitting here like a china doll doing nothing while you have to do all the work."

"Listen, you have no need to worry. A young person who is not covered in hair and who actually talks is a much better bet than a grunting ape from the geriatric men's ward. No offence to hairy, elderly men of course," said Maria.

Again, I was in awe of these people.

Zoë and Maria were soon chatting ninety to the dozen about the leaving party they were off to for one of the nurses. Zoë was single and we started talking about what they should wear. I was soon pontificating at length about the little extra touches that make a difference, about accessorising and going the extra mile.

"Then you'll swan into that joint and give off an air of someone who oozes confidence. You'll be beating men off with a shitty stick!" I vowed to her.

While she was taking this on board, I caught a glimpse of myself.

I had greasy wet hair, white skin-tight medical stockings (on up to my thighs), deflated breasts with stitches and drains coming from my sides and velcroed to my calves, and I was giving this gorgeous twenty-something young woman advice on how to look good?

It was too much for me. I started to laugh and couldn't stop. The two nurses looked at each other, smiling in a bewildered fashion.

"If all else fails," I choked out between giggles, "you could always bring me in a wheelchair looking like this and you'd both look even more amazing than you do now! Jesus, the men will be flocking to you!"

We fell around laughing. When we had gained some composure, one of the nurses asked where my shampoo was. I instructed her to take everything out of my monster wash-bag.

With my delighted permission, they opened all the bottles and sniffed and argued until they agreed I was a "Jo Malone" girl that day.

So I had "Lime, Basil and Mandarin" shampoo, conditioner and shower gel applied. The fresh citrusy scent was heavenly. They gently sponged my body down, taking care not to interfere with the stitches or drains. The fruity, delicious fragrance filled my senses and removed the yellow stains of iodine from my skin. The cloying hospital antiseptic fug was washed down the plughole (through the garden seat) and I was left feeling like a queen. The Velcro was removed from my legs, they patted me dry and I was able to put on some pyjamas. They were my button-through revolting and horrendous ones, but in comparison to the surgical gown, they were couture!

With my hair turbaned in a towel, my wash-bag was packed up and we all emerged from the bathroom grinning like gobshites. I was aided to shuffle back to my bed, feeling like a million dollars. I felt ready to go to the Oscars. An original Valentino design wouldn't have made me feel better. I felt like a princess.

I later wondered if these nurses have any idea of the impact they make on people's lives. They made such a difference to me that day. The human outreaching, the extra mile of appearing with a hairdryer and asking me what way I liked my hair done.

"I can't promise any miracles," said Maria. "My training didn't stretch to hairdressing – but I'll do my best!"

Little did she know, the miracle had already been performed. She'd made me laugh and feel good about myself.

I sat in my chair smiling. I'd say I must have looked like a total moron beaming away to myself in the corner like that, but I didn't give a hoot. I was so happy.

I was over the operation. I know I had a long way to go. But any road can be travelled with clean hair and a body that smells of "Jo Malone" shower gel.

I sent a text message to all my friends telling them that I was still alive and doing well. I requested no visitors. I am usually the type of person who loves to be surrounded by people, but this time was different. I needed the time to recover. My immediate family came in regularly. I felt that was enough. My mobile phone rang non-stop, so I was able to keep in touch with everyone.

I hired a TV from the TV man who came round the wards. So that kept me going too. I had the concentration of a gnat anyway, so I just spent my time flicking from one mind-numbing programme to the next.

Betsy proved to be a lovely roommate. She was up and about and going up and down the ward for little walks. She always stopped by my bed for a quick chat.

"It's good to see you up and about. Did you enjoy your shower?" She regarded me with her head to the side.

"I'll never take soap and water for granted again," I answered.

Johnny, her husband, arrived the next day to collect her. They looked delighted to be reunited. She strolled over to me before she left.

"Good luck with your recovery, child. I hope you'll be up and about again soon. It was lovely to meet you." She patted my hand.

"Good luck yourself, look after her, she's a special lady," I told Johnny.

"You wouldn't need to be a genius to know that. Sure, I'd be lost without her." Johnny smiled proudly at his wife.

On Thursday the drip was removed and I was thrilled. Every wire and foreign part they removed from my body was a step in the right direction. A small, personal milestone.

24

Emily

Human Spaghetti Cheese:
Take person doing an impression of a bag of spaghetti. Slowly, day by day remove bits of spaghetti from human holder. Eventually leave free of appendages, garnish with a large cheesy smile.

It was day five after my surgery. I was still in my bed by the window in the hospital ward. The drains were the last appendage hanging from my sides and once removed would leave me a free agent. As the days passed, there was less and less fluid in each drain.

"I'm satisfied that you're not producing enough fluid to warrant these fellas being attached to you any more, Emily," said Maria. "Would you like them removed?"

"That sounds like one of the most exciting offers I've ever had in my life so far." I smiled at her in glee. No more baggage to drag to the bathroom!

Maria came with her trolley of goodies. She had bandages, little kidney bowls of sterile saline, cotton wool balls and snippers. Tia would have played for hours with the trolley and its contents. It reminded me of a child's nursing kit I owned when I was about five. Many teddies and dollies had been saved with that kit.

This was the real thing, being allowed to work on real live people. It gave me a tiny insight into the reason some people wanted to be nurses.

For a split second, the organisation and equipment took me back to my childhood games. But the sheen wore off immediately when Maria started to remove the drains. They were sewn in place, so the stitches had to be removed and then the tubes loosened.

"This is going to cause a pulling sensation," Maria warned.

With three tugs, the metal-ended tube was gently pulled through what felt like muscles and nerves until it became visible under my skin. With one final tug, it appeared in the nurse's hand. It wasn't painful, just an unbelievably weird sensation. Also seeing the metal structure moving under my skin was odd.

She kept saying how well I was doing and apologising for hurting me.

"I'm sorry, darling, you're doing so well," she muttered while concentrating fully on the job in hand.

"It's not sore, just utterly weird," I explained. It was such a peculiar feeling.

As I'd now been freed of anything scary-looking, I phoned Robbie and asked him to bring the children in after school. I was yearning for them. I missed them dreadfully.

"No problem, we'll be there at around three thirty."

I was so excited. The time dragged – it was like the clock had stopped.

I heard them coming way down the hallway, tripping along beside their dad, chirping away, asking questions constantly. They spotted me at the end of the room and broke free from Robbie's hands and ran to me.

"Mummy, you're here!" Louis shouted, recognition registering on his face.

"Mummy, hi!"

For the first time I realised I couldn't hug them. I felt the tears burn my eyes and the lump was at bursting point in my throat. I longed to bend onto my hunkers and envelop them in my arms. Instead I had to stand and let them hug my waist. It would have to do.

"Hi, you two, I'm so happy to see you both. I've missed you so much. How are you?" I used all my might to remain in control.

I was struck by how small they were. When I see them every day I am obviously so used to them that I forget they are still so young. Tia just slipped her little hand into mine and wouldn't take it away. Louis jumped onto the bed and took a computer game out of his pocket and began to play it.

Eventually Tia did a tour of the ward. I watched her talk to each person.

"Hi, my name is Tia. I'm five." She then returned with all the questions.

"Why are you all sleeping in the same bedroom, Mum?"

"This is called a ward. Hospitals have lots of wards where ladies and men and even children all sleep together, so we can all be minded by the doctors and nurses."

"What is wrong with the other ladies?"

"Well, they all have different things wrong with them, but the doctors are fixing them, so they can go home soon."

"Why do you have a blue blanket on your bed when you are a girl? Do the nurses not know that you are a girl?"

This upset her. I didn't want her to go home worrying about the fact that my blanket was wrong. I also knew Robbie wouldn't understand why that bothered her so much.

"Well, why don't we go and ask the nurse if they can find a pink blanket instead?" I took her hand and we went off to sort it out.

I brought her to the nurse's station and asked if I could have a pink blanket when they changed my bed.

"We can do better than that. Will you come to the cupboard and help us find a pink blanket and we can change Mum's bed this minute?" Zoë asked.

"Yes, I will." Tia was delighted.

"You'd better put on a paper nurse's hat and come this way to help me. It's very lucky you came in today or we might not have known Mum had the wrong colour." Zoë put the hat on Tia's head and took her hand, winking at me over her shoulder.

Tia got a plaster and a sticker on the way and trotted back down my ward with an impish little grin on her face.

"Now, I will need help changing this too," said Zoe. "Can you pull that blue cover off for me?" she asked Louis.

He was trying desperately to look uninterested, but he couldn't quite manage it. Hurriedly, he leapt off the bed and ripped the cover off. Dumping it in a heap on the floor, he helped Tia and Zoë tuck the new blanket in place.

"Thank you both for all your help," Zoë exclaimed, scooping the offending blue article off the floor.

"You're welcome," Tia and Louis chorused, delighted with themselves.

They rooted in my bedside locker and found a packet of boiled sweets and a bar of chocolate, which they demolished. For the first time in my life I was actually in a position where I was able to leave chocolate uneaten. Miracles really do happen. I am usually able and willing to consume my body weight in chocolate.

It started to snow outside. Big fat tumbling flakes, quickly making the rooftops white and sparkly.

"I think we should quit while we're ahead with the children. Before they start running up and down and fighting," Robbie whispered.

He was right, they should go home. I wanted to see them off, so agreed to go in the lift as far as the hospital entrance. I walked one corridor and half the length of the next. I was exhausted. I couldn't go any further.

"Mummy's legs are still a bit wobbly after the operation," I said. "I'll have to wave from here." I had to stand with my back against the wall and steady myself. The pain was dreadful, but I was desperate not to frighten them.

They cheerfully accepted this and covered my stooped face in slobbery kisses. Like two puppies they bounced and skipped away, all the time turning to wave avidly. I blew kisses and they caught them and spat them back.

I thought I'd find their leaving heartbreaking, but it had been so lovely to see them I only felt joy and love. They were one of the main reasons I was doing this, and seeing them now compounded my determination to get through this process.

I shuffled clumsily back to my bed, my head filled with happy thoughts and a smile on my face. It was a wonderful reminder of how lucky I was. Having my husband and my two beautiful cherubs. They were the best reason I needed to fight on.

The sister arrived shortly afterwards with news.

"You're on the move, Emily, a room has become vacant, so we'll take you down there now."

"Sounds great."

We piled all my belongings onto the bed and two nurses wheeled it to the private room. Two huge bouquets of flowers arrived as if on cue. One of the food-service ladies came in and arranged them in vases and placed them around the room. I felt like I was in a hotel. I had my own bathroom and no curtains around my bed. Luxury!

Laura came in and brought a book all about garden fairies, with little envelopes to open and fairy dust in another little pocket. We pored over it for ages. Who said you have to be three years old to appreciate the world of the fairies?

"Now, I know you are looking at this in a cutesy and superficial kind of way, Emily. But there's a lot to be said for having an angel and fairy presence in the room with you at a time like this."

Oh Christ, Laura was off on one of her tangents. While I didn't mind her waffling on about angels with me, I was kind of hoping she stopped before Robbie came in. With all this going on, I didn't think he'd be that open to Laura and her quirkiness. She was also wearing a particularly odd outfit, even for her.

She was in "head-scarf" mode as she put it herself. She was wearing a bright turquoise one with acid green edging and little bits of gold-coloured mirrors stuck to it. She had a large apron in shades of pink wrapped around a long flowing denim pinafore. Her favourite red and white stripy tights, Birkenstock shoes and ankle chains (over the tights) completed the look. She basically looked like a migraine headache personified.

"I was planning on bringing one of the cats in to see you too, as I thought it might cheer you up, but then I reckoned she'd hate the bus journey."

There was a knock at the door and the dinner lady brought in my afternoon tea tray.

"Would you like a biscuit?" she asked as she was leaving.

"Oh yes, I'd love one." Laura was already pouring herself a cuppa. "Why is this only water? Do they not give you tea in this place?" She was opening the little metal pot and poking around for the tea bag.

"No, I put my herbal tea bags in myself. Grab one from the locker there, will you?" I nodded towards the bedside table.

After a lot of clattering and spilling, Laura produced two small cups of tea. It made me smile to watch her. She'd always been the same. She was constantly surrounded by turmoil and mess. She'd dribbled the tea everywhere, not just on the tray, but all over the bed and the floor too. When she'd finished with the tray, she went into the bathroom for a look.

She stuck her head back into the room. "My boiler in the flat is on the blink again. Do you think anyone would mind if I had a shower?"

"I don't know, Laura, but maybe you should ask, just in case it's not allowed," she made me smile. No one else would want to have a shower in hospital unless they had to.

A few minutes later she arrived back into the room, looking a bit annoyed.

"No, apparently I can't get into your shower, in case of infection. I had a shower the day before yesterday – it's not as if I'm full of scabies or anything."

By now I was knackered. But Laura wasn't taking the hint, so I had to tell her to go.

"I don't mean to be rude, but I don't have the attention span or the energy at the moment. You don't mind, do you?" I didn't want to upset her.

"No worries at all, Em. You know me, I mean well but can be as thick as pig-shit at times. I'll scoot off and leave you alone. I'll be in touch, okay?" She kissed me on the cheek, and in a flash of colour and stripes she was gone.

After she'd gone I realised she'd put the book in the middle of two vases of flowers, almost making an altar. A shrine to fairies everywhere!

All the nurses who came in immediately ran to pay homage to the book but one of the male nurses muttered about insanity and shook his head in disgust. Well, there's just no accounting for taste.

So I had found myself in the nearest thing to the Ritz imaginable at that moment in my life. The silence was golden. The nurses put my bags away and wheeled my TV in. There was nothing for me to do except relax. I spent the evening reading – well, flicking. I still had the concentration of a goldfish, the room hadn't changed that.

Before I knew it, it was time to take the bedtime painkillers and sleeping tablet.

Although I was making progress every day, I was still very incapacitated. I vowed I would do something every day that I couldn't do the day before. That made me feel better. It was important to have a goal each day, no matter how small.

True to my vow, I asked if I could have a shower on my own. I was allowed to try, with the knowledge that I had my alarm to yank if I collapsed in a heap or got stuck in a difficult position. My private shower was a lot more posh than the communal one, in that it had its own fold-down, soft rubber seat. So I wasn't having to balance on a deck chair while busily avoiding my stitches and trying to wash my hair. I had to take a deep breath to lift my arms up to my head. They didn't really want to do that movement, so I had to push them a bit. I got as far as the sides of my temples and decided that would do nicely. I tipped my head to the side to meet my wobbly arms and, hey presto, I was able to wash my hair.

Now, I wouldn't have won any awards with Toni & Guy for the job I did – in fact a few days later I ended up with a head like a snowstorm my dandruff was so bad – but I had managed to wash my own hair, shower and dry myself and even dress myself. An Olympic gold medal wouldn't have felt better than this. I had to go for a glory lap around the wards afterwards. I met several people who nodded kindly at me as if to say, "God love her, she's completely off her rocker". But I didn't care. I shuffled up and down the corridors with my simple person's grin. Slowly but surely I was getting my independence back.

25

Susie

Pretend Pudding:
Arrange to speak to your father for the first time ever. Pretend on the outside that you've got it all sussed. Melt and broil until almost disintegrated on the inside. Serve with a day's work and serious desire to cope.

It was Thursday, the day that we had agreed Jim was going to phone me. I woke that morning with butterflies in my tummy and almost that same sense of anticipation I used to have before running to see what Santa had left on Christmas morning. I arrived at my surgery feeling lighter mentally than I had for a long time.

I had a full schedule including two new patients, which meant a lot more work. I would also have to try and bond with them. If they didn't like me and trust me, I would be no use to them as a therapist. Some days this was daunting and, like with any other job, there were days when I wished I could just curl up into a ball and not be there.

Today was different. I had no idea how my talk with Jim was going to go. At least with my patients, I was trained to deal with them and their problems. My experience afforded me a pretty good shot at being successful. My impending conversation with Jim was a different story altogether. I hadn't even any guarantee he would definitely call. But, in spite of myself, I was looking forward to finding out about this man.

Luckily my heavy schedule meant that I didn't have time to clock-watch. The first opportunity I had to pour myself a glass of sparkling water and look at my watch, it was four thirty.

"Your final patient has just phoned, she has to cancel today," my secretary said. "I've put her in for next Monday's clinic instead. She said it was unavoidable. Shall I charge her for today? She's missed the twenty-four hour cancellation threshold."

"No, don't bother. She doesn't make a habit of it, so that's fine. I'm going to head away early in that case."

I was going to go home and have a shower and light the fire and make some dinner, and wait for the phone to ring.

By the time I'd negotiated the unrelenting traffic, I hadn't actually managed to gain much time at all. I had figured out a long time ago that it was worth my while to take one more patient and end my day slightly later, and still get home around the same time.

By the time I'd popped a fish pie into the oven (made lovingly by a well-known luxury supermarket chain) and had a shower, it was almost a quarter to seven. Before I had time to wonder if he'd actually call, the phone rang. I rested my hand on the phone and let it ring twice before pressing the green button to answer.

"Hello?" I knew my voice sounded slightly odd, but I was so nervous.

"Is that you, Susie?" I heard a man's voice with a slight twang of a country accent.

"Yes, hello, Jim. Thank you for ringing. I wondered whether you would or not."

"Oh, of course I had to. I've been looking forward to speaking to you. It was hard to wait this long to call." He laughed nervously.

"This is kind of unusual, isn't it? I'm not sure what to say to you without sounding like I'm either interviewing you or behaving like a moron."

"Oh, I know what you mean. It's not the type of thing you can ask many people's advice on either. It's not the most run-of-the-mill situation, is it?"

"No, but I'm glad we're in contact. I can't believe I am actually speaking to my father."

"Likewise, believe me. I never imagined I would ever be having a conversation with my own daughter." He sounded emotional.

"I saw in your letter that you don't have any other children. Was that by choice, if I may ask?"

I heard him draw breath sharply.

"My circumstances meant I wasn't in a position to have children." He sounded uncomfortable discussing the subject.

"I'm sorry to put you on the spot like that. Let's change the subject. What would you like to ask me?" I tried to turn the conversation before I lost his confidence. *Damn*, I berated myself, *I should know better than to mess up and say such a stupid thing at the beginning of a conversation*. Jesus, I did this every day of my life and got paid for it. Why the hell was I making such a pig's ear of this conversation?

"Oh, wow, where do I start? Did you have a stepfather growing up? Is there someone you call Dad?" He sounded vulnerable.

I zoned back in, trying to keep my cool. "No, Mum never met anyone. She had some boyfriends on and off, but they never lived with us and she was always careful never to have any of them in the house."

"Did you ever think of what your father should be like? I suppose what I'm trying to find out is, what do you have in mind by way of a father? I'm more than a little worried that I mightn't be what you want or need. You've obviously done so well without my help. God, I'm so proud to think that I have a daughter who is a psychotherapist." He hesitated. "I'm sort of wondering why you want to know me at this stage of your life."

I shut my eyes and smiled. I could feel my eyes welling up and my heart felt like it was going to burst with pride.

"The reason I want to get to know you is for the exact reason you have just mentioned. Apart from the doctor who I trained under, no man has ever told me he's proud of me. Until you said it just now, I never realised how amazing that feels. Even if we never speak again or never meet, which is not what I would like, you have made me feel good about myself in a way I hadn't thought would matter so much." I felt like a weight had been lifted off me. It's hard to describe why his comment had touched me so much.

Mum had always loved me and had done her best by me. But she was a one-person-show. I was used to her loving me and encouraging me. I took her love for granted. It had always been there. But here was a whole new concept, a father.

"I'm glad I've said the right thing. I'm desperately trying to choose my words correctly, because I know you'll be able to analyse me and I don't want you deciding I'm a lost cause before we even meet." He was openly struggling.

We chatted for a few minutes longer. Well, we had a game of emotional tennis, both trying to wrestle the words out to each other, without giving in and totally losing it and bawling like children. In order to end our talk on a positive note, I purposely kept it short.

"I think we should leave it at that for tonight. I don't mean to sound like I'm speaking to a patient, but let's speak again really soon. Is that okay with you?" I was feeling quite emotionally drained.

"That's perfect, I've really enjoyed talking to you, Susie," I could hear him smiling down the phone. "Even though we've both been quite nervous for most of the conversation, I'm pleased with how it's all gone." He sniffed and I heard him sigh heavily.

I took his number and agreed to call him in three days' time.

"It will give us both a chance to digest our conversation and know a little more how we feel about talking to each other again. I think the best way to take this is slowly, do you agree?"

"Absolutely, sure aren't I dealing with the best? I'll go along with whatever you think is going to work." He chuckled, sounding more confident and assured.

I put the phone down and sighed. One of those deep-rooted ones, which comes right from the centre of your soul. A monstrous, deep, cleansing breath.

I went to sleep with a smile on my face that night. I had a kind of warm cosy feeling inside. So far, I liked the sound of my father. It was very early days, but at least he was willing to get to know me and I was aware that he was being very accepting. If I found out I had a child and no one chose to tell me, I can't say for sure I'd be so understanding about it. He seemed like a genuinely nice man.

The next day I arranged to meet Mum for lunch. I wanted to sit with her face to face and tell her about my conversation with Jim. I wanted to make sure I kept her in the picture, so she couldn't accuse me of shutting her out, or dumping her for Jim.

As we sat in the crowded coffee shop, I was pushing my salad around the plate. Mum was horsing into a sandwich, only half listening to what I was telling her. She was looking around at the other people eating.

"Isn't that little girl a dote? Look at the matching ribbons in her hair and the tiny hearts on her tights. The clothes and accessories available for children now are extraordinary, aren't they?" She held her head to the side and stared mistily at the child.

Anger and resentment suddenly bubbled through me like a volcano threatening to erupt.

"Yes, she's a lovely little girl. Good for her. Yes, accessories have come a long way since the seventies. Mum, sorry if I'm boring you. You seem very uninterested in what I'm telling you, which I have to say baffles me. What is the story with you? Are you finding this upsetting or uncomfortable or what way are you thinking?" I stared at her expressionless face.

"I'm not upset, Susie, not at all, dear. I just don't really want to get involved with the whole Jim issue. I already told you how I felt about it. If you can see it from my perspective, I never knew him to start off with, so it's not like we have any previous history to draw from. If all this makes you happy, that's fantastic, but I don't have a lot of thoughts about him either way." She shrugged and smiled.

"And that's it? You're just listening with one ear, while distractedly looking around the coffee shop, and it never occurs to you that this might just be important to me?" I shook my head in disbelief. Tears of anger and resentment began to prick my eyes. Drawing a deep, incensed breath, I ground my feelings down. I refused to let her do this to me. She was not going to push me into causing a scene in public. And anyway, I didn't cry. But right at that moment I wanted nothing more than to box her right between the eyes.

"As I've said, love, if it all makes you happier, that's fantastic," she smiled.

Mum really did live in a total dream world. That was how she survived. But at times like this, when I needed a little more input and opinion and depth, she still didn't falter. I couldn't take any more.

"I'm going now, Mum. I have a lot of work to do." I scraped back my chair and grabbed my handbag.

"Are you not eating your lovely salad, dear?" She looked at it with interest, picking up her fork to start poking at it.

"No, I'm not that hungry at the moment." I knew it sounded sarcastic, but it went over her head totally.

"Okay so, waste not want not." She leaned over the small vase with dried flowers badly arranged in it and started to stab the salad with her fork. "Bye for now, love. I'll see you soon." She waved distractedly as she continued to root through the lettuce for something tasty to pick at.

Feeling tears burning my eyes, I fled the scene. As I drove away, I wondered to myself how I'd managed to grow up with any ability to deal with real-life situations. Mum lived in La-la Land. Now more than ever, I was curious to meet my father. Would he be any different? Impulsively I dialled his mobile number.

He answered after the second ring.

"Hello?"

"Hello, Jim, it's me, Susie."

"Hi, Susie, that's a nice surprise. Everything all right with you?"

"Yes, thank you, fine," I lied. "Listen, if it's too quick or if you feel I'm being a bit pushy, please be honest with me, but how would you feel about meeting me?"

"Oh, Susie, I'd love that. Really I would. You've made my day now. I've discussed meeting you with Jean, and we both agree it would be very exciting."

"Jean is very welcome to come too if you like," I added.

"Ah, no. I think it would be better if we meet on our own first. Jean might feel a bit stuck in the middle."

"Well, feel free to say it to her if you like," I said.

"Thanks, Susie, but I think I'd prefer to meet you on my own. I know that might sound a bit mean, but it might cloud things a bit if we complicate it too much at first." He coughed.

"Okay, whatever you think." I thought he was sounding a bit odd, but maybe Jean was very bad socially, or maybe she was struggling a little bit with my turning up and she needed a bit of time first. "I'll tell you what, why don't we meet in a restaurant or hotel the first time? That way we are on neutral ground?"

"Good idea. I'm actually working this Saturday, so I have Friday off. Do you work on Friday afternoons?"

"No, I don't, so that would be perfect. Why don't we meet in the hotel in Portlaoise? That's kind of halfway for both of us, isn't it? Say at two o'clock?" I could feel my heart thumping with excitement.

"That sounds very exciting. Thanks, Susie."

"For what?" I was a bit taken back.

"For contacting me and for wanting to meet me. You've no idea how thrilled I am to have found out about you."

"What a lovely thing to say! Well, ditto. I'm really looking forward to Friday. See you then!"

"See you then." He hung up.

I squealed when I put the phone down. I couldn't remember the last time I'd felt so excited about anything. It was all a little surreal. Only a few weeks ago I'd no idea my father was even alive, and now I was two days away from meeting him for the first time.

An image of Mum flicked through my mind. She was an issue I knew I had to deal with. Her flippant, devil-may-care attitude was really getting to me. I also realised I had a lot of built-up anger and resentment towards her, which I would have to deal with sooner or later, or it would end up destroying our relationship. Not that's she'd even notice, the way she was behaving lately.

Her behaviour just now in the coffee shop had been inexcusable. Even if she genuinely didn't have even a flicker of interest in Jim (which

I really couldn't fathom), why could she not muster up some interest just for me? There was no way on earth she didn't grasp the fact that this was important to me. Forcing the image of her poking at the salad and babbling to herself out of my mind, I tried to relax my shoulders and think of my impending meeting with Jim. I had only two days to go before we would be face to face. Father and daughter. United for the first time.

26

Emily

Beef Salad a là Misadventure:
Take one post-surgery patient. Add two pounds of confidence and filter
through to the brain. Decide you're invincible and pour into dressing
gown and slippers. Send out into big bad world. Wobble like jelly and
have full-on panic attack.

Life in the hospital developed into a routine. I gradually began to feel stronger. I was going for regular trots around the ward and I felt I'd turned a corner both physically and mentally. So I decided to go on an adventure to the shop in the hospital lobby.

It all started when I ordered a beef salad for my evening meal. Big mistake. Christ almighty, it was unfathomable how revolting it was. The food in general was absolutely fine. My appetite wasn't amazing anyway (a fact I took great delight in, as like most women I spend my life trying not to put on weight). But I also knew I needed to try and eat in order to get better.

This beef salad was beyond me though. There were some very sad soggy leaves with a large piece of gelatinous playdough sitting on top. The garnish was an ice-cream scoop of hard dry lumpy, green-tinged potato salad, a sliced tomato and an array of shredded plastic-type stuff. I did try to cut up the playdough and pretend to eat it, but it just wasn't going to happen. It was too vile.

So I decided to go down to the shop in the hospital lobby and buy a yoghurt or a sandwich or something less offensive. I put on my dressing gown and slippers and took some of my money from my wash-bag. I shuffled down the corridors to the lift. I met no one on the way until the doors opened on the ground floor. I stepped out gingerly, a crowd of impatient visitors pushing by me. Feeling slightly shaky, I made my way to the shop.

I felt terrified and, worst of all, invisible. I had stupidly assumed that my uniform of pyjamas, dressing gown and slippers would be enough to warn people that I was delicate and sick, but no. I was shoved and barged into.

At one stage, while I was looking in the open-fronted fridge for a yoghurt, a young gouger pushed me out of his way and I lurched forwards, missing my footing and falling. My arms were so weak and unable to move quickly I thought I was going to go straight down on my face but I managed to find my footing and stabilise myself.

I grabbed what food I could, paid and left as quickly as possible. By the time I got back to the lift, I was sweating. I was astonished by the terror I felt.

By the time I got back to my room, I couldn't eat. I was exhausted and traumatised. I just wanted to shut the door and never come out again. It was a reality check for me. I'd thought I was doing so well, that I'd come through this surgery with no problems.

But I wasn't invincible.

The moral of that story was to be very careful of what you order for tea. I vowed to stick to sandwiches from then on.

I phoned Robbie, needing some reassurance.

"Why the hell did you go off on your own like that? I'm on my way in now! I would have brought you something. Stay in your room and I'll see you in fifteen minutes." Robbie hung up.

I knew it was stupid, but I had felt better and I hadn't anticipated being mowed over like a piece of invisible lint.

On the Tuesday I was allowed to go home. I had mixed feelings about this. I really wanted to be in familiar surroundings and in my own bed again. I was longing to see the children. But at the same time, I was in a routine in hospital. All I had to do was worry about myself. I hadn't been in that position for over six years. Not since I was pregnant with Louis.

I wouldn't miss having my blood pressure and temperature taken constantly. Not to mention that little bastard of an injection each morning – the one to stop my blood clotting. It was a tiny needle, but bloody hell it was a stingy little git. I had lots of little black bruises all over my tummy from that. Having blood taken each morning wasn't a crowd pleaser either. I suppose it's safe to say I'm not a huge fan of needles and generally being poked, so it would be a relief to stop all that. I also had to wear the revolting white unsexy stockings all the time, to ensure my legs didn't fill with blood clots. I wouldn't miss them either.

Robbie came to collect me. I said goodbye to all the nurses and we made our way down the corridor to the lifts. I felt like I was being released from a secure mental home. I was excited but strangely nervous about facing the outside world.

"You stay here and I'll run over to the multi-storey car park and get the car." Robbie grabbed my bags and strode off.

Sitting on a bench outside, I looked on at the world of the smoker. They were huddled like vermin in the wooden gazebo, with grey smoke billowing out from under its wooden roof. It baffled me how these people, a lot of them seriously ill, with drips and machines attached to them, could drag themselves out here to smoke. I understand that nicotine is a serious addiction. I know that smokers will go to any lengths to get their fix, but this was just taking the piss. It was February. It was freezing. They were in their pyjamas.

Robbie beeped and waved frantically at me, snapping me back to reality. I shuffled stiffly to the car. Opening and closing the car door was a challenge. The seat belt hurt, so I had to hold it away from my body. Every pothole and speed ramp was another jolt and stab of pain. By the time we got home half an hour later I felt like I'd been run over by a bus. We had collected my painkillers on the way home, so I was able to get into bed and take my drugs.

Everything looked so luxurious. The carpets were like enormous blankets on the floor. Looking out my bedroom window, the garden looked like it had been digitally enhanced. The colours were so vivid. The trees looked fake they were so green. The grass and flowers were like something a druggy on acid would do in a painting by numbers. I was having a *"hey, man, the earth is so beautiful"* experience. After the bland calm of the hospital this array of colour was incredible.

I was exhausted but so excited about seeing the children again. I'd bought them each a little present which I'd wrapped and hidden under my bed before I'd gone to hospital. They weren't coming home for two hours and I felt like the time would never pass. Robbie made me a cup of herbal tea and brought it up to the bedroom.

"How does it feel to be back home?" He was staring at me as if I was an alien.

"It's good. A bit strange though, if I'm honest. I feel almost institutionalised after my hospital stay. It'll just take a bit of getting used to. I'm really looking forward to seeing the kids. Did you tell them I was coming home today?" I sipped my herbal tea.

"Yes, of course I did. They're very excited."

Robbie was being quite strained. I supposed he'd been through so much and I was sure he was exhausted having to deal with the children all on his own over the last while. Maisy was a great help, but I had no doubt they'd been stuck to Robbie like glue with me gone.

"They were fine when you were gone though. They ate all their food and went to bed each night without fighting. To be honest, they act up a lot for your benefit." Robbie was busy examining his nails.

I looked sideways at him. Either he was trying to annoy me or he was just being a bit thick, but I had to push the thoughts to the side. Was I being paranoid or was he trying to let me know that they'd all been happier without me?

"I'm off to collect the kids. Do you want anything in the shops on the way back?" Robbie was pulling his coat on and grabbing the car keys.

"No, thanks, darling, I'm fine."

"Okay, see you in a while." He bent and kissed me briefly.

When they arrived home, Louis and Tia bombarded me like little bouncing balls of electricity. They leapt and pointed at me like excited puppies.

"Hi, Mum, you're back again! Why are you in your bed?" Louis wanted to know.

"Mummmyyyy!" Tia jumped up to hug me.

I put my arms out to hug them to me, and remembered sadly that my arms wouldn't go out properly and that I couldn't hug them. I saw their faces register that there was something wrong. They froze and stared at me, waiting for me to make everything all right again.

"Mummy's silly arms are still a bit broken from the operation, but I can give big standing-up hugs," I suggested brightly.

They waited for me to stand up, and they wrapped their little arms around my legs. Thank God they were munchkin size, so my legs were at a huggable level. I pointed out that there were some presents under my bed with no one to open them, so they scrambled underneath and ripped open the parcels. Delighted, they skipped off to play.

By their bedtime that evening, I was exhausted and very stressed. I had become institutionalised and accustomed to the silence and tranquil setting created by the nurses. It was a serious shock to the system to join the real world again.

"Emily, dinner's ready! Do you want to come down or will I bring it up for you?" Robbie shouted up the stairs.

"I'm coming down, thanks."

I tried to sit in the kitchen with the rest of my family, but the chairs were too uncomfortable and the noise level was shocking. I had to excuse myself.

"I'm sorry, Robbie, I'll have to go back to bed. I'll try and join in with bath time in a while." I ruffled Robbie's hair and made my way back up the stairs.

I figured I would be able to sit on a bed while they were in the bath in our en-suite bathroom but it turned out I was too wobbly and weak.

"Mummy, why is your face looking so sad and sore?" Louis asked. "You have a big line here." He pointed to the space in between my eyebrows.

I realised I was wincing and therefore frightening him. He was only six, but he was far from stupid.

My two babies knew me better than anyone. They knew I was suffering. So instead of freaking them out, I figured it would be better to retreat a little until I was stronger.

Day by day, I managed to do more. Before I left the hospital, the physiotherapist had come around to show me some exercises. They involved raising my arms above my head, pulling my arms up to shoulder level and other similar stretches.

"These are not going to be pleasant, Emily, but you must force yourself to do them. If you don't, your mobility won't return. It's your job to retrain your muscles. No one is going to check if you are doing this, only you will know. It's for your own good."

Now, at home, I took out my exercise sheet and did as many of the stretches as I could. I was very limited with what I could do in general. I quickly realised that I needed to use my energy to its maximum potential at the times it was most needed. The children were getting more and more conscious of the fact that I was unwell, and it was upsetting them. They were feeling threatened and worried.

They were stopping themselves from running when I was around, conscious that I might get a bang.

Louis was beginning to scold Tia. "Don't jump now, Tia! Mummy's coming and you might hurt her."

They were nervous of me, and I hated it.

So I made it a priority to be able to get up and eat breakfast with them before they went to school. Although I was in my dressing gown, I felt it was better to be up and acting as normally as possible. Showering and dressing took a lot out of me. By the time I'd done all that and put on make-up, I was ready for bed again. But that didn't matter. I would allow myself an hour back in bed or even on the bed. Then I would be able to function again for another short spell.

My sleeping pattern was totally erratic however. I was also terrified that Robbie would roll over onto me during the night. Not that he'd ever done that in all the time I'd known him. But I felt incredibly vulnerable, and couldn't help feeling nervous of being banged. I also couldn't get comfortable.

Not knowing what else to do, I called the breast care unit in St Theresa's Hospital.

"Breast Care, Hayley speaking."

"Hi, Hayley, this is Emily Cusack."

"Hi, Emily, how are things?"

"All fine, except I can't sleep," I explained.

"Okay. Did they tell you about the 'V' shape with the pillows before you left the hospital?"

"No, but it sounds very exciting."

"Okay, you need to put three pillows, one on top of each other behind you in the normal position. Then put one either side of you, so you can rest your arms, bent at the elbow, on them. This will prop you up and take the pressure off the expanders, while supporting you at the same time. The other thing is to make sure you are in the middle of the bed, so you're not nervous about falling out."

"You mean, ask Robbie to get out?" I was astonished.

"Oh good lord, he shouldn't be in the bed anyway! That would make you too nervous. No, he'll have to go into another room or another bed, just for a few weeks."

"Well, I didn't want to hurt his feelings, but it would make me less nervous, I must admit."

"It will probably be a relief for him too, if you think of it that way. I'm sure he's worried about hurting you."

I hadn't really thought of it from his point of view. I'd say it was really tough for him, not wanting to rock the bed too much while getting in and out. And maybe being afraid he might roll over on me. I would bite the bullet and suggest it to him.

As it turned out, Robbie was fine about it all. He understood I wasn't banishing him to the shed or anything. He promised to bring home a single bed that night. We organised to borrow one, and that was that. It actually gave us a bit of a laugh that night. It was like sleeping in a dormitory. We put the single bed beside our bed, making it look like a boarding school.

"Make sure you put your light out by ten," I warned him.

It was kind of weird, but in a way it was a huge relief. I had been very worried about being hit. It only became apparent now that I was able to lie and relax in the middle of the bed. I definitely slept better that night.

I vowed we would only make this a short-term arrangement. I didn't want to drive a wedge between us, or make Robbie feel he was being pushed aside.

The children thought it was brilliant.

"Are you two having a sleepover?" Louis wanted to know the next morning.

"Sort of. Dad is having his own bed for a little while until Mum is feeling better." They just accepted this, without any questioning. I think the fact that we were in the same room still made it seem more normal.

27

Susie

Apprehension Punch:
In a large bucket, mix as much self-scrutiny as possible. Douse with
fear, excitement, uncertainty, a decent bout of the trots and a good
measure of cold sweat. Using a small trowel, ice entire face with as
much make-up as skin will absorb. Panic. Repeat said panic tenfold.

Friday morning finally arrived. Today was the day when I would meet my father. God, it was daunting and so surreal. I had agonised over what to wear. I didn't want to look like I was going to meet a patient. That would be too formal. I certainly didn't want the "sexy vamp" look. It was winter-time, so I couldn't arrive in a simple cotton dress, which would have suited the occasion perfectly, so I went for a Diane Von Furstenberg wrap dress, with tights and boots. Simple and elegant, yet not too over the top. I did of course paint on the make-up with a heavy hand. All gals know that a good dose of make-up adds a sense of confidence.

I had two patients to see that morning, which I was grateful for.

Otherwise, I knew I would have left the apartment at nine and arrived in Portlaoise, the small midlands town, hours before our meeting, giving myself too much time to get myself in a knot.

As it turned out, my second patient ended up taking a lot longer than I'd anticipated, so I had no time to ponder. By the time I'd negotiated the already building weekend traffic which engulfs Dublin on a Friday, I was only just on time. I pulled into the Hotel Portlaoise car park at a quarter to two. Quickly pulling a brush through my hair and spritzing myself with perfume, I checked my make-up in the rear-view mirror. Raising my arms I sniffed my armpits. I didn't want my father's first impression of his daughter to be a nice whiff of BO.

I'd have to do. I was definitely at a disadvantage meeting my father at this advanced age. Most girls met their fathers naked and screaming in a hospital room where they both fall in love instantly. I was a ready-made version, warts and all, and it wasn't guaranteed he would like me.

As I pulled the large, brass-handled door towards me and walked into the foyer of the hotel, I nervously glanced around to see if I could spot Jim. Glancing at my watch, I realised it was still only five minutes to two. He probably wasn't even here yet.

"Susie?"

I heard his voice and I turned to my right. And saw Jim for the first time.

"Hello, Jim." I held out my hand. As he took it I realised he was very tall. A good head and shoulders taller than me, which doesn't happen often. He was wearing dark blue denims with a crisp white shirt and a chocolate-brown leather jacket. His hair was exactly the same colour as my own, not red, not brown. He had a trendy haircut for a man his age. He was better looking than his photos.

I tried not to stand like a total gobshite, staring openly at him, but it was difficult not to. I felt a huge whoosh of emotion, which was almost like a physical force moving me backwards. I glanced nervously sideways, to check if anyone else had noticed. The small hotel seemed to be continuing to function regardless.

The two uniformed girls behind the reception desk were going about their business. A man in a suit walked past me talking on his mobile phone. There was a babble of conversation filtering through from the bar area. No, the rest of the world was still turning. Taking a deep breath (but trying not to make it visible) I willed myself to speak again.

"I'm sorry, I'm sure I'm staring at you, but I'm trying to take all this in."

"I know. Me too." He laughed easily, stepped closer and kissed me on the cheek, while holding my hand. "God, it's great to meet you!" He looked slightly shy.

"Yes, you too."

We stood staring at each other again. Neither of us speaking. Both of us trying to drink in as much of each other as we could.

Clicking back to reality, Jim broke the silence first.

"Let's go into the bar and get a drink and some sandwiches. I'm sure you're parched after your drive."

He led me towards the bar, at the back of the hotel.

We settled at a small round table at the end of the room. It was one of those patterned-carpet, patterned-clashing-curtains, and stripy-wallpaper hotels. The whole place was like a pot of maroon and navy paint in various stages of obscenity. They'd also put brass railings and fittings in every possible spot. The stained-glass windows in conjunction with the dark colours made the place seem like it was already night-time.

"Why do they make these places so dark?" I asked, looking around.

"I suppose it induces more daytime drinking. It makes people feel less guilty, sitting in here in the middle of the day, sculling pints of beer. If the sun is bleeding in and making them feel they should be outside, they're not going to fill the cash register as readily, are they?" He glanced at the bar food menu as a waitress approached.

"True," I agreed.

We ordered sandwiches and coffee. I sat back in my chair and regarded him. The atmosphere wasn't tense; we were both just trying not to say the wrong thing.

"I have to admit, when I received your letter a few weeks ago, I was stunned," he said.

"I'd say you were. I hope it didn't cause too many problems between you and Jean?"

"No, Jean is very open-minded and level-headed. The type of person who can deal with whatever life throws up. I'm more the one who freaks about things. I'm a bit of a perfectionist. I like to be precise and on time and I find it more difficult than Jean to deal with shocks or unplanned events."

"I'm quite like that too. Certainly with the perfectionist thing. Mum is the exact opposite. She's very easy-come-easy-go, and it drives me mental most of the time."

"Does she know you're meeting me today?" Jim looked a little nervous.

"Yes, of course. Does Jean know you're meeting me?"

"Yes, it was with Jean's encouragement I even answered your letter. I wasn't sure what to do about you. Frankly your letter and your existence frightened the living shit out of me. I wasn't sure if I should block you out or face you head on. Jean thought I should at least give you a chance, and then I could make an informed decision." He was smiling.

"Well, please thank Jean for me. I'm glad you took her advice."

I noticed Jim shifting in his seat and wondered if he was nervous after all. I was too, but my job probably gave me an advantage – I was used to dealing with people who were feeling vulnerable. But this was so different. Jim was not a patient, and I was not his therapist.

We asked each other fairly guarded questions at first. By the time we'd finished our sandwiches and coffee, we were firing the questions back and forth. Once the initial ice had been broken, I was like a starving person grabbing at food. I wanted to crawl inside Jim's head. I would have loved to grab a blank hard drive and download all the information about him and his life, past and present. I wanted to urge him to stand on a box and let me look at him properly, so I could form a proper image and impression of my father.

But of course that would make me sound like a total freak. I was so terrified of messing this up, and yet a larger part of me was so desperate for knowledge it was painful to maintain my restraint.

Jim asked me about where I'd grown up and how I'd managed to get into my job. I asked him about his life. He was open and easy to talk to. There was one burning question I wanted to ask, but I wasn't sure if it would be too invasive for a first meeting. Curiosity got the better of me however, and he seemed so approachable.

"Do you mind me asking why you and Jean never had any children?" I asked.

He paused and scratched the back of his head, which both worried me and totally freaked me out. That was what I did when someone made me nervous. Some people twitch, some cough, some laugh, I scratch my head. So did Jim.

"That's a difficult one for me to answer. Would you mind if we talked about that the next time? I'm sorry if I sound like a mental case, but can we come back to that another time?" He looked apologetic.

"Of course. I'm sorry, it's none of my business really, I shouldn't have asked. I was just curious. I suppose I'd wondered as soon as I knew about you whether I had any half brothers or sisters. If and when you're ready to tell me, we can talk about it." I tried to look unaffected. It was so strange, I was so able to hide what I really thought when I dealt with patients. I had a mask which was totally impermeable. I was good at not making people uncomfortable when they spoke to me, my livelihood depended on it, but this was different. I was doing a terrible job of keeping myself in check. I berated myself inwardly: *Keep it together, Susie, don't fuck this up.*

"What about you? I know you're not married, but do you have a significant other?" he asked.

"No, I've been busy building my career I guess. There just isn't time to fit it all in, is there?" I looked at him.

He regarded me with his head to the side. "I think you haven't met the right person. Maybe you will some day. It would be a pity if you never let yourself find someone. It can be very nice to have someone to share things with. There is a good side to being attached."

"I'll take your word for it, but it's not something I think about much."

As I said the words I knew they weren't completely true. Often I looked at Emily and Robbie and what they had together. They had their bad moments, sure, but they were happy. They had Louis and Tia and they adored them. Mum had always managed on her own, and she didn't seem bothered. But I was starting to realise that Mum had really made herself into an island. That wasn't right either. She was pretty emotionally bereft. Ever since I'd told her about Jim, she'd just trundled along the same way as before. Nothing seemed to phase her but nothing seemed to make it through to her heart, her core, her emotions. Was I going to end up the same way? I always thought Mum and I were so different in every way, but maybe I was wrong.

That night a couple of weeks ago, when I'd sat with Jim's letter in my hand, I had yearned for someone to share the moment with. Someone to support me. Someone to be there with me if the news had been negative. I was happy most of the time, but I knew Jim was right. Sometimes it would be nice to have someone.

We parted company about an hour later. We agreed to keep in touch by phone and to meet up again sooner rather than later. We kissed on both cheeks as we said goodbye.

Jim smiled warmly and held my hand. "I'm so glad to have met you, Susie. Let's do it again soon."

"I'd love that. You've no idea how much this has meant to me today." I struggled to stay calm. That huge lump was rising in my throat again. *Keep it together, Susie. The last thing this man needs is a blubbering mess in front of him. Don't fuck it up.*

He walked me to my car and after I'd sat inside he closed the door and stood waving me off. Nobody had ever done that for me before.

I drove out of the town feeling lighter than air. I was a girl with a father. I was his daughter. The whole idea of it filled me with an insatiable glee. I heard giggling and saw shoulder-shrugging and hair being tossed around. I was astonished to realise it was all being done by me.

I was about to call Mum and tell her about our meeting, but my hand moved away from the phone. Clicked into its hands-free cradle, I could have called her easily. But I didn't want to speak to her. Not yet. I was feeling too resentful towards her. She had lied to both myself and Jim. She had played God and decided to keep us apart.

I couldn't change the fact that I'd missed out on having a father. No one could, but her lack of remorse and emotion about it bothered me. I wanted to wait and figure out how to handle Mum before I phoned her.

By the time I got back to Dublin I was physically and emotionally wrecked. I picked up a Chinese takeaway and a bottle of wine and settled down by the fire.

I had high hopes of developing a relationship in the future with Jim. I felt a warmth inside at the thought of that. It was a new and yet easy feeling.

28

Emily

Real World Hors D'Oeuvres:
Dust off the flour of surgery, pour into real clothing, i.e. anything but pyjamas. Coat with make-up, serve with a forced smile. Practice makes perfect. If you keep trying, it eventually comes naturally.

It was two weeks after I'd escaped from hospital. The hospital smell was well and truly gone from my skin. I felt like I was ready to face the world again. My desire to see people came back a few days later. I was now managing to dress myself and put on my war paint again. I knew I looked more human, and more like myself. Deciding not to waste the make-up, I began to phone the troops. Friends were all eager to come and visit, so all it took was a text message from the "send to many" option on my phone and my diary began to fill up.

It was wonderful to see everyone again. It felt like I'd been gone on a round-the-world expedition for ten years. People looked so glamorous and fresh. I caught up on all the gossip. It was amazing. The world hadn't been on hold while I'd been missing in action. People were still getting pissed at dinner parties and making fools of themselves. The shops were still stocking clothes people had to buy. The same annoying cows were still upsetting everyone. Cakes and chocolate still made people fat.

I was glad nothing had changed. I had been put in the freezer for a short while, but I was beginning to defrost and all the familiar things I loved about my friends and my life were there waiting for me. All I needed to do was regain my strength, and I could slot right back into place. I was dusting myself off and sluggishly rising from the ashes.

My friends were all astonished at how well I looked.

"We really didn't know what to expect. But you look quite normal."

They had all arrived at my house in trepidation, wondering if they'd have to lie through their teeth by telling me I looked well.

I was very flat-chested at this stage, so my clothes did look a little baggy and odd.

It reminded me of being a skinny teenager again. I looked like I was only beginning to develop, with small, sad boobs.

The questions flooded in from my friends.

"So are you in pain all the time?"

"Not really, I'm still on painkillers."

"Are you feeling spaced from the painkillers?" Deirdre asked while moving her hand around in a circle in front of my face.

"Deirdre, they don't give me heroin or anything. I'm feeling quite normal really."

"So, million dollar question," said Susie. "Are you glad you did this?"

There was silence in the kitchen. They all moved in to hear what I was going to say.

"You bet I'm glad. I feel like I've defused a bomb. It's been ticking away in here." I held my hand to my chest wall. "Ever since they told me I had this gene I've felt the pressure building up inside me. I have no regrets. In fact it's much better than that. I feel like a physical weight has been lifted off me. I can't ever imagine regretting what I've done." I smiled, and I was genuinely happy.

The only dampening of my happiness came from Robbie. He was becoming more and more distant. He was still phoning me several times a day to see how I was getting on. But he was different. He was subdued and uneasy in my company. He came home later and later from work each night.

I tried to talk to him one night. "Are you all right, Robbie? Are you coping with everything?"

"I'm fine. Work is just crazy at the moment and I'm having to put in the extra time to keep up. That's all. Why?" He looked grey and strained.

"You don't seem to be in very good form. If you were having a tough time, you'd talk to me, wouldn't you?" I looked across the room to where he was sitting on his single bed reading a report.

"Everything's fine, Em, stop fussing. I need to get this done, okay?" He pulled his fingers through his hair and continued reading.

I was called back to the hospital to start the muscle expanding, two weeks after the surgery.

The doctors were going to use my own breast muscle to create a pocket shape, which would eventually hold a breast implant. During the surgery, this muscle had been peeled off the chest wall and an expandable bag was slotted in behind it. So at that moment, my breasts consisted of my skin and nipples on the outside, just like before. Then underneath, instead of breast tissue, which is soft and squashy – especially after two babies, I would now have a curved, shaped mound or pocket created with my own muscle.

I was to have saline injected into a port, situated under the skin. This port was like a hard plastic button-shaped device, which I could actually see under the skin, just below the scar. This button was at the top of my ribs on either side. The saline solution, which is exactly the same water they use in drips when people are dehydrated, would fill up the expander or shaped bag under my muscle, and thus stretch my skin and muscle forwards. Gradually, the water would push my muscle outwards to create a pocket, which would house an implant. Then I would be done. This process would take at least six months though.

So at that moment I was almost totally flat-chested. Every two weeks

I would attend the hospital so they could inject a little more saline solution through the port. This would make my muscle expand and therefore, make my breasts look bigger and more normal. Once I had reached the size I wanted to be in the end, they would expand slightly further. The reason behind this was to allow for a more natural-looking droop. All normal breasts drop down in a tear shape, as opposed to standing up to attention like soldiers. So the doctors advised me to create a slightly larger pocket, so the size I wanted would have room to drop downwards a little, providing a more natural result.

In between times, I would have to go in and have my ovaries out. Or an "oophorectomy" as it is called. The fallopian tubes were to go too. Apparently they can harbour some ovarian cells so I could still manage to develop ovarian cancer even without ovaries. Naturally I would be one of the tiny percentage who would do that too. Go to all this trouble and still end up in a wooden box, with *"She was the 2%"* on my headstone.

But, before any more surgery could happen, I had to become expanded (without the use of chocolate). I attended the "wound clinic", which sounded utterly barbaric to me. I imagined war scenes of people with gooey, bloodstained bandages slumped in the hallways moaning deliriously to themselves. Of course I found it to be very organised and civilised, with efficient, perfectly groomed nurses, checking patients in by computer and asking you to take a seat and help yourself to a cup of coffee and a biscuit. Not a bandaged head or severed limb in sight.

"This is quite nice really, isn't it?" I whispered to Robbie as we stood in the hallway.

"Yeah, could be worse," he muttered.

I was given a bed in the day ward. So I perched on it with my clothes and shoes on. Robbie sat in the armchair and got stuck into that day's Sudoku.

I read a hospital copy of *"Women's Bits"* or some such nonsense magazine.

"Before you go in to see Mr Green for your first round of expansion, we need to take your blood pressure and temperature." The nurse wheeled the familiar blood-pressure machine towards me.

"Which side was your mastectomy, Emily?" she asked.

"Both, I've had a bi-lateral mastectomy," I answered matter of factly.

"You did not, you poor auld creature." The nurse looked agog.

"'Fraid so," I smiled.

"Well, you'll have to make sure you have your blood pressure taken on your leg for the rest of your life. The side of a mastectomy must never be pressurised by a blood-pressure monitor, so both your arms are out of bounds from now on." She wrapped the black Velcro around my ankle.

"Now that you mention it, they did use my leg all the time while I was in hospital, but it never occurred to me that that was unusual. That's interesting, isn't it, Robbie?" I nudged him, knocking his wrist and making him scribble across his Sudoku puzzle.

"Watch it!" he said grumpily.

I had to put on a sexy tie-up-the-back gown. It was luckily a different design to the one I'd donned for two days post-surgery. This one had more muted colours and looked stunning with my skinny designer jeans.

When I got home from hospital, one of the first things I did was to retrieve my Victoria Beckham jeans from where I had hidden them from Robbie – and my own guilty conscience. I couldn't wait to see how good they would look now that I had lost some weight. Gleefully I put them and to my shock and horror they were as snug as they had been the day I bought them. I couldn't believe it. They still looked great but I had smugly expected to have lost about half a stone. I got out of the jeans and on to the bathroom scales. Oh no, two effing pounds! *Two pounds.* For all the pain and eating very little for two weeks, I hadn't ended up in a position where I had the doctors advising me to eat chocolate cake and cream pies for breakfast, to build myself up. But, oh no. Two pounds was my lot. Lousy, mean and utterly unfair if you ask me.

Anyway that's nothing to do with the injecting.

I met my surgeon, who is a sweetheart and sent by the angels. He shook my hand and told me not to be nervous, while he busily readied himself.

I was perched on this table, draped in a green sterile blanket with a hole in it, with one little shrivelled boob poking through.

"How've you been doing?"

"Fine, thanks."

"How are the kids getting on? Happy to have Mum back home again?"

"Yes, once I'm there they seem to relax. The first couple of days were a bit strained, but they're used to my lack of mobility now."

"Children adapt very quickly, don't they?"

He was one of those rare breeds of surgeons who didn't have a personality transplant when he qualified. Either that or he forgot to take the pretentious-asshole tablets.

I tried not to stare at the trolley full of needles and syringes beside the bed. I took off my designer robe and had my wounds checked. They were fine, nothing to report.

"Okay, are you ready? This is only going to cause a pricking sensation and after that it won't be sore. You'll feel a tightening as the muscle is being pushed forward. If this tightening is too much just yell." Mr Green gave me a thumbs-up signal and readied himself.

He inserted a thin metal hollow tube, a little bit like an epidural needle. It did indeed cause a minor pricking feeling, in fact it made an audible popping noise, but that was it. Then came the horse-tranquilliser syringe. It was like a blown-up version of the Fisher Price kids' doctor's set.

"Now, Mr Green, where do you think you're going with that enormous contraption?" I yelped.

"I'm not inserting it anywhere, don't worry! It's only going to hold the saline solution, which we will inject into the porthole."

"Are you telling me the truth? I may be incapacitated and all that, but I can still kick you in the chops if I have to!"

"No need for any Kung Fu for the moment. I'll tell you what, if I hurt you feel free to give me a good hard kick, how does that sound? I am so confident this won't hurt, I will put my ass on the line, literally," he laughed.

Nonchalantly he picked up the offensive device and began to fill it with saline from a sterile bag, just like a drip bag.

"So how much will we try and put in?" he enquired.

"Well, seeing as I haven't had my breasts removed and put back before, that is a pretty difficult question to answer. Can I phone a friend?"

"Cheeky pup! Most people have about forty to sixty mils put in at a time."

The competitive little green alien in my head woke up. "Okay, let's go for that to start off with," I instructed him.

"Fine, let's start." He began to push the syringe and the liquid began to pump into the expanding bag inside my breast. "That's sixty mils now, Emily, how are you doing?"

"I'll see your sixty mils and raise you another forty mils," I challenged.

Smiling, he began to push more liquid in. I'd thought it would be a very smooth process, but this was no light-hearted affair. He had to get his full weight behind the syringe and push with all his might.

"I'm having to push this behind a muscle which doesn't want to move." He gritted his teeth as he pushed hard on the syringe with the heel of his hand.

Beep, beep, beep!

It was his beeper.

"Dr Lucy will take over," he said. "I'm sorry – I've been called to emergency surgery. I'll see you again in two weeks' time. Take care, Emily." He patted my hand and in a flurry of white coat was gone.

Dr Lucy, the nurse and myself all looked at each other.

"I hope one of you knows what you're doing," I said.

We all looked at my poor breast protruding from the hole in the sterile blanket. This poor little bee-sting had a metal tube and wire threading out of it, with a syringe suitable for putting a cow to sleep attached.

I discovered it was their first time too. Maybe nerves kicked in, but we got incredibly giddy. It was quite hysterical. Dr Lucy tried to push the saline in behind my muscle, but nothing was happening. We were all encouraging her as if she was in labour.

"Push, Lucy! Good girl! You can do it!" I shouted.

"You're not helping matters, Emily! Stop yelling in my ear and for goodness' sake stop laughing – you're shaking the syringe," she giggled.

A student nurse poked her head in the door.

"I was supposed to observe . . ."

She broke off and retreated backwards out the door.

It took us a few minutes to compose ourselves. It must have been the happy endorphins, but I kept Lucy pumping and we managed 120 mils in each side. I actually had a bit of shape. I was starting to look like I did before.

"Now, Emily, you will feel sore tonight and tomorrow," Dr Lucy warned. "This muscle is being stretched and shoved into an unnatural shape and position. So that is going to cause discomfort. Take your painkillers and make sure you rest up."

I was then handed a supply of bandages called "Tubigrip" bandages. They were thick-ribbed, stretchy, cream-coloured bandaging like wrist or ankle supports – exactly the same idea as one of those sports injury bandages, except wide enough to go around my torso.

"These guys are going to be your closest friend for quite a while to come," said Dr Lucy. She explained that they needed to be worn over the top of my breasts for at least six weeks.

"When the breasts are expanded, there is a danger that the expanded muscle will allow the expanders to meander upwards. This would leave you with a very high-looking result."

"So my breasts would look like two melons, up towards my collar bones. In other words, I'd be like one of those A-list celebrities with the prominent breast jobs, with fabricated-looking breasts and a cleavage which starts too high up!"

"Got it in one. Once they travel up the chest wall, they can't be put back either. So this Tubigrip is vital. Keep it right here." Dr Lucy pulled a length of Tubigrip over my head and gestured to me to pull my arms through, which I painfully did. "It sits here under your armpits. I know it's tight, but that's what we want." She fixed it in place.

"It will leave a red mark on your skin when you take it off. Just like the mark an elastic band would leave on your wrist if you left it there too long. That's normal."

"Do I have to wear it all day?" I asked.

"You have to wear it all day and all night as well. The only time you can remove it is during bathing and showering."

"But it's so uncomfortable," I moaned.

"You have your choice – it's up to you."

I had to rationalise this. It would only be for a short time and it would ensure the best results. I had to do what they were telling me. God, it added to the pain though. How was I going to sleep with this? It was quite thick and encompassing. How would I dress so people couldn't see it? On the other hand, everyone knew I'd had surgery. I could explain why the Tubigrip was there, and that would be that.

I waved goodbye and we all congratulated each other on getting through the first ever saline-expansion session.

Robbie was still sitting doing his Sudoku in the armchair in the day ward. I quickly dressed and we escaped home. That night I was really bloody sore, as in a seizing, cramping feeling in my chest. The poor muscle was obviously thinking "What in the name of God is going on here?" It was desperately trying to contract and return to where it had been removed from. I took all the painkillers I could and just went with what my body told me to do. I had hot showers, I paced up and down, I lay down, I stood up, I slept fitfully. Luckily there are only about eleven hours of darkness so the daylight came along with the general hustle and bustle of life.

I edged out of bed and decided to try and ignore the whole thing.

29

Emily

Polo Neck Tagliatelle:
Take one post surgical, stiffly beaten girl. Add a tight polo neck. Turn
up the heat until both the top and girl resemble human tagliatelle – as
in tangled and messy. Serve soured and distressed.

I had a bit of an incident with a polo neck. The polo-necked jumper won. As part of the stretching exercises, I had to try and lift my arms up above my head. I was getting quite good at this, so I assumed I'd manage to put on a polo neck and jeans. I'd pulled on the jeans though the button was a bit hard to close – not because I was too squidgy for them but whatever muscle is used to close jeans buttons, it kept contracting and rubbing against the plastic muscle expanders inside me. It produced a revolting crunchy type sensation. So I had to brace myself for the crunch (and not stamp around in a circle flapping my hands making raspberry noises which, as we all know, makes the nauseating sound go away).

Jeans on, I felt cocky enough to go for a polo neck. Seeing as I was a non-post surgery gal (in my own head) this wouldn't be a problem. I pulled the sleeves over my arms and scrunched the torso part into a fat pleat, ready to be pulled over my head. This all went very smoothly until I got my head stuck in the base of the neck part. It was stretched over my face like a second skin. My arms were locked in a T-shape from my shoulders and nothing could move. I didn't have the strength to pull everything downwards and release my head. I was getting a bit hot and bothered at this stage so I had to stand up against a wall and take deep breaths and try to figure out how to get out of this. Houdini himself would have had trouble with this one. I was then faced with the added threat of all my stitches pulling. I was anticipating a ripping noise under my arms – and not from the jumper. I released one locked arm at a time and finally freed my head. My hair was matted and static, my face red and puffy so I looked a bit like a boiled duck's arse. I put on a cardigan.

The specialist's secretary phoned to say that Mr Green needed to see me. He wanted to go through the operation and discuss formally what way the reconstruction would go. Robbie took more time off work to come with me.

We were ushered in to see Mr Green. He had a folder full of test results in front of him.

"Hi, Emily and Robbie, thanks for coming in to see me. I have a bit of news for you." He looked me in the eye.

"What is it?" I smiled.

"Your tissue test results have come back from the pathology lab," he said calmly. "They're not clear, I'm afraid."

I felt the entire room beginning to spin. Silently I prayed, don't tell me I've already got cancer.

"What does that mean?" Robbie leaned forwards.

"We have found a large clump of pre-cancerous cells."

"Were they in my left breast?" I asked him immediately.

"Yes, how did you know that?" he asked, surprised.

"I'd been having pain there on and off, during the run-up to the operation. But I just assumed it was psychosomatic, because I knew about the altered gene," I answered.

"That's interesting to know. You certainly weren't imagining the pain. The cells were burrowed deep inside the breast tissue, behind the nipple. If the cancer had had a brain and it could have worked out where to hide so it couldn't be detected, this would have been the best place."

"I bloody knew it," I said.

If I ever needed justification for what I had done or if any of my family and friends did, there it was.

I got an overwhelming sense of someone or something looking down on me. One of my angels had come through for me. I do believe things happen for a reason. I was just meant to have this surgery.

"I'm very shocked." Robbie was sitting with his head in his hands.

"Well, it is very shocking for me too." Mr Green was tapping his pen on my file. "Emily, you would have had cancer in six months if you hadn't had the mastectomy, that's the bottom line. You're a lucky woman."

"Wow! That's amazing." I burst out laughing. I don't know why, but I felt utterly elated and thrilled. I felt like the person who'd missed the plane which then crashed. Robbie and I thanked Mr Green and drove home.

"That was a close one, wasn't it?" I said to Robbie on the way home.

"You did the right thing after all," Robbie said quietly.

His comment bothered me, but I decided to let it go. What was the point in pushing the issue? It was all over now.

I called my parents and Robbie's parents from the car.

"My God, that's kind of chilling, isn't it?" Mum was stunned, as was Dad.

Robbie's parents were equally flummoxed by the news. It was a strange feeling for us all. Of course we knew the odds were very high for me to have breast cancer. That had been the deciding factor for having the surgery in the first place, but the knowledge that I was on my way to having the disease was still scary.

I had begun to go out on adventures. My first outing was to Tesco with my dad and Tia. Dropping Louis to soccer practice, we descended on the supermarket. I was über-organised with my list. It was beautifully written on a proper piece of paper, as opposed to the torn end of a utility-bill envelope, which then gets lost in my metropolis of a handbag.

Dad was in charge of pushing the trolley and Tia, sensing the weakness, was in charge of behaving like an octopus on speed.

She grabbed every forbidden packet of biscuits, sweets, chocolate and boxes of cereal with more nutritional value in the cardboard than the contents. I was so excited to be out and doing something "normal" that she got away with it. Her eyes shone and her impish little grin displayed her pleasure and comfort in the fact that Mum was out again. Not forgetting that fun-sized people also adore getting one over on adults. Granddad was a dreadful pushover at the best of times, but I was usually a tougher target. So she couldn't have been more satisfied with the whole situation.

"Mum, can we buy these chocolate cakes to eat for lunch?" Tia's eyes were dancing.

"Yeah, sure. Why not? Let's have chocolate cakes for lunch today." I laughed at her astonishment and delight.

We bought enough to feed an African village for six months along with the usual necessities like scented candles, pink pot scrubs, wooden hanger sets and other such items which will spend the rest of their lives in the utility room, before being put in a skip. Dad packed my shopping and drove me home. I was throbbing and exhausted but it felt good to have escaped, even for a short while.

That trip out broke the mould. I hadn't melted or disintegrated, in fact I'd enjoyed it. So I started to organise more outings. My gorgeous yummy mummy friends from Louis and Tia's school invited me for coffee and scones. I was collected and delivered home as I still couldn't manage driving myself. It was a joy to see them all again, and to hear all the school gossip.

Realising I was ready to be reunited with Dunmahon was a momentous occasion for me. The home of the jeans.

"Susie, are you booked up this afternoon?"

"No, I was supposed to do some paperwork, why? What do you need?" She sounded tired.

"I need to go to Dunmahon, are you up for it?"

"Get your ass in gear, I'll be there in fifteen minutes!" She sounded thrilled.

Her car arrived outside my house and she jumped out, looking stunning as usual, in a navy silk and cashmere trouser suit.

"The lady is looking stylish today!"

"Not really, Emily. I think you've just spent too much time in your pyjamas." She smiled all the same.

We drove the short distance to Dunmahon.

"Are we allowed to park in the disabled spaces, do you think?" Susie eyeballed a space right beside the main doors.

"We'd better not. What would we do if we got questioned – take off my top and show them my scars?"

Cackling like witches, we linked arms and Susie helped me along.

I bought party shoes for Tia, a toy for Louis, birthday gifts for kiddies' parties and a jacket for myself. It was too expensive for what it was – a casual, to-go-with-jeans jacket, but what the hell! I felt I'd earned it. And my Victoria Beckham jeans deserved it. It was also an item I could wear at that moment with a lack of boobs and later when I inflated more. So really it was a very sensible investment.

Of course it had opened a whole can of worms for me, in so far as I would have to get a top and some accessories to go with it. Shoes would be useful too. I only had about eighty pairs. The light was changing too, so some new-season lip colours would be in the pipeline of course. It was a tough call, but I'd manage. It would all take me about four weeks at the rate I was going, but I had all the time in the world now!

I had this image of myself in this new outfit, looking tanned (that would have to come from a bottle), toned (highly unlikely as I could barely make it around a shop never mind a gym or pool), blonder (possible, would phone my hairdresser) and deliciously relaxed (well, it was only an image). Oh well, it was worth dreaming.

30

Susie

How to Whip Up an Interesting Life:
Take one friend, chop to pieces and discharge from hospital. Take another friend, mix with a long-lost father and jiggle all her emotions around until she doesn't know which way is up. Place both girls in a shopping centre and mix with coffee.

Emily and I decided to go on a little shopping trip to our beloved Dunmahon centre. I was so glad to see my darling friend up and about. Fair enough, she was pretty wooden and delicate, but she still did it.

Over coffee I filled her in on all the gossip about Jim Lynch.

"I'm dying to meet him. When are you going to have an unveiling?" she asked.

"I'm not sure. We've spoken on the phone a couple more times and we're ticking along nicely. He's actually asked me to his house next weekend."

"For a sleepover or just to call in?"

"Jesus, you're talking more and more like Louis. No, not for a sleepover. For lunch and to meet his partner, Jean. She sounds really nice and is happy to meet me, which I have to admire her for. I don't think I'd be so understanding if my partner turned up with a long-lost daughter."

"What about Pauline? Will she go with you or would that all be too awkward?"

"No, Mum is driving me insane actually. She's doing her ostrich impression with the whole Jim issue. I'm finding her impossible to deal with at the moment. She's acting as if none of this is happening. If I call into her and try to talk, she's more interested in showing me another vile, clashing knitted cushion she's made, or telling me about what a wonderful shop TK Maxx is. She's for the birds, Emily!"

"She's never been any different, in fairness to her, but I wonder if she's acting like this to hide the fact that she's finding it all a bit difficult. What do you think?" She paused and added, "You're the psychologist after all."

I felt her last remark was a bit pointed. But she was right. When it came to my mother, all my psychotherapist skills went out the window.

"You might be right," I sighed. "I'll try talking to her again. I know you think I'm quite mean to her but, believe me, she's bloody annoying when she's your own mother. She just buzzes about in her own little world and has no interest in anything else and at times it's frustrating, you know? Your mum is so clued in and normal. So it's easier for you to be sympathetic towards my mum. But, believe me, she's bloody hard work to have as a mother."

So that was why I was now on my way out to Bray. To try and give Mum the benefit of the doubt. To try and include her in the whole Jim thing. To give her an opportunity to express herself. I was able to be open-minded with my patients, so I needed to afford her the same courtesy.

I pulled up outside her cottage and braced myself. Put on your understanding and open-minded hat, I thought to myself.

"Susie, how are you, dear? You look smart as usual. Come on in, I was just going to have some tea. Will you have a cup?" She left her door open and walked the short distance to her kitchen.

"Thanks, Mum, I'd love one. I've just come from Dunmahon – I was there with Emily." I plonked myself into a chair.

"That's nice, dear. How is Emily these days?"

"She's okay. Getting there. She looks terrible. I wouldn't tell her that of course, but she's still fragile. She's dealing with it all really well though." I smiled at the thought of Emily.

Mum was busying herself, making tea and opening ancient biscuit tins. She had a collection of tins going back to my childhood, which she used for stashing her culinary delights. She never worked on the "best before" idea, so I always checked things for mould if they weren't freshly baked.

"Mum, I've spoken to Jim Lynch a couple more times," I began.

"Oh? Right. How's all that going then?"

"Fine. He's invited me to his house for lunch next weekend, so I can meet his partner, Jean. He's said to invite you if you'd like to come too. How would you feel about that?"

"Ah, no, I won't bother. Thank him for the invitation but I've organised to go to the garden centre with Nuala from the library on Saturday. I'll leave it, maybe another time. Or if he comes up this neck of the woods it might be better." She didn't even falter. She continued to make the tea and hum to herself.

I decided to put her on the spot. "Mum, don't you think you're acting slightly strangely about all this?"

She turned and looked at me in confusion. "In what way, dear?"

"You haven't asked me a single thing about him. You seem to have no thoughts about him at all. Aren't you even slightly interested in hearing about him or seeing him? Or is it that all this is making you uncomfortable and you want to stick your head in the sand?" I was doing it again. Getting impatient and annoyed with her.

"I'm not sticking my head in the sand at all, Susie. He sounds like a very nice man, by all accounts, but I really don't give him much thought. If it makes you happy to get to know him, that's lovely. But it's not really anything to do with me. I know he's your biological father, but as I've told you I never knew him. I just don't see the point in getting all excited about a man I don't know." She plopped the teapot and two chipped mugs on the table.

"Mum, have you always been so emotionally bereft or is it only in recent years?" It came out before I could stop myself.

Mum looked mildly surprised. "I didn't think I was emotionally bereft."

"Well, I have to tell you, I find your attitude kind of odd. You seem to live in your own little world and you don't give a toss about anyone else. You never met a man for instance. Have you never felt lonely? Have you never felt you'd like someone to share your life with?"

"Well, I met a few gentlemen friends over the years. But none of them ever really blew me away. I have Nuala and the girls at the library. I meet people most days when I walk on the beach. I don't feel lonely, to answer your question. I have you as well. You bring me great joy of course. You always did." She smiled at me.

"But Nuala is married, the people on the beach aren't your friends, I don't live with you. Don't you ever wish you had a companion?" I was feeling exasperated again. She always made me feel this way. The familiar wall was up on her part and the rising sense of frustration was bubbling inside me.

"Well, I could ask you the same question, dear. Why don't you have a partner? Aren't you lonely?" She held her head to the side.

"Well, to be honest, Mum, I never used to want anyone. In fact, poor Kevin was just in the way when we were together. I was so intent on making my mark career-wise that I had no extra time for anyone else. So I will admit that I did shut people out. But I was a lot younger then and I had a set goal. I am slowly realising that I might like to let someone in. That it might be nice to have someone to share my life with. I don't want to end up in a dark seaside house, with nothing but a few plants to talk to!"

"Well, I'm sorry if you think my existence is sad, Susie, but I'm perfectly happy. That's all I can say to you. If you see my life as being so awful, then by all means change your own. Make sure you don't end up like me." She looked hurt.

"Mum, I'm sorry. That was uncalled for. I shouldn't have attacked your life like that. I've no right to judge you and question your happiness. That was horrible of me." I felt cruel and yet like I'd hit a brick wall with Mum. I had hoped to shock her into submission. I had hoped that if I pushed her, she'd open up to me and tell me how she felt.

But I was wrong. There didn't seem to be any great secret to her existence. Plodding along in her own little world was what she chose to do. Nobody was forcing her to live in her dark little cottage. Nobody was telling her to travel around on a twenty-year-old bike. Nobody had broken her heart and forced her to live without a partner. It was all her own choice. She was happy that way. I'd messed up again. I'd ended up being nasty and making an unpleasant scene. Mum was still humming and buzzing about. I was anxious and still none the wiser for our conversation. Mission un-accomplished.

I had realised, though, that I hated the thought of ending up on my own. I would like to find the happiness that Jim seemed to have with Jean. I thought of Emily and Robbie. The day they got married, I'd kind of sneered at her – only in my own head of course. I would die if she knew I'd thought that way. But I had always thought she'd done the stereotypical thing. Getting married and having kids. I had in my own conceited head-up-my-own-hole way, thought she was baling out. I had, deep down, thought I was the stronger, more hardworking, modern go-getter of the two us. But now I was ashamed to realise that being happy to share your time and love with another person was a privilege. I wasn't sure if I'd ever experience that, but I was certainly ready to be more open to trying.

31

Emily

Mixed Grill with Rasher:
Take one shag-obsessed kitten, mix with an ounce of rancid poo, add to innocent cushions and try not to vomit. Learn lots of ways to avoid explaining to small children what the cat is up to. Become a walking thesaurus filled with alternate words for bonking, like hugging, playing, scratching, sniffing, bouncing . . .

April brought brighter longer days. The blossoms were bursting forth on the trees. The daffodils and bluebells were in full bloom. The garden was alive again. The bare trees were full of acid-green baby leaves, the birds had all returned and were busily building nests and going about their business. The winter had firmly passed and the spring was in full swing.

Rasher the kitten had turned six months. Apart from trying to eat all the little baby birds, he'd discovered his bits and was systematically shagging the cushions, jumpers, duvets and anything generally comfortable. I adore cats and in my mind there are few things cuter than a kitten, but this constant humping of furniture was decidedly off-putting.

It just made me want to chuck him out the window – while wearing rubber gloves. The other really irritating habit he'd started was wandering around the house at half three in the morning, meowing at the top of his lungs. This not only woke myself and Robbie, the au pair and the kids, but also caused mayhem. He'd yowl like a banshee until we were all awake. We'd all lie in bed ignoring him. Then he'd get bored and make a beeline for a bedroom. Jump on the handle and open the door, run in and proceed to run about like a turbo-charged, electrified eel.

Within minutes we'd all be either in the hallway looking dishevelled with backcombed hair and squinty eyes, or one person would be under a bed whispering, "Pish, pish, pish!" and attempting to coax the little shit out.

He'd seem delighted about having someone to play with and his boredom would ease, his dancing glassy eyes beaming. After a lot of thumping and words sounding like "fire-truck" and "rollox" he'd be caught. He'd howl and bawl all the way down the stairs. He'd be put into the kitchen, as Tia and Louis cried too.

"Don't be mean to Rasher, he only wants to say hello to us!" Tia would wail.

"It's three thirty in the middle of the night!" Robbie would shout. "Everybody go back to bed. It's sleep time now." Robbie hadn't wanted Rasher in the first place and he was not endearing himself to his master. "I told you anything coming from Laura's house would be insane, Emily! Was I correct?" Robbie stomped back to bed muttering about possessed creatures.

Our doors, bar the bathroom, don't have locks so we couldn't turn a key to keep him enclosed. The next eight nights we put everything from kitchen chairs to a shelving unit up against the door to keep him in. This just generated more noise. He'd jump at the door handle to open the door and then follow the action with a good twenty minutes of head-butting and wailing. Eventually the persistent little git would emerge triumphant. And the aforementioned shenanigans would begin – again.

Robbie and I were on the point of throwing him out at night but then, if he ran off, trying to explain his disappearance to the kids was just too much to bear. They would be traumatised, so I didn't want to take the chance. I felt they'd had enough upheaval. We were about to buy locks and chains to contain the little toad when Robbie had a brainwave. He bought a little black, plastic doorstop for €1.25. We shoved that into the door from the outside and the night-time problem was solved. After a few nights of fruitless attempts to get out, the little wretch gave up and stopped yowling too. It was such a relief. It was almost as good as the first night your baby sleeps all night. The doorstop did not however, do anything for the old shagging problem, so I phoned the vet.

"Hi there, I was wondering if you could help me?" I was praying the vet would have some type of medication which might stop Rasher from humping the sofa. "Our kitten seems to want to mate with all our soft furnishings. Have you come across this problem before?"

"Yes, a lot of male kittens do this. Really the only solution we know of is to have him neutered." The vet sounded deadpan.

"Well, that sounds fabulous. When can I bring him in to you?" If all it took was to have his pockets picked, then I'd go for it.

I phoned Robbie to tell him the good news.

"The cat's going for the snip. The vet thinks it will stop him trying to shag the furniture. Sounds like a good solution, doesn't it?" I thought Robbie would be thrilled.

"Ah dear, poor little bastard! When are you taking him down?" Robbie sounded genuinely sorry for Rasher. Typical male, feeling sorry for him because I was interfering with his manhood.

My mum was bringing the children to school each morning and I asked her to take Rasher to be neutered. He was delivered and we were told to phone at two to check on his progress and to book a "home time" for him. When I phoned, the secretary took it very seriously.

"I was ringing to enquire about our kitten. He came in this morning to have his pockets picked." I thought it was funny.

"What is your kitten's name please?" She wasn't laughing.

"Rasher," I answered.

"Ah yes. Rasher Cusack. He's doing well. He's a bit groggy still. But he's in recovery and is feeling a bit sore. He should be okay to come home at five o'clock."

I didn't ask her how the hell she knew Rasher was sore. Did she speak Cat?

My dad collected him at the allotted time and returned Rasher in his carrier cage, looking really pissed off. He'd had a bit of complication in so far as his snip went well, but one of his knackers hadn't descended, so they'd either removed it or forced it into position. I wasn't sure which. He'd to go back to have his stitches removed in two weeks and had to be kept inside the house for three days.

I offered him food and he just stood swaying in front of the dish bug-eyed, stoned and confused. Poor little bastard, there's nothing more pathetic than a sick animal apart from a sick man. I felt so mean. I was certain he wouldn't be jumping on door handles or bonking cushions for a few days at least.

The following day after a silent night, he managed to make his way up to my room. I sympathised with his pain and we spent a rainy grey, miserable morning silently understanding each other. I liked him more again.

The next day I changed my mind. His stitches were obviously annoying him and I know he was only an animal but he was behaving in a revolting manner. He was doing lots of licking his bits with his leg in the air, followed by dragging himself around the carpet by his front paws with his back legs in the air. I know he was obviously having a sensation which he wasn't used to, but having stitched arses dragged across the rug is too much for me. I just couldn't allow it, so I locked him in the utility room with some food and milk and his bed. Feeling utterly mean a couple of hours later I let him out.

He immediately made a beeline for the sitting room, jumped onto a cushion and began to shag it.

Oh bloody hell, all my hopes were dashed. I'd been promised by the vet and other people with shag-prone cats that having their pockets picked would stop this revolting behaviour. But no, Rasher was destined to be a shagger by the looks of things.

The next morning he tried to bonk my dressing gown. I threw him outside. I know he was supposed to be kept in for three days, but I felt if he was well enough to bonk and climb curtains, he could bloody well go outside and be disgusting out there, where I couldn't see it and be appalled by him.

It was Week Four to the day when I started to feel more myself. More "normal". I'd come off all painkillers and was generally stronger. The green pallor had left me and I even began to look alive, as opposed to a corpse with make-up on.

32

Emily

Stuffed Breasts:
Fillet breasts by removing all natural tissue. Gradually replace breast tissue with saline solution. Watch carefully as pancakes turn into small melons.

On the Tuesday I went back to St Theresa's Hospital for the next session of reconstruction or pumping as I liked to call it. I'd suffered after the last time, so we all agreed to put in sixty mils on either side. Bringing my grand total to 260 mils, each side.

I had to reach 400 mils before the expansion was complete, so I would need two more trips for reconstruction before I would be fully inflated. I was still having to wear the Tubigrip. I was now good at disguising it under my clothes. As it was trussed around the top of my new implants, it had a habit of peeping out of my clothing, making me look like I was wearing an ugly vest. I'd become very deft with a needle and thread. I could tack it carefully into the top I was wearing, so it couldn't be seen.

The relief when I could take it off for a shower was incredible. Because of that, I'd been showering twice daily for the last few weeks. My skin was a bit like sandpaper from all the water, but it was worth it for a couple of minutes' relief.

Next time I saw Mr Green I was asked if I would mind having my picture taken. Not in the normal sense – this was for the Breast Book, the book which was shown to other breast patients, or the *Little Book of Horrors* as myself and Robbie liked to call it. Apparently mine turned out very well, so in a way they didn't represent the full picture of what most women will end up with. But if it'd help, of course I was delighted to do it. I had to sign forms to consent to having my breasts photographed.

"You will be treated with sensitivity and the photos will never be used for anything other than patient viewing on the hospital grounds." Mr Green was speaking in his serious voice.

"Well, I'm a bit disappointed." I used my serious voice too. "What the hell is wrong with my breasts? Why aren't you selling them to *The Sun* for use on page three?"

Smiling and shaking his head, he called the photographer by internal phone.

"Hi, Patrick, can you come over to the day ward and take some photos for me? Just to warn you, you might be nervous of this patient – she's a little scary."

"*Moi?*"

"Now, Emily, be nice to Patrick please. He's quiet and nice, so don't freak him out."

Meanwhile the trolley with the same horse tranquillisers and needles appeared. The cattle-injecting syringe was produced and the saline was pumped in. The difference this sixty mils made was incredible. The whole breast took shape as if by magic. It was like inflating a balloon. My breasts went from being a bit sad and dejected-looking to pert and a hell of a lot more normal-looking.

"That looks brilliant, even if I say so myself," said Mr Green, admiring his own handiwork.

"I'm thrilled with them – you're a genius!"

242

If I'd been told two years ago that I would be sitting on a medical couch with four people, two of whom I'd never met before, prodding and discussing my breasts, I would have thought it impossible. But here I was, ecstatic about the whole idea, and relishing the fact that I was chosen to have my picture in the *Little Book of Horrors*.

That night, I had a night of hell again. I feel like my skin was crawling and I was going to explode. I had a major temperature and a slightly gritty throat. I was getting paranoid that it was withdrawal symptoms from coming off all the pain relief. I felt like a junkie coming down off heroin. My nerve endings were like they were fizzing all over. I couldn't get comfortable and had an unrelenting urge to wriggle and move non-stop.

I decided to have a bath for what must have been the first time in seven years. I am not a wallow-in-water type. I know it's meant to be relaxing, but it just doesn't do it for me. I decided to have a shower to alleviate the sitting-in-own-dirt syndrome first. Then I ran a bath and filled it with purifying, relaxing Dead Sea salts.

I sank into the soft water and tried not to notice all the scratches on the bath and the streaks of supposedly wash-off crayons from my children's bath time, which had engrained themselves in the sides of the bath and the surrounding tiles. I closed my eyes and tried to relax. It's not easy with Spiderman and Barbie looking at you. They're on transfers on the wall above the taps. Tia and Louis seem to find this acceptable, but I have to say Spiderman is a bit vacant looking. Barbie is just unnerving with her perfect figure, and her stunning white smile. She is a bit smug too in her own way. Grinning at me as if to say, "My life with Ken is just spiffing. I'm going to ballet, then I'm going to be an air hostess and drive my pink Beetle to a fabulous pool party with my other model-tastic friends. You enjoy wallowing like a hippo over there, I don't mind!" Cheeky cow.

I did quite well once I blanked Barbie, but very quickly I had a sweat moustache, felt a bit light-headed and iffy and just had an urge to get out. So I did. I can't honestly say I felt any better, but it was something to do.

I went driving – on my own. It was as exhilarating as the first time I was able to drive a car by myself after learning. God, it was a buzz to be able to go around the block on my own. I realised I'd have to go to places where I could go in fairly straight lines for the moment, but I could work around that. Turning the wheel was a bit of a strain as the muscles that were being pushed out by the expander came into play big-time. But I had to start somewhere and the pain was worth the result. Being able to be mobile and on my own again was marvellous. I stopped at the traffic lights and made eye contact with another woman. I nodded and smiled at her. She looked at me as if I had just asked her to have an illicit lesbian affair with me.

She nervously looked away and became very busy looking at the floor of her car. Of course this encouraged me, so I kept staring at her and raising my eyebrows until the lights changed. It didn't take a huge amount to entertain me at that time.

It was a big breakthrough for the kids too, because it meant I would be able to drop them to school and collect them again. Any further scrap of renewed routine was vital to them.

As each piece of the jigsaw was slotting back into place, their behaviour was becoming less erratic. I phoned Robbie to tell him the good news.

"I just drove around the block, I'm so excited!" I yelled into the phone when he answered.

"Emily, I'm in a meeting. I'll call you later." He was gone.

I tried to push the feeling of deflation to the side. Robbie had become more and more distant over the last couple of weeks, working long hours and spending less time at home.

I had quashed the fear that he was avoiding me for the last while. But it was reaching a stage when I would have to speak to him about it. I had a sudden stab of fear. Was he having an affair? Had my mutilated body and my lack of energy driven him to the arms of another woman? Once the idea came into my head, I couldn't shake it.

33

Susie

Sautéed Emotions:
Take one mother who goes by the cloud-cuckoo-land recipe book and gently fold into a whipped-up daughter, who lives by the no-bullshit book of life. Watch as the mixture curdles rapidly.

My attempt at a frank conversation with Mum had upset me. I had driven away feeling like I'd been a nasty cow and she, as usual, seemed utterly unaffected.

I had phoned her the next morning and told her I loved her and that I was sorry if I'd sounded harsh.

"Don't give it a second thought, dear. I haven't. You were always volatile as a youngster. That's your way and you don't need to apologise for who you are. I know you love me and I love you too, very much. At the end of the day, that's all that matters, isn't it?"

She then began to talk about her impending trip to the garden centre with her friend Nuala. So what happened? Yes, you've guessed it. I ended up hanging up the phone in bewildered awe – was I mad or was it Mum?

Because I was really missing something with her. She seemed to have an impermeable coating surrounding her. Making her impenetrable to emotion. I decided I would have to try and picture her as a rag-doll. A very sweet and lovely thing, which was easy to love, but would never have a conversation with me about feelings.

I had to put Mum's oddness on the back burner. I had a lunch to attend, in my father's house. It just felt and sounded so new still. My father.

Saturday was one of those awful April-shower days. The sky was black and the rain was lashing down, with no sign of stopping. It was that time of the year when you just don't know what to wear. It's still not that warm but it could get kind of muggy in the afternoon. As I drove towards the Midlands, I peered out the top of my windscreen to search for a patch of blue sky. The odd brave bird flew just above ground level, as if trying to avoid the heavy drops of rain.

With the Scissor Sisters blasting at full pelt on my car stereo, I tapped the wheel and imagined what Jean was going to be like. I wondered if she was anything like Mum. I somehow imagined their house would be a bit of a seventies throwback. I knew it was a three-bed semi-detached, and so I had a picture in my mind's eye of a pristine yet slightly hicky house. With maybe a moss-green three-piece suite with tassels and arm covers. I envisaged plenty of little statues and figurines, carefully placed on slightly yellowing linen doilies. Their lack of children made me think they'd have tons of trinkets and neatly placed items, which had never been smashed by tiny hands. The kitchen, I thought, might be dark wood, with a more country kitchen than modern edge to it. With a heavy wood kitchen table and matching chairs. I could see Jim drawing heavy chintz curtains at night, after lighting the real coal fire.

I had brought a bottle of Chianti and a bottle of Chardonnay, and a hand-tied bouquet of all-white flowers. At least if they had a very colourful and busy décor, the white wouldn't interfere with anything.

Jim had emailed me directions, and I followed them with ease. He was precise and to the point, and I pulled up outside his house with ten minutes to spare despite the awful rain. It was a typical 1970s' semi-detached, with white pebble dashing at the front, white-painted window surrounds and small immaculate front garden. The windows had been upgraded to add double gazing. There were no gnomes or over-the-top water features of vomiting cherubs or peeing fishermen. So far, so good.

I had a fleeting sensation of apprehension. I hoped that Jean was comfortable with meeting me. I hoped Jim hadn't told me everything was fine, while he'd been rowing with her constantly hoping she'd eventually give in.

I dashed to the front door and huddled under the protruding roof of the small front porch. As the doorbell rang, I heard footsteps accompanied by a symphony of barking approaching.

"Girls, girls, girls! Calm down!" I heard Jim scolding the dogs.

As he flung the door open, two little black and white cocker spaniels leaped and bounced towards me.

"Hi, Susie, welcome! Isn't it vile out today? Excuse the girls – they get very excited when we have visitors. Come in from the rain, how lovely to see you!" He stood aside and I stepped into the hall. "Miranda and Charlotte, stop that silly carry-on! Go to bed!" He clapped his hands firmly and the two dogs click-clacked down the hallway, their nails drumming on the wooden floor.

I looked around in surprise. It was not what I'd expected – at all. The hallway was floored in wide oak, waxed boards and the walls were painted a pale ice-cream pink. The stairs were made of chrome and oak and large skylights made the place seem bigger. Even on such a dull dreary day, the place was flooded with light.

I followed Jim down the hallway. He pushed open a heavy varnished wooden swinging door, to reveal a large open-plan kitchen and living room. The entire room was floored in cream high-shine tiles and the kitchen units were muted pale wood, with glittery black marble tops. The focal point in the centre of the kitchen was an oversized bar, with cream and chrome stools.

The living area housed squashy cream leather sofas and nests of unusual-shaped tables. The rugs and accessories were cream and burnt orange. In the corner, there was a shining chrome vase, with six-foot-high orange silk flowers arranged in it.

"Wow, your house is so cool!" I looked around in awe.

"What were you expecting? Brown velvet and clashing patterned sofas, with china things with dead fish eyes looking at you from every angle?" he chuckled.

"Yes, quite frankly. I'm pleasantly surprised. You're quite a trendy bastard, aren't you?" I teased.

"Well, I can't really take all the credit – it's mostly down to Jean. I'm not exactly Mr Astute when it comes to colours and textures. I just kind of do what I'm told in that respect," he grinned. "Jean will be back shortly. Can I get you a coffee while you're waiting?"

"Sure, that'd be lovely." I handed him the wine and left the flowers in the sink. "These are for Jean, and I wasn't sure if you liked red or white, so I brought both." I perched on a barstool.

"Thank you, you shouldn't have. Cappuccino or Americano?"

"Cappuccino would be delicious. God, I'm so envious, you have a Gaggia machine! They make the best coffee but they cost a bloody fortune.'

"It's worth it though. I can't stand the burnt nasty taste of instant coffee. I'd rather have a glass of water." He busied himself making the coffee.

As he set the two cups on the counter, he took a deep breath. He turned towards me and hesitated.

"Susie, there's something I need to tell you, and I really hope it's not going to shock you too much. We're only getting to know each other and I would hate to spoil that, but I have to be honest with you."

He looked a bit nervous but not as nervous as I suddenly felt.

"Right," I said. "Well, keep in mind that I make a living out of people coming to tell me their problems, some of which are pretty shocking."

"It's about Jean," he began.

Oh no, my worries were going to be confirmed. She didn't want me in their lives.

"What about her?" I tried to look impartial.

"Well, that's just it. She's actually a he."

There was a lilting silence as the penny slowly dropped.

"I'm gay, Susie. Jean is my long-term partner. We've been together for a very long time and we're very happy. I just hope you don't have a problem with my being gay."

"Jesus, no wonder you don't have any kids!" I was gobsmacked.

"Yeah, it might have proven a little difficult all right. Although times have changed. Plenty of gay couples adopt successfully these days, don't they?" He was still searching my face for a reaction.

"But you don't look gay or even sound gay. I'm kind of amazed, I'd never have known." I was quite thrown.

"Why? Because I don't walk around wiggling my bottom and hips with a limp wrist, lisping and shrieking and crying a lot?" he said, smiling.

"No, don't be silly. God, I'm sorry. I feel a bit stupid that I didn't see it. Mind you, I do remember being utterly devastated when I found out George Michael was gay. I didn't see that one coming either!"

"Yes, a lot of women found that one difficult to fathom, although I always thought the gold-lamé shorts in the "Wake Me Up Before You Go-go" video was a dead giveaway." He paused, looking me in the eye. "So you're not upset then that I'm gay?" The poor man was still waiting for some reassurance.

"Oh God no. Of course not. I'm sorry, I should have clarified that first off. It makes no difference to me who you choose to shag!"

"Who is he shagging now?"

I turned around to find a small round man with curly hair standing in the doorway. "Is it safe to come in? Are we out of the closet?" Jean had entrancing brown eyes and a cheeky grin.

"You're firmly out," I said, hopping down off my bar stool, "and I was just telling Jim that it's all fine with me."

We shook hands and Jean came and sat beside me.

He spotted the bouquet. "Oh, did you bring those divine flowers?"

"Yes, they're for you, I hope you like them."

"Anyone who brings me flowers is welcome here any time. So how are things going?" Jean looked from me to Jim.

"Great," Jim answered immediately. "I'm relieved that you know, Susie. I felt I was keeping you in the dark beforehand but I just wasn't sure how you'd react to finding out your long-lost-dad was gay." He shrugged.

"Well, in fairness, I think I still win on the bomb-dropping stakes.

Your being gay doesn't even come close to my announcing myself as your long-lost daughter."

A thought struck me. "Hey, is your name actually Gene then, as in Gene Kelly?"

"Yes – Eugene. But I changed it to Jean years back."

I was glad. The very word "gene" had a bad connotation for me at the moment because of Emily's faulty one.

We chatted easily and I spent a lovely afternoon with the two men. They were friendly and open and seemed very happy with each other. They'd led a pretty normal life. Jean worked in an interior design shop. They travelled twice a year and seemed to live life to the full.

"How is Pauline doing?" Jim asked.

"She's okay. She's kind of sitting on the fence when it comes to our meeting up." I didn't want to tell Jim and Jean that she didn't seem to give a toss what we all did, that she was so away with the fairies that none if it affected her either way.

"It's just, I remember you saying to me that the reason she never told me she was pregnant was that she was afraid our parents would have made us get married. Just for the record, I agree with her. Of course I would have loved to have known about you, so I could have seen you grow up, don't get me wrong. But my parents were very old school and they just wouldn't have understood. They're both dead now, but my sister still lives in Dublin. I see her from time to time, and she accepts me the way I am. What I'm trying to say is that Pauline made the right choice for both herself and me at the time. I know it's probably hard for you to understand what it was like in the seventies, but it was very different. Our parents would have made us get married without a shadow of doubt. Considering I'm definitely gay, can you imagine what kind of a marriage we would have had?" Jim took my hand. "I can see that you're angry and confused about why your mother held her silence for so long, but I think we all need to try and move forward. As I'm sure you are well aware, considering your profession, dealing with the past and then moving on is the most healthy way of coping with things." He was looking at me hopefully.

"I am angry with Mum. I think she should have told me about you and vice-versa a long time ago. But that's an issue I will have to come to terms with in my own head. I know we can't get back the years we have missed but we do have the future to look forward to. It would be great to think that you'll both be a part of that." I sighed. What was the point in carrying my anger and bitterness forward? The only person who seemed to be annoyed was me. Mum and Jim seemed to be managing to accept the way things had gone.

"Why did you sleep with my mother, just as a matter of interest? Was it to confirm in your own head whether you were actually gay or not?"

"She was my one and only female encounter. Although she might not want to be told that. I'd hate her to think that our union resulted in the confirmation that I wasn't ever going to be in the vagina business. It wasn't as if she was the reason or anything – I just needed to know for sure."

"It's okay, Jim. I am aware, as is my mother, that gayness isn't acquired by shagging women on top of frozen veg!" I laughed.

"Christ, she actually told you that?" Jim looked shocked.

"Yep, I know I was conceived on a freezer cabinet."

There was an awkward silence for a few seconds, until Jean piped up, punching my arm playfully, "Besides, two dads are better than none!"

"Not a bad day's work, I suppose, going from being fatherless to having two," I agreed.

It was dark by the time I said goodbye. I'd enjoyed our afternoon and I felt a lot of ghosts had been laid to rest that day.

Just wait until I told Emily! She already thought I was living a soap opera. I couldn't wait to tell her about Jean. I also knew I had to call Mum and fill her in. Knowing I had at least an hour and a half in the car, I dialled Emily's number and clicked my phone into the hands-free cradle.

"Hi, it's me, can you talk?"

Emily's house sounded unusually quiet.

"Yes, Robbie and Maisy have taken the kids out for a runabout and to pick up some takeaway. How did your meeting with Jim and Jean go?"

"Great! Jean was lovely. Cuddly and friendly. Very open-minded and delighted for Jim. And gay."

I waited for the reaction. There was a pause.

"And *what?*"

I giggled. "And gay."

"Jean is gay?"

"Jean and Jim are gay."

"Bloody hell, were you shocked? Did it not occur to you that he was a bit camp or anything before he told you?"

"No, not for one second. You'll get to meet him soon and you can judge for yourself. I just assumed they had no children because Jean, or Eugene as it turns out, had gynaecological problems or something." I yawned as I turned the car on to the main motorway to Dublin.

"Well, she does, I suppose, in so far as she's a man. That's the most insurmountable gynaecological problem there is really!" Emily chuckled.

"Shut up, smart arse! How are your inflatable boobs? And how's Robbie?"

"All fine. I'm a bit sore, but that's the story of my life right now. It'll pass. Robbie's out as I said."

"Are you sure everything's okay?" I thought I could sense a slight edge to Emily's voice.

"Yes, Miss Psycho Analyser, everything's ticking along nicely here. Look, you go and ring your mum and fill her in on this week's episode of your fabulous life."

I realised she had changed the subject.

I was too tired to press her further about Robbie. I felt a bit like a wet rag, having taken in so much today and having to drive in the rain. I let Emily go and dialled Mum's number, albeit reluctantly.

"Hey, Mum, it's me." I tried to sound nonchalant.

"Hello, love, how was it all then?"

"It went really well. I hope this won't shock you too much, Mum, but there's something Jim wants me to tell you."

"Oh really? What's that now?" She sounded all chirpy and happy.

"He's gay and has a live-in lover. He has done since I was born pretty much." I left a silence, waiting to hear if she'd explode or cry or be astounded.

"Good for him." There was another silence.

"Are you all right, Mum?"

"Oh yes, dear. Just fine. I'm in the middle of altering a lovely skirt I picked up in Oxfam this morning, so forgive me for sounding a bit distracted. You know me and needles. I'm forever stabbing myself."

Feeling the blood rising to my face, I had to bite my tongue to stop myself yelling at her.

"He was very understanding about your decision not to tell me he existed, which I thought was big of him," I gritted my teeth. There was still no reaction on the other end of the phone.

After a couple of seconds she answered. "Well, all's well that ends well. Isn't that great then? I'm glad he has a nice partner and that they're both happy." Then there was a silence.

Was that it? She didn't want to know about his house or how long they're together? Nothing. Blank wall. Again.

But then she came up with what seemed like a more interesting question.

"Are they going to get married, do you think?" she asked.

"I don't know, why?" I was delighted she was showing an interest at last.

"Well, you know Elton John and his partner had a beautiful wedding. I know there wouldn't be any dresses, which is a terrible shame, but at least they could go to town on the floral arrangements to make up for it." She had her airy-fairy voice on again.

I scratched my head. All she could think about, with all this news, was whether or not they'd like to have a wedding.

"Maybe you could ask them. I'm going to have them up to my apartment for dinner soon. I thought you might like to join us?" I held my breath.

"I'll see, Susie. They mightn't want me cramping their style. It mightn't be such a good plan."

"It would mean a lot to me. I know it might be a bit strange at first, but it would be a thrill for me to have both my parents in the same room together. Will you at least think about it?" I was gritting my teeth.

"Well, I won't commit to it yet, I'll see how I feel nearer the time.

Now, you should go, dear. You shouldn't really be shouting into the roof of your car while you're driving. It's a bad old night out there. You need to concentrate." She was brushing me off again.

I didn't have the energy to argue with her. I would have to take it up with her again. I was sure of one thing though. I liked the idea of having both my parents in my apartment.

As I sped towards home, I started to plan the menu. I knew it wasn't going to be a traditional family dinner, but it was the nearest thing I would ever get to it. Maybe I could do a real roast dinner with gravy and stuffing. Just like Emily used to have in her house.

34

Emily

Madwoman's Ratatouille:
*Take one post-operative madwoman. Blend with a wardrobe of clothes.
Decide all the clothes are overcooked. Scrape almost every piece into
black bags.*

I decided to clean out my wardrobe. Spring-clean and remove
outdated/hideous/never worn/too big/too small garments which didn't
pass my "Would I go out in this right now if I had to?" inspection. I
vowed if it didn't make me want to put it on, it would have to be made
to go away.

I was ruthless and merciless, and all sorts of old friends were banished
to a black sack. Destined for a mothball-smelling charity store. After the
pruning was over I put the remaining contestants in order, all skirts
together, all trousers in a row, shirts, jackets etc. I had severe difficulty
in parting with one old friend: my beloved medicine-pink-coloured
velour tracksuit, bought when the Spice Girls were the living end.
Sourced on the Kings Road in London many years ago. It had turned

into a very sad creature in the last five years. Stretched beyond its capacity, leaving it with an elephantine arse and saggy knees, it was not the most delicious outfit in existence, but in fairness it had served me well. It was never meant to be an item of high fashion and beauty. In fact I'd never gone out in public in it. It was purely for wearing in the confines of my own home while relaxing and being a slob. But Robbie took huge offence to it and referred to me as Barbie on Acid when I wore it.

But it had to go. This was a new life, a new me.

Round three of expansion was completed six weeks after surgery. This time I took on serious shape and was instructed to wear non-underwired bras. So I drove myself to Dunmahon shopping centre on the way home and made my way to a large chain store's underwear department.

I longingly passed all the pretty stuff that one actually wants to own, and made my way to the "hideously unattractive" area, with Quasimodo as the mannequin. All the "non-wired" bras were made for naughty people who have sinned against the God of Breasts. They were nasty little strung-up hankies in a box, and I had the enviable task of picking out three. Ooh, it was a tough choice, which one would I go for?

I decided to go for colour, one white, one black and one flesh-coloured. Now, whatever about the white and black ones, the flesh-coloured one was always going to spend its life as a passion killer and was made abysmally sad by the lack of lace, padding and wire. It was lucky my breasts had been removed at this point because I'd say they'd have jumped off and scuttled across the shop making a loud squelchy noise.

I purchased my delicious gear and, feigning an upbeat disposition, made my way as fast as my legs could carry me out of the shop and into the abyss of the shopping centre.

I had an image of a dainty, white, lacy dress I wanted to buy for the summertime, which would have been so handy at that moment in time, in the torrential rain with furry, unwaxed, blue tinged legs.

But the nausea set in. I'd had a slight dose of it the last two times after expansion but this time it was severe. I decided to stop at a chemist and buy another box of soluble painkillers, the amazing ones with codeine and paracetamol in them. I staggered into the nearest coffee shop and grabbed a bottle of water and a paper cup.

Guzzling my bitter, now-familiar foam, I tried to relax and breathe in the codeine. I knew relief would come swiftly, but it could be difficult to avoid clenching the muscles and making the sensation worse.

By this stage of reconstruction my breasts were like two concrete mounds which would withstand the force of a sledgehammer. The buttons, which had firmly lodged themselves in my ribs, were protruding like two plastic ring-pulls on either side. But the stitches were healing well and from the outside I looked totally normal. So that was a positive slant to take. I wasn't finding it easy to remain optimistic at that moment though. In fact I felt sore, miserable and very sorry for myself. My temperature was rocketing but I'd say that was largely due to the panic I was feeling.

I went to a corner of the shopping centre, dropped my bags at my feet and rooted for my mobile phone. I held it to my ear, pretending to have a conversation. This afforded me a right to loiter in the corner, without drawing unwanted attention to myself. Taking deep breaths, I tried to restore a little calm to my harassed system. I was doing quite well when the bloody phone sprang to life and belted into my ear. I must have jumped two foot into the air. It was also apparent to the onlookers that I'd been pretending to talk to someone on the phone. It was Robbie.

"What the hell do you want?" I barked, alarmed and mortified. "You've just made me look like a total moron!"

"Well, hello to you too, darling – yes, I am having a wonderful time today. Thank you for asking, it's great to speak to you too, I'm so glad I phoned."

"Sorry, I'm having a terrible day. My boobs feel like they're going to explode. I'm standing in a corner of a shopping centre. I was pretending to talk on my phone and then you rang and frightened the living daylights out of me . . ." I trailed off, too hassled to go on.

"Okay," said Robbie. "Look, why don't you call me when you're making some sort of sense, and we'll pretend we haven't had any conversation at all, how would that be?" He was gone.

Fuck him anyway. Why did he always have to take offence when I least needed him to? He should try going to hospital and having the muscles in his chest injected with saline and see how he liked it. Feeling sore and utterly miserable I made my way to the car and drove home.

I tried on a bra when I got home and realised I had a new sensation to contend with. The band at the bottom of the bra was in a perfect position to dig into the blasted buttons. So I had this dull, digging sensation where the elastic was straining against the hard plastic with the thin film of skin between the buttons and the bra stretched to capacity. This did not improve my state of mind.

That night I had another night of no sleep at all which was par for the course those days. The only positive thing was that one night in every four I would end up so knackered that I'd be forced to fall into a semi-coma, due to utter exhaustion.

The children were doing quite well. Tia was my little shadow though. She appeared most nights and got into bed with me. She didn't speak or make a big deal of it. She would just appear and I would feel her little arms attaching to my arm.

"My Mummy," was all she'd whisper and promptly fall asleep.

Louis was coping well. I had been making a point of trying to talk to him about how I was feeling. "I'm much better today, Louis. That's good news, isn't it?" I'd wait for him to reply, but these artificial conversations seemed to make him uneasy so I decided it was better to just behave normally. I hoped he would come and talk to me if he needed to.

But Robbie and I were becoming more and more strained. The fun had gone from our relationship. He never smiled any more. He looked like he had the weight of the world on his shoulders all the time.

I tried to broach the subject one night. "Robbie, are you okay?"

"I'm fine, why?" He didn't look at me. In fact, he didn't take his eyes off the television.

"You seem very distant at the moment. Do you want to talk about anything?" I hoped he would sigh and confide in me.

"Everything's fine. Just perfect." He turned the volume up on the TV.

I left the room. What was the point? I didn't have the energy to fight with him. I certainly didn't need him treating me like I'd done something wrong. I was using all my inner strength to fight for my own health and to look after the kids. I just didn't have any reserves to deal with Robbie.

I was due to have the ovaries out three weeks later. In the meantime I went to the hospital for the final breast expansion.

Afterwards I looked bigger than I'd ever been in my life. I felt a bit like Pamela Anderson, but the result was better than I could ever have hoped for. Although they were large, they looked natural and I was sure that no one would ever suspect what I'd been through. The only thing that made my breasts seem fake was the fact that they were absolutely rock hard. I could feel the pressure immediately this time. The stiffness in my muscles was more pronounced also. I thanked the triumphant team of nurses who shared my joy at being finished this leg of the race.

"We have exciting news for you today, Emily." Maureen was smiling at me. "You're allowed to get rid of the Tubigrip bandaging at this point. And there is no need for you to wear the bras any more either."

So the Tubigrip torture and the sensation of having marbles digging into my ribs were things of the past.

Mum was waiting for me when I came out of the clinic.

"You look pleased with yourself, how did you get on?"

We linked arms and walked out to the car park.

"Brilliant. The expansion is over and I'm allowed to remove the dreaded Tubigrip, and to top it all off, I don't have to wear the bras."

"That's great news! Will we go to Dunmahon for a coffee to celebrate?" Mum was always open for a quick shopping fix.

I had a bag full of vouchers which needed spending and was fully intent on doing so. By the time we'd reached the ground floor, the pain was moving across my chest and around to my shoulder blades. I was having darting pains in my breast muscles and my temperature was rising. We made our way to the pharmacy and I quickly downed some painkillers.

Hoping to distract myself, we headed to the first clothes shop. In no time my two shoulders were clamped into my ears and my left arm was cramping down as far as the elbow. The intensity of the pain, especially in my left breast, was agonising. I felt a dull thudding sensation in my temples, my ears were playing a tribal drumming thud, my eyes were dimming in and out of focus and I could feel saliva rushing around my mouth. I felt heat rise from my toes in a flush to whoosh through my cheeks. A hot knife of pain was tearing through my chest. I had to catch my breath to stop my mouth from moaning involuntarily like a wounded animal. I wanted to curl up in a ball on the shiny, cold tiles and groan. Knowing I'd attract a serious amount of attention and possibly get arrested, I decided against this.

"I'm sorry, Mum, but I have to go home. Can you give me the car keys and I'll meet you there when you're finished paying?" I felt awful as Mum's face dropped. The shopping expedition was ruined.

Partly trotting on my tippy-toes, almost dribbling with pain, I made my way to the car park. I managed to open the car door and sit inside. Relief flooded me. I was away from the watchful stare of the public and able to shut my eyes and drink in the pain.

By the time I got back home and into bed I felt utterly seized up. The ache was coming under my armpits from my shoulder blades and over my shoulders, down through the core of my breasts. The left side was considerably worse than the right.

I eased myself into my nest of pillows and tried to relax, closing my eyes and concentrating on breathing. The pain intensified and began to send jolts down my left arm and into my rib cage. Saliva rushed into my mouth and I staggered into the bathroom in time to vomit.

Feeling like a wet rag, I stiffly lowered my body into bed and lay and shifted and lay and shifted, desperate to decipher which position would cause the least pain. If I'd stood on my head it couldn't have been more uncomfortable.

I raided my stash of painkillers and took a cocktail of every sort possible simultaneously, not caring if my liver fell out my arse. In fact, death would have been something less sore to contend with. After about forty minutes I managed to fall asleep. I only knew I'd slept because I woke with a snort of surprise to find two green eyes and a furry stripy face staring into mine.

Rasher was very excited to find a victim to pet him. Forgetting I was having a muscular seizure I swiftly sat up to shoo him off the bed. Dear Lord, the throbbing agony which followed was unnatural. I sounded like a Tourette's Syndrome sufferer. The language which tumbled out of my mouth was astonishing. I actually shocked myself.

Deciding that lying down was a hideous idea, I rose from the ashes and peeled my jeans off. Yes, I'd been in bed in all my clothes – I had managed to take my boots off, but that was it. I donned a soft cotton lounge-about suit, a gift from two gorgeous friends, and hobbled down the stairs like an arthritic puppet. I wandered in and out of all the rooms, put the kettle on and felt knackered.

Louis and Tia arrived home from school. I gave them half an Easter egg each, ushered them out onto the trampoline with the au pair and dragged myself back up the stairs to bed.

That night the clock stopped. Time seemed to stand still. People say a minute can be like an hour, but my God, this was taking the piss. I couldn't bear the TV any longer. I couldn't concentrate on reading a book. I was sick of magazines and their ongoing bullshit of what diet we should all be on, what not to wear, who not to look like, where not to go, what car not to drive, where not to live. If you listened to even half of what they told you, you'd undoubtedly end up in a loony bin.

Eventually, dawn broke. Robbie softly closed the bedroom door and crept down the stairs and straight out the door to work. Soon afterwards my door opened and Louis crept in.

"Mummy, do all families get dead at the same time?" he enquired, wide-eyed and worried.

"No, Louis, they don't. But no one in our family is going to die for a very long time."

Seconds later Tia appeared, her tiny frame hovering by the bed, the back of her hair fluffy, her cheeks flushed, her eyes droopy with sleep.

"Are you allowed to have a hug now, Mummy?" she asked, rubbing her eyes.

I explained it was very early and that we all needed to cuddle up and have a little rest. I lay like a board in the middle, with my two little hot-water bottles either side of me. For about five minutes they were still and silent. That was how long it took them to wake up fully. It was six fourteen. Gradually I felt the electricity flow through them and they began to wriggle and fidget.

"It's very sad that Tia has no willy," Louis sighed.

"No, it's not, I don't want one, they're silly," pouted Tia.

That was it. They taunted each other back and forth, reaching across me to biff each other until I yelled, "That's it! Enough!"

I fumbled for the remote control and turned the TV on. Apart from a gobshite in a raincoat, wearing little round wire glasses speaking German, it was all news and programmes about living on the Aran Islands in the sixties. We settled for cartoons in Irish. They shut up for a minute or so, their brows furrowing until Tia asked what planet the cartoon was from.

"It's Irish," I explained, desperately trying to stay awake.

Good old Murphy's Law – just when I wasn't allowed to sleep any more, my body and brain decided to bugger everything up and try to switch off.

Not too put out by the fact that they couldn't understand a word of the Irish programme, the children lay and let the lilting language flood over them. I woke at seven forty with Maisy standing in the room, nervously saying, "You late, you sleep too much, you need get out of bed, it time for school."

Fuck, fuck, fuck. I jumped out of bed and pushed myself into the shower. My muscles ached, I was dehydrated from all the painkillers and my head was throbbing. I had all the signs of a serious hangover, without having had any of the fun the night before. I managed to beat the children out the door, badly dressed and eating Nutella sandwiches on white bread, while drinking cartons of apple juice. It did occur to me to care, but the thought process stopped there. We arrived at school with two chocolate faces and Tia sucking on a lollipop, again courtesy of Maisy.

Louis bounded into his classroom, dumped his coat on the floor beside the coat rack and immersed himself in a game with two other little boys. Tia was happily sucking the lollipop and skipping beside me like a little fairy, smiling at all passers-by. We reached her classroom door and the bad fairy appeared. She refused at the first fence and dug her heels in at the doorframe. Seeing the tirade about to begin, her teacher came over to scoop her up and take her away.

But Tia was one step ahead of her. She wriggled free and bolted out the front door towards the busy car park. There should have been bionic noises coming from me as I pegged after her. Mastectomies are utterly irrelevant when your five-year-old is heading at full tilt towards oncoming traffic. She was just at that height where she couldn't be seen over a car window either. She was at a perfect stage to be completely flattened.

"Tia, stop! There are cars coming!" I yelled.

Managing to grab her by the arm, I stopped her in time. We had a group of three other mothers in tow. We all came to an abrupt halt. Looking at each other in that knowing way, the others doing the supportive, isn't-she-a-little-monkey-look, me doing the I'm-taking-her-to-the-vet-to-be-put-down look. I started to coax her back towards the door. Pouting and yelling "No" while stamping her foot, she crossed her arms and stood her ground. Against everything I knew I was capable of doing at the time, I picked her up like a spear, head first, kicking legs going through my arms and hitting me in the back every couple of steps. I staggered down the hill to the front door of the school. Her teacher grabbed her like a baton in the relay race and muttered "Run, Emily!"

I did.

By the time I climbed into the car and exhaled, the stabbing pain hit.

I felt like the muscle expanders were going to burst out my sides and explode out the front of my breasts. Touching either side of my breasts, I checked for blood, water or any other substance running down my sides. I was dry and blood free. Okay. Calm down. It was all okay. Take a deep breath. In and out. Easy does it.

My mobile rang ten minutes later. It was Tia's teacher.

"Hi, it's me. Just to let you know she's making a mouse out of a toilet-roll insert, while humming "Twinkle, Twinkle, Little Star". Hope you're okay."

"I'm fine, thank you so much for letting me know."

I was glad she had got over the incident but a part of me wanted to burst in the door of her classroom and shake her until her teeth chattered.

When the children got home from school, we did painting. It meant we could all be calm and stationary and I could join in. Standing at the side of the trampoline was no longer enough for them. They just assumed I didn't want to bounce and this upset them. So I decided to make a conscious effort to do things which I'd be able to join in with better. Highlighting my inabilities at the moment was not the way to keep them calm. So we did lots of creative stuff. I bought little kits for making masks, collages, painting by numbers, paint your own piggy bank. We made little buns and iced them. We beaded jewellery. Well, Louis thought that "sucked" so he didn't join in. But I know that my full participation in any activity was the key to them not noticing I was running on low batteries. This, in turn, stopped the bulk of the questions about families "getting dead" and when did I have to go the hospital again?

As part of my "getting on with things" I had agreed to go to an art exhibition with Laura that evening, but when the time came I just wanted to go to bed and stay there for about two months. Knowing it would make the whole ordeal much easier if I could promise Daddy would be home, I picked up the phone and called Robbie.

"Robbie, can you please try and be home by six thirty tonight? I'm going to this exhibition and it would make life so much easier if you could put them to bed for me."

"No-can-do, Emily. I've two big jobs coming up. Maisy can do it, can't she? That's what she's there for." Robbie was distracted and clipped.

"Yes, Maisy *can* do it. But I'd like you to do it. The children need you around more. You're never here at the moment." I didn't want to always be the bad guy, the one who said the wrong thing. But Robbie was at home less and less.

"Look, Emily, all you do is nag me. Every time you phone me, you either tell me how much pain you're in or give out. It's getting a little boring, to be honest with you."

I was stunned. This was not the man I'd fallen in love with. He had become so hard and negative.

"Robbie, I'm sorry if I say that I'm in pain. But the fact of the matter is that I actually am a lot at the moment."

"And whose fault is that?"

An enormous silence hung in the air between us. I felt like I'd been slapped in the face.

"What's that supposed to mean?" My voice was calm and quiet.

"Look, Emily, you brought this all on yourself. No one told you to go and have all this surgery. Stop trying to blame me and everyone around you for the fact that it's all a lot harder than you'd figured."

"Robbie, I'm hanging up now. I sincerely hope you have a long hard think about what you've just said to me. That is unforgivable and callous and nasty. You know as well as I do that I did this for all our sakes. I'd be a hell of a lot more 'naggy', as you put it, if I had cancer and was undergoing chemotherapy and radium right now. Which, in case you are forgetting, is what would have happened." I slammed the phone down and burst out crying.

Is that what Robbie really felt about the whole issue? Obviously it was. He was angry beyond belief at me for what I'd done. He felt I had brought all the pain on myself. Did he not see my reasons for doing this at all? Why the hell had he not voiced all this properly before now?

I felt hurt and betrayed by his words. He was more and more sullen and spending less and less time with me and the children. I had stupidly put it down to his workload. But it was now obvious he was avoiding me and the "problem" he obviously thought I'd brought on myself.

I spent the day mulling our conversation over and over in my head. What was I going to do? Robbie was always the one I could turn to when I need to talk. I didn't want to tell my parents either. They would worry too much. I didn't want to tell Susie because she'd go mad. She'd phone

Robbie and rip him to shreds. That wouldn't solve anything. Maybe it would all blow over. Then Robbie would be back to the happy-go-lucky man I'd fallen in love with. I didn't want anyone to hate him either. He was usually so kind and loving. This was surely just a glitch.

More for a distraction than anything else, I decided to go out that night as planned. Laura and I were to stare at some art belonging to another friend, followed by a casual bite to eat. I wanted to shower and change and put my face on, all before leaving the house at seven thirty. Maisy had bathed and dressed the kids in their pyjamas, so I just had to usher them up to their bedrooms. By the time I got Louis into his room, brushed his teeth, read him a quick story and left him to read a book for a while, Tia had escaped back downstairs.

She was sitting naked apart from goggles and a snorkel, playing marbles with the cat.

"Please, Tia, Mummy needs to get ready to go out," I implored.

Her little mouth turned into a pout and she began a torrent of reasons as to why I couldn't possibly leave her and go out.

"But, Mummy, we can't go up the stairs ever again, the bears will eat us." She was quite convincing, I have to hand it to her.

"There are no bears, now go upstairs please, Tia," I ordered.

"But the magic green man just jumped out of my ear, and he's running around upstairs putting slime on the carpet. We'll slip on the slime and then we'll get dead," and she nodded earnestly.

"Tia, I'm going to count down from five. If you're not up those stairs by the time I hit one, there'll be big trouble, do you hear?" I tried to look annoyed, which wasn't hard.

She promptly burst out crying. I tried to soothe her while inwardly feeling like yelling, "Just shut up and go to bed for Christ's sake!" Instead I coaxed her up the stairs, found her pyjamas and then we argued about why she couldn't wear those exact ones. We found the pink "Dora the Explorer" ones and she let me put them on.

Eventually I got into the shower and the hot water massaged my tight neck and shoulders. Time didn't afford me much lingering, so I hopped out and proceeded to have a frustrating fracas with my clothes. Everything I owned belonged to the other woman who used to live in them. The new woman who had rock hard, rigid mounds a bra-size bigger, didn't fit in anything. I vowed to go on a shopping trip and buy some Ballet wrap-tops, which would adjust to fit my mountains.

I arrived at the art gallery ten minutes late but Laura wasn't there yet, so I accepted a glass of sparkling water and tried to drum up the interest to look at the pottery and art work. I really didn't give a shit about the clay formations, which if I was honest resembled scrunched turds. But who am I to comment on "art"? My daughter's bedroom is cough-medicine pink with a Disney Princess plastic canopy over it. So I am obviously lacking in the appreciation gene.

While standing and staring into space, quite relaxed in my trancelike state, in fact nearly asleep, I was joined by a loud and brash American woman. She was about forty-ish, with a teased beehive type hairdo. You know the one, puffed up and backcombed and then sprayed within an inch of its life? I actually didn't know there was anyone in existence who could still do this kind of damage to her head. It was dyed that wonderful Tango Man meets a peach, with some random stripes of white throughout. I couldn't be certain but I could swear I saw a squirrel looking out at one stage. Anyway, she was standing and staring at a sculpture of a nondescript blob and raving about its beauty and how wonderfully clever the artist was. I was trying to discreetly slip by her when she turned around and asked if I could possibly hand her a glass of wine. Wondering if I had "waitress" or even "asshole" written on my forehead, I tightly informed her there was a bar just behind her where she could help herself, as I didn't actually work there.

"Oh no, sweetie, you don't understand," she drawled. "I'm not able to reach out, I've just had surgery and I can't stretch much, would you be so kind?"

Not necessarily feeling "so kind" I turned and grabbed a glass of wine and shoved it at her. Hoping that would be the end of our contact, I tried to escape again. But guess what? We were new best friends. Hurray! Thrilling and enthralling, just what I needed. Weak and injured as she was, she was still able to grab the top of my arm in a vicelike grip and in her best little girl, whingey voice tell me all about how much pain she was in and what a terrible trauma she'd been through.

Softening a little, but still really not wanting to get involved with this brash, loud, orange person, I put on my best poor-you face and resigned myself to having to listen to her moaning.

"Victor, my poor husband, has been so supportive over the last month, you know. Surgery is a serious thing for a gal to endure."

I nodded in agreement and made lots of sympathetic grunts when necessary. I knew I had to get away from her ASAP. I know it sounds harsh and all of that, but she just made my skin crawl, I couldn't help it. Nothing she was saying or doing was helping her cause.

"I mean, he told me he would be there for me wholeheartedly from the beginning. He even paid for me to attend the best hospital. But men just don't understand the half of it."

"No, they don't." At least I wasn't lying there.

"But I have tried to cope. I've used up a lot of my inner strength. My back-up reserves are depleting at this stage. I'm close to the edge, you know?" She still had my arm in a dead-man's grip.

"Right. I'm really not the person you should be talking to at the moment –" I tried to get away from her.

"Look, honey, take it from me. Your time will come. You won't be young and pert forever. So don't dismiss some advice from a lady who knows the pitfalls." She glanced around and then muttered from the side of her mouth, "I've had a boob job. They were done six weeks ago, and I know it will all be worth it in the end, but at the moment I am going through hell. It's a cross I have to bear and I know women in general go through a lot of pain during their lives, but this one is different. I wanted them to be more like they were when I was twenty. They now are but I am suffering, darling, suffering!"

She fiddled with her jacket, trying to strain the skimpy fabric across her manmade shelf. She was still wittering on to herself and I only zoned in on her when the babbling stopped. She was looking at me expectantly. Her mouth was shut and there was no more noise, so I supposed she was waiting for an answer. What seemed like an eternity elapsed, with no sound from either of us.

"I asked if you liked the results, and whether you wanted my surgeon's number," she spat huffily. "I'll take it from your silence that you have a problem with my new breasts. Jealousy will get you nowhere, young lady."

Almost afraid to open my mouth in case I lost the run of myself or boxed her in the face, I coughed gently.

"Listen, lady, the result is definitely a personal taste and I won't need the number of your surgeon. Thanks anyway." I smiled fleetingly, rubbing my temples, where a vicious headache was beginning.

"You'll thank me in five years when you are not feeling so smug." She winked and nodded while tapping the side of her nose and smiling at me.

Feeling my blood begin to boil, I tried to steady my temper and resist the urge to damage her. "Each to their own and all of that, but a boob job wouldn't be high on my agenda," I delivered through gritted teeth.

"You don't know until you try, honey. Take it from me, it's a whole new world for you and your body. I thought mine were fine, but they were merely two saggy, poached eggs in a hankie compared to the beauties I've got now. Don't dismiss me right off, I know what's good."

Sweet Divine Land of the Leaping Jaysus, did this woman have a death wish? I felt the colour rise in my body, from my toes through my neck and face and out the top of my head. I wouldn't have been surprised to find steam burns around my ears.

"Look," I seethed in a whisper, "I've just had a double mastectomy and am undergoing reconstruction at the moment. What you choose to do with your body is entirely your own decision. I am thrilled that you are happy with your new bazookas and that they have fulfilled your life in every way. I do however think you should get a grip on yourself and reality, and stop using the fact you chose to have cosmetic surgery as a tool to torture that poor bastard you are married to and everyone else who happens to encounter you. You are not suffering from a debilitating illness, apart from the obvious malfunctions in your brain. Now, please, step away from me before I am forced to deck you one."

Flushed, shaking and feeling like I wanted to die, I gathered myself and just as I was about to steal away, she wrapped herself and her shelf around me – well, as best she could with both our chests in the way.

"Oh my goodness, why didn't you say? We're the same! We've both had breast surgery, how exciting!"

I was abso-fucking-lutly stunned, flabbergasted, astonished, amazed, staggered and astounded. Dear Jesus, this woman was from Planet Zog. I didn't know whether to laugh or cry. How in the name of Jehovah could she possibly equate what I'd been through with what she'd done to her body?

I managed to continue speaking to her without punching her little fat pug face. At the first opportunity, I wriggled free and ran. I made my excuses to the artist and drove home. I rationalised that the lady was a loudmouthed foghorn and to be ignored, but I was upset. In spite of myself, she had bothered me.

As I was approaching home my mobile rang.

"Hey, Em, are you on your way to the exhibition? I'm running a bit late but I'll see you there okay." Laura, I'd forgotten about poor Laura.

"I'm sorry, Laura, I just had a bit of a row with a mad American woman who was trying to convince me to have breast augmentation and had to flee the scene. I'm on my way home. Can we meet up another night instead?"

"No probs. Did she upset you? Would you like me to mess with her karma?" Laura was her usual upbeat and uncomplicated self.

I was relieved she wasn't one of those people who became mortally wounded if you broke a date.

"Give me a buzz when you're feeling better. Are you all right?" She sounded genuinely concerned.

"Not a bother, darling. Thanks anyway, I'm being silly really. I think I'm just tired, I haven't been sleeping well and I think the mad old bat just tipped the scales. You know yourself?" I felt awful to stand her up, but I knew she would go along anyway and probably end up in the pub until closing time with a group of people she'd never met before.

35

Susie

Seminar Soup:
Take one frazzled psychologist, sweat gently and pour into an uncomfortable business suit. Place in a stuffy room and leave to ferment. Add a little sprinkling of magic. Feel the heat rise.

From time to time, I had to leave my practice and go to seminars. Most of them were a load of horseshit and not worth the money it cost to pay for flights and hotels and other expenses. But there was a really interesting one in Munich which I was hoping was going to be of some benefit.

The lecturer had published many books on addiction and I was looking forward to meeting him. On the way to the airport, I phoned Mum.

"Hi, Mum, I'm just reminding you that I'm off to Munich for the next couple of days. The management company for my apartment has your number, so don't be worried if they phone you and say my alarm is going off."

"Oh, yes, that's fine, love."

"Mum, you won't forget the dinner at my place at the weekend, will you?"

"No, Susie, I won't forget. I'm not really looking forward to it though. I know you want me to meet Jim and his partner but I'm really not sure I know what it's going to achieve."

"Look, we're not going to figure out a cure for cancer or plan world peace, but it might be enjoyable and who knows, maybe you'll even get on well?"

"Right, I suppose so, Susie. If you think so." Mum sounded like she was already thinking about something else. She had her distracted I'm-not-listening-to-you voice on.

"Bye, Mum. I'll talk to you when I get back from Germany."

The following morning I got up at six thirty and went for a quick swim in the hotel leisure centre. The pool was quite crowded with other likeminded people, so I did a few lengths and got out.

By the time I'd finished breakfast in my room and dressed in a trouser suit, it was time to go to the conference room. Taking my printed name badge, I found a seat about a third of the way down the room. I wasn't there long before I was joined by tall, well-built man. I assumed he was either French or German. His hair and skin were dark and his tousled Hugh Grant type hair made him look foreign. He nodded at me and sat down.

He was a big man. His legs only barely fitted under the desk in front of him. He wasn't fat – just a large man, broad and imposing.

After he'd taken some paper and pens out of his brief-case, he turned and offered me his hand.

"Hi, I'm Walter Blake," he said.

I was surprised to realise he was in fact Irish.

"I'm Susie Rosedale, pleased to meet you." I found myself looking at his left hand and promptly blushing. What the hell was wrong with me? Looking for wedding rings. Jesus, was I going insane?

I was aware of his presence the whole way through the seminar. Every time he moved his arm or wrote something down, I noticed. I actually found it difficult to concentrate on what the lecturer was saying. Wafts of spicy aftershave came my way every now and then. I found myself discreetly trying to make sure I wasn't creasing my suit too much or breaking into a sweat.

When the lecture stopped for lunch, we were all herded into the large dining room. As it was designated seating, I waved to him and agreed I'd see him afterwards.

I was disappointed I couldn't sit beside him, although I probably wouldn't be able to eat any lunch if I knew he was watching me. This was crazy! I had only just met the man, he was probably either married or gay or both. In fact, there was no way in hell a man that attractive could be single, and even if he was he probably wouldn't have any interest in me.

I spent the lunch trying to coax conversation out of an elderly German doctor who was very pleasant, but after Walter Blake he was a poor second. I was delighted when the meal finished and we were all ushered back for the second half of the lecture.

Walter was already sitting down when I found my seat. He had to stand up and move to the side to allow me pass.

"Sorry for disturbing you," I apologised, suddenly very aware of the size of my arse as I pushed past him.

He leaned over and confided, "Believe me, Susie, you can disturb me anytime. I've just spent that lunch with a Frenchwoman who has a serious problem with men. I'm relieved to get away from her and back beside someone normal."

I was surprised at how happy I felt that he liked sitting beside me. It brought me back to school and being allowed to sit beside the popular girl. I had never been the one people wanted to sit next to. I found the present situation stupidly thrilling. Before we could chat any further, the lecturer took the podium and we had to concentrate.

By six o'clock, the seminar finally wrapped up.

I stretched my legs and yawned.

"Jesus, that was heavy going, wasn't it?" I said.

"Yeah, they certainly don't go in for tea breaks every two hours, do they?" he agreed.

"It was good though," I said. "There are a lot of ideas that will work very well for me with some patients in particular."

"Where are you based?" he asked.

"I have a room in the Rochestown Clinic."

"Wow!" Walter whistled. "I'm impressed. You must be the youngest specialist by ten years in that place. I'd say they were all delighted to see such an attractive young woman walk through the doors when you arrived."

Normally a comment like that would get my back up and make me snap a nasty response, but somehow I didn't feel Walter was being condescending or sexist.

There was an announcement that dinner would commence in less than an hour.

"They don't do things by halves here, do they?" I said. As usual with the German organisers, every detail was covered and the entire seminar was timed with precision. "I'd better go and freshen up. I might see you during dinner?"

"Sure thing," he replied.

As I showered, I wished I'd brought something a little more glamorous than the black wrap dress and simple heels. I applied my make-up carefully and took extra care with drying my hair. A long time ago I'd realised that these seminars were usually male-dominated and I hated the idea of men looking down my top, rather than treating me like an equal. Hence the conservative dress for this evening.

As I sat at the table for dinner, Walter approached and sat beside me.

"We meet again, Ms Rosedale." He took my hand and kissed it.

We chatted easily for the whole meal. He was based just outside Dublin and had some really good ideas. I thoroughly enjoyed chatting to him and found myself laughing and relaxed, something that never usually happened at a work thing.

After dinner we moved into the bar and continued our conversation over a drink or two. When I glanced at my watch I was astonished to see it was almost midnight. I didn't want the day to end, but at the same time I wasn't going to sit in the bar until four in the morning with him. It just wouldn't be the right thing to do, in my book. I had a professional demeanour to maintain after all.

Pushing my chair back, I could see he was surprised I was leaving.

"I have an early flight in the morning and a full clinic tomorrow afternoon, so I'm going to hit the sack. It was a pleasure to meet you, Dr Blake." I held out my hand and smiled.

He rose to his feet and took my hand, then leaned forward and kissed me on the cheek.

"May I call you when I return to Dublin, Ms Rosedale?" he whispered in my ear. I was delighted that he had to bend down to speak to me. Most men had to lean their heads up to talk to me. "I think I might have started to suffer from an addiction myself – do you think you can help me out?" He was grinning.

"I think I can manage to fit you in, yes." I looked him in the eye and remained serious. I fished in my handbag and gave him one of my business cards.

Spinning on my Gucci heel, I sauntered away, wishing I'd spent a little more time in the gym last night. *Keep it together, Susie, pretend you love your arse. It's probably not as big as you think.*

I went to bed thinking about Walter Blake and imagining his strong arms wrapped around me. I found myself hoping he'd call me.

I had a full clinic waiting for me on my return, so I didn't have much time that day to think about whether I would see Walter again. I had a late appointment at six o'clock, which went on until after seven.

Just as I was logging off my computer, my secretary buzzed me.

"That's a Dr Walter Blake on line one. Will I tell him you've already left or do you want to take it?"

"No, that's fine, thanks, you can put him through."

Making sure the call was actually on hold, I balled my fists and punched the air squealing like a teenager. Panting quickly to steady my voice, I closed my eyes and sat bolt upright. Of course my posture would have a huge impact on our conversation – not.

"Dr Blake? What can I do for you?" I tried to sound formal.

"Ah, good evening, Ms Rosedale. I was hoping I might catch you. I was wondering if I could make an appointment with you? Say, tomorrow night at eight o'clock in Lorenzo's on Baggot Street?"

"I reckon I can fit you in, that sounds fine. I'll see you there." I hung up the phone and squealed again, jumping in the air and clapping.

I glanced at my watch and had a sudden urge to go to Dunmahon shopping centre and buy something new to wear.

Within half an hour, I was trying on clothes. I settled on a pair of heavy linen trousers and a turquoise bustier with a little bolero cardigan to match. I knew the vibrant colour was good with my auburn hair. The outfit was understated and yet had enough glamour to make me feel dressed up. I reckoned it was what the fashionistas would call a classic outfit.

Skipping home, I jumped into the shower, scrubbed my skin and applied a quick layer of fake tan. My sallow skin only needed a couple of weeks of sitting on my balcony to turn a golden colour, but as it was only May I needed a little help.

I decided not to tell Mum or Emily about my impending date. It was so long since I'd dated anyone, I was worried they'd get carried away. Mum would, no doubt, get out her wedding scrapbook. It contained everything from cut-outs of flower arrangements to table settings and of course, page after page of wedding dresses. She'd had no reason to inflict it on me for quite a while, and I knew she'd use any excuse at all to produce it.

Emily would be very excited for me, but I just wasn't ready to spill the beans yet.

I had the "family dinner" on Saturday night too, so I didn't want to have to discuss it with everybody then. I wanted the focal point to be on all of us meeting and trying to get to know each other. Knowing Mum, she'd hone in on the whole date issue and bring her blessed scrapbook along and harp on about weddings for the night. That would make me tense and annoyed and I'd end up wanting to kill her – again. No, it was best to keep my little date to myself for the moment.

36

Emily

Trying to Follow a Recipe Book:
Using the internet, look up far too much about surgical procedures which usually take years of training to understand. Convince yourself after several hours of surfing you are now practically qualified. Add a pompous surgeon and feel yourself being stripped back to an uncomfortably vulnerable state. Serve with confusion, mild upset and general feeling of personal attack.

My oophorectomy was coming up. I was starting the countdown to my next surgery and next milestone. After searching through Google for many hours, meandering from website to website, I had come to the conclusion that I should possibly have a full hysterectomy. I was going halfway there, having the ovaries and fallopian tubes removed. The womb would be left on its tod wondering where its friends had gone.

From what I'd read, there could be some problems stemming from this. Fibroids very often occurred. Prolapsing is another delight. When at rest (as in not full of babies, fibroids or any other such delicious stuff) the womb is the size of a small pear. Allegedly.

They can blast the ovaries and fallopian tubes with a laser and suction them out with a medical type Hoover thingy. So I reckoned while they were at it maybe they could loosen the womb and remove it by suction vaginally too. I knew it could be done as I'd read about it on the internet. So of course it had to be possible if the internet said so, hadn't it?

I was supposed to have a conference call with my surgeon the next day to discuss this. I was to compile a list of "relevant questions". In other words I couldn't ask: "Can you do liposuction on my stomach and thighs while you're at it?" or "Can I stay in hospital in a private room for two months after the operation with a TV and regular supply of magazines and chocolate?" or "Can you write to my husband and tell him I am very lucky to be alive and that he's to remember this every day of our lives?"

I had decided to get Robbie to take the kids to school that morning, because it would be just my luck if she phoned when we were in the car on the way to school. Louis would have instinctively known and started shouting about bums, willies, poo and all his other favourite subjects. He would have taken the opportunity to ask her what colour blood a beetle had or what Martians eat for lunch on the moon. It would have been too messy.

I woke early the next morning and showered and dressed, ready to face the day and ready should the phone ring. Robbie took the children to school, which delighted them both.

"We're going in Daddy's car, so we can have really, really loud music and drive so fast!" Louis was thrilled.

"Please don't drive like a maniac, Robbie. Make sure you bring them into the classroom too. Don't leave them on the side of the road outside the school gate like last year."

Robbie smiled and kissed me briefly before leaving. He was still in very quiet form. Every now and again, just like then, I would see the faint hint of the man I knew. After a lot of soul-searching, I figured it was probably safer to try and jolly him along rather than pin him against the wall and make him talk about how he was feeling.

I had invited some friends to lunch, so I busied myself with preparing that.

At eight thirty the phone rang. It was the secretary to tell me she was waiting for Ms Mulcahy to come in to make the call.

The morning passed and the phone remained silent. It reminded me of waiting for a guy to ring when I was a teenager. Just like most of the guys I'd met before, this lady didn't call either. The secretary raised my hopes by calling.

"I'm sorry, Emily but she's been called into surgery and she'll try to call at twelve o'clock. Will you still be able to take the call at that time?"

"It'll be just bang on the time my friends are supposed to arrive for lunch, but I can go into another room," I assured her.

As they trickled through the door shortly afterwards, I explained I might have to leave the room for a few minutes if Ms Mulcahy called. They all had a glass of wine. I abstained, thinking it might be better to be sober while speaking to her, just in case I agreed to have a limb removed as well.

The wine early in the day took its toll on my friends and we got incredibly giddy. They suggested putting the phone on speaker and leaving it in the middle of the table, so we could all ask questions. Like did she do group rates for those of us who were finished with our bits? I was glad she didn't phone at that stage.

By school collection time, we all piled out the door and after a chorus of beeping and frantic waving we trundled off to collect our offspring. When we met in the school, the ten-minute car journey had done nothing to make any of us any more sensible. When the children came out the doors of their classrooms, we were all a mess. The look of disgust on the children's faces was fuel to our madness. The kids all started inching away from us, while looking out their eyelashes in revulsion. For me, it was the first time Louis had ever been totally and utterly embarrassed to be near me. If he could have jumped into his school bag to get away from me, he would have.

"What's wrong with you?" he muttered as if talking to a deranged slug.

"I'm just in a happy and giddy mood, having fun with my friends, isn't that good?" I beamed.

"You're too old to have friends, and you shouldn't do giggling when you're a grown up," he sighed.

Knowing I'd finally hit the point where I was an embarrassment to my children was a poignant and satisfying moment. The amount of times I'd found my own parents mortifying as a child was countless. I knew this was the first of many of these moments for Louis. He just wanted a Jedi knight to swoop down and obliterate me and my friends, and stop us behaving in this offensive and disgustingly happy way. Mums were not supposed to have this much fun, and if they did, it was supposed to be done quietly without drawing any attention to themselves. Or preferably when he wasn't around at all. With his head bent low, to avoid eye contact with anyone else, he forged ahead and stood waiting unhappily at the car. I noticed a few other kids doing the same thing. I pointed it out to two other mothers, and of course this set us off again.

I finally had my conference call with the gynaecological surgeon. She was pompous, superior and aggressively argumentative.

I was back to the usual behaviour of consultants. I'd become so spoilt by the relaxed and informative attitude of Mr Green. He was a normal individual who was capable of having real conversations. He was even of the belief that patients were human beings with a brain. That they are competent and in control of their faculties and able to discuss their procedures.

This wench, on the other hand, was condescending, aloof and in spite of her qualifications and medical background, kept her head firmly up her arse. Unfortunate, for both herself and anyone who had to be in contact with her. Sure, she knew what she was doing, she wouldn't be there if she didn't. But, like a foreigner on the news, she needed a translator. She needed to have a PR person who could speak to patients while she sat and spouted.

Her opening line to me was a sarcastic: "So you want a hysterectomy, do you?"

"No woman in her right mind *wants* a hysterectomy," I retorted in the most controlled manner possible. "I merely wanted to ask you if there would be any advantage to having it done along with the ovaries and fallopian tubes."

"No. No advantage. The recovery would quadruple. I do not recommend this surgery."

"Perfect," I clipped. "That was all I wanted to know, thanks for that." Before I could say another word, she had hung up.

After I'd calmed down and finished pacing up and down the house clenching my fists in frustration, I was rational enough to be glad I was only having minor surgery and the attack on my body was going to be minimal. Especially when I had another breast operation in five months' time – my exchange surgery, when they would remove the muscle expanders and replace them with implants.

It galled me so much to be made to feel I was almost a hypochondriac who was bored and sitting around, drinking tea and dipping chocolate digestives into my blue and white stripy mug, deviously planning which bit of my body I could have removed next. Did this self-important, arrogant, offensive cow not realise that all I wanted was to protect myself and my family from having to repeat history? I felt it was very unfortunate that she had to be the one to operate on me at all. I just found solace in the fact that I'd hopefully be unconscious next time we met. Knowing she was meant to be one of the top surgeons in Europe wore a little thin when she was so revolting to deal with. I just hoped the cantankerous old goat was as good as her reputation.

The time for the children to get summer holidays was drawing closer. They were crotchety and tetchy. They were tired and ready for their holidays. I had hoped to have the oophorectomy over with before they were around full time. That wasn't going to happen. The hospital bed crisis was at its height. *Prime Time* was dedicating full programmes to the plight of gravely ill patients on trolleys in hallways. The beds were just not available. I was at the mercy of the sinking system.

37

Susie

Lurve Potion:
Allow yourself to open your heart, just a little. Try to swallow the fact that you might be feeling a wee flutter. Bake in a case of new clothes and a positive inner feeling. Serve with delicious wine.

For the first time ever, I was wishing my day away in work. My job had always been the first and last waking thought in my life. I took it seriously but I also loved it. It was my provider but in a lot of ways it was my family too.

On Thursday, however, all I wanted was to get home and change into my new outfit and try to make myself look presentable for meeting Walter.

Willing all the traffic to hurry up, I drummed my nails on the steering wheel.

"Come on, come on," I muttered. "Got people to see and places to go!"

I felt like a small child at Christmas, as I skipped out of the lift and negotiated the door of my apartment.

When I'd finished applying the last of my eye make-up, I stood in front of my full-length mirror and surveyed the result. I couldn't decide if I liked the look or not. I ran out of time and, hoping to God I didn't look like a colour-blind giraffe, I had to leave.

I'd ordered a taxi so I could have a couple of glasses of wine. I needed a bit of Dutch courage to help me along. When I walked in the door of the restaurant, I spotted Walter immediately.

He approached and kissed me on both cheeks.

"God, you look great," he said, nodding in approval.

"Not like a colour-blind giraffe?" I asked, cringing slightly.

"Not what would have sprung to mind, no."

He led me to a table. Shortly afterwards a waiter arrived with a bottle of champagne.

"Is this okay with you?" Walter asked.

"Oh, I'll suffer along," I smiled. "I'm impressed, Dr Blake."

"Well, I kind of felt you needed impressing, you and your rooms in the Rochestown Clinic and all that," he teased back.

"Cheers!" we clinked glasses.

The evening passed with alarming speed. He made me laugh and we jumped from one subject to another, from décor to psychology and back again.

"I've really enjoyed seeing you again. You're a lot less scary than the last time I met you," he confided.

"What do you mean? I'm not scary!" I laughed.

"Oh yes, you bloody are. It took a lot of courage to muster up the gumption to speak to you the first time. I was glad we had to sit through that seminar. It took me the full day to be able to approach you that evening."

"Well, I'm sorry if I appeared rude." I wasn't quite sure where this was going.

"No, you weren't rude, quite the opposite. You were quietly, confidently polite. When you told me about your practice, I was a bit bowled over. Beauty and brains to match. If I'm honest, I was trying to see if you were married. I couldn't believe my luck when I realised you were single." He searched my face for some inclination I might be interested.

"Well, I'm sorry for scaring you. I suppose I'm not mad about those conferences and I usually tend to keep myself to myself. I nearly always get stuck with some old goat who wants to tell me how little women know and blow his own trumpet. I suppose I just kind of switch off automatically. To be honest, I tried to switch off this time, but I was too aware that you were sitting beside me."

"I know it's early days but I have a good feeling about this, Ms Rosedale," he said, taking my hand.

"Me too," I answered.

We finished our wine and decided to move on to a local bar for last drinks. I changed to water, knowing I had to be on the ball for my patients the next day. I was relieved to see that Walter was happy to do the same. We chatted openly and I even told him about finding Jim recently.

"That must have laid a lot of ghosts to rest for you," he said.

"Yes, it's all kind of coming together. I need to get through this dinner on Saturday night and I'll at least be able to relax in the knowledge that Mum and Jim have finally faced each other after so many years." It felt so good to be able to talk about it all with someone who didn't want to judge me or my unusual situation. It felt like we'd only been talking for five minutes when I realised it was one in the morning.

"I'm sorry, I'd really love to stay, but it's a school night, you know yourself. It's not great to have an appointment with your psychologist and have her asleep face down on the table while you spill your heart out!" I reluctantly began to put my coat on.

"I understand. I'm in the hospital tomorrow all day so I need to be clear-headed myself. Can I see you again?" His voice sounded calm but his eyes had taken on a definite urgency.

"I'd really like that." I felt my heart flip. It actually did a flip!

I never, ever believed in my cynical head that falling in love could actually feel this good. Whether I liked it or not, I was falling in love with Dr Walter Blake. Judging from the impish grin on his face as he put his strong arms around me and kissed me slowly, I kind of thought he might be feeling the same way.

38

Susie

An Alternative Dinner Party:
*In a small apartment, mix one daughter, two shag buddies from the
past, one gay partner and a struggling married couple. Pray to God
everyone behaves. This recipe is not for the faint-hearted.*

On the morning of the dinner party, I buzzed around my compact
apartment and sprayed polish on whatever I could. I added a new
air freshener to the bathroom and cleaned the loo, sink and shower. Not
that anyone would be sniffing around in the shower, but you know
yourself, the paranoia kind of takes over.

By two o'clock, there was nothing left to clean. I walked around to
the local Spar and bought some fresh bread and some chocolates to go
with the coffee after dinner.

The caterer came at four and delivered the food, wine and mineral
water.

"Would you like me to set the table while I'm here? It won't take me
a minute?" she asked.

"Well, if you don't mind, that would be great. I'm not the most creative person and it'll probably take me two hours and it'll still look a mess."

Within minutes she had transformed my kitchen table into a beautiful dining area. The flowers arrived and she put the finishing touches to the table. She even snipped the head off one of my lilies and placed it in a tiny dish in the bathroom, along with some tea lights. It all looked gorgeous.

"Thank you so much, that's beautiful. All I need now is for my mum and dad and my dad's boyfriend to arrive." I was smiling at the table delightedly when I realised the poor girl was in shock. "Oh feck, sorry! My parents aren't together – my mother knows my father is gay. It's a long story."

I knew she just wanted me to pay her and let her get the hell out of my air space, so she could text all her friends and tell them how insane I was.

As I shut the door on her retreating back, I got a fit of the giggles. She might have jumped out the window if I'd told her my parents didn't actually know each other, apart from a shag on the frozen peas.

Emily and Robbie arrived first, which was not surprising as I'd told her if she wasn't there half an hour before everyone else I'd never speak to her again.

Next came Jim and Jean. They were both immaculately dressed and they brought a bottle of vintage Moët champagne and a beautiful floral sculpture in its own vase.

"I hate being handed bags of flowers, with all that crunchy cellophane and water and sachets when I'm trying to organise drinks. At least you can just dump this anywhere and the work is done," Jean said and kissed me dramatically.

"This is my best friend, Emily, and her husband, Robbie. Em and Robbie, I'm delighted to introduce you to Jim and Jean."

There was a lot of shaking hands and air-kissing, with Robbie sticking firmly to the handshaking, I noticed.

Just as everyone was finishing their first glass of wine, the buzzer went and I was glad to see Mum had arrived.

"I was beginning to think you weren't coming," I hissed.

"I wasn't. Well, I was, then I decided against it. I had taken my coat off and then I knew you'd be so cross with me so I made myself come. Are they here then? Jim and his fancy man?" She peered down the tiny hallway.

"Mum, it might be a good idea not to refer to Jean as a fancy man," I whispered. "They're also only gay – they're not deaf as well and I don't live in a palace with a west wing. Keep your voice down!"

Emily appeared from the living room and made a big fuss of Mum.

"There you are, Pauline! How are you, sweetie? You look lovely as usual, come on in and have a glass of wine!" She grabbed Mum and dragged her inside before she could blink.

"Hello, Pauline. How nice to see you again. Gosh, you look exactly the same, how are you?" Jim stepped forward and held his hand out for Mum to take.

Mum looked him up and down. "Hello, Jim. I'm well, thanks. You look great. You've grown into yourself, do you know that? You were a bit kooky when you were younger."

Oh fucking hell, I could feel the sweat starting to pour down my back. Why the hell did Mum always have to say the wrong thing to people? Why couldn't she just say hello like any normal person?

Jim tossed his head back and laughed. "Do you know what? You're dead right. I was an awful awkward-looking geek when I was younger. It's all the gangly arms and legs – they're made for an older man – it's taken me a while to grow into them. This is my partner, Jean." He stood aside and allowed Jean to shake hands with Mum.

"I, on the other hand, was given small arms and legs which fitted quite well when I was younger but have become sadly shorter and squidgier over the years," Jean joked.

The conversation and the wine flowed. The atmosphere in the room was thankfully light and easy. By the time we sat down for dinner, everybody was relaxed and a bit tipsy.

The food was delicious and I could have easily taken the credit for it all, except for the fact that Jean asked me what the secret ingredient was in the Boeuf Bourguignon.

"If I hadn't drunk five glasses of wine, I'm sure I'd be able to make something up, but I'm too pissed to think of a lie. Sorry, Jean, I actually used a caterer."

I laughed and so did everyone except Mum.

"Susie, how much did that set you back? My goodness, it wasn't caterers and fine wine you were reared on!" She rolled her eyes up to heaven.

Everyone laughed, but I felt like boxing her.

As I was serving the dessert, which was a meringue roulade, I decided it might be nice to open the bottle of champagne Jim and Jean had brought.

I popped the cork and, when we all had a glass, I made a small toast.

"Here's to the future and all the happiness I hope it may bring!"

"To the future!" they all chimed in.

I heard my mobile phone beeping in the bedroom so I excused myself and went to check who was texting me.

Hope ur night is going well. Hope ur parents r behaving themselves. Can we meet tomorrow? U can fill me in & also I really want to c u x x W

I immediately texted him back.

So far so good. Luv 2 c u 2moro. Meet u in Bewleys 4 breakfast @ 10.30? C u then x x Suze

I wandered back to the living room and got caught by Emily.

"What are you up to? You look like the cat that got the cream? Anything you'd like to share with me?"

"Come over here!" I grabbed her arm and dragged her into the hall. "Don't scream or draw attention to us. I've met a man."

I had to hold my hand over Emily's mouth.

"Where? When? Do I know him?" she cried when I released her.

"I met him at the conference last week in Munich. He's a psychotherapist too, his name is Walter Blake. We've had one date and it went really well."

"Have you shagged him?"

"No, we were in a bloody restaurant in Baggot Street. Give me a chance!" I laughed.

"But you want to, don't you? I can see it in your eyes!" She was quite drunk and giddy.

"Emily, you are behaving like a child. All in good time. At the moment, we are getting to know each other. But, if you must know, if I have my way it won't take too long!"

We both cackled like witches.

Realising it looked bad, we rejoined the others in the living room. Mum and Jean were chatting like two old women on the sofa.

"Looks like those two have hit it off," I said to Jim.

"They're talking about weddings," Jim raised his eyes to heaven.

"Oh Jesus, no! I can tell her to stop if you like?"

"Listen, Jean would probably still be sitting there looking as animated as she is this time next week, if he had his way," Jim smiled. "He's obsessed with weddings and organising them. In fact, he's been thinking about taking a redundancy package in work and setting up a wedding planner's service. So if he can find someone else who is as interested in talking about it, that suits me fine. I'm all wedding-ed out at this stage, and I've never even had one!"

"My God, I don't believe it!" said Emily. "Pauline has found a soul mate at last and he's the gay boyfriend of her ex-shag!"

I laughed heartily. But, yes, it was amazing.

By the time Jim and Jean decided to leave it was two thirty in the morning. Emily and Robbie had left an hour earlier.

"I wish you'd taken me up on the offer of a room for the night. It seems such a waste of money for you to stay in a hotel," I said.

"Next time, we'll definitely stay. We thought it would be better the first time to leave the option open in case it all went horribly wrong and we had to make an excuse and leave at nine thirty," Jim confided.

"Fair enough. I would have done the same thing myself," I agreed. "Mum, you're staying, aren't you?"

"Yes, dear. That would be lovely. Although I'll have to open the windows if you don't mind. I find this place very hot and dry. I don't know how you stick the heat in here." She swatted her face with her hands.

"That's just because I have a thing called central heating and my bedrooms aren't crumbling with damp," I teased.

We all hugged and kissed in the hallway and vowed to meet up again soon. As I shut the door, I felt an overwhelming sense of relief and inner calm. The evening couldn't have gone better. I was delighted Mum had relaxed and the fact she'd found a fellow wedding enthusiast in Jean was an extraordinary bonus.

"Emily and Robbie were kind of quiet, weren't they?" I said as I filled us each a glass of water to take to bed.

"I thought they were fine," said Mum. "He's a great fellow, Robbie. Chats away. Emily is fantastic as usual. You'd never know she was going through any trauma. Although she's surprisingly open about it. She didn't seem to mind Jim asking her questions about her surgery. Well able to chat about it all, isn't she?"

"Yes, well, she did decide right from the beginning she didn't want it all to be a taboo subject. She's right too. It would eat her up if she had to internalise it all. It wouldn't be healthy for her." I yawned and scratched my head.

As I fell into bed, I looked at the text message Walter had sent me. I was really excited about meeting him in the morning. I was pleased with my night too. I fell asleep almost immediately. If I did dream that night, I don't remember. All I know is that I slept more soundly than I had in years.

39

Emily

Au Revoir Ovary Pie:
Mix a large dollop of pink with a carefully selected group of girls. Add alcohol, good food and several pounds of slurred advice. Cover entire pie with more pink and fluffy stuff. Revel in the knowledge that friends are sublime. Taste the sweetness that togetherness brings.

Whoever invented school holidays should have been shot at birth. He or she certainly didn't have kids, that's for sure. With the long summer days a chorus of "I'm bored," "Where are we going today?", "Who's coming to play?" and all the usual moaning that children who are five and six come out with ensued. Although I was utterly blessed to have the support and back-up of an au pair, it was still tough.

Quite unexpectedly I received a call from the hospital to say they had a bed for me the following week for the ovary removal surgery. We had a holiday in the country booked for two weeks at the end of July, and it now looked like I'd be operated on before then. Things were starting to fall into place. I felt that after a spell of stagnant and frozen

293

time the hands of the clock were rustily beginning to tick around again.

I hadn't realised how much I'd been mentally holding my breath until the date was announced. I felt an enormous sense of relief both mentally and physically.

I organised a "girls' dinner" at my house on the Friday night before the ovary operation. A hen night for my ovaries, as such. Nine close friends were invited. I dug out my box of decorations and strung pink heart-shaped, fluffy lights all around the kitchen and living room. I bought candy-pink tablemats and rose-tinted wineglasses.

It was my husband's idea of a nightmare realised. Being a minimalist and an avid hater of the colour pink, it was as effective as garlic to a vampire in keeping him out of the way. The added terrible thought of having a house full of gaggling and gossiping women was enough to send him off to find his own entertainment for the night.

By nine thirty and several bottles of pink bubbly later, we were pretty loud and raucous. There were ten conversations going on at once, each lady determined to get her story out. One particularly curious friend who was intent on getting the full low-down on my breast operation, begged me to show her my scars. Not wanting to put everyone off their food, I told her I'd show her another time when there were fewer people there to be freaked out. That was met with a chorus of reassurances that no one would be in the slightest bit bothered by the look of the scars – in fact they'd been dying to see them since the surgery.

Fuelled by the wine and bubbly, I decided to show them. I hadn't noticed one of my friends who was sitting at the opposite end of the table to me. She was apparently rooted to the spot when I was encouraged to show and tell. Being very squeamish, it was her idea of living hell. But she didn't have to guts to say so. Intending to leave the room quietly, she found her limbs didn't work quickly enough. We all knew of old that if any of the "having babies" stories began, Tamara would either have to stick her fingers in her ears or leave until we'd finished. On this occasion she felt no different but she became paralysed by fear. She didn't make it out of the room.

As I lifted my top to show the girls a side-profile of my new boobs, we heard a thump as Tamara's head hit the table with a bang.

"Tamara!"

We raised her head from the table but she was out cold.

"Think quickly," I said. "What are you supposed to do with someone who faints?" I felt quite stricken, although rather pissed from all the wine at the same time.

We decided to shake her. Her floppy head lunged backwards and forwards dangerously. Her head looked like it was going to fall off her neck.

"I think we should stop doing that, we're going to give her whiplash!"

Slowly, Tamara began to come to, moaning and groaning. "Where am I? What happened?" she looked around, genuinely confused.

"Emily flashed at you, and you conked out," said Susie.

"Oh God, Emily, I'm so sorry, I didn't mean to offend you. I feel very sick." She really didn't look well.

"Pour her a big glass of red wine there and we'll get her to drink that," I said to the others. "It's full of iron and the alcohol would be good for her too."

So we more or less force-fed her the glass of wine.

Astonishingly, she perked up after that.

"Oh God, I'm so sorry, Emily. I can't believe I did that." She kept apologising for fainting at the sight of my boobs.

"I'm highly insulted," I teased her. "You'll be laughing on the other side of your face in thirty years' time. I will be reeling at the sight of your boobs, drooping down past your knees. You'll be able to lift your skirt to show me yours by that stage, and mine will still be pert and happy looking. We'll see who faints then!"

The incident didn't dampen our style that night. In fact, I think it added to the fun. We all agreed it was the best reaction I was ever likely to get and that I ought to be rather proud of it. I knew I would be able to use it against Tamara for a very long time to come.

40

Emily

A Second Helping of Pain Relief:

Drag now well-versed woman into surgery. Gouge out ovaries and fallopian tubes. Leave in violent pain with brain-dead moron.

The alarm sounded at 6.30 a.m. I dragged myself out of bed with a feeling of butterflies in the bottom of my tummy. The sensation could have been attributed to a birthday, going on holiday or a fun day ahead. Quickly I remembered I was going to hospital.

I'd had to shower the night before and fast from midnight. Robbie laboriously chewed through a bowl of muesli as I tried to look out the kitchen window and think of nothing at all.

The house was in a rare state of silence. No little people to bounce noise and energy from its walls.

"Looks like it's going to be a better day weather-wise." Robbie was chatting as if it was lunchtime.

I urged him to speak quietly so as not to wake the children. I hadn't told them where I was going. The operation was being treated as a one-day case. I would come home that night, if all went to plan. As I was only staying in for one day, I thought it better to say I was going to work and would see them later.

Tia and Louis were going to my parents for a sleepover that night, so they were fully focused on that. All the same, I didn't want to meet them on the way out the door. They would sense there was something happening and I hated that feeling of leaving them behind.

Robbie was still talking at full volume and thumping around the house.

"Why do you feel the need to shout? I'm sitting right beside you, keep your voice down. I'll be in a right pickle if you wake the children," I hissed.

"Calm down, I'm only trying to make conversation with you. Jesus, you can be a cranky cow at times." He chomped on his cereal, savouring each bite.

"Shut your pie-hole, Robbie, and stop eating like a warthog. Talk about rubbing it in that I'm not allowed to eat!"

He looked at his spoon and bowl of food in confusion. Then looked back at me.

"What the hell do you want me to do? Starve just because you're fasting?" He looked astonished and outraged.

"Yes, I do want you to starve too, if the truth be known. You can go to the coffee shop in the hospital when you drop me off."

"Well, sorry for living." He shook his head.

I know it wasn't his fault, he was only eating his breakfast and let's face it that's hardly illegal, but I was more nervous than Robbie realised.

"Look, Robbie, I'm very nervous I'm going in for more surgery and I need some kindness and support right now. I know I can be narky and tetchy but I think I have good reason at the moment, don't you?" I stared at him, wondering if he was appreciating any of what I was feeling.

"Yes, Emily. It's all about you, isn't it? I am well aware of how much it's taking out of you. Everywhere I go and everyone I speak to is telling me how great you are, how strong you are, what a great thing you're doing. Well, sometimes that all gets a bit galling. Especially when I'm stuck here dealing with it all the time!" He flung his chair back, picked up his cereal bowl, dumped it roughly into the sink and walked out.

I stayed in the kitchen rooted to the spot. I was stunned. Robbie was getting more angry and less supportive by the day. This was the last straw for me.

It was not the time or the place to behave like this. I was hurt and very angry. Grabbing my coat and handbag, I followed Robbie out to the car.

I wanted to whiz through time and get this surgery over with. Having Robbie not speaking to me and driving like a maniac made the whole situation much worse. We didn't pass a single word for the entire car journey.

The registration and subsequent wait for admission seemed to go on forever. Like with any anxious wait, time seemed to stand still. Eventually, about twenty light years later I was ushered to a bed and given a designer gown and disposable knickers to put on. I was ready and willing to go. I felt like the day should be half over but for most normal people the day would only be beginning.

Robbie was sitting in the chair beside my bed, still silent.

"Just go, Robbie. You're not helping and I don't need to deal with you right now." I went to the bathroom to put on my surgical gown.

When I returned he was gone.

I was relieved. At least I didn't have to try and think of what to do about our lack of communication. I needed to focus on what was happening. Once I got through this operation, I would have to address our problems.

I found myself in the pre-surgery room once again. Then the mask was over my face, the pliable plastic uncomfortable and claustrophobic. It smelled like those clear almost rubbery plastic packs you buy knickers in, in chain stores. I wanted to push it away and make them stop holding it there. The oxygen, which was wooshing through the corrugated tubing to the mask, was nauseating and made my throat dry. The almost antiseptic taste of the anaesthetic hit me and I felt my body flopping and being taken over by the drug. My limbs became incredibly heavy and my entire body became too large to function, so I gave in and the drug-induced slumber over took.

The next thing I remember was waking up to the distant sound of someone calling my name. I tried to ignore it a few times, but it was persistent and growing louder and louder.

"Emily? Em-i-ly? Emily? Emily? Hello, Emily?"

It ranted on and on. It didn't stop. It didn't want to go away.

Reluctantly I decided to open my eyes and answer the voice. It was a male nurse, who greeted me by babbling chatter.

"Now, that's a great girl. How's it goin'? Grand that you're awake again. How are you feelin'? I'd say you're a bit groggy. Now, I'm going to fire ahead and take your blood pressure and look at your levels – right so, let's do that so." He rabbited on about heart rate and a total warble of other incomprehensible stuff.

I'm sure I must have been just lying there staring at him with a look of, "*Are you fucking insane?*" because he stopped abruptly, sniffed indignantly and shut up. Instead he busied himself with scribbling wildly on my chart and clipping it on the side of my bed.

"Now, if you can keep your attention on me," he began.

I'd rather not, I thought to myself.

"If ten is excruciating pain and zero is no pain at all, where on the scale do you think your pain is now?"

"Oh, about six hundred," I answered. My voice was croaky and seemed to belong to someone else.

"No, I think you're kind of like, missing the point, you know?" He flapped his hand around and rolled his eyes. "If ten is –"

"I heard what you said. My answer is still six hundred. I feel like a combine harvester has gouged through my insides and ripped some vital bit out on the way. My pain level said au revoir to ten a long time ago. In fact if and when it ever has the luxury of reaching the excruciating level of ten ever again, I will throw a party. *Comprendez vous?*"

Not being deterred and not wanting us to deviate from his question he rolled his eyes, sighed and flapped his hands.

"If ten is excru –" He was on a mission.

"Look at me," I urged. "I am not interested in playing higher and lower with you. This is not a game. I am in fucking agony and if you don't give me some serious pain relief rapidly I am going to muster up all my strength to yell continuously until you do."

"Right so, would you say a nine maybe?" he probed, with his head to the side.

"Yep, whatever you say, a nine sounds spot on, if that makes you happy." I closed my eyes and tried not to curl into a ball as the dull, thudding ache ripped through my side and continued through to my tummy.

"I'm going to give you a tiny amount of morphine," Eye Roller slurred. "Not too much, mind you, 'cos you'll be going home in about an hour, d'ya know?"

This robotic gobshite had obviously been programmed that I was in for one day and that I would have to go home and nothing was going to make him change his mind. Nothing was going to interfere with his programme.

He topped up the morphine twice more. It didn't work. At all. It didn't kill the pain to any degree. It just made my head feel fuzzy. I tried to tell him so. As on the Night of the Orange Claws, morphine was not my friend.

He just topped up the morphine again.

I made one last gigantic effort. "Listen to me. Morphine is not my friend, it is not stopping the hurt, not making me feel better, not bringing the pain level below five. Can you comprehend that at all?" I was so, so tired. It was taking a lot out of me to try and get through to this moron.

He sighed. "I don't know what else to do with you at this stage, to be totally truthful." He waved a limp hand in my direction and dramatically dabbed his forehead with a tissue.

"Well, I'm sorry to be such a nuisance, with all this pain and all, but I'm afraid I'm not in the market for lying and saying I'm feeling fabulous, just to please you. Please go and get Ms Mulcahy, I want to talk to her."

"Okay, okey-dokey, righty-oh, I'll call her if that's what you would prefer." He hurried across the room to find Ms Mulcahy.

When the surgeon arrived, she astonishingly believed me that I was not having a fun time.

"You really look like you're in terrible pain. You don't find morphine much use for relieving the pain then?" She was reading the scribbles on the chart. "Right, we need to change Emily's pain meds."

"While you're here, Ms Mulcahy, might I also point out that I am not, under any circumstances, going home today. Although Robot here has decided I am on my way in less than half an hour, that cannot happen. I am not in a fit state to be seen by my children. I might be mad, but I am not giving a five-year-old and a six-year-old more reasons to be freaked out by their mother. The thought of walking now makes me want to die and I am not capable of pretending I am fine."

Yet again the surgeon was reasonable and agreeable.

"You won't have to go home if I don't feel up to it. Let's see how you're doing. I'll be back into you in about twenty minutes and I'll assess the situation then. Is that okay with you?"

"Would you translate that into Dalek so this robot can understand, as he doesn't appear to speak English?"

She glowered at the robot. "It is not a previously decided fact that a patient should always go home on the same day as surgery."

Robot still didn't seem to understand and continued to talk about pain levels being between ten and zero. I thought the surgeon's eyes were going to pop out of her head as she led him a few steps away from my bed.

It was a bit like in a soap opera where two characters stand and discuss another character who is in the same room about four feet away. I decided to play the part and pretend I couldn't hear what was going on. I did have the advantage of having just come round from anaesthetic, so it was easy to play dumb.

The surgeon proceeded to rip Robot to shreds, gesticulating wildly and explaining the importance of listening to patients.

"All operations differ and all people have different reactions. Pain relief was invented for a reason and this was one of them. It is inhumane to leave a person without pain relief for two and a half hours. I am most upset and annoyed. Your handling of this patient leaves a lot to be desired. I will return shortly to assess the situation. Is that clear?"

I was stunned. I had no idea I'd been battling with Robot for so long. I also wished in a way I hadn't got him into so much trouble. Well, that's not true, I was bloody delighted, but I just wished I didn't have to be there with him when he was being told off.

The surgeon came back (from all four feet away) and apologised for my discomfort.

"The surgery has been successful and there were no complications as far as I am aware. I can assure you you will be made more comfortable. I agree with you that you are not in a fit state to go home. I think it would be advisable at this point to organise a bed for you to stay in overnight. I'd like to make sure you get enough pain relief over the next twelve hours. Is that any better?" She looked at me and actually wanted to know if I was okay.

"This is all marvellous news. Thank you for sorting it all out." My only problem now was the fact that the surgeon and her team were starting to walk off, leaving me on my own with Robot Man.

Oh Christ, what if he decided to have his revenge? What if he wanted to put a pillow over my face or inject me with rat poison? I decided I'd better take the bull by the horns and have it out with him.

"I'm sorry if I got you into trouble there but I did try to tell you I'm in pain, and that I wasn't relishing the thought of going home," I tried tentatively.

"Yeah," he rolled his eyes and wagged his limp hand around, "all patients differ and some people just react differently." He was quoting the surgeon and acting as if this was all coming from him. He didn't seem to be in the least bit bitter with me and appeared to have no intention of killing me. He merely busied himself organising some pain relief and pottered about his business as if nothing negative had been said at all. I was hesitantly relieved, but being quite evil myself thought he must be seething inside and remaining outwardly calm while he plotted my murder.

Luckily, he was either too robotic or dense to do me in. Within half an hour I was feeling less pain, and found myself being wheeled by a man dressed as the green giant in clogs up to a ward.

The ward was cluttered and smelled of a cross between feet and cabbage. It was nothing like the place I'd been previously, for the breast surgery. I soon discovered I was also stationed opposite the local nutcase. With wild, unkempt wiry hair to her waist, most of her teeth missing, obesely overweight and the maddest green eyes I'd ever seen. Using two wooden walking sticks she clacked over to my bed.

"Heweye, love?" she whistled and spat through her gappy gums.

"Not great," I muttered, avoiding eye contact.

"What happened to ya, were ya in casualty or did they chop ya up?" By this time her face was uncomfortably close to mine. Her breath stank of cheese and onion crisps.

"I'm not in the mood for chatting at the moment, I'm too sore." I shut my eyes tightly and hoped to God she'd bugger off. I felt her breath on my face as she tried to fathom what I'd said to her. I opened one eye slightly and she leaned a little closer.

"Tell Gina all about it." She smiled and nodded her head. She looked like an enlarged toad.

"I'll tell you all about it later on when I've had a sleep, okay?" I really had to make an effort to be polite while badly wanting to shout "Fuck off, Gina!"

Luckily for all concerned Gina decided to go away. I felt the air clear as she speared the ground with her sticks and clacked back to her own bed. I realised I hadn't spoken to my angels much since I'd come out of surgery. I silently apologised for ignoring them and quickly asked them to surround me and help me out. My answer came quickly. A nurse came and pulled the curtains around my bed and I began to drift into an addled slumber.

I know it's probably not ethical and probably against the angels' theories, but I also asked them to keep the crazy cow away from me too.

Robbie arrived and asked all the usual questions. It turned out the hospital hadn't thought to inform anyone that I was out of surgery or that I was still alive. So poor Robbie and my family had spent all that time wondering what the hell had become of me.

"We didn't know what to think," Robbie explained "We were hoping they hadn't found something sinister or that you weren't bleeding to death down in theatre."

"I'm fine, it all went well. I just couldn't convey the concept to the Mush-for-brains in Recovery that I needed more pain relief. In the end I had to call Ms Mulcahy out from surgery and get her to call the shots. I don't know why you weren't told I was out of theatre though. I think I'll go back down and tell that doorknob what I think of him." I made a half-hearted attempt to sit up. Everything was really difficult. Moving, speaking, breathing, thinking. "I'm going to do that any minute now. I am a little bit knackered though, so I might just have a quick few minutes' sleep, if that's all the same to you."

"I'm going home, Emily. I'll call you later on, have a good sleep."

I heard Robbie telling me he was going home. It did register but I couldn't respond, so I grunted and continued to sleep.

By the time the food came around I was in an even worse state. The smell and the clattering made me want to claw my way out of bed and yell like a madwoman for everyone to get lost and leave me alone. I longed for a dark, silent cupboard where I could lock myself away. Preferably a nice soft, squishy hot press, lined with fluffy towels and marshmallows. So I could lie down and let my muscles and bones relax. If only I'd been born a squirrel, I could easily go to sleep for a really long time, only to be woken up after six months' hibernation. That would suit perfectly, then all the pain would be gone and the wounds would have healed. I lay and reasoned with my own mind. I told myself that this time next week I'd be so much better than I was now. That this time next month I'd be even better than that again. This time next year I probably wouldn't even remember this pain. I was looking forward to the complacency and the hindsight.

Instead of hibernating, however, I had a polite conversation, trying not to slur my words, with a large hair-netted lady in a housecoat, about the fact that I had no appetite. I courteously joined in with the farce of pretending that the congealed plate of sweet and sour goo with rice looked delicious, but sadly I couldn't possibly eat it as I'd been fasting since 1954 and toast might be a wiser first option.

Kindly, the dinner lady left the plate, patting my forearm and suggesting, "You try just a little, honey, it might make you feel better. Line your tummy." She disappeared.

It might work well to line wall cavities in a new building but it was not going near my tummy, of that I was certain.

I shut my eyes again and once more hoped the plate of gunk might go away. I was woken abruptly by a nurse buzzing through the curtain, yelling and waving her arms about.

"Don't eat that, darlin'! You haven't had a thing in your tummy for a long time. That'll just come back up, looking much the same, except all over your sheets!"

The sticky, orange gloop was removed. A tray with a little metal teapot (the same type as before, which piddle tea all over the tray and into the saucer as you pour, leaving enough liquid to fill half a cup) appeared, together with a plate of toast triangles and a small metal dish (with the little circular foot underneath, like jelly and ice-cream dishes from the school canteen) filled with butter patties and individually packed jam portions.

I requested a jug of cold water and asked her to remove the tea, as the smell of tea makes me want to vomit at the best of times.

The water arrived and I tentatively sipped it. I fumbled the gold-foiled butter open and managed to spread it on the polystyrene toast and topped it with a scraping of jam. I was almost too exhausted to eat it at the end of the palaver. I managed a triangle and a few more sips of water before giving up and lying back on the crunchy mattress and springy pillow.

The pain continued to sear through me. I felt like it was never, ever going to go away. It was intense and so bloody sore. I wanted to curl into a ball and howl. I physically couldn't curl, due to the incisions in my abdomen and the expanders in my breasts. So that was out, and I knew if I'd started to wail, Mad Annie across the way would see it as a green light to come back and annoy me.

The nurses changed shift and the night nurse came to introduce himself.

"Hi, how are you doing? Are you in any pain?"

"Hi, I'm bloody awful – yes, I want drugs and a sleeping pill – I am in agony."

He just stood staring at me, looking slightly confused.

"Listen, I am not trying to be dramatic or to piss you off but you did ask if I needed any pain relief, is that not correct?"

"Yes, I did." He looked really perplexed by the whole conversation.

"Well, the answer is yes, I do need pain relief, so the general idea now would be for you to go and get some, how would that grab you for a suggestion?" By now, I had really come to the end of the line with people who didn't want to give me drugs. I was not circling a nightclub looking for ecstasy to give me a buzz to pass the time. I was in hideous pain and unless I was more deranged than even I gave myself credit for, painkillers were for this exact scenario. Why the hell was it so shocking to these people that I wanted some? Was I supposed to be really Irish about it, and not say what I really meant? Do you want some pain relief? Ah no, sure you're grand. I'll just have a cup of tea and lie here in agony, and then complain about my pain to everyone I meet for the next twenty years. Well, I wasn't in the market for playing silly beggars that day. I wanted to try and abate some of the pain. Was that so wrong?

He buggered off and didn't come back. I waited. I know quite some time passed, because the light was starting to fade outside. The TV was pumping out the World Cup, and all the other inmates were huddled around the blaring box, enthralled with the men in matching outfits chasing a ball. Not being a soccer fan at the best of times, I knew I would now always feel a special hate for it after that night.

I pressed my buzzer. I hated ever having to press my buzzer. I felt like I was intruding on someone else who might be sick, or interrupting something urgent, but the pain was refusing to go away and I wanted to sleep.

Instead of the usual methodical footsteps approaching, the nurse's voice came from in front of the television.

"Yeah, do you want something?" He threw his head backwards, not moving from his chair.

"Yes, please," I muttered through gritted teeth.

He reluctantly hauled himself from the chair and sloped to my bed, stopping at the gap in the curtain.

"Yeah?" He stood tapping his foot and looking pissed off at being disturbed.

"I want painkillers and a sleeping tablet, if it's not too much trouble."

"Yeah, the trolley will be coming around shortly and I have to get a sleeping pill written up by an in-house doc, so you'll have to wait till they come around, right?" He stood staring for another few seconds to see if I had anything further to add, before wandering back to sit in front of the television.

All I can say is that he is a lucky man, that I was so incapacitated. If I'd had the energy I would have leapt out of the bed and rugby-tackled him to the floor, grabbed him by the hair and bashed his face off the ground. Not a very Christian or ladylike thought I know, but I am not religious and I never claimed to be a lady.

The sleeping pill and the painkillers never came. The night passed very slowly. I had a snorer of earth-quaking proportions in the bed beside me. The lights were left on all night and it sounded like a small child was running up and down the corridor for hours with a metal box of spoons on a metal trolley, while negotiating speed ramps. The noise was horrendous.

Dawn broke and soon afterwards the breakfast arrived.

I was offered a boiled egg or corn flakes. I took the small tin bowl of cornflakes and poured the miniature jug of what tasted like warm yaks' milk over the top. How can they manage to make even cornflakes taste that bad?

One of Mr Green's team called in on spec to see me, to find out how I was getting on.

"Christ, you look rough," she greeted me.

"That's a coincidence because I feel like an utter bag of shit," I answered her.

I explained about the lack of pain relief and how it had coincided with the World Cup.

Within seconds she returned with mega-blaster pain relief and apologies for the behaviour of the night nurse.

By that stage, I just wanted to get out of there. I wanted to go home and sleep, in a bed that didn't crackle with rubber sheets and most importantly before I was accosted by the crazy-lunatic opposite. I had to wait for the gynaecological team to come around and release me.

Meanwhile I called Robbie and instructed him to get his ass into the hospital as soon as possible in anticipation of my escape.

"Bring a rope ladder in case I have to shimmy out the window. I'm not staying in here a second longer than I have to," I whispered down the phone to him.

"I'm on my way, but we might be boring and go out the door, if that's all the same to you. I'm not in the mood for scraping bits of you off the footpath at this hour of the morning."

Within two hours I was home. I was dizzy with relief but, also, just dizzy. I felt slightly drunk and a little imbalanced.

At first I thought it was just my imagination but after a while I was certain my equilibrium was off. I was clipping myself off walls and missing things I tried to pick up. I was also beginning to feel quite seasick.

I lay down, fully sure that I would be engulfed by a feeling of comfort and safety. I was horrified to realise it made the feeling worse. The nausea rose through my body like a tumbling, rolling wave, gaining in momentum until it hit my throat and caused a flood of saliva to fill my mouth. I staggered to the bathroom and vomited three times. This, believe me, was some achievement. The violence of the vomiting was astonishing. I had no idea how many muscles get involved in the process. It's only when most of them are stitched or stretched you realise what they all do. Looking on the bright side, I was learning all about what my muscles are really for.

I could have dictated to a cunning children's book author, and we might have written a bestseller entitled *"How Clever are my Tummy Muscles?"* Feeling a lot better, I staggered back to bed and flopped like a wet rag, hoping to either fall asleep or die. Either would have suited me perfectly.

Just at that moment the bedroom door burst open and Louis and Tia bounded in.

"Mummy, you're back, did you get us a present?"

They leaped onto the bed and flung their arms around me, hugging and bouncing and shouting and chattering, utterly oblivious to the fact that I was green and slicked with cold sweat.

This is one of the things which never ceases to amaze me about children. They either point out that you have a funny red thing on your chin and it wasn't there yesterday. Or else they don't notice a damn thing because they are so delighted to see you. I am convinced they have an image of Mummy in their little heads and unless you have a large boil or an extra eye, they still see you as Mummy. This time, there were no appendages so they wittered on about a new movie they would like to see in the cinema and showed me a worm they were holding hostage in a matchbox.

"So we're going to try and find a friend for Mr Squirmy Wormy. Can we go to the cinema after that?" Louis raised his shoulders and scrunched up his face in a pleading way.

"We can't go to the cinema today, darling. But we'll go really soon. I promise." Luckily he was a bit too busy with the worm hunt to argue, so they scuttled away chattering.

Astonishingly, knowing they were around and that I was still their mother gave me a fresh kick to fight the feelings of hopelessness which were attempting to creep into my head.

With the best will in the world and the most positive slant I could take on the whole situation, there was a part of me which had started to think, what have I been left as? What have I done to myself? I had to stop myself feeling like a mutilated freak. I had to not see that image. I had to quash those feelings. I was fearful. I was afraid it had all gone too far. I was worried Robbie would decide I was too damaged to want me any more.

Maybe it was the hormones, or maybe reality was just hitting.

But I felt much lower after this surgery than I did after the breast one. I didn't feel the surge of relief or the totally self-assured positive energy. I had to make a conscious effort to pull myself up by the bootlaces and force a smile and not let the situation beat me.

The nausea was exactly the same as morning sickness. I vomited for seven days. The thought of food filled me with dread and the smell made

me gag. Having spent my whole adult life on a diet and forcing myself
to be disciplined about what I ate, this was a new experience for me. I
had often wished I'd been one of those people who could go all day
without remembering to eat. Who could walk into a hand-made
chocolate shop to ask for change for the parking meter and not even
realise the whole room was wafting the tantalising aroma of melting
chocolate. I thought that would be a fortunate way to be. I thought I
would love to be that lucky. But this was depressing. The aromas,
flavours, textures, colours and appearance of food made my stomach
turn. I realised what huge pleasure I took out of food and eating and
savouring that joy. I didn't just eat to survive, I enjoyed the whole ritual
involved.

I phoned the hospital and explained how I was feeling. It was all
"normal". I don't know if I was relieved or upset to learn this. I had to
wait six weeks while my hormones deregulated before they could start
the hormone replacement therapy or HRT.

41

Susie

How to Change a Stodgy Pudding into a Fluffy Soufflé:
Open the freezer you currently call your heart. Try to banish the ghosts
of bad relationships past. Pray you have the right ingredients this time.
Try to let go.

Walter and I had met for breakfast. We ate sticky buns and drank frothy coffee and then decided to go for a walk around St Stephen's Green, a lovely tranquil park with a duck pond right in the centre of Dublin city. The sun was shining so we bought some newspapers in a nearby newsagent, and found a sunny spot to sit and read.

We didn't manage to get much reading done in the end. We snogged like two teenagers. We tickled and poked each other and rolled around on the grass together.

Walter looked at me. "Would it be really presumptuous of me to ask you back to my place?"

"No, but my place is nearer, so let's go there."

I kissed him and we scurried off to find a taxi.

By the time we'd gone the two floors in the lift and reached my apartment door, we were almost ripping the clothes off each other's backs.

Falling onto my bed, we made love frantically.

Afterwards, Walter cradled me in his arms. He made me feel like a little girl – but not in a creepy way. I liked it.

"I don't feel like I have to fight to be myself when I'm with you, it just happens." I looked up at him and stroked his dark face.

"I hope you never feel like fighting with me. I'd say you're pretty scary when you're angry. Do your clothes rip off and do you turn green and uncontrollable?"

I swatted him gently. "Don't annoy me and you won't have to find out!"

We eventually moved into the living room where I opened a bottle of wine.

"This is all rather naughty – it's only three o'clock in the afternoon and we're drinking already," he said, nuzzling up to me on the sofa.

"No one's forcing you, Dr Blake. I'll pour yours down the sink if you like?" I raised an eyebrow and stared him in the eye.

"No, I'm not complaining for one second," he said, gently tucking my hair behind my ear.

I filled him in on my family gathering and told him I would love him to meet Jim the next time he was around.

"I'd love that. Your mum sounds like a bit of fun too. For the birds, but lovely." He stroked my feet as I lay on the sofa.

The days turned into weeks, and Walter spent more and more time in my apartment. By the time we'd been together a month, I asked him to move in officially.

"I know it's kind of quick but we're not sixteen. What's the point in delaying? What do you think?"

"I knew from the first second I sat beside you in Munich that I would like to live with you. But you were scary back then and you didn't know me so it wasn't appropriate to move in with you at that stage. I'm more than ready. Half of my stuff is here anyway, so all it will mean is collecting up my other bits and pieces and renting out my own place."

I called Mum to tell her the good news.

"That's wonderful, Susie. He seems to be a lovely man and I hope you'll both be happy together. Hey, I have a little bit of news myself." She sounded very excited.

"Really?" I was intrigued.

"Yes, a bit of a new beginning! Jean and I are going to open a wedding-planning service. We made the final arrangements this afternoon. We are opening in a small premises near Portlaoise. We'll do full wedding packages and have a small bridal boutique, selling once-worn gowns and suits, along with shoes and accessories."

"Mum, that's wonderful news! I'm delighted for you both. With your obsession and Jean's enthusiasm, there'll be no stopping you."

"I know! We're calling it the 'One Stop Wedding Shop' – what do you think?"

I thought it was a bloody awful name and a hideous idea, but it made them both happy so who was I to argue?

"I've handed in my notice at the cottage," she said. "There's a little one-bedroom flat upstairs above the shop, so I'm going to live there too. It'll be a whole new beginning for me. I'm glad Walter is moving in with you. At least I won't have to worry about you!"

"I'm sure you wouldn't have fretted yourself into an early grave over me, but it's nice of you to say it," I answered.

Either because I had Walter now or because Mum was so much happier, or maybe it was a combination of the two, but she didn't annoy me the way she used to.

Things were changing at an alarming rate, but it was all for the better. My life was going better than I could have ever imagined. The only person who was really concerning me was Emily.

I had tried to speak to her about Robbie a few times but she always fobbed me off. She was wildly protective of Robbie and would never admit if he was behaving badly.

I could sense that she wasn't happy though. All I had to do was find a way of getting her to talk about what was going on. I had to be careful though. If she thought I was trying to treat her like a patient, she wouldn't thank me for it.

42

Emily

Holiday Turnover:
Pile husband and children into the cars, with most of the contents of the house. Turn up the heat and remove all patience from children after approximately one hour. Continue to drive for what feels like another year. Arrive frazzled and ready to butcher anyone who looks sideways at you.

The following week, we took the children away to the south of Ireland to a gourmet food establishment. The thought of having to be in the restaurant every night and face food filled me with dread. But day by day, I gradually began to feel better. The sun seemed to know I needed it to shine. So it did.

The children made friends with other small hotel guests, and played from cockcrow to late in the evening, falling into bed each night exhausted from all the fun, fresh air and sunshine, their little bodies brown, their hair the colour of straw, with a healthy glow induced by the wonderful food and country air.

Robbie and I were at a total stalemate.

We were sitting in the garden having coffee one morning, watching the children playing with two other guests, when I decided to broach the subject.

"Robbie, how long can we continue like this?" I looked him straight in the eye.

"Like what? Living in a hotel?"

"No. Like we're two strangers. Or two people who share a house. When are we going to actually talk about the fact that we have no communication and no life together any more?"

He didn't move in his seat. He didn't flinch either. He just remained motionless. Looking into space, acting like I wasn't there.

"You're doing it now. You're trying to block me out and not even acknowledge my existence. Do I repulse you since all the surgery, is that it?"

"No." He didn't sigh. He didn't act as if the conversation was ripping his heart out. He was cold and unemotional.

"Is that all you have to say? 'No'?" I could feel hurt and anger welling up inside me, bubbling and raging.

"What do you want me to say, Emily?"

"I want you to tell me how you feel. Why are you shutting me out all the time? You're not even letting the kids in. You barely answer them when they talk to you. You never play with them any more. You snap at them all the time. If you're angry with me, then that's one thing. But the children have done nothing wrong, so don't punish them. They're only little. They don't deserve to be shunned."

"I don't shun them." He was still ice cold.

"Yes, you do. You shun me too." I could feel the tears welling up in my eyes.

"If I'm such a dreadful husband and father maybe I should just leave then." He smiled sarcastically and raised one eyebrow.

"Is that what you want?" I was stunned. Who said anything about leaving? I didn't.

"Sometimes. Yeah. I think you'd be better off if I wasn't around cramping your style and getting in the way of your 'journey' as you call it."

I felt like I'd been smacked across the face.

"So are you telling me that you feel left out because I am having lots of surgery? That I am on some sort of voyage of discovery with no room for you?"

"Well, you make room for Louis and Tia some of the time. But in a nutshell, yes. You are on a serious trip for one. Come on, admit it. Where do I fit in with all this? I'm allowed to take you to hospital and wait around for hours wondering if you're dead or alive. Then I can bring you home and watch you writhe around in pain until you have enough stamina to pretend to be okay. That's all fine, but I am supposed to be a silent partner in all this. I am supposed to just grin and bear it all and act like it's the best thing that's ever happened to us. Well, guess what, Emily? It's not." By now he was shouting. "It's fucking terrible. It's a total nightmare. It's horrendous. You keep spouting to people about how lucky you are to have all this done. You're not fucking lucky. Winning the lottery – that's lucky. Being maimed and mutilated is not lucky."

The children had stopped playing and were looking at him with their mouths open.

The other children's mother approached gingerly.

"We've just ordered coffee, so we'll be here for a while. Would you like me to watch the children so you can go and talk?"

"Thank you so much. I'm sorry for the scene, would you mind awfully?" I felt so grateful to the woman for reaching out and being so thoughtful.

Robbie flung his chair back and stomped off.

I trailed after him. We walked to our room in silence. Shutting the door quietly behind us, I sat on the bed.

Robbie paced up and down, clenching and unclenching his fists.

"What do you want me to do?" I asked him sadly. "I had no idea you felt so left out. You should have said."

"And you would have listened? Did you listen when I told you I didn't want you to do all this?" He waved his hand towards me.

"But Robbie, the breast tissue results showed a large pre-cancer tumour! I would have had cancer by now if I hadn't done this! Does that not make you realise it was the right way to go?" I was astonished at his anger.

"No, Emily, if I'm honest. No. It doesn't. I never wanted this to happen. I thought it was a barbaric thing to do. I still do. It's been horrendous, every step of it. From having to look at photos of other carved-up women to sitting for nine hours while you were being chopped up. Trying to be cheerful to all the friends phoning to enquire. It's been a living hell. Now I'm supposed to sit in this fucking hotel for two weeks and pretend everything is hunky dory. I can't fucking do it any more. I can't pretend it's all fabulous. It just isn't."

He thumped the wardrobe, making me jump two feet off the bed. He was still pacing up and down like a caged tiger.

"But I'm nearly there now. I've only one operation to go." I was feeling panicked.

"You might be nearly there, Emily, but I sure as hell am not." He smirked bitterly, shaking his head.

"Well, what do you want to do about it? Do you want to go to counselling? Maybe Hayley can organise someone for us to talk to in the hospital."

"I am not going to see anyone else in that bloody place. I've spent enough time in there without finding another reason to sit there like a fool."

"Well, what do you suggest then? Tell me how you're going to fix it then?" I stood up and stepped in front of him.

"Maybe there is no 'fixing' this one. Maybe we have actually just gone in two very separate directions." He looked me in the eye for the first time in weeks.

The room fell silent. The wardrobe, bed and curtains held their breath.

"I can't stay here. I'm going to pack up my stuff. I can't live in Mary Poppins Land any more. Things are not right and I'm not playing the game for a second longer." He strode across the room and started to throw his clothes into a suitcase.

"So that's it, is it? You've had enough so you're leaving? Right now, in the middle of a holiday? Just buggering off and leaving me here with the children? What's that going to solve?" I felt like killing him.

"You'll be fine here. I'll see you when you get back and we'll talk then, when we've both had a bit of space and time to think." He seemed quite calm and happy with himself all of a sudden.

"Well, I'm glad all the burden has been lifted from your shoulders, Robbie. I'm thrilled for you that you're feeling a bit better now. What a relief it must be for you not having to spend the next two weeks with your maimed wife and children. You just bugger off and leave me here to pick up the pieces. That's really mature and thoughtful of you. Do you know what? Go. Sort your head out and don't come near me until you do." I walked out of the room, tears spilling down my cheeks. I couldn't take much more of this. I walked at a speedy pace, down the avenue of the hotel to God knows where.

My stomach hurt as I pounded the ground. I didn't care. I needed to put some physical distance between Robbie and me. I had a sudden panic attack about the children. Were they okay with the other lady? I couldn't go too far. I had to go back and get them.

As I stood with my hands on my hips, gulping in the air, I actually felt a slight tinge of relief flood through me. The atmosphere was so strained with Robbie. He was bringing an air of moroseness to everything. He was obviously so clogged with anger and pain, it was stopping him from being able to function normally.

I didn't have the energy, either physically or mentally, to deal with him. He would have to go and work it out in his own head. I couldn't do it for him. I couldn't reverse what I'd done now either. I also didn't regret it. I was still very glad I'd had the surgery. I was still very sure of what I'd done. It was a turning point for me personally. After the ovary operation when I'd felt so sick and low, I had wavered for a spell. But the row with Robbie made me realise that I was glad I'd done what I did.

Robbie would have to work it out for himself.

I know it sounds crazy but maybe I was a bit numb. I couldn't face thinking about what was going to happen to us as a couple. I simply didn't have the resources or energy reserves to go that far. I had to plod along and make it through the here and now.

I turned robotically and walked back to where the children were playing. Miraculously I managed to rustle up a smile and apologise to the lady for leaving her with them.

"Sorry about that. My husband is having some difficulties at the moment and he's had to leave. Thank you so much for minding the children for me."

"No problem, sure we all have days like that." She smiled and didn't ask any probing questions.

I silently thanked her for being so discreet.

"Come on, you two, we're going on a trip to the zoo." I put my hands out and Louis and Tia ran and grabbed one each.

We returned to the hotel room and Robbie was gone, along with all his stuff. Pre-empting the confusion I sat the children down.

"Daddy had some really important stuff to do in work, so he had to go home in his car. But we're going to stay here and finish our holiday and have loads of fun anyway. Starting with the zoo right now!" I was astonished at how easily I could lie to them and jolly them along.

Of course they accepted the scenario and loved the idea of a day trip. So far, so good. Thankfully we had travelled to the hotel in two cars, so at least I wasn't marooned in the hotel for the next ten days.

We drove to the zoo. The sun was shining and children were in great form. We meandered around. In fact, the children were more interested in the playgrounds than the animals. We stopped at the food area and bought revolting food consisting of semi-cooked frozen chips and mechanically reclaimed yellow stuff posing as chicken.

We sat on the little train and went around the entire park in ten minutes. By five o'clock the children were exhausted and I was in pain and fit for the bin.

I opened the car windows and put the radio on at ear-splitting level to keep the children from falling asleep on the way back to the hotel. By the time I got them out of the car they were whingeing and hungry. I took them into the bar and ordered sausages and chips for the three of us.

"With two apple juices and a glass of white wine please."

I needed a drink. My head was pounding and I felt so deflated I was sure I looked a foot smaller. Robbie hadn't phoned or texted. Not a word. Anger was starting to rage through me. How dare he leave me here, still in recovery, with two children to cope with, on my own, in a hotel. What a pig!

"Are you okay, Mummy?" Louis was staring at me, his short legs dangling from the high bar stool. "You have a line right there." He traced his finger down the frown line in between my eyes.

"I'm just tired, Louis, after our busy day." I ruffled his hair lovingly. Whatever happened, I had my two angels. If Robbie wanted to miss out on that, he was even more stupid than I thought. When had he turned into such an asshole? It was an awful revelation to suddenly see your husband as such a weak and selfish git.

"Do all grown-ups get that line when they're tired?" Tia was examining my frown lines.

Jesus, I'd have to make sure I started saving for my face lift now – they'd make me so paranoid by the time I was sixty that I'd have to have a fund in place.

"Lots of grown-ups do, Tia. When we get older our skin gets a bit baggier and that's why we get wrinkles."

"Why don't you glue them then?" She was looking right under my chin now, poking my skin with her little cold finger.

A deep-fried basket of food and two glasses of wine later, I led the children back to our room. After some serious splashing and yelling in the bath, I managed to settle them in their adjoining room.

"Can you ring Daddy so we can say night-night?" Louis was yawning and rubbing his eyes.

I froze. What could I do? They always phoned him to say goodnight when he was away with work.

"Of course. I'll get my mobile." I dialled his number and handed the phone to Louis. I couldn't face talking to him yet.

Louis launched into a full conversation the second Robbie answered. "Hi, Daddy. We went to the zoo and went on the train. The elephants did huge poos."

At least he had answered the phone. That was a start. Louis finished his chat and handed the phone to Tia.

"Hi, Daddy, where are you?" she looked confused.

I could hear him struggling to mollify her.

"I'm at home, Tia, I have work to do, but I'll see you when you finish your holidays, okay?"

"Okay then. Do you want to talk to Mummy?" She handed me the phone.

"I'm just putting them to bed. I'll talk to you another time." I didn't wait for a reply. I just hung up. There was nothing I wanted to say to him. Good or bad. I just needed to not hear his voice or be near him.

After reading a bedtime story, I settled them both and, leaving the adjoining door ajar, showered and changed into my nightdress. I tried reading a magazine but couldn't concentrate. I turned off the light and tried to relax. Robbie's face kept creeping into my mind. He was so angry and bitter and twisted. I hadn't realised until today how much he resented me for what I'd done.

Instead of feeling sad or guilty about it, I felt anger and disappointment towards him. He was not the man I'd thought he was. He was showing himself to be selfish and above all else weak. I hated him for that. If he'd been having such an awful time accepting all the surgery he should have had the decency to do something about it.

He should have either talked to me or someone else. Why had he let it get this far? I wanted to grab him and bash his head off a wall. I wanted to shake him by his ankles until all the self-centred venom fell out and my loving and kind man came back. Was that lovely man still there at all? Had he gone for good? Did I even want him back? I felt betrayed by him. The one time in my life when I really needed him, he'd fallen at the first fence. Would I ever be able to forgive him? Would I want to?

43

Susie

Boiling Up Anger:
Listen to a distressed friend. Feel your insides bubbling to your throat.
Explode and spill out inner thoughts. Try to regain composure.

I was pacing up and down my office. I thought I must have steam coming out my ears. Emily had just phoned to tell me that Robbie had left herself and the kids on their own in some hotel in the middle of nowhere.

"I'll fucking kill him! Who the hell does he think he is?" I shouted. "For fuck's sake, Emily, this is the very time that you need his support. Christ, he really picks his moments to decide he can't cope any more! Oh Emily, what do you want me to do?"

"Nothing, Suze, there's nothing anyone can do at the moment. He needs to go and sort his head out. He's been a total nightmare to live with for the last while. He's distant, moody and unbelievably sullen. It's been putting a huge strain on both the kids and me for a while now. In a way, it's a bit of a relief that he's gone. At least the atmosphere will be brighter here now."

For all her brave words, I could hear that Emily was fighting back the tears.

"But how are you going to manage on your own with the kids? Jesus, he's a selfish git!"

"We're in a hotel, Susie. I don't have to do any cooking or cleaning or entertaining. The kids have met other little ones to play with. So it'll be fine. It'll give us all a bit of space to think. I really think Robbie needs to decide whether he's out or in. If he's out, at least I'll know. If he decides he wants in, then he needs to change his attitude towards me. I'm not prepared to go on the way things have been. Nothing is worth that."

"Emily, why didn't you tell me things were so bad?" I was so upset for her.

"I kind of thought it would all go away, that we'd wake up one morning and Robbie would be in good form again. But it's time to take my head out of my arse and start facing the music."

What was the point in having a husband if he behaved like that?

"Promise me you won't ring Robbie or call in to him. It's imperative that you do as I ask. He needs to decide what he's going to do. I know you have my best interests at heart but please don't go for him."

"Okay, but I have to say I think he's a gutless wanker for doing this to you, Emily."

It made me shudder. What had I let myself in for, moving in with Walter? If I ever needed him, was he going to let me down? I'd always thought Robbie and Emily had such a good relationship, and look at them now.

But deep down I realised it was already too late to back out of my relationship with Walter. I was already in love with him and leaving him now wouldn't protect me from future hurt.

I decided to sleep on it but the following morning the whole situation didn't seem any better. I was furious that my friend was being put through so much shit by Robbie.

Going against my promise, I picked up the phone and dialled Robbie's number.

"Hi, Susie." Robbie sounded deflated.

"What's going on, Robbie?" I was trying to maintain control.

"Nothing. I just need a bit of time away from the whole situation. It's stifling me. Emily is intent on being upbeat all the time and acting as if nothing's wrong. I can't do it any more." He sighed heavily.

"Look, I know I'm supposed to remain objective here, but don't you think she's doing her best? What do you want her to do? Sit around and mope all the time? Fuck off and leave you and the kids and spend two months in a home convalescing? With her feet up, thinking of nobody but herself? She can't, Robbie. She's not in a position to bugger off and leave the kids on holiday in a hotel on their own. So what gives you the right to do that?"

"I couldn't take any more. The whole situation is just too damn much. You're not the one living with it twenty-four seven." Robbie was really angry now.

"Neither are you, Robbie, if we're going to be technical about it. But Emily is." I paused. "Look, this is futile, us arguing. The fact remains that Emily is there on her own struggling to cope. You are having a breakdown and –"

"No, I'm not having a breakdown! I just need some breathing space!"

"I think it might benefit you to speak with one of my colleagues. It won't work if you come to me. It would be better for you to see someone who doesn't know you personally. Will you let me arrange it for you?"

"No thanks, really. I'm not in the mood for telling some stranger about my life. I appreciate that you think you're helping, Susie, but I really just need to be left alone. If that's okay with you."

Before I could answer, he'd hung up.

I was angry and sorry for him in equal measure. It would be much easier to empathise with him if he wasn't married to my best friend.

Meanwhile, the One Stop Wedding Shop was almost ready to open its doors.

Mum was in charge of the wedding gowns, shoes and accessories. She had a mixture of once-worn and new dresses. Although she had no business experience, her own cop-on was enough, along with Jean's business knowledge. He was in charge of designing the website and organising the business end of the shop. They both intended to travel to various venues and hotels, putting together price packages for prospective couples.

Jean had been on the local radio station, promoting the business.

It was early days but it looked like Mum was already making a mark for herself in the world of nuptials. Her enthusiasm and love for everything to do with weddings was paying off.

"I always knew my wedding scrapbooks would come in handy," Mum gushed. "I was also thinking, maybe you and Walter could be our first clients? We could do you a good deal?" She had a twinkle in her eye.

"I think you can forget that for the moment, Mum. Walter and I are ticking along nicely and I don't need you poking your nose in or making constant comments. I don't see myself planning a wedding in the near future. You'll have to drum up some business elsewhere!"

I was happy with Walter, but the thought of getting married still didn't appeal to me in the slightest. Especially in light of Robbie and Emily's current situation. The thought of being abandoned, while ill, with two small children in the back of beyond was chilling. The whole marriage and kids lark was a big gamble. What Walter and I had at the moment was controllable and only involved us consenting adults. He still owned his flat and I owned mine. There were no bridges burnt if we needed to turn back. I was still in a position to go back to the way things had been before if I so wished. Nothing was set in stone. I had no intention of changing any of that, not for a very long time.

44

Emily

Catering for One Less:
Have massive row with husband. Have him leave you high and dry. Season with a weird sense of relief. Attempt to switch off the cooker of emotions stewing in your head. Leave consequences for chewing over another day.

After Robbie left us high and dry at the hotel, things became much simpler for me. I hadn't realised quite how tense I'd become. I'd been walking on eggshells with him for weeks.

At least when I knew he wasn't going to turn up, the kids and I could suit ourselves. When they woke in the mornings, I turned on the television and a couple of times we didn't even make it out of the room until after eleven o'clock. I had breakfast delivered and we all ate it in bed, in our pyjamas.

"This is fun, isn't it, Mum?" said Louis. "Having a picnic in bed, when everyone else is up and outside being busy."

"It's great for a change all right."

"We're on holidays and we're allowed to do whatever we like, isn't that right, Mummy?" Tia bounced up and down on her knees in the middle of my bed.

By the end of two weeks, I felt like a different person. I was able to eat, wine tasted good again and things were looking up. For the past few weeks my stomach problems had taken away from the pain of the muscle expanders in my breasts, thus proving the age-old theory – if you've a pain in your head, stub your toe and your head will suddenly be fine.

I was reaching the stage where I was really looking forward to having the muscle expanders removed. The exchange operation was on the horizon. All going well, I had less than three months to go. Then I would be in line for the third and final operation. The muscle pockets would be sufficiently stretched and an implant could go in to replace the rigid expanders.

I returned home with the children. As it was a Friday and mid-morning, Robbie was at work. I had one brief exchange of words with him the day before to confirm that we were coming home. He hadn't asked how I was and I hadn't asked how he was.

The children were delighted to see all their toys and reunite themselves with Rasher.

"Look, Mum, Rasher is wearing a fairy tutu and sitting in my dolly's pram!" Tia was thrilled to have her stripy live baby back.

Louis was on the trampoline, bouncing high in the air, delighted with life.

I unpacked the suitcases with Maisy's help. As usual there was a never-ending pile of dirty clothes.

At four o'clock, Robbie arrived home.

"Hi, you guys, where's my hug?" At least he sounded cheerful towards the children, which was something.

"Daddy!" Tia bolted from the playroom and ran to hug him.

"Hi, baby girl, where's your brother gone?"

"He's out in the garden with a stick whacking everything." Tia, still in his arms, pointed out the window to where Louis was absentmindedly swatting flowers with a piece of bamboo.

"Hi, little man, how are you?"

Louis ran and wrapped himself around Robbie. They sat on the grass and chatted for a few minutes. I busied myself with rooting in the freezer for something to rustle up for dinner. The fridge and freezer were of course empty.

"How are you doing?" Robbie was standing in the doorway, leaning against the jamb.

"Fine, and you?" Seeing him, I realised I didn't actually care how he was. I wasn't ready to speak to him. I still wanted to throttle him.

"There's nothing here for dinner. Why don't you go with Maisy and the children for something to eat? I could do with some breathing space, seeing as I've had them twenty-four-seven for the last two weeks." I shoved past him and went upstairs. I heard the children cheering at the news of a meal out and within minutes I heard the car doors closing and the engine starting up.

Exhaling slowly, I flopped onto the bed. I knew there was no way Robbie and I could just carry on as if nothing had happened. I couldn't live with such a farce. I needed to speak to him and tell him how let down I felt. I also needed to find out what the hell was going on in his head.

Two hours later they all returned with plastic toys and balloons. Maisy took Louis and Tia for a bath, leaving Robbie and me on our own.

"Do you want a hippy tea?" Robbie was putting the kettle on.

"No, Robbie, I don't. I need to talk. I can't live like this either. Before we go one second further, I have to tell you that."

There was a dead silence. Neither of us looked at the other. Neither of us moved. There was so much emotion pending and it was just a matter of who was going to say something first.

True to his recent form, Robbie just said nothing. At all. His face was like stone.

"Have you nothing to say? Nothing you feel you should say after leaving me in a hotel on my own with the children?"

"Not a lot, no." He was unbending and certainly unrepentant.

"That says it all then. I suggest you pack your bags and go. I am certainly not staying under the same roof as you, if that's all you can come up with after your behaviour."

I didn't wait to hear his answer. I walked out the front door and got into the car. I drove around the corner and parked the car in a laneway.

I hoped Robbie would be gone when I got back. I couldn't deal with him and his awful cold hard demeanour for a second longer. I realised I would rather be on my own than with a man who didn't care about me. I was not going to put up with being treated like that.

Operations or no operations, I was not going to stay in a loveless marriage. I had not been brought up to be treated with malice. I had survived before I'd met Robbie and I was determined I would survive without him. An image of our two beautiful children came to my mind and I felt a physical pain at the heartache it would cause them. But it would be better than having them submersed in a house of rows and hate. Because that was exactly what would follow if Robbie continued the way he had been.

Calling Susie, I cursed as her phone went to the message minder.

I drove home twenty minutes later to find the children playing snakes and ladders with Maisy.

"Hi, Mum, were you at the supermarket? Did you buy chocolate biscuits?" Tia looked behind me for evidence of treats.

"No, Tia, I just had to go to do a quick job. I'm back now." I looked around for signs of Robbie having left.

"Robbie has gone to his business trip." Maisy didn't meet my gaze.

I didn't react. I sat down and pulled Tia on to my knee and helped her with the game. Having spent the last ten days without Robbie, I wasn't finding his missing presence unusual.

I didn't speak to Robbie for two days after that. I had nothing to say to him. He'd left when I needed him. I didn't forgive him. In fact, right at that moment, I hated him for what he'd done.

As I was getting into my car to go shopping a week later, Robbie approached me. I hadn't heard him drive up to the house, so I was surprised to see him.

"Emily, we need to talk." He seemed less hard and less aggressive than before. "Can I get in?"

I motioned to the passenger side of the car. He walked slowly around and got in.

"How have you been?" He looked at me for the first time in a long time.

"Do you actually care? Or are you just saying it to make yourself look better?" I met his stare coldly.

"You know I care." He coughed uncomfortably.

"Oh, do I? That's funny because you've a bloody strange way of showing how much you care. I'd hate to see how you treat people you don't give a toss about."

"Look, we need to try and work things out." He was facing me now.

"Well, let's start with some honesty then. Why the hell did you not tell me you were so against everything I've done? When were you going to let me in on the thoughts flying around your brain?"

"It all built up on me. I couldn't stand seeing that hospital any more. I couldn't have one more cheerful conversation about how wonderful everything was and how lucky you are. I don't think any of this awful shit is lucky. I think it's a bloody nightmare. I can't carry on with this farce any more, being cheerful and delighted about each hospital trip." He pulled his hands through his hair and sighed deeply.

There was so much going through my head. I was trying to see it from his point of view, but it was bloody difficult.

"Well, however difficult it's been for you to watch, I'm the one who's been actually going through it. I need your support right now; so do the children. Blanking us and blocking it all out until it goes away is a really intelligent way of dealing with it all. If you're not careful, Robbie, you're going to end up on your own. I can't deal with this right now. I am peddling as fast as I can. I am trying to keep all the balls in air. I'm sure you are going through a lot and I'm sorry if it sounds cruel but I don't have the reserves to keep you afloat as well." I actually felt like slapping him.

"I didn't ask you to keep me afloat. I just need to try and get to grips with all this."

"Well, that's nice for you. I suggest you sod off and do that, and when you're ready to behave like a husband and father you can get back to me. I can't guarantee that I'll still want to see you or even be in the same room as you, but that's a chance you're going to have to take."

Robbie sat looking straight ahead. It was utterly weird. We weren't shouting and yelling at each other. It was all a bit surreal. I didn't have the energy to fight either physically or mentally. I just couldn't deal with anything else. I wanted him to get the hell out of my car and decide what he was going to do. In his own time and his own space.

My mother called in that afternoon for a coffee.

"How's, Robbie?" she asked.

Was that a loaded question or not? I hadn't actually told my Mum that Robbie was not at home at the moment. I hadn't told anyone except Susie.

If anyone had told me two years ago that Robbie was going to leave and I wouldn't bother to tell anyone about it, I would have laughed and thought them insane. Yet here I was in a husband-free situation and I'd hardly told a soul.

Mum was sitting looking at me expectantly.

"Oh, Robbie's fine, I'm sure." I waved a hand in the air absently.

"What do you mean 'I'm sure'?" Mum was looking a bit confused.

"Robbie's not living here at the moment, Mum. He can't deal with all the shit that's going on so he's moved out for a bit."

"What? Since when? Why didn't you call me and tell me?" Mum had tears in her eyes. She was reeling with shock.

"I don't know why I didn't tell you, Mum. Sorry about that. Really I am, but I don't want to deal with Robbie and his Amazing Technicolour Breakdown right this minute. The way it's been left, as of this morning, is that he's going to try and figure out who or what he wants and whether he's capable of being a husband and father. He's getting back to me on it." I continued to place coffee cups on the table along with milk and sugar.

I was opening a packet of biscuits when Mum came over and put her hand over mine.

"Emily, this is crazy. Sit down and tell me what the hell is happening here."

"Mum, I don't know if it's because I'm trying to keep myself and the children going or what it is. But I am not able to enter into any of this at the minute. I know it may sound bizarre to you, but I am simply putting it all on the back burner. I am leaving it in a box in the back of my mind to be dealt with at another more convenient time. I would never have thought I was capable of doing that, especially when my marriage could be on the rocks. But that's what I'm doing. I think it's called survival."

I was amazed at myself. I used to be the type of girl who would spend the day phoning all and sundry to discuss what a boyfriend had said, how he'd said it and what it might mean. I would analyse everything in my life. But right at that moment, I didn't have the strength or mind space to get into that.

Maybe I had shut him out. Maybe I had assumed he was big enough and old enough to mind himself. I suppose I had been concentrating on myself and the children. I'm sure a lot of this was my fault. Yes, I had brought this all on myself. Robbie was right there. But I had no regrets about it. I certainly was not going to feel bad about it.

Feeling suitably harassed and sweaty and annoyed, I arrived home to find a message from a close friend on my answering machine, saying she'd be in the vicinity later that day and she'd drop in on the off chance I was in. If I was busy or out, she would simply go away. She was one of a dying breed, in so far as she didn't possess a mobile phone. She also lived in the middle of nowhere, with no television, a four-year-old, two-year-old and now a four-day-old baby.

I was thrilled at her impending arrival and had a parcel of tiny, soft pink things for the new baby to puke all over. I busied myself wrapping the beautiful pink outfit in the "Welcome New Baby Girl" shiny wrapping paper. I tied bows with ribbon and wrote the card. Just as I was securing the card to the gift it occurred to me that this would be my first time being in contact with a newborn baby since my oophorectomy. I wasn't fearful of my reaction, but I was thoughtful.

I was conscious that in its own way this would be a small step for me to take, a bit of acceptance would have to take place in my own head. I hadn't ever wanted a third child, but now I didn't have a choice any more. I wondered if I would have any pangs of regret or envy or sadness. Would I feel like an empty vessel beside my friend who was still intact? She still had all her bits. Mine were in a jar in the hospital floating around peeking out at a lab attendant. Would I find this visit difficult to swallow?

Before I had too much time to ponder, the doorbell rang. It was Shauna.

"Hi, babes, did you get my message? If it's a bad time I'll be gone, are you busy?" she stood with one foot facing the driveway, her whole body language telling me she was staying only if it suited me.

"I'm delighted to see you!"

I hugged her and walked with her to the car.

We opened the door and the four-year-old and two-year-old spilled out full of chat. In familiar territory they ran into the house looking for Louis and Tia, or even better just their toys.

There in a tiny Rock-a-Tot was the most perfect little angel.

"Meet Rosie." Shauna smiled down at her proudly.

The infant lay sleeping like a little flower fairy in her seat. Gently untangling the seat from the belt, I raised her up to my height so I could have a good look at her. The tiny baby smell wafted up at me. Her precious little face with long, dark lashes, serene as she slept.

"Bring her in, bring her in," I begged excitedly.

Shauna carried her into the house where she was placed on the kitchen table. Why is it we all do this, even though it has printed on most baby Rock-a-Tots not to put the seat on high surfaces? We all know a story about a friend of a friend who ended up in the children's hospital with a baby with a fractured skull caused by a toppling Rock-a-Tot.

Anyway, Rosie was dumped on the table. I shoved the gift at Shauna and resumed my position, gawking at the baby. Drinking in every detail of her tiny person.

"Can I take her out?" I surprised myself by asking this.

"You can do what you like with her!" Shauna waved her hand backwards at me as she ripped open the pink paper. She oohed and ahhed at the clothes while I gently scooped the infant into my arms.

She was warm and pliable and soft. She smelled sweet and delicious. She made me smile involuntarily. I instinctively rocked her from side to side while cooing at her. Her eyes tried to open drunkenly for a second before she gave up and continued to sleep.

I would be lying if I said I didn't feel a pang of emotion. There somewhere deep in my psyche was an oddly uncomfortable twinge of slight regret. There was certainly a wrenching of some sort happening.

It's definitely true to say that you always want what you can't have. I had years of opportunity to have another baby. I could have delayed the oophorectomy to have a baby had I wanted to, but I didn't.

I knew this was just a moment that I had to experience. It wasn't what I would call pain, but it was a deep and slightly sad acceptance of what my body had now become. My tummy looked the same from the outside, but the factory was shut. Never to produce again. Did I care? Yes. I did. Not that I wanted another child. I was delighted and grateful with the two perfect kids I'd been blessed with. I knew I didn't want more. But it's always easier to be sure of your ideas when you know there's room to change your mind should you wish to do so.

I was not going to dwell on this though. I needed to remember that I was incredibly fortunate. I was lucky to be well, I was lucky that I didn't have cancer, that I wasn't having to face the fact that I might not see my children grow up.

That was the reason I'd made the decision to do all this. As soon as I reminded myself of this fact, I lifted myself out of my self-pitying drain of despair. I kissed the tiny infant on the forehead and placed her back in her seat.

Taking a deep breath, I put the kettle on and proceeded to chat to Shauna about the lack of sleep and shredding of nerves that was happening in her house. The older two were both wetting the bed in honour of the new arrival. Orna, her two-year-old, was also a liability and couldn't be left on her own in the room with the baby.

"She has already taken an adjustable spanner to the baby's toes and had tried to feed her a chocolate mousse from the fridge. All in all, I'm feeling quite suicidal. My tummy is like a deflated balloon, the world is falling out my arse and I'm yearning to drink a bottle of red wine with two sleeping tablets, and hide for twenty-four hours." Shauna looked quite deflated in more ways than one.

I fed her strong, freshly brewed coffee and chocolate biscuits. A poor substitute for alcohol and drugs, but the best she could hope to ingest in her lactating state.

The baby woke up, the other two children and my two ran around the house like lunatics. They were wearing masks and screaming endlessly, running away from imaginary monsters. This in turn frightened the living daylights out of baby Rosie who howled in terror. Tia tripped over the long dressing-up outfit she was wearing and launched herself at me, crying forcibly for sympathy.

Forty minutes later, when Shauna shoved her yelling children and wha-ing baby into the car and drove off, I felt my shoulders slowly release from my ears and I exhaled the breath I'd been holding for a dangerously long time.

I'd changed my mind. I was right the first time. I didn't want another baby. I knew I'd thought that one through. I felt at peace with myself in a funny way. It was like I'd passed that test. I was sure there would be times in my life, yet to come, when I would feel a tugging or a certain sense of loss. But my security in knowing I would not die of ovarian cancer bridged that gap like nothing else in the world.

45

Susie

Just Desserts:
Meet live-in lover for relaxed meal. Glaze with love. Enjoy.

Walter and I were sitting in a little cobbled area at the back of a restaurant in Donnybrook one evening. We'd just finished a lovely meal, consisting of fresh seafood and home-made brown bread. I was commenting on the beautiful sweet pea, which was winding its way up the trellis beside us.

"Aren't the colours so beautiful? Emily loves sweet pea, she always said they should be baby fairies' party dresses." I sat and smiled as I remembered us as children. We lived in such a cocooned dream world when I thought about it. We hadn't a care in the world and we thought everything was all lollipops and frills. I was lucky to have had such an idyllic childhood. In my line of work I realised so poignantly how many people were left scarred by cruel and heartless treatment during childhood.

Walter was unusually quiet that night. I focused on him and realised he had been staring at the table for quite a while, absent-mindedly tinkering with a teaspoon.

"Penny for your thoughts," I smiled. "That's kind of a redundant phrase here now, isn't it, with the Euro and all that?"

He didn't smile in return.

"What's the matter, Wal?" I asked, suddenly feeling a bit uncomfortable.

"I need to talk to you about something, but I'm worried about how to broach the subject with you."

He looked at me and I could see sadness in his eyes.

"You can tell me anything. What's the matter?" But I was suddenly very nervous.

"I want to ask you something." He was staring at the teaspoon again. "But I'm not sure if you're going to like it." He hesitated. "I've realised for quite a while – well, since the first time I met you, in fact – that I love you." He looked at me again.

"Right . . ." I held his gaze.

"The more time I spend with you, the more I realise I don't ever want to be without you. Basically, I've never felt this way about anyone else. I didn't think it was possible to feel this way. But it's freaking me out, because we don't have any solid commitment. I want to ask you to marry me, Susie, but I'm afraid if I do you'll feel trapped and end up hating me and leaving. But if I don't ask you, I'm worried you won't realise how much I love you, and maybe you'll get bored and leave anyway." He was speaking at a hundred miles an hour and looked so vulnerable.

"Oh, Walter!" Tears pricked my eyes and I was overcome with relief. "I'll tell you what – I'm going to go to the loo – and when I come back why don't you propose to me and we'll see what happens?"

He looked so stunned and shocked at the thought of being left on his own at that moment that I couldn't help laughing.

"I'm sorry!" I got up and went over and sat on his knee. "I didn't know this until you just asked me, but I would love to marry you," I whispered.

"Are you serious?" He whooped and hugged me back. "So do you think you might like to look at the box I have in my pocket then?" He grinned and fumbled in the inside pocket of his jacket, which was hanging on the back of his chair.

"No way!" I yelled.

"Susie, will you marry me?" he asked formally, as he opened the navy velvet box. Inside, like a shining star, was the most beautiful, clear twinkling diamond I'd ever seen. The setting was high and simple, in white gold, showing off the sizable diamond to perfection.

"Oh Jesus, that's beautiful! It's a serious rock too – that must have set you back a few euros. Did you really pick that yourself?" I was beyond impressed.

"Yes, I did, you cheeky cow!" He was thrilled with himself.

"God, you're a talented boy, aren't you?" I let him place the ring on my finger. I felt a shudder go down my spine. But unlike the last time I'd been engaged, this time it was a shudder of excitement and pleasure. "Oh God, I love it, and I love you. I never thought I'd say this, but I can't wait to marry you." I looked at my ring from every angle. "Oh, can you do me a favour?" I asked him, becoming serious for a minute.

"Sure, what is it?"

"Can we not tell my mother until tomorrow?"

"All right." He sighed and shook his head. "You're so mean – she's going to be so excited."

"I know, I'm a bitch, but I want to just enjoy being engaged on my own, nicely and quietly before all hell breaks loose. She's going to want us to have the wedding of the year, you know? She'll be unstoppable once she gets wind of this."

"I know, but what harm? It'll make her happy."

"I'll restrain myself and hold my tongue. Suffice it to say that if you'd grown up in a house with my mother, you would know that this is going to be the biggest day of her life, even though I'll be the bride." I smiled at the thought of how excited Mum would be. "I took the nose off her only the other day as well – she'd tried to suggest we should get married and I told her I'd no intention of it. Well, it was true at the time." I kissed Walter and felt like I was going to burst with joy.

I stared at the magnificent ring on my left hand. Jesus, diamonds really are a girl's best friend! I'd been denying myself a lot by not owning any up until now. I felt almost entranced by its kaleidoscopic beauty, the glittering and twinkling filling me with a most amazing sense of anticipation and joy. Quite apart from the fact that the ring was utterly magnificent as an object, it was offering me a promise and a new life. Only a few short months ago, I would have laughed if someone had told me I'd be engaged and delighted about it.

Emily had always said to me that one day I would meet "the right person" and that would change my mind. I had always pooh-poohed the idea and deep down felt she was just a foolish romantic. But she was right. I hadn't met the right person. I also hadn't been ready to let myself fall in love. There really was a right time and right place for things to happen. Right at that moment I figured I'd never been as happy. If a foot was to come through the sky and squash me like a flea, I'd die a very happy little bug.

46

Emily

Can a Ruined Dish Ever be Rescued?

Take well-baked and burnt-to-the-core relationship. Examine for signs of salvation. Attempt to scrape shreds of love from the bottom of the pot. Try not to get your heart burnt.

The balmy weather still trying to hold on by its fingernails. An autumnal breeze was gently curling itself through the fading green trees. The evenings were already shortening noticeably.

The phone rang. It was Robbie's brother Mark calling from France. Himself and Sandrine his wife were coming home for a few days and would it be okay for them to stay? What could I say? Yes but don't bring that miserable cow of a wife with you?

"Sure, of course you can." I was forcibly pleasant. "Especially if you don't mind camping in the playroom, you're very welcome. The spare room is now occupied by our au pair."

"That's perfect, Emily, we'll see you in three days. I spoke to Robbie briefly earlier, he couldn't talk as he was in a meeting and said to call you. Hope you don't mind being put on the spot."

"Not at all, Mark, see you soon." I put the phone down and dialled Robbie's number. I was fit to kill him.

"Hi." He sounded nervous.

"I've just had a call from Mark who is arriving to stay with us in three days' time. Why didn't you tell him you're not actually living here at the moment?"

"He hardly ever comes home and I didn't want to go into everything with him. I'll explain when I collect him from the airport."

"Robbie, what kind of a spanner are you? Are we supposed to just plod along and pretend everything's okay just because Mark is there?"

"No, but I do think we should try and sort everything out between us. Can we meet for dinner tonight?"

I have to admit it was getting difficult with the children. They were beginning to ask questions about where Daddy had gone. We would have to make some decisions either way and tell them. My mother had become silent on the whole issue. Thankfully she was not the interfering type and had wisely realised there was no point in pushing the issue with me.

"Fine. What time?" I sighed.

"I'll call over after work and spend some time with the kids and we'll head out when they go to bed. Does that suit?" At least he was making the first move.

"Okay."

"Right. See you later then."

We hung up and I carried on with what I was doing. I was still on survival mode with Robbie. As in, I was so busy keeping my head above water with everything else I still managed to push our flailing marriage to the depths of my mind. I sat down for a cup of coffee about half an hour later and allowed myself to think about what I wanted to say to Robbie later that night.

I did still love him. I realised that. I was just feeling very let down and hurt by his reaction. But I had to try and put myself in his shoes. If I had to watch him go through a load of surgery, especially if I didn't agree with his choices, would I react the same way? The answer was definitely no. That was where the problem lay for me.

I would never do to him what he'd just done to me. Even if I hated his choice I could never leave him when he needed me the most. I had to decide whether I was willing to forgive him and work at making our relationship work. Did I want him back? Did I want to be married to him any more?

At five o'clock I had a shower and put on a simple summer dress, retouched my make-up and dried my hair. Maisy was in the garden with the children when I heard Robbie's car arrive.

I saw Tia and Louis swarm at his car, both covered in sticky wet mud. "Dad, come and help us make a mud pie!"

Robbie laughed and followed them to the back garden. I sat on our bed and tried to steady my mind. I felt strangely nervous. It was almost like a first date. Was Robbie nervous too? Did he have an amazing speech ready to try and make me forgive him? Was he even sorry? Did he want to come home?

I painted my nails, just for something to do. I was fidgety and wanted to get our talk over with. I decided to go down to the garden and get Robbie to come and talk to me upstairs.

I stood and watched him with the children. "Hi, Robbie."

"Hi. You look summery." He was never very good at compliments.

"Can you come upstairs for a minute?" I turned and walked on up.

He arrived up and stood awkwardly in the doorway.

"I didn't think we could talk in a public place, so let's just get it over with here." I was still feeling quite angry. I realised I needed him to help me feel better about all this. It was up to him. The ball was in his court.

"How are you?" He looked at me as I sat on the bed.

"I'm fine, you?"

"Okay. I want to come home, Em. I'm sorry for the way I've behaved. I know I've been useless. Can you forgive me?"

He sat beside me. We didn't touch each other. We both sat staring straight ahead.

"Is that it?" I looked at him sideways.

"What do you want me to say? I'm sorry. I should have behaved differently." He was still holding back.

"That's not good enough, Robbie. I need you to open up more. You said you blamed me for bringing all this on myself. That you don't agree with what I've done. That I've brought all this hassle upon us both. If we're to move forward, you're going to have to come to terms with all that and talk about it. All this is not going away and we have to be on the same level with it or our marriage is never going to work."

"I know."

We sat in silence for what seemed like an eternity, each of us deep in our own thoughts.

"Do you still love me?" I asked him quietly.

"Of course I do. I'm sorry I tried to blame you as well. It was wrong of me. I knew it when I said those things. Of course you've done the right thing, but it's very hard to sit and not be able to do anything. I'm used to being in control and being able to fix things. I hate being so useless."

"You only became useless when you left, Robbie."

"I deserve that."

We sat in silence again. It was the strangest situation. We weren't yelling and screaming. We weren't looking to fight with each other. We just needed to find a common ground and to understand how we both felt. The pressure the surgery and the altered gene had placed on us had quashed our relationship. It was all so huge it had actually drawn a line in the sand between us. I had been trying to survive it in my own way and I had obviously shut Robbie out.

He had struggled enormously with the vast journey I was taking and had felt I wasn't including him. We were both sinking. We needed to hold each other up.

"I need you to stop resenting me, Robbie. I need you to stop treating me like a criminal. I am doing what I hope is the right thing for me and all of us. I can't cope with you turning that on its head and blaming me for wrecking our lives. That was the furthest thing from my mind when this all started. Don't let the gene ruin us. If we do, then in a way it's won and we've lost out. I'm nearly there now. The hard part is over. Why are we letting it all beat us at this stage?"

"I hear what you're saying and I agree, but it just got too much. I couldn't stand it any more. But I don't want us to break up. I never wanted that. I promise to make more effort to be supportive and positive. But you have to stop shutting me out and being a one-woman-road-show. Let me in. Let me help you."

He took my hand and I let my head flop onto his shoulder.

At that second, Tia burst through the door looking like a mud monkey. Her face and hair streaked with dirt. Her clothes were long gone, apart from a pair of pink "Tinkerbelle" knickers.

"Look at me, I'm a brown girl!" She was about to throw herself onto our white bed. Both Robbie and I jumped and yelled "No!" at the same time.

Maisy arrived looked red-faced and covered in mud.

"Sorry, Emily, she run away very fast. I put her in bath now. Come on, Tia, we make you clean girl."

"I think the shower might be better, Maisy, to get all the mud off."

Louis appeared looking even dirtier, but equally delighted with himself.

"Who's that muck monster, Dad?" I glanced at Robbie who, taking the cue, grabbed the wriggling child and ran into the bathroom.

"Maisy, we're going to head out. Can you heat up the sauce and make a pot of pasta in a while?"

"No problem, Emily, I see you later."

I pulled on a pair of shoes and grabbed a light jacket. I appreciated having Maisy there. It made life so much easier to have back-up.

After kissing the cleaner children we walked out the door. We walked to our local Chinese restaurant and settled at a table for two.

"I'm going to the loo. Back in a minute." Robbie slipped away.

I sat munching prawn crackers and looking around at the other diners. The restaurant was owned and run by real Chinese people. The girls were all like little dolls, dressed in exquisite silk dresses with Mandarin collars and black silk shoes, their shiny black hair pulled into high ponytails or cut in perfect silky bobs. As one girl set a jug of water on the table, I admired her tiny brown hands and perfect skin.

Robbie appeared, looking pleased with himself. He was closely followed by a man with an ice bucket and a bottle of champagne.

"I know we have a lot of work to do, but I thought we could start afresh with a bottle of bubbly."

He looked so vulnerable and delighted at the same time. I was thrilled that he was making an effort and obviously wanted things to work.

"That's lovely, Robbie, thanks."

He sat down and I leaned across the table and kissed him.

Our dinner turned out to be very little food and far too much booze. We finished the bottle of champagne and drank a further two bottles of wine. Staggering out into the dark balmy air, we linked arms. More for support than affection. It took us almost an hour to walk the two-mile journey home.

That night as we made love there was genuine affection between us again. Nothing would be fixed overnight, but I knew we were in a much better place than we had been for a very long time.

The following morning we were woken by Louis.

"Daddy, you're here. Are you not having a divorce any more?" He stood staring at Robbie.

My eyes shot open and Robbie sat up and lifted the side of the duvet to coax Louis in.

"No, of course not, Louis," said Robbie, croaking both from emotion and dehydration from all the wine.

"Damien's mum and dad got a divorce and his dad lives in a different place just like you were doing, so I thought you might be going to live with Damien's dad." Louis hugged Robbie happily.

I felt so guilty and mean. Louis hadn't mentioned any of this to me over the three weeks Robbie had been gone. I had brushed over it all and assumed the children hadn't noticed much. I'd really had my head up my arse lately. I needed to get with the plot and pull things back to normality before we were all irrevocably affected.

The atmosphere in the house was considerably better. Robbie and I were making a huge effort to talk to each other. We also decided to have a bit of a routine with going out. Wednesday night was "date night". We went to the cinema or for a meal out, making sure to find some time for each other. So far it was working. All the resentment seemed to have gone and Robbie was far more relaxed.

47

Susie

How to Deepfry a Frenzied Mother:
Take one wedding-obsessed mother, who has long since given up on her only daughter giving her a day out. Announce your engagement, watch as she froths and boils over with excitement.

The day after Walter proposed, we had driven the hour and a half to Mum's new flat and work premises. The place looked amazing, I had to hand it to her – and Jean no doubt. What had been a fairly nasty premises now looked bright and gorgeous. It was all decked out in ice-cream colours: creams, pale pinks, pale green and pale blue. They had created a bevelled effect in the once rectangular ceiling with clever draping of soft and flowing materials. Beautifully hand-decorated sparkly silk screens sectioned the room into different areas. Scented candles and soft lighting, with slow murmuring music, made the place calm, romantic and inviting.

A dramatic cream and gold chaise-longue with draping around it formed a wonderful centrepiece to the room.

"Mum, this is wonderful, congratulations!" I swivelled slowly around, taking in all the detail.

"Thank you, we're thrilled with the result. Jean and I are just on the same wavelength. We have similar taste and when we sat down and started to talk about the mental image we both had of this place, it was a match made in heaven," Mum was oozing with pride and delight.

She was so busy showing us all the new stock and explaining about the way they were planning on presenting things, it took me a while to even get a word in with her.

"Mum, can we tell you something?"

"Yes, dear. What is it?" She stopped and looked at me.

"Walter and I got engaged last night." I extended my hand with the ring on for proof.

"What?" She looked from my hand to Walter and back to me. "Now this isn't your idea of a sick joke, is it?" The colour had drained from her face and she flopped onto the chaise-long with a dull thud. With one hand on her stomach and the other on her forehead, she stared at us both as if we were little green men.

"A joke? No, Mum. Jesus, you must think I'm a right bitch! I know how you are about weddings. I wouldn't dangle the carrot at you and whip it away again!"

"Well, you did before," she sniffed.

Counting to ten, I chewed my lip as I tried, as usual, not to get annoyed with my mother.

"Well, things were different then," said Walter. "Susie wasn't ready to be married, and besides, she hadn't met me!"

"So it's really happening? A real live wedding, involving my own family?" Mum had gone a funny florid purple shade.

"Yes, Mum." I raised my eyebrows and grinned.

"Oh fucking hell! Oh excuse me! Oh Jesus, Mary and St Anthony, I don't believe it! This is incredible. This is the best news ever. Oh, where are we going to start? Susie," she grabbed my arm in a vice grip, "now promise me you won't go off to the Caribbean or Vegas or Rome or anywhere like that, so there's no organising to be done!"

"Mum, we really haven't discussed venues, but I don't think we'll be having a foreign wedding, will we?" I turned to Walter.

"Well, my mum has a bad hip and she's not keen on flying, so I think we can safely rule that out." Walter nodded very sagely at Mum, while trying to keep a straight face.

"Thank God!" gasped Mum. "So who knows? Who have you told?" She was like a headless chicken.

"Nobody, bar the three of us standing here. We thought you ought to be the first to find out."

"Thank you, darling. That's gorgeous." Her hands flew up to her mouth. "How many bridesmaids would you like, do you think? I saw the most amazing shimmering yellow silk the other day, but I'd say there might only be enough for five dresses left in it."

She was off.

"Mum? Hello? Mum?" I took her two hands. "I won't be having more than five bridesmaids, and I don't want to be rude but I can't see myself standing in the middle of a flock of canaries. We haven't decided on a date or even a year for this wedding, so don't start to panic, okay?"

The little bell on top of the shop door pinged and Jim and Jean walked in, carrying arms full of stock for the shop.

"Hello, hello," Jim greeted us cheerfully. "This is a nice surprise! Are you here to check up on us?" He kissed me on the cheek and shook hands with Walter. "Nice to see you again," he said. They'd met for a quick drink a couple of weeks previously.

"Emily and Walter just got engaged!" Mum was bouncing up and down with excitement, clapping her hands.

"That's wonderful news, congratulations both of you!" said Jim, looking absolutely delighted.

Jean was beaming.

After we all hugged and the men banged each other on the back awkwardly, amidst plenty of shuffling and deep coughing, Walter took me aside for a second.

"Was I supposed to take your father for a drink and ask for your hand in marriage, do you think?" His eyes were twinkling.

"No, he's only known my hand for a short while so I don't think it's really necessary!" I laughed.

"Seriously, though, will you ask him to give you away?"

"I don't know, really. I honestly haven't thought that far and when I was a little girl Mum was the one who talked more about weddings than me, so I never really had an image of myself walking down an aisle or who it would be with. I'll need to think about that one a bit more."

I watched all the people in the room and thought how strange the gathering was. A year ago, if someone had told me I'd be standing in my mother's wedding shop, with my father, his boyfriend and my fiancé, I think I would have wet myself laughing. But, here I was, and dysfunctional as it might seem from an outside perspective, I felt very lucky to have my odd-ball family together – sort of.

Slipping outside, I made a quick call to Emily.

"Hey, Em, how are you today?" I asked.

"Not as well as you are, judging by the tone of your voice. Have you been drinking?"

"No, not yet. But I have news!" I knew I was sounding like a squealing teenager.

"What?" Her voice was rising by the second.

"Walter and I are engaged!" I yelled.

"Fuck off!" she shouted.

"'Fraid so." I had to hold the phone away from my ear as she screamed.

"Oh, that's amazing news, Suze. I'm delighted for you both. It's about bloody time too. I was beginning to think I'd have to buy you a husband on the internet or something! Did he give you a ring?"

"Sure did. Not shabby either, I might add," I boasted.

"Bitch. You see, that's what happens when you wait eight years – the hubby-to-be has less kid and more cash which translates as a bigger piece of ice. I'm dying to see it. Ring me later on when the dust settles and we'll meet up for a quick examination session. Oh, I'm so, so happy for you, Suze! You deserve the best. Ring me when you can."

"You're on. Talk to you later."

By the time I'd rejoined Walter and the others, I could see he was looking a bit shell-shocked.

"I think I need to get away from here," he said. "They're going mad showing me dresses and suits and talking about venues and music and finger-food and cakes. I don't think I can take any more." He looked a bit green.

"Okay, let's head off. I have a work thing this evening, so I need to go home and prepare," I lied.

"You bloody spoofer! I hope you don't think you'll get away with telling me lies, Ms Rosedale!" Walter pinched my bum as we retreated from the One Stop Wedding Shop.

I'd say it might have taken Mum and Jean quite a while to even realise we were gone, they were so hysterical. The flapping and arm-waving and hi-pitched bouncing was all a bit much for me. I sincerely hoped Mum would get all that out of her system and return to earth fairly swiftly. I was beyond ecstatic with my news and impending wedding, but I was still never going to be frenzied about the whole thing. My only hope was that the business would take off with a bang and Mum would actually be too busy to pester me constantly.

48

Emily

Detergent Frappé:
Mix one small child with forbidden detergent. Survey damage while trying to remain calm. Wonder where the recipe book on how to raise a "normal" child has gone.

My appointments were looming closer all the time. My follow-up appointment with the gynaecological surgeon was three weeks away. I would be starting my hormone replacement therapy at that stage. I'd managed incredibly well so far and had escaped with few symptoms. I wasn't having hot flushes – quite the opposite, I was having cold shivers. The heat would drain from my body, my hands would go completely numb and my lips would go blue. It made me feel like I'd been standing at a bus stop for two hours in the middle of winter with no coat on. That chilled-to-the-bone feeling where you can't imagine ever being warm again.

I was suffering from headaches a bit, which was something I'd never had before. But the worst thing of all was still the muscle expanders in my breasts. I was longing and craving for a night's sleep where I could move comfortably onto my side. I kept waking up with pain searing through me, as the hard plastic buttons threatened to rip and pop through my skin. I felt like the whole of my breast was in danger of exploding at times. My back was suffering due to the rigid sleeping position. I was also starting to experience pain underneath the fold of my breasts, a slight stinging, tugging sensation, which I hoped would disappear when the less rigid implants were put in.

I don't know if it was just psychological, but I was reaching a point where I just couldn't stand the expanders any more. I was more than ready to have them removed.

It's a bit like the feeling at the end of a pregnancy, when you've coped brilliantly with growing this baby for a whole nine months and suddenly at the end an impatience and astonishing desire takes over and you just want that baby out. It could come out any orifice, you're not choosy at that point, you just want it out!

The children kept me sane though. I hauled myself around the supermarket and as I was attempting to unload the groceries, back home, a little vision appeared. I stifled a scream when I saw her.

"Look at me, Mummy, do I look booti-ful?" She had her face turned upwards, and eyes shut to show off her make-up. She had gloops of purple, pink and green all over her face. There was glitter everywhere. She was wearing a sparkly vest top of mine, which was pulled down to her navel, tucked into a pink bikini bottoms, which she'd put on over pale green woolly tights. Her tiny feet were stuck into my one and only pair of Jimmy Choo silver sandals and she was in serious danger of snapping the heels off them. The ensemble was completed by her hairstyle. She had stiff, crispy hair, which smelt alarmingly like loo cleaner.

"I'm a disco dancer, and I'm doing a show on the coffee table right now. You're invited. Come on!" She tugged my hand and I realised her hands were both gritty and sticky at the same time. A quick glance at her fingers revealed her self-manicured nails. She'd managed to paint the entire backs of her hands with a plum-coloured lacquer. Already in the sitting room, with a similarly made-up face and a head full of clips and bobbins was our long-suffering au pair Maisy.

"Hi, Maisy, you look divine. You should go out like that on Saturday night – you'd have to beat the men off with a stick."

She grinned and sat back good-naturedly. She was an amazing girl. She genuinely didn't mind when Tia covered her in gloop and made her sit in it for hours on end. There had to be a big squashy satin seat in heaven for Maisy. I was Tia's mother, so it was my job to be made to look and act like a total moron, but this girl was no blood relation and yet she allowed herself to be attacked on a regular basis. However, in this case I was wishing she was less tolerant.

"Ladies and gentlemen. Please welcome, all the way from the playroom, Princess Tia the Great!" Tia yelled at the top of her voice.

Maisy and I had to clap and cheer fervently.

Thrilled with herself, Tia proceeded to fling herself on and off the coffee table. After a few minutes and just as my ear drums were beginning to perforate she stopped.

"My eyes feel funny, Mum." She staggered towards me picking at her eyelashes. Examining her closely I realised she had stuck the glitter to her eyelids, eyebrows and forehead with school glue. Great big dollops of the stuff.

"Oh Christ, upstairs, Tia! We don't put glue on our own or anyone else's eyes or face, do you understand?"

I took her by her sticky arm and led her up the stairs. The quickest and easiest solution I could come up with was to remove the revolting outfit and put her in the shower. From there I put gentle eye-make-up remover onto a flannel and dabbed the congealed glue from her eyes, picking the bigger lumps off with my nails. As the water hit her hair, it began to foam. Disgusting smelling orange bubbles began to pour out of her head like a waterfall.

"Tia, what did you use to make your hair so pretty," I enquired gingerly.

"The same stuff I used to wash my curtains and carpet," she answered matter-of-factly.

Grabbing the showerhead off the wall, I directed the spray onto her head, and ensured none of the detergent went into her eyes or mouth. Fumbling for the shampoo, I put a tiny amount onto her hair and rinsed it clear. Then I wrapped her in a towel, guided her out of the shower and called Maisy upstairs.

"Can you please dry Tia and put something clean on her. She's been washing things while I was out."

Maisy's face dropped.

"The only time I leave her, Emily, was to put wet clothes on line in garden. When I come inside, she upstairs. I call her, she come down and she have this clothes on with hair sticky. I just thought she put gel." The poor girl looked panic-stricken.

"Don't worry, Maisy," I patted her arm. "We'll get to the bottom of it."

As I approached Tia's room, the smell got stronger and stronger. When I opened the door the stench of orange-scented, all-purpose cleaner stung my eyes and nostrils. There were spongy pools of bubbly mess in puddles around the carpet but she'd done a fine job on the curtains. They were streaked from about three feet down with a putrid murky violet colour, where the orange cleaner had mixed with the once-purple fabric. I opened the windows and backed out, shutting the bedroom door. On automatic pilot I walked down the stairs and found the number of the carpet cleaner. He answered after two rings.

"Hi, Peter, it's Emily Cusack," I informed him.

"How's it going, Emily? What's Tia done now?" he chuckled down the phone.

"Don't laugh, Peter. I haven't reached the stage where this is funny yet," I seethed.

I had to hold the phone away as he boomed into my ear with laughter.

I explained about the curtains and carpet. As usual, he promised to call over on his way home from work and do what he could. I hung up. I knew he was still laughing. This man had been called to our house at least five times a year since Tia had been able to physically move. She had sprayed, spilt, squirted and poured most types of cleaner known to man on most surfaces in our house. I had tried cupboard locks, child-lock containers, locking the cleaner in the shed. Although come the wintertime, that just didn't work. It was bad enough having to clean the house without having to be soaked or snowed on as well while retrieving cleaners from the garden.

I'd been lulled into a false sense of security by her in recent months, as she seemed to have grown out of it. I had stupidly taken my eye off the ball, thinking she had got the cleaning bug out of her system. Well, more fool me.

I had to rationalise the situation, and once again thank my lucky stars she hadn't blinded herself, or ingested the stuff. We were all intact and that was the main thing. It didn't stop me wanting to beat her senseless and dangle her out her bedroom window by the ankles, just to frighten the living daylights out of her. Of course, I didn't do any of those things.

I waited until Maisy had dressed her and then called her into my bedroom.

She skipped in gleefully. "Hi, Mummy-pummy!"

"No, Tia, I am very angry and shocked with your behaviour. Peter has to come again with the big machine and try to save your curtains and carpet. Putting cleaner on them like that is a bad idea. It ruins things and I've told you before not to do it." I wagged my finger at her.

Utterly unperturbed, she answered, "But Maisy told me to do it. The room was filthy so I made it all clean. That's all. Don't worry about it, Mummy, it will be all better in the morning, you'll see." She patted my head and skipped out.

I didn't have the strength to argue with her. She'd just end up screaming and then I'd have to calm her down. Peter was on the way. I'd deal with her later. Feeling like a wet rag, I made myself a cup of hippy herbal tea. Of course, it tasted like stewed grass, and certainly didn't make the situation any better.

49

Emily

Blood Bath Bake:
Fillet ovaries and fallopian tubes. Measure six pounds of pain. Add to abdomen. Garnish with nausea and a good coating of fear.

I began to bleed. I was doubled over with cramps and nauseous as hell.

"Robbie, am I supposed to be bleeding, do you think?" I asked him at breakfast.

Looking at me, with his eyebrows raised, mid-chew, he spat, "Do I look like a gynaecologist? I am also trying to eat, so would you kindly stop talking about things that I should have no conception or knowledge about?" Poking his red-berry muesli, he dropped the spoon, not hungry any more.

Men are just marvellous. If he'd been bleeding he'd have a megaphone and a flashing red light on his head, running up and down the kitchen shouting, "Mayday, mayday!" But there's no point in even going there. We all know the population would have ceased centuries ago if men were to have babies. Their colds are life-threatening, all their illnesses are more serious than women's and no one understands them.

I drove the familiar route to the hospital a couple of days later and sat myself down in Ms Mulcahy the gynaecological surgeon's waiting area. As usual it was completely full. Women of all ages, sizes and colours waited nervously to discuss their bits with this woman.

"So what's been going on?" Ms Mulcahy asked, settling herself in a seat and gesturing to me to sit opposite her.

"I've had some abdominal cramping and some heavy bleeding over the last three days, but I wasn't sure if this was normal or not, so I rang your secretary and she told me to come straight in." I finished, feeling a little stupid. I knew I was supposed to be entering menopause which in itself is a cessation of menstruation, but I didn't know when that would happen. I was expecting her to sneer at my ignorance and tell me I could expect to bleed monthly for quite a while.

But she didn't. She didn't even seem to think I should be made to sit in a corner weaning a hat with a big "D" on it.

"In short, Emily, you shouldn't be bleeding, and you are not stupid to ring and come in to see me. I am a consultant gynaecologist, you are not. Therefore you are not expected to know all the answers to these questions. We'll leave that up to me." She smiled kindly. "I am going to prescribe you Cyklokapron. It acts as a coagulant, and so will clot your blood to stop the bleeding. I want you to take the pills three times a day for four days."

"Okay," I answered, relieved and a little surprised that I had in fact been right to come in. I was also delighted to have something to take and to be told it would stop the bleeding.

"Having said that, if you feel any more pain, and the bleeding hasn't stopped by the day after tomorrow, I want you to call my secretary first thing in the morning and come straight back in, do you understand?"

"Sure," I answered, feeling better. It's a great feeling to have someone competent take over and tell you what to do. Maybe the old goat wasn't so bad after all. She did have her uses.

I took the pills and the bleeding stopped.

My journey was coming to an end. Well, the end was in sight. The final hurdle had to be jumped and we'd be on the home stretch. I was also within spitting distance of my hormone replacement therapy or HRT appointment. I was having more and more menopausal symptoms. The hot flushes were now keeping me awake at night. Any time I managed to get to sleep they woke me up. I was uncomfortable with the breast expanders, but this internal furnace was another problem altogether. It started at a volcanic source right in the core centre of my body, from whence it bubbled and rose through my flesh. It was like molten lava was raging through my soft tissue, setting it almost on fire. I would immediately retaliate by kicking off the duvet. It would take a few seconds for the cool air to hit my skin. Then the shivers would take over causing teeth-chattering, bone-racking movement. Retreating under the covers the heat would rise again immediately. By now, I would be wide-awake, exhausted and frustrated. Sometimes I would go back to sleep at once, other times I would lie awake, listening to Robbie sleep and the odd drunk person pass by the window outside. I would zone in on things I needed to do. I would try to stop my mind from whirring but I would often get in a rut and find myself being so annoyed at being awake that I had no hope of falling back to sleep.

Night terrors had taken hold also. I was having vivid and colourful nightmares, which would wake me with a thump. I would sit up deranged and disorientated to find myself sweating – again. It was a vicious circle and was now bothering me so much that I was beginning to dread going to bed. Every four nights I would allow myself to take half a sleeping tablet. This afforded me a night free of dreams, solid slumber and a whole new approach to the world when I woke up.

I was hoping that HRT was the magic wand I had been told it was. I was having in-depth conversations with women twenty and thirty years my senior about menopause. It was enlightening and humbling. They were in the same boat as me, but we looked very different from the outside. They had so much more life experience than me.

I felt almost like an impostor or the villain in *Scooby Doo* who gets her mask removed at the end of the programme and they reveal it's the young upstart after all. All I was missing was: "I would have gotten away with it, if it weren't for those pesky kids."

50

Susie

Wedding-Flavoured Fever:
Take one frenzied Mother of the Bride, mix with a wedding-phobic daughter. Watch as nerves are grated.

Mum had begged me to come and have lunch and chat about my wedding. We'd only been engaged a wet week and there was plenty of time to organise things but as far as Mum was concerned there was no time like the present.

"Go and meet the poor woman and put her out of her misery," Walter had said.

"Well, what type of wedding were you thinking about?" I asked. "Before I go and meet her, I need to have some iota of an idea, or else she'll take off and we'll end up in a cathedral with three hundred people we've never met before."

"I dunno, maybe a smallish church followed by a country house. Something more on the demure side than Disney Princess side, if that suits you too." He looked worried.

"Right, that sounds about right. Why are you looking at me like that?" I asked suspiciously.

"I just hope you don't feel dragged along by pressure like you did with Kevin all those years ago," he confessed.

"Honey, you and Kevin are light years apart. I was a different person then. I wasn't ready and I didn't actually love the poor guy. It was all wrong from start to finish. This is different. You are different, and more importantly, so am I. I love you and I can't wait to marry you. I would rather we did it quietly with a handful of people, all of whom we actually know and like. But I think a registry office and a table for twelve might just break Mum's heart. But we won't be too silly about it all the same."

Mum was sitting at an outside table, with a glass of white wine and an array of brochures, magazines and folders. She was busily sorting things into piles and humming away to herself.

I stood for a second and watched her. She was so happy with her new job – it had given her a whole new lease of life. I was glad for her. She was a funny fish. She annoyed the crap out of me in so many ways, but deep down I loved her so much. She had great spirit and wasn't afraid to be herself.

She looked up and spotted me.

"Oh, there you are, Susie, come and join me. I've so many exciting ideas I want to share with you. I've had a bit of an unsuccessful morning too, so I'm kind of hoping you'll be more enthusiastic." She looked a bit dejected for a second.

"Why, Mum, what happened?" I kissed her cheek and sat beside her.

"Oh, I finally met a client and the deal fell through – she's decided her mother is making everything and they're keeping it simple." She thumbed through more pages as she spoke. "But, anyway, back to your wedding. Have you decided on a date or a time of year yet?" She was off.

"No and no. Look, before you lose the run of yourself, Mum, we're not having a cathedral, glass coach, white horses, two thousand guests or swans and ice sculptures."

"Right. How many are you thinking of and we'll work from there." She was holding her breath hopefully.

"Well, I'm not sure until we sit down and work it out properly, but I can't imagine having more than about sixty. We're thinking a small church and a country house."

"Okay. Well, I know of two which would be gorgeous. I have brochures here . . ." She began to sift through the glossy clear plastic pages of a ring-binder folder. "The deciding factor would really be the time of year. One would be better for a winter wedding and the other would be better for the summer." She tucked her pen behind her ear as she thumbed through her file.

I was mildly impressed with her professionalism. She'd really found her niche.

"Well, seeing as it's the start of autumn now, we can either go for a winter wedding and do it maybe around Christmas time, or we can wait until next year and have a summer wedding. Those are the options really." I was trying to sound like I was really excited.

"Ah, Susie, you're going to have to muster up a bit more excitement than that! You *are* going to have a wedding this time, aren't you?" Mum looked over her reading glasses at me, with her *I'm warning you, young lady* face on.

"Yes, Mum. I'm fully planning on getting married this time. It would also be really helpful if you would stop talking about the last engagement. It freaks Walter out and it's not something I'm that thrilled to bring up over and over again. Can we both decide that it was all very unfortunate and not feel the need to bring it up any more? Unless you'd like to have one final big discussion about it? Maybe then we could lay it all to rest?"

"No, that's all right, dear. If you say you're going to go through with this one and you're happy about it, then I think I can get over the last unfortunate one." Mum sighed and looked like she was dealing with a huge personal struggle. "Although at the time I thought I'd never get over it. I really thought you were making a grave mistake. But I always want you to be happy and that's why I'd never say anything."

Once again, I had to quash my annoyance at her. I knew she wasn't deliberately trying to annoy me but she always managed it all the same.

"Just thinking aloud, Mum, I wonder would it be nice to do the wedding around Christmas? Emily should be finished with all operations and it'll be the start of a new beginning for us all. We could even try for New Year's Eve. That could be lovely. Nobody ever knows where to go and what to do on that night, so why not do it then?"

"Oh, that sounds gorgeous! You could have fireworks and a big exciting countdown to midnight! That sounds so romantic!" Mum had tears in her eyes just thinking about it. I nearly had too but not for the same reason. The thought of some plank with a microphone, shouting ten, nine, eight . . . Oh Jesus, with everyone in a circle on the wooden dance floor holding crossed hands ready to sing Auld Lang Syne. Oh, it made me shudder. They might even try to push me into the middle of the floor and make me stand there like a meringue with a head as all the florid drunk faces beamed at me.

"Mum, hang on and let me phone Walter before you get too emotional." I dialled his number and waited to see if he could speak.

After a brief conversation where he categorically stated that he didn't care where or when we got married, just so long as we did it, we agreed New Year's Eve would be fine.

"We might have difficulty securing a venue as it's a popular date, you know." Mum was off in her telephone voice, with her glasses balanced on her nose, and she wasn't even on the telephone.

After another hour of wedding talk, I'd had enough. The venue was actually available and we made an appointment to go and see it the following week. There was a small eighteenth century church just beside the grounds and it was also available.

"That's all the major things sorted. Until we go and see it, there's nothing else we need to do for now, is there?" I yawned and stretched.

"Susie, Susie, Susie! For an intelligent girl, you really don't have a clue about weddings and the amount of preparation needed, do you?" Mum was enjoying the role of me being a half-wit and her being the controller.

"Well, I'll tell you what, Mum, I'm hiring you to sort it all out. Once we've seen the venue and agreed it will do, you can organise the rest. All I ask is that you think demure rather than Disney. You put the package together and I'll approve it. It will be a business arrangement and I can rest easy that you will think of every detail, especially the ones I've never heard of. What do you think?" I looked at her hopefully.

"I'd love that but of course I won't be charging you, silly minx. You can be my official practice run, how's that? All I'll ask you to pay for are the costs, and I'll waive the fee. What do you think?" She looked so proud and excited.

"I think that's amazing. Thanks, Mum!" I leaned across and hugged her. "I'm very glad you're so happy. You seem to have found your niche in life, haven't you?"

I pulled back and saw the twinkling delight in her eyes.

As I drove away, I phoned Emily to see how she was. When I explained to her about the idea of having a New Year's Eve wedding, she was delighted.

"Brilliant idea, I'll be happy to say goodbye to the last year I can tell you. That sounds wonderful."

"Now I'm only testing the water to see how you feel, but would you like to be my matron of honour?"

"Oh, Susie. Of course I'd love to! But please just promise me we'll pick the dress together."

"We can, but I'm the bridezilla here, so you have to go along with what I say. I think a layered bright orange number, which makes you look the size of a house is in order."

"Bitch. I wouldn't put it past you," Emily laughed. "Seriously, that sounds amazing though – winter weddings are lovely. It can be dodgy organising a summer wedding in Ireland. I know we all say we're not going to take the weather into account, but it must be hard not to think your marriage is doomed if it's the middle of August and there are thunderstorms and grey skies."

"True, and this way we can go down the log fires and cosy house with mulled wine and comfort food route. Much easier!"

Emily was laughing.

"What?" I said.

"You're about as romantic as a kick in the head, do you know that?"

"Ah, shut up, Em! You know I don't do this stuff. It'll be great on the day and I'll have a ball and all of that, but I just don't have the head for all this frills and skipping through the meadow crap. It doesn't mean I won't make a fantastic wife, mind you. I can heat up a ready meal just like the next woman. I can give my laundry to the 'Mr Suds' van on a Tuesday and accept it all back on a Thursday."

"Have you thought about the children issue?" Emily asked.

"Yes and no. I have of course thought it will probably have to happen, but I'm not really going to sit and plan it down to the last second. Walter has made no secret of the fact that he'd like kids. And I love kids – I just couldn't eat a whole one!"

"Or you could do what Robbie and I did, and plan not to have any for a while, and then get pregnant that day. Apart from almost dying of shock, it worked perfectly for us."

As I finished my chat with Emily and entered my apartment, I looked at it all with fresh eyes. I loved and adored my little place. It was mine and I'd earned every square inch of it, but times and circumstances change. I knew that one day, and it didn't have to be this week, but one day I would be ready to leave it behind and move on.

I had dreadful feelings of nervousness about being a mother. But I had felt the same way about getting married for a very long time and now look at me. I knew I was the closest I'd ever come to meandering towards the direction of motherhood. I knew Walter would be able to handle me too. He would sweep me along with him, we'd do it together. Be positive, Susie, I thought to myself. Life is what you make it. I flicked on the kettle to make a cup of coffee and realised I was humming.

God, I hope I'm not turning into my mother, I thought.

51

Susie

Curdled Wedding:
Whip two cups of wedding-loving weirdos with one cup of wedding-weary wanderers. Watch as the mixture threatens to curdle and spoil.

Walter and I went with Mum, Jean and Jim to view the country house in Meath, which was about an hour's drive from Dublin. It was quaint and leaned a little bit more towards the *Fawlty Towers* side than the Hilton side of things.

It was run by third-generation owners, all of whom were charming and rather batty. They didn't go in for fancy convoluted food and said they'd "do a nice dinner, using ingredients that were in season". They weren't keen on loud discos until six in the morning and they'd very much appreciate if the guests could refrain from parking near the back field, as a car had got stuck there last year and it had taken two tractors to pull it out.

Apart from that, it seemed they didn't care what we did. They suggested having an official brunch on New Year's Day at around twelve o'clock, so everyone could join in.

"There's nothing worse than not knowing what you're supposed to do the day after a wedding. Should you skulk away in your track suit or get all dressed up and stand around shaking hands making polite conversation?" said Henry the owner. "Make it easy for them. Give them a nice hot hangover cure, full Irish breakfast, plenty of home-made stodgy breads with sticky home-made jam and send them all on their way. It cuts out all the messing."

"That sounds like a lovely idea. How many can stay here?" I asked.

"We can sleep twenty-six in the house and then we have converted stables which will sleep a further sixteen. Along with the three guesthouses within walking distance, you could comfortably have fifty-six guests."

Walter and I looked at each other.

"Done," we said together.

With the venue booked, and the date set, I felt really excited.

"Because it's a small number, we can pay for everything," Walter suggested. "All the accommodation and food and drinks. That way, all the people invited will be getting a proper night out with no expense for them."

"I agree," I said. "The other thing is, I don't want twelve toasters and a revolting dinner service. Let's put a no-presents request on the invitation."

"But, Susie," Mum piped up from the back of the car, "you might get some lovely keepsakes!"

"Yes, that's what I'm afraid of. No presents and that's final." I was adamant I wanted a no-frills affair. I could hear Mum sighing in the back seat of the car.

"But you can request vouchers or do a lovely wedding list. All the exclusive stores have wedding list departments. It's easily organised and you and Walter could make a day of it. Go and choose a beautiful family heirloom dinner service together. One you could leave to your grandchildren, then have a delicious champagne lunch together. It would be so romantic."

Mum was trying to entice me, but the thought of traipsing around a shop looking at gravy boats filled me with horror.

"Mum, you'll just have to find yourself a man to marry and then you can have the full fairytale day, with all the frills and fuss imaginable. It can be my idea of a total nightmare and you can do your worst."

"You are going to wear a dress and veil, aren't you?" Mum ignored my jibe and decided to see how far she could push me.

"I haven't decided any of that, Mum, and we're not discussing it in front of Walter. It will ruin the surprise." I was relieved to have a scapegoat.

"Oh of course, sorry, dear. I shouldn't say any more. I'll just work away quietly and I'll fill you in when I've got some suggestions." She beavered away in the back seat.

We stopped for lunch on the way home and I had a bowl of seafood chowder. The others had chicken and chips in a basket.

By the time we arrived back at our apartment less than an hour later, I was beginning to feel slightly queasy.

"Do you feel sick after that lunch?" I asked Walter.

"Not at all, do you?" He peered around his newspaper.

"Yes – in fact –" I ran and just made it to the toilet bowl. That was the first of a series of vomits that day. In fact, I managed to vomit right into the night as well.

I was feeling dehydrated, so I kept allowing myself sips of water. I soon realised that one tiny sip equalled another bout of dry retching. So I gave up and fell into bed like a wet rag.

I slept fitfully and woke the next morning, feeling like a wrung out-sponge. My tongue was fuzzy and stuck to the roof of my mouth. Walter was snoring soundly as I padded into the kitchen to get a glass of water.

Gingerly, I raised the glass to my lips. I was almost afraid to drink it in case the whole process started again.

The water felt cool and relieved my tight throat and parched mouth. I could feel the coldness trickle down my oesophagus and enter my stomach. My tummy reacted by gurgling violently. Feeling a bit hot and sweaty and light-headed, I sat on the sofa. I must have been sitting there with my greasy hair and dead-fish-eye-stare for almost half an hour before Walter appeared.

"Good morning, vomit pants," he said. "Is it safe to sit near you?" He gathered me into a hug.

"Hug at your own risk, I'd say I smell."

"Ah, you're still beautiful to me," Walter grinned.

"Get a grip, I look scary," I swatted him and inwardly thanked him for his ability to pretend that I wasn't a germ-infested mank-bag.

I spent the day in bed, sipping flat 7UP, which seems to contain magic powers. By that evening I was able to eat some toast and drink a mug of tea.

"Jesus, I thought I was going to die last night. It was definitely the seafood chowder too. Every time I think of it, I cringe. I don't think I'll ever be able to eat it again."

We went to bed to watch a DVD but only managed to watch the first ten minutes, deciding instead to turn to our own personal form of entertainment.

52

Emily

Menopausal Mince:
Take one thirty-year-old woman. Remove ovaries. Leave to sweat.
Add cramps, bleeding and a general feeling of confusion. Mix with a
Rottweiler carefully disguised as a surgeon.

My appointment with Ms Mulcahy had dawned. As usual, I waited for hours to be seen, becoming a dazed, red-faced, vacant-looking dumpling.

"Emily Cusack?"

I was being summoned finally.

"Hi, Ms Mulcahy, how are you today?" I tried to smile at her.

"Sit down, Emily. Sorry about the delay there." She didn't smile. "Your pathology results have come back, you are in the clear. Everything went to plan. I will prescribe your hormone replacement therapy and you can leave." She didn't look at me. She barely drew a breath.

"I've been having hot flushes and a lot of headaches. I'll be glad to feel a bit more normal," I ventured.

"Well, that's all normal, due to the ovary removal. Here's your prescription. If you have any problems, ring my secretary." She scribbled on a notebook and stood up, handing me my prescription.

"Thanks, lovely to see you again. I feel a bit like Charlie, from the chocolate factory." I gave her a slightly too hard dig in the top of the arm.

"Pardon?" She looked me up and down as if I was insane.

"I've got a golden ticket!" I sang waving my HRT prescription.

"Quite." She glowered like a bullfrog.

"Well, it's been a pleasure as always." I banged her on the back and walked out to her secretary.

Jesus, she might have her uses but she was a rotten, grumpy old trout. I had enjoyed poking her in the arm and would have happily given her a swift kick in the butt as well. But the main thing was that I didn't have ovarian cancer. All had gone to plan, and I had my HRT. Thank goodness. I was hoping to feel normal again.

All the reports I'd read and anyone I'd spoken with had told me it was like magic. That it restored feelings of normality pronto. I was looking forward to saying goodbye to the hot flushes for a few years. In the greater scheme of things, having a numb bum from waiting and dealing with a grumpy trout were a drop in the ocean. I suppose any woman who spends her day chopping other women's bits off is bound to be a tad odd.

53

Susie

Tolerance Terrine:
Mix one wedding-crazed mother with one wedding-phobic daughter.
Peel patience and chop up tolerance. Hope everything doesn't spoil.

Mum was getting more and more frenzied about my wedding as the days went by. There was plenty of time but she was getting her knickers firmly in a twist.

"Mum, I am not ready to count down yet. By the time the wedding happens, we'll all have died of boredom."

"Well, speak for yourself, young lady. I happen to be very excited about the whole day. I don't mind telling you, I am starting to seriously panic about your dress."

"Why?" I was flicking through my patient files for that morning.

"You haven't tried on one single dress – you don't even know what your style is. Some girls come in to see me with a set idea in their heads of what they want, only to discover that's not their style. So they have to change their whole mindset and image of what they're going to look like in their photos. That can be very upsetting in its own way. So the more time you give yourself the better."

"Okay, Mum. I'll come in over the next few days and try some on, how's that?" I just wanted to fob her off.

"Susie, you are just the limit. Why did I get lumbered with such a difficult daughter? Any other normal girl would be thrilled to have a mother with a wedding shop. I don't know what's wrong with you, that you won't let yourself be caught up in all the delicious glamour and romance of it all!" Mum sounded quite exasperated with me. Again.

I was suddenly drawn to a file. Henry Sweeney, a lovely widower, was coming in to see me that morning. He needed a few sessions to help him after his wife had passed away two years ago. She had died slowly of a degenerative progressive brain disorder. He had, understandably, come to me suffering with trauma after her death.

He was quite old-fashioned in a lot of ways and a real gentleman. He now came to see me every six months, to keep himself in check, as he put it. With a sudden blinding flash, I thought he'd make a gorgeous partner for Mum.

I told Mum about him, and said it was a pity I wasn't in a position to introduce them.

"Susie, I think you're getting as mad as your patients if you think I'm going to start dating any of your mental cases. Do you think I'm that desperate that I'd need to go on blind dates with lunatics?" she shrieked.

"Mum, calm down, you're overreacting here. Firstly, I am not going to set up a blind date. Secondly, Henry is not a lunatic or a mental case. You are so narrow-minded when it comes to my work. You decided years ago that all the people I deal with are somehow subhuman, or so insane they foam at the mouth and go around trying not to murder people. For your information, a lot of my patients are a lot more level-headed and normal than you at times. They all want to be the best people they can be. That's why they have therapy. You need to get your head out of your arse and stop judging everybody. You live on your own planet and that's fine, but don't look out your own little squinting window and wag your finger at everyone else. I know my wedding is very important to you. I know you believe what I am wearing on the day is of life threatening significance. Fine. If you feel that way, that's up to you. I don't go around telling you that what you do is pitiable or futile. But that's how you've always made me feel about my job. I'm sick of you judging me and disapproving of me because I don't want to be Cinderella. Face it, Mum, the slipper doesn't fit. It never will. If you want a fairy tale, look in the mirror. Go and find your own prince. Leave me out of it. And before you go off phoning Walter, I am not calling my wedding off. I am simply going to do it my way. I no longer require your services. Use your time and energy on someone who doesn't hang around with lunatics for a living."

I hung up and instead of feeling guilty and mean, like I used to. I felt liberated and free. Mum was excited about my wedding, but there was more to it than that. She so obviously craved to be a bride and live the life she now thought I was about to have. But I was not going to be her puppet any more. She needed to grow up and face the music. She needed to get out more and mix with the real world. I knew I was being harsh, but at the same time I was not going to be bamboozled into having *my* wedding for her. Enough was enough. If she didn't piss off and leave me alone, I would end up not speaking to her for a long time. To be perfectly honest, it would be no skin off my nose.

That night, Walter and I were sitting sharing a bottle of wine on the balcony, when the phone rang.

"Hi, Susie, it's me, Jim."

"Hi, Jim! How are things?"

"All fine this end, how are you?" He paused. "Look, your mother was on to me earlier and she's very upset about your row today. She means well and she thinks you don't want her to be your wedding co-ordinator any more. I offered to give you a buzz and try to clear things up. What's the deal?" Jim sounded awkward and not overly happy at being dragged into our domestic.

"Jim, I appreciate your acting on Mum's behalf. But she's right. I don't want her to have anything more to do with my wedding. She's driving me nuts, she's like a dog with a bone and all I can say is that she'll have to learn to listen to people a little more if she wants to make her business work. I'm sick of her sighing with disappointment because I prefer reading books to discussing shoes. I am as fashion-conscious as the next girl but it's not my entire life's work. Also, since about the age of six, the allure of weddings and everything to do with them was brutally stamped out of me, due to her obsession. I was willing to let Mum play with our wedding to a certain point. But it has reached a stage where she's phoning me twice and three times a day and berating me for not doing things and not jumping up and down about it all. It's one fucking day, Jim. It will be a super day for all concerned, I hope. But it's months away. I have no intention of walking up the aisle naked. I will have flowers, the cake will be ordered. I'm not going in a stagecoach, helicopter, stretched pink Hummer or any other ridiculous contraption she comes up with. It's Walter's and my day and we will spend it the way we want. End of story." I exhaled.

There was a brief silence. I heard Jim cough nervously.

"Erm, right, so. Yes, okay," he stammered.

"Sorry, Jim. I shouldn't rant at you but as you can tell I've had enough of all this bullshit." I relaxed, glad it was all out in the open.

Walter was grinning.

"What the hell are you smirking for, Walter Blake?" I glowered at him.

"Oh, don't mind me, I'll just sit with my fingers in my ears and hum. Then I'll turn up at the church on the day and wonder why your mother's not there. I quite like the idea of you walking up the aisle naked though, if I might say so!" He started to laugh.

"Shut your hole, no one asked you!"

"Who? Me or him?" Jim asked.

"Not you, him!" I shouted.

Both Jim and Walter thought this was hilarious.

"Look, Susie," said Jim, "for what it's worth, I have to agree with you. I think the whole wedding hype is a little too much. But your mum is so excited and she just wants to make it special for you both."

"Jim, sorry to sound nasty, but considering I've known her a lot longer than anyone, she's actually not thinking of me at all. She's thinking of herself. I am not backing down on this one. She can come to the wedding, by all means, but I'm not letting her take over and do what she wants."

There was silence and I knew Jim was in a bit of a position. I was sure Jean was on my mother's side. In fact, they'd probably both been discussing what a horrid nasty girl I was all afternoon.

"While we're on the subject, Jim. What are your thoughts on walking me down the aisle to give me away? I had always assumed Mum would do it. But given the circumstances, I would like you to do it. What do you reckon?"

"That's very kind of you to ask, but why don't we leave that to nearer the time. I am available of course, but things are a bit raw at the moment. Let's wait until closer to the time and see what the best thing might be. Don't box yourself in. If you work things out with Pauline, she might be terribly hurt if you tell her I've stepped in. After all, she was the one who reared you. She may never forgive either of us if she feels pushed out on the day. Angry as you may be now, you don't want to hurt her unnecessarily. I'm only the newcomer in your life. I know you're very angry with her right now, but I'm sure you'll sort out your differences in time."

We spoke for another few minutes and I promised Jim I would keep an open mind about the whole wedding. He was very calm and diplomatic. He had a wonderful way of smoothing things over in an unruffled way.

Not for the first time since finding Jim, I was grateful I'd got him in my life now.

"Jesus, I think we should just run away to Rome for the weekend and get married without any of them," I confided in Walter. "That way we can wear our jeans and eat pizza and drink wine with nobody to annoy us."

"It's not a bad idea. It is possible. Why don't we just do nothing for the moment and see how you feel in a couple of weeks' time? If you still hate the idea of a wedding and things aren't better with Pauline, then we could do it." Walter looked serious.

Right at that moment I loved him more than ever. I knew he would jump through hoops if that would make me happy. I slid down into the chair and took a big slug of wine. Closing my eyes I tried to think happy thoughts and put my mother and her wedding stresses out of my head.

Walter was right, I had months before the invitations needed to be sent out. I would work it all out before then. Right at that moment, I needed to clear my head and get things in perspective. Otherwise, I'd be sitting in my chair in more of a mess than any of my patients the following morning.

54

Susie

Stinger (Shaken not Stirred):
Take one very controlled consultant. Add copious amounts of uncontrollable vomit. Leave shaken to the core.

I could hear Walter talking to a client on his mobile phone in our bedroom. He ran his clinic in a very open-house way. If his patients needed to call him on the mobile, he encouraged it.

Seeing as it was only six thirty in the morning, I decided to drag myself out of bed and spend the time having a shower and shaving my legs, rather than hearing Walter talking a patient through a panic attack. I had a whole day of my own patients ahead of me. I didn't need to take his on board also.

As soon as the hot water hit the back of my neck, the saliva started to run into my mouth.

I pulled the shower screen back and managed to make it to the bowl in time. Dragging myself off the floor a few minutes later, I turned off the running shower.

Wrapping myself in a towel, I staggered back to bed. Walter had finished his call and was all ready for a cuddle.

"Don't, I'm sick. I think I've got food poisoning again. I was in the shower and I suddenly had to puke." I was shivery and miserable.

"But I ate the same chicken dish as you last night and I'm fine," he said, puzzled.

"I'm thrilled for you," I answered flatly. "I've a full clinic today too, so I don't know what I'm going to do. I really need to try and get around to hiring someone else to fill in when I'm away and to generally alleviate things. I'm too busy and it's getting to a stage where it's all becoming too much for me."

"Well, see how you feel – what time is your first appointment? Would it help if I filled in today? I'm supposed to be off today to look for new premises, but I can give you a dig out if you like?" He rubbed my arm gently.

"I don't know. I'm not sure how the patients would take it. If they don't know you it might throw them off balance. Thanks for the offer, but I'll have to try and drag myself in after a while." The room was spinning and I felt like I needed at least twelve hours more sleep.

I woke to the sound of Walter's voice.

"Susie, you'll have to decide what you're doing. It's nearly eight. If you're not going in you'll have to either let me go for you or notify your patients."

Feeling less ill, I sat up, rubbed my eyes and stretched. I was feeling a little bit better. If I didn't eat anything, maybe I'd be all right.

"I'll jump in the shower and see how I feel," I mumbled.

By the time I'd managed to get dressed I was still shaky, but starving. Knowing I didn't have time for breakfast, I grabbed my coat and kissed Walter.

"I'll manage today. Why don't you call in and see me at lunch-time? I've only a half-hour gap today, but I'd love you to bring me a sandwich or something if you're in the area."

"I thought you had food poisoning?" He looked at me quizzically.

"It's obviously gone from my system. I'll be fine."

"Okay. I'll pop by with some lunch. See you later on." He waved as I backed out the door.

I drove the short journey and as I stood up out of my car, I had a sudden head rush, which caused me to lurch forwards. Grabbing the open car door to steady myself, I managed to stay on my feet. As I walked in towards my clinic, I was worried about passing the bug on to my patients. It was actually really irresponsible of me to go to work with a tummy bug.

By the time I managed to get into the lift and stop at every floor on the way, I was only just in time for my first patient.

Rushing into my office, I had time to grab the first file and call my patient straight in.

As we began the session, I felt queasy again. Pouring myself a glass of mineral water, I had to sip it slowly and concentrate on not throwing up. I knew I must have looked a bit bug-eyed and strained, but what could I do?

By twelve o'clock I was feeling a lot better. Thank God. It was a relief the retching had stopped.

My patient was leaving the room when everything started to spin. I could see and hear the lady standing in front of me but it all started to slow down. Her voice began to drone and go deep. Like an old record player winding down.

"Ms Rosedale?"

I knew I was falling to the floor, it all happened in slow motion, but I couldn't stop it at the same time.

The next thing I remember was opening my eyes to see my secretary and patient looking down at me.

"Oh, sorry. What happened? Why am I on the floor?" I asked, feeling very foolish and embarrassed.

"You've just fainted. Try and sit up and put your head between your knees. It will help to get the blood flowing again," the patient said.

Doing what I was told, I leaned forward, delighted to be able to hide my face. I felt so unprofessional and stupid.

"I'm fine now. I'll show you out and let you make another appointment." I smiled and clambered up. I steadied myself and, using the wall of the small corridor to the waiting-room as support, managed to make my way to the desk.

"Are you sure you're okay?" My secretary was having none of it.

"I'm fine now, emergency over," I tried to smile. I waved to my patient and told my secretary to hold off my last patient of the morning for a minute.

Making my way into the small bathroom, I locked the door and using the paper towels for drying hands, I dampened some and mopped my forehead. Taking deep breaths, I closed my eyes and tried to relax.

Somehow I got through the last patient of the morning and called Walter.

"Hi, Walter, listen I'm okay now but I've had a bit of a black-out. Are you on your way in here with lunch?"

"I'm just pulling into the car park. I'll see you in a minute. What happened?" He sounded surprised and concerned.

It was weird, as soon as I heard his voice, all I wanted to do was cry. What the hell was wrong with me? I heard my voice crack and I stifled a sob.

"I'd say it's just this bug I have," I managed. "I'll see you in a minute. I'm free so just come on in." I put the phone down and the tears just flowed. I wasn't making them come, they just arrived on their own. It was all totally involuntary. What the hell was wrong with me? I didn't cry. Ever. This just didn't fit.

By the time Walter arrived with a picnic lunch, I was hysterical. I knew he was coming in and I did honestly try to stop the tears, but they wouldn't comply.

"Jesus, Susie, what's happened?" He dropped the lunch stuff on my desk and rushed over to me. He wrapped his arms around me and that made me worse. Howling like a small child, I let him hold me and rock me backwards and forwards.

As soon as he knew I was calmer, he flicked open his mobile phone and dialled a number.

"Peter? Hi, it's Walter. Listen, Susie isn't well. She was vomiting this morning and she's just had a black-out. She's a bit distressed. Can you see her this afternoon?"

"I can't, Walter, I have a clinic," I tried to interrupt.

"Okay, you're a star. Thanks, yes, she's here in Rochestown Clinic.

Perfect. Thanks, I really appreciate it."

Walter clicked the phone shut and smiled.

"Bingo, my friend Peter is ten minutes away. He's a doctor. He's going to swing by and have a quick look at you."

"What? Are you fucking mental?" I felt so angry it wasn't natural. "I'm not having your friend come and poke my bits and then have to sit in the pub with him and act normal. That's so inappropriate, Walter. How could you do that to me?" To my shock and disgust, I burst out crying again.

Looking like a drowning man, Walter backed out of the room and took refuge with my secretary. I heard them discussing my afternoon clinic. Two of the patients were new and one wasn't.

"Phone them all and explain that I am standing in today, so if they wish to reschedule to see Susie specifically that's perfect – otherwise they can see me today."

He walked back into the room.

"You can't do that, Walter. People won't appreciate being messed around like that. It's out of the question!"

"It's happening, Susie, so just relax."

To my own astonishment, I didn't have the energy to argue. At least he was notifying the patients and offering them an alternative.

Peter knocked on the door a few minutes later. Himself and Walter shook hands and banged each other on the back. Walter left the room, and I could hear him talking to my secretary.

"So what's going on then?" Peter pulled up a chair and sat down, resting his elbows on his knees to scrutinise me.

"How do I know?" I barked.

"Okay, let's start at the beginning," he said, ignoring my rudeness.

"I woke up this morning to Walter conducting a counselling session from our bed, so I went for a shower, threw up, then fell asleep. I rushed in here late, have sipped water, haven't puked since. I was showing a patient out and wham I woke up on the floor." Then the tears started to flow again. "And to top it all off, I'm crying more than I did when I was a baby and I don't know what's wrong with me." I shrugged my shoulders and continued to sob – involuntarily.

Peter regarded me thoughtfully. "Is there any possibility you might be pregnant, Susie?"

"No, God no. I'm on the pill. I took my last pill only two days ago. I'm on day two of my seven-day break. I'll get my period either today or tomorrow."

"And you took all the pills in the packet, on the correct days this month? You didn't miss one?" he asked while rooting in his bag.

"Peter, I am capable of taking one pill a day, especially when the days are marked on the packet."

"Okay, then. Just pop into the loo and pee on this to rule that out. It could be a number of things, but this will just tick one box for me." He smiled calmly.

Snatching the stick, I went and did the business. Before I'd even managed to wash my hands, the second blue line had appeared.

Guess what? I started to cry – again.

"Susie, are you all right in there? You've been there for a long time, are you sick again?"

It was Walter.

I unlocked the door and opened it a fraction. He pulled the door open and poked his head in.

"Okay?"

"Walter, I'm pregnant," I blubbed, hunched on the closed toilet seat. "I took all the pills, I did what I always do, I wasn't trying to make this happen, I didn't try to trap you, I wasn't trying to trick you into anything." I knew I was babbling.

"Come out, Suze. Come back into your office." He grabbed my hand and pulled me back into the privacy of my surgery.

Peter was sitting with one leg crossed over the other, not looking surprised.

"How did you know?" I muttered to him.

"Well, the early morning vomiting and passing out. All good solid signs," he grinned. "But it was the tears that really gave it away."

"But I took all my pills . . ." I trailed off. "That bloody food poisoning. I was puking for the whole night. I take my pill at night . . ."

"That'd do it all right. Make sure you eat small amounts regularly, it can be easier to digest and your blood sugars won't drop so much." Peter got up and shut his bag. "I'll leave you to it. Am I allowed to say congratulations, or are you still in shock?"

"Oh, yes. I suppose." I tried to smile, but I just wanted to cry – again.

"I won't tell anyone, don't worry. I know it takes a while to get used to. When we had Vicky, it took us both a month or so to get our heads around it."

"Thank God you've said that, I'm in total shock I must admit," I managed.

Walter walked him out to the lift. By the time he came back into the room, I was sitting on my desk, staring ahead like a mute sack of spuds.

Walter came over and hugged me.

"Bloody hell, that's all a bit of a surprise, isn't it?" He cupped my face with his hands and raised my gaze up to meet his.

"You can say that again. What the hell are we going to do?" My bloody lip was wobbling again.

"Well, it looks like we're going to be parents – that's what we'll do," he grinned.

"I don't have time to have a baby. Not at the moment. It's going to make things very awkward," I began to splutter, "and if I'm supposed to spend the next nine months going around whingeing and blubbering while vomiting, I'll have to kill myself." I tried to regain control, but it just wouldn't bloody work.

"You'll have to make time and you're not going to be on your own. I'll be with you. Your mum and Jim will help, I'm sure. Emily's done it all, so she'll be great too."

"I suppose," I pouted.

"For now, I'm taking your clinic this afternoon. The two new patients will see me, your three o'clock lady has rescheduled for Monday. So you can go home and have a rest." He hugged me. "I'm actually very excited. Imagine a little Susie or Walter running around! And he or she will be the most level-headed person in the planet with two psychologists as parents!"

"Either that or it'll be a complete psycho, and we can spend the rest of our lives trying to make it a normal child!"

I had mixed feelings about leaving Walter in my clinic. It was mine. My baby. The only baby I'd ever had until now. It was difficult to allow anyone else to step into my shoes. I felt so vile though that I reluctantly conceded and left.

As I walked down the stairs (deciding the lift would make me sick) I tried to come to terms with the idea of being a mother. My own relationship with my mother was so strained, I was very dubious about what kind of mum I would make. Feeling too freaked out to go home and sit by myself, I quickly dialled Emily's number. Luckily she was home and said I could drop in.

As I pulled up outside her house, I surveyed her front garden from a fresh perspective. I noticed a small bike, a hula-hoop, one Barbie boot-skate and a sandpit filled with muck along with abandoned spades and buckets.

I knew I was rooted to the spot and probably staring at the toys like a madwoman. I nearly peed myself with shock when Emily knocked on the passenger side window of my car.

"Jesus holy Christ, are you trying to kill me?" I barked at her.

"What's up your hole?" Emily looked at me, puzzled.

"Well, a small foetus as it happens," I told her while looking at the ground.

"Whaaaaaat?" Emily started to bounce up and down, while waving her arms about in a rather possessed manner.

I, of course, started to cry.

"Oh, God, Suze, I'm sorry, are you not happy about it?" Emily looked concerned as she took my arm and led me into the house.

I kind of stumbled and let her be in charge. I knew I looked like a stunned chimpanzee as she warned me to lift my legs for the steps.

She put on the kettle and fussed about putting biscuits on a plate and I sat and the tears continued to roll down my face.

"Hiya, Susie!" Tia ran into the room and flung her arms around my neck. "Why are you crying? Did you fall off your bike?"

"No, Tia. I'm just being a bit silly. I don't usually cry and now I can't stop," I babbled.

"Well, you're very good at it, aren't you?" She stared at me with her head to the side, nodding gravely.

"Why don't you go and make Susie a picture in the playroom, Tia," Emily said.

"Then do you think she might stop crying?" Tia asked her mother.

"Yes, I'll try," I sniffed.

As Tia ran off to do the picture, I got a sudden burst of jitters. Emily had given birth to that little girl and grown her. She was her total responsibility. She was a lovely little girl. A pretty little scrap too.

"Fucking hell, Emily, what if my baby is really ugly? I know everyone says you love your own child. But if it was totally and utterly butt ugly, you'd know deep down, wouldn't you?" I burst into fresh tears. "My baby is going to look like a peeled toad, I just know it will."

"Susie, look at yourself, a tall auburn goddess, and Walter is divine. I'd say you'll be putting a bag over the child's head all right, but only because it'll make you look like a hag in comparison. There's no way your children are going to be mingers!"

"God, that's really shallow of me, isn't it?" I suddenly realised I was thinking all the wrong way. "All I should be concerned about is whether it's healthy, not if it looks like a bulldog's arse-hole. Emily, I'm going to be a shit mother, I'm already bad at it!" And more tears started to spring from the newly grown fountain in my head.

"None of what you're experiencing is weird or wrong. I had all these thoughts when I was pregnant with Louis. It's such a shock. You weren't trying either, so it's not like you have even sorted the whole concept out in your head yet. Give yourself time. Believe me, nine months is a bloody long time. By the end of it, you won't care what orifice it comes out or if it looks like it's hit every branch of the ugly tree as it fell. As long as it gets the hell out of your womb, you won't be in a position to care about much else." Emily banged the coffee pot and milk and sugar onto the table.

"What if it hates me? Let's face it, I'm not exactly close to my mother. I'll probably piss it off and it'll hate me." I wasn't able to control all the crazy thoughts which were whizzing around my brain.

"It'll be a baby. It's too small to hate you. Mine still both like me which is astonishing. I'd say you've a good seven to ten years before they really hate you. So I wouldn't deal with that concept just yet." Emily was smiling.

"Stop smiling at me, you psycho! You're enjoying this, aren't you?"

"Yes, quite frankly, Miss-Psychologist-oh-so-together, I am," said Emily as she dipped a chocolate biscuit into her coffee. "I've never seen you so manic and out of control. It's good for you. I think this child is going to be the making of you, Susie. Whether you like it or not."

"Emily, what if I have awful post-natal depression and end up in a mental hospital, and Walter has to bring up the baby on his own? If it's a girl, he'll dress it in boys' clothes and bring it to the barber for vile haircuts. If it's a boy, they'll be like two louts, eating pizza out of cardboard boxes and he'll have no idea how to behave with women. Oh Jesus, Emily, what am I going to do?"

Emily came over and simply put her arms around me and rocked me back and forth. She didn't speak for a long time and neither did I. When my tears finally subsided, for a few minutes anyway, she handed me a baby wipe.

"This will cool your face," she said, smiling gently.

"I don't want that – give me a piece of kitchen paper instead. I'm not ready to touch anything to do with babies!" I was shocked by my own shock, if that makes sense.

"If it helps, it took me about six months to come to terms with the fact I was actually going to be a mother when I had Louis." Emily held my hand.

"I remember you being a bit freaked out all right but how come I didn't realise how terrified you were?" I looked at Emily in shock.

"You can't possibly understand what another person is going through, unless it happens to you too, I suppose."

We spent the afternoon chatting about life and how it can throw things at you when you least expect it. I left Emily's house and she promised not to tell anyone about my baby until I was able to come to terms with it a bit better.

I got home and immediately flicked on one of the health channels. There was a birth programme on, where women were discussing the run-up to the birth. One was having a home birth and the other was going down the hospital route.

There was no way I was giving birth on the sofa or in a blow-up

Winnie the Pooh swimming pool in the apartment, that was for sure. I was going to the best hospital in the world, a place where they knock you unconscious and wake you up when the baby is six months old if possible.

As I was pacing the room, behaving like a caged animal, my phone rang. I let it go to the answer machine. I wasn't in the mood for pretending to be normal. The speaker on the machine clicked into action and I heard the caller draw breath and hesitate before speaking.

"Hi, Susie, it's Mum. Walter just phoned me and told me about your little surprise. He told me that it's all a secret for the moment, so I've only told Jean and Jim and they've promised to keep it under their hats. Mum's the word," she giggled. "Give me a call when you get a minute, I can't believe how excited I am. Although I'll have to figure out what the baby is going to call me. I don't feel like being a granny or nana. Maybe Grandma Pauline would be nice? What do you think? Give me a call, bye, love." The phone clicked.

Bloody great. Why on earth had Walter told Mum? I wasn't planning on telling her for quite a while. Although at least this way I didn't have to call her and go through the whole pretending to be thrilled charade.

I must have fallen asleep on the sofa, because I woke up a while later and the apartment was darker and I was stiff and cold.

Peeling myself upwards and swinging my legs to the floor, I realised I was starving. Not normal, hungry-type starving. Oh no, this was a feeling like I hadn't eaten for a week. This was wild-animal-who-hasn't-had-a-kill-in-over-two-weeks type of starving. Pulling the cupboard open, I found a packet of biscuits, which would normally not interest me in the slightest. I munched on those as I put on water to make pasta.

Just as I'd finished a huge bowl of pasta with tomato sauce, Walter phoned.

"Hi there, how are you feeling?" he asked.

"Hungry, can you stop and get a take-away?"

"Sure," he laughed. "What do you feel like eating?"

"Everything. You decide. Just make sure there's loads of it and get back here as soon as you can, before I eat one of the curtains."

By the time Walter arrived with a bag of Chinese food, I was ravenous again. We sat and munched, and Walter had a glass of wine. I didn't, I was too afraid of damaging the baby.

"How am I going to survive the next nine months without drinking?"

"I'm sure you can have a glass of wine the odd time," he said.

"No way. I won't be doing anything that could jeopardise the baby. I couldn't live with the guilt. If it was born missing an arm or with an extra eye, I'd blame myself. But it's going to be a right pain in the arse all the same."

"It'll be worth it though. I can't believe we're going to be parents, can you?" Walter hugged me.

It was all right for him to be all lovey-dovey and delighted. He didn't have to grow the baby and then push it out a very small hole. Knowing I was a brimming psycho, I decided to try and consciously keep myself in check and not be a complete bitch all the time.

I suddenly remembered he'd taken my patients. "How did today go?"

"Really well. The Rochestown Clinic has a lovely atmosphere. I'd love to work there." He sipped his wine.

"Well, why don't you then? I need someone else on board, especially now that Junior is making an appearance. You're looking for a new spot and I need another doctor. We won't be working together, as only one of us will be on duty at a time, so we can't kill each other. What do you say?"

"Do you think the board will go for it?" He looked excited.

"If I propose you and it means the clinic isn't going to be messed up by my maternity leave," those words made me shudder, "I don't see why they'd have a problem."

I knew I could trust Walter. He would do his best to keep my clinic running smoothly and it would mean I could always have first-hand information on what was going on. He was the person I trusted most in the world and I knew he was also a damn good doctor.

"I don't know why I didn't think of it before," I added.

The atmosphere in the apartment was now jovial. Walter was like the Cheshire Cat. I was a bit of a sinking ship though if I was honest with myself. I really wasn't finding it easy to take in all this pregnancy lark.

So much was about to change. I wasn't sure if I was ready for it all. Our wedding was a couple of months away, and I wasn't sure if I wanted to go down the aisle with a bump.

I was really happy with the idea of Walter coming in on the business with me. That felt right. But the whole baby thing was different. I knew millions of generations of women had coped before me, but I just wasn't sure if being a mother was something I wanted to do. More to the point, I wasn't sure if I *could* do it.

55

Emily

Freezer Moments:
Do the good mother thing by preparing nourishing meals and place in the freezer. Have a satisfied domestic goddess moment, while knowing deep down your work is a total waste of time.

It was November and the sense of cosiness the winter brings was setting in. The day of my exchange operation was finally approaching. I'd filled the freezer with home-cooked food, and left a list the length of my arm of instructions for Robbie and Maisy.

But I knew deep down Maisy would give them sherbet dip-dabs and crisps for breakfast. They would have chocolate spread and jam sandwiches, with orange squash instead of water in their beakers for lunch. They wouldn't eat a single morsel of the food I'd spent time preparing. Tia would refuse to let Maisy brush her hair for the entire week. So I would come home from hospital to a child with a backcombed toilet brush for hair. They would sit and play video games for hours on end. Go to bed two hours late. Get up half an hour after the proper time and refuse to get dressed. No homework would be done. Well, I suppose I couldn't expect Maisy to learn Irish poems. She was having enough trouble mastering the English language as it was.

Both school coats would be lost. Half of their books would go missing. Tia would paint her carpet with my best nail varnish. Rasher the cat would probably end up wearing my most expensive evening dress, while being wheeled around in a dolly's pram.

Louis would use words like "crap", and "you stupid thick" as often as possible. Their teeth wouldn't be brushed at all, from one end of the week to the next. But none of it really mattered in the greater scheme of things. All that mattered was that they were all happy. Sherbet and chocolate for breakfast every now and then is a bloody marvellous idea. Especially if you're five or six years of age.

I knew they would miss me. I would miss them terribly too. But we would all live to tell the tale. We would muddle through and come out the other end. I had weeks, months and years to make them eat porridge in the mornings and preach about water being the best liquid for the human body.

Acting on an impulse, I grabbed my car keys and yelled to Maisy that I'd be back in five minutes.

I drove to the local shop and filled a basket with sweets, crisps, biscuits, chocolate and general rot-gut.

I drove home and hid the forbidden stuff in drawers around the kitchen. I knew by the second day I was gone, Louis and Tia would go looking for prohibited items. I wanted them to find some. It would give them a little boost. Everyone likes to win some of the time. At least this way I was providing the nutritious and nourishing meals, which would remain in the freezer. They were to soothe my responsible, adult conscience.

The sweets and junk would delight and enthral the children, easing my dreadful guilt for not being there.

So much had happened since February. It was only eight months ago, but in a way it felt like a lifetime. I had changed. Of that fact, I had no doubt. I wondered had it had as profound an effect on my children?

I knew it had affected Robbie profoundly. He had buckled under the pressure of the operation. The whole experience had been too much for him to bear. But I would have to subject him to copious amounts of drugs or severe Chinese torture to ever find out about it. God forbid that he might actually open up and say how he felt. It would be a chilly day in hell before he would get into a deep conversation about what had been going on in his head and exactly how he'd felt. Maybe some day I could get Susie to prise it all out of him.

Did men ever really open their hearts and minds to others like women do? Maybe it will never change. Women will probably always drink copious cups of tea and coffee, while putting the world to rights. Men will probably always swig pints and swing golf clubs while uttering very few words. *C'est la vie*.

"Mummy, when you go for this operation next week, will Dr Green let you go to sleep before he cuts your skin with his scissors?" Louis asked as I tucked him into bed.

"Well, firstly Dr Green doesn't use a scissors. He uses a tiny sharp knife, which is used especially for performing operations. It's so sharp that it has to be put away in a special place in case anyone cuts themselves with it. It's called a scalpel, and you must be very clever and skilled to use one."

"Wow, I want one of them for Christmas. That sounds like a great thing. Could I cut Tia's ear off with one if she annoyed me?" He looked thrilled by the prospect.

"No, that would be illegal and not very nice. If you want to own a scalpel, you had better start studying now. It takes a lot of work to be allowed to own one of those."

Next morning, I went into Tia's room to try and coax her out of bed. The usual running order involved kissing and stroking her little face until she woke up. I would then carry her into our bed and leave her there watching cartoons while I had a shower. This way she had a few minutes' grace to wake up properly. This made life more pleasant for her and, more importantly, for everyone else around her. Tia was not a morning person. She was reluctant to go to sleep at night, and even less happy about being woken up in the mornings. If rushed or pushed in her semi-conscious state, she could be quite scary and nasty. She could fly into a violent rage, with small arms and legs flapping like uncoordinated propellers.

So this method had proved to be less distressing all around. By the time I'd showered, I could dress in my room while talking to her and making suggestions that she should start to dress herself.

This morning, I bundled into my bedroom with a towel turbaned around my head, all ready to start the coaxing process. The bed was empty.

"Tia? Where are you?" I called.

"I'm getting dressed in a few minutes, Mum! I'm just packing my bag," she shouted from her darkened room.

"What are you packing a bag for?" I walked into her room and flicked the light on.

"Your operation, silly," she smiled and nodded at me knowingly.

"What do you mean, sweetheart?" I asked her.

"Well, you're going into St Theresa's again, for more operations on your lady-boobs. I'm coming too, so you will have someone to talk to when you wake up. I like you coming to talk to me when I'm waking up, so I'm going to mind you back. Okay?" She smiled and busied herself stuffing random items of clothes and toys into a bag.

"Tia, that's a great idea, but the doctors won't allow anybody in while Mummy is sleeping. But how about Daddy brings you in to see me, as soon as I wake up? Maybe you could wear your nurse's outfit and bring me in a magazine and something to drink when I wake up?"

She thought about it for a few seconds. I was expecting her to fly off the handle and refuse that idea but thankfully she seemed to buy it.

"Only if you get Daddy to bring me in straight away after you get woken up," she warned.

"It's a deal, I promise." We shook hands.

She would of course be brought in when I didn't have any scary drips or wires hanging out of me. But that would be an easy one to swing. She would believe Robbie if he told her I was still asleep, until it suited to bring her in.

Hayley phoned me that day to confirm my surgery.

"You'll have to come in as a day case again, I'm afraid. There just aren't any beds on the wards. The only thing is that you'll be admitted and allowed to stay if you're not well enough to go home, so keep that in mind."

"Won't I be a bit too groggy to go home after one day?" I was a bit stunned.

"No, you should be okay, but as I said the ward staff will admit you if they think it's necessary. You'll have to be very careful of yourself after this operation to avoid rejection."

"That's okay. I still have my au pair so I'll be in a position to take it easy."

"When I say you must behave, I mean you don't do a thing. You don't take a chicken out of the oven, you don't hang clothes on the line, you don't wash the floors, you don't do any housework. If you stretch your arms upwards, you are in danger of rupturing the stitches. If this happens, even the tiniest tear can lead to an infection. In turn, an infection will lead to the implant being rejected." She paused. "Are you with me so far?"

"Yes."

"You won't be able to drive for at least three weeks, so you need to keep that in mind."

"That's okay, my family will be on stand-by for school runs and all the other necessary driving."

"You will have to wear Tubigrip for two to three weeks after the surgery again, to stop the implants rising up the chest wall," she went on.

"Oh great, I'm looking forward to that again."

The thought of the tight binding being strapped down over the tops of my breasts again filled me with dread. I could feel the tightening in my shoulder-blades once more from the strained fabric.

At least this time the portholes or my 'buttons' would be gone. I was hoping this might make the whole feeling less painful.

"What other factors lead to rejection?" I asked Hayley.

"Chemotherapy but you're not having that so you're safe there. Infection is the biggy. You will have to be very careful that you don't jeopardise your chances." She laughed and added, "I know it will be a new concept for you but you must be sensible if you can manage that!"

"I'll certainly try if it means an end to surgery. At this stage, I'm more than ready to stop visiting theatre with all the little men in green outfits with matching masks and clogs."

My skin had decided meanwhile to erupt. I had spots in places I had never dreamed spots could form. I got a really nasty, pus-filled one by the side of my eye. I was sincerely hoping all this was due to my hormones being utterly do-lally. Whoever gets a spot in their crow's-feet?

The eye crater was not alone. It had first cousins, neighbours, grannies and aunties all around my nose, chin and forehead. My face was a holiday camp for pus. "Zit Zone" – bring all your friends! Kids-go-free option this week!

I went to the chemist and tried to find some products for "pizza-itus" but all the products are aimed at teenagers. So I bought a facial wash, packaged in shocking pink and purple boxes, with pictures of children wearing make-up on the front.

After two days of washing my face with this stuff, the spots were still thriving – in fact, more had appeared. I binned the stuff.

When I woke up with two cold sores to add to the fray, I had reached a point of no return. My lip was swollen to three times its normal size. I looked like I'd been hit with a rugby ball, producing a devastating impact.

I set out for Dunmahon shopping centre but I felt too unattractive, so I went home and watched morning television. I took off my jeans and boots and fitted jacket, and put on a tracksuit instead. I felt more comfortable in my slobby clothes.

I knew the Victoria Beckham jeans were not happy about having to hang around with all the pus. They didn't actually tell me that, but I could just tell from the dejected way they lay on the floor when I took them off.

56

Susie

Pregnant Pear Melba:
Take one previously normal woman, add pregnancy hormones, watch as the whole dish goes utterly pear-shaped.

It was two weeks since I'd found out that I was pregnant. I was still freaked out. In fact I think I was worse. The word had spread like wild fire, despite my request to keep it all quiet. It was like a rocket that just took off on its own and I couldn't control it.

I was feeling so negative about it that I'd ended up having to lie to everyone and feign delight. But inside, I was panicking and struggling.

The signs of the pregnancy weren't showing on my body yet, which I was thankful for. I wasn't ready to look like a walking beach ball yet.

Walter had decided to make the move to my practice and my bosses at the Rochestown Clinic were all in total agreement that he was the perfect candidate to join me. That was fantastic. In fact, it was my one positive thought, which I forced myself to concentrate on when people talked to me about the baby.

I felt like a heel. I also felt alone. More lonely than I ever thought it was possible to feel. I just couldn't tell people that I hated the thought of my own baby. That sounds callous and hateful. But I couldn't help it. My true feelings were dreadful.

Now I was standing in the shower, taking deep breaths, to try and stave off another bout of early morning vomiting. Every morning bar one I'd welcomed the day with my head stuck in the toilet bowl. That of course wasn't helping me to feel thrilled about the pregnancy either.

As I patted my skin dry and tried to breathe through the retching, I felt heat on my legs. Looking down, I realised there was blood all over the shower and my legs and feet.

"Oh, Jesus! Oh no! Please, no!" I began to cry and panic. Rushing into the sitting room I grabbed my phone and called Walter, who'd just left for work ahead of me.

"Walter, I'm bleeding. It's all over my legs and I don't know what to do!"

"It's okay, Susie, I'm turning back. Try and dress yourself, I'll call the hospital and tell them you're coming in," he answered calmly.

"But, where will we go? I haven't seen a gynae yet!" I panicked again. I'd put off going to see one, purely because I'd felt it was another step towards accepting the whole baby thing.

"The National Maternity Hospital will see you, they'll know best," he said.

Hanging up the phone, I shuffled into the bedroom and grabbed a tracksuit. My hands were shaking and I struggled to dress myself. I quickly cleaned myself up and found some sanitary towels.

I pressed the button for the lift and came outside as Walter pulled into the apartment block.

"Get in, I've rung ahead, they're going to take you straight in for a scan – that should tell us what's happening."

Before I could even click my seat belt into the holder, we were speeding towards the city centre hospital. Within minutes, we pulled up outside.

A security guard approached us.

"She's bleeding and we're afraid she's miscarrying!" Walter shouted.

"Leave me your keys and you go on inside." The guard obviously knew the drill.

A wheelchair appeared from nowhere and we sped to the outpatients area.

"Just lie up on the bed like a good girl and we'll put some gel on your belly and see what's happening." The nurse, who looked too young to know how babies got in there, never mind look after them when they did, helped me onto the table.

After a small amount of fumbling and digging with the scanner, a dull blob appeared on the screen.

"There's your baby." Shuffling the scanner to the right slightly, she smiled. "And there's the probable reason why you've had a little bleed – another little one. Both sacs are intact and looking fine for this stage. Looks like you're having twins there, Mum."

"Fuck off!" I said, before I could stop myself.

Grinning, she wiped my tummy and moved the back of the bed to a sitting position.

I looked at Walter who was now like a stunned rabbit.

"Are they going to be all right?" I asked.

As the nurse answered me, I realised for the first time that I desperately wanted her to tell me they were. I had been so terrified of losing my baby, it had shocked me into submission. I now knew that I wanted it. Them.

The realisation that the baby had turned into two babies hit me.

With tears springing again, I put my arms out to Walter and he came and hugged me.

"Oh dear Lord, what have we let ourselves in for?" I cried and laughed at the same time.

"It'll be fantastic." Walter sounded very unconvincing. Now it was his turn to look like he wanted to run as fast as he could, far away to the Land of Nowhere.

"Have you been very sick, Mum?" The nurse was filling in a file.

"Yes, actually. And then starving, as in not normally hungry. I go from being violently ill to being so starved that I can't get enough food into me."

"That's all normal. I'll get a specialist to come and look at you as soon as possible. I'm going to admit you for a day or two. Don't be alarmed, everything looks fine now, but we just need to take extra special care of you, as twins puts you in a high risk category." She patted my arm and excused herself, promising to return shortly and tell us what room I'd be in.

I patted my tummy and exhaled. "You do know I'm going to look like a beached whale very soon, don't you?" I asked Walter.

"Ah well, we're not married yet. I'll just leave now before it all gets too hard," he teased.

"Don't even joke about that!"

"Susie, this is the most amazing thing that's ever happened to me. I'm going to have you and two little shrimps, why on earth would I want to leave?" He kissed me tenderly.

By the time I was settled in a room two hours later, I was exhausted.

"See you later, Daddy," I waved as Walter left.

I felt more serene and optimistic than I'd felt for a very long time. The fear of losing my baby had jolted me into touch. I was ready to be a mother after all. I wasn't sure if I'd be any good at it, but at least the babies wouldn't know any better. We could learn and do it all together. If I turned out to be the worst mother in the world, they could hate me together.

Patting my stomach, I drifted off to sleep, realising I was blessed. I wasn't sure how I would cope with my new life, but I was really looking forward to finding out.

57

Emily

Iced Fearful Fancies:
Find one fearful mother. Remove from bed in the middle of the night.
Add a computer, pour out heart.

The night before my operation, I went to bed at eleven o'clock, which was late for me. I figured if I tried to stay awake for a little while longer I might fall asleep. Of course that didn't work at all. I couldn't sleep.

Robbie was unconscious beside me, so I decided to get out of bed and do something. It was two forty-five and the house had taken on an eerie silence. I checked on Louis and Tia and stroked their little faces gently. I meandered downstairs not really knowing what I was going to do. I found myself at my computer and began to type.

Dear Louis and Tia

I hope that you never get to read this letter. If you are reading it, that means I am gone. I need you both to know that I love you with all my heart. You mean the world to me. I did try everything in my power to stay with you, but sometimes wishes don't come true.

I was blessed to have my two babies. Every day of your lives you gave me joy and love. Nothing in the world could have prepared me for the way you both made me feel. I hope that you will both be happy and learn to carry on without me.

Try to remember me with happiness and know that your mummy loved you. I will be watching over you and loving you for the rest of your lives. It's just going to be different because you can't see me any more. Help Daddy to smile again, I know you can do that. You are my little angels sent to brighten up my world and I never wanted to leave you. Sometimes people have to go and become a star in the sky. I will twinkle and shine down on you both forever.

I know you are both going to turn into wonderful people and I hope that some day you will have children of your own, so you can truly understand the feelings of love that I have had for you. I have gone to a place filled with sunshine and laughter. I will try to be happy too, but I will be waiting for you until we meet again.

Thank you both for making me a better person. I love you both so much there are no words to explain it. Try your very best not to be sad for too long after I am gone. All I ever wanted was for you both to be happy. Look after each other and make sure that you are always there for each other. I am sorry that I had to go. Please forgive me. I love you both, my precious children.

Your loving mum,

Emily x x x

I had this sudden compulsion to write to them. Just in case it was one of those freak operations where I didn't wake up. I'd been lucky so far, yet I didn't want to be complacent. I quickly printed the letter and closed the document without saving it. I found an envelope and put the letter inside. Sealing the envelope, I placed it in my bedside locker. If need be, the letter would be discovered. I considered writing to Robbie and my parents and Susie, but decided against it.

Louis and Tia were the only ones who really didn't understand what was going on. I knew someone would explain it all to them in years to come, if I was gone. But I wanted them to know I loved them and didn't want to leave them. Feeling slightly more at peace with myself, I crawled back into bed and snuggled into Robbie.

After checking in and answering all the usual questions, I took my place by a bed in the day ward. I smiled and nodded at the lady opposite me. All the other inmates had been taken to surgery already, so the beds lay empty.

I had an idea and came up with a post-it note to stick on my chest for Mr Green. I wrote: *"Sorry about the face, but the legs are smooth and hair free"* ↓ I then drew two eyes and a nose and big smile on my knees. If nothing else, it might spur him to never want to see me again, and hence do an extra good job of my reconstruction.

Robbie sat and shook his head as I finished colouring in the last eye on my left knee.

"You know you'll probably be locked up," he said seriously.

"You should be so lucky," I answered, as the man in green with the facemask approached me.

"Emily Cusack? Ready to go for it?" he asked brightly.

"Sure am." As I smiled at him, the butterflies rose in my tummy.

I bent and kissed Robbie, feeling less emotional or nervous or upset than I'd been since this whole journey had begun.

Robbie's and my eyes met. We smiled at each other.

I followed the orderly to the operating area. I was relieved of my dressing gown and slippers and put onto a wheeling operating table.

The room was empty when I arrived, but quickly filled up with other victims. Fellow lambs to the slaughter. The area had a most strange atmosphere. There wasn't silence, as people were constantly milling around, but there was an unnerving falseness to the place – orderlies and doctors and nurses all being forcibly cheerful to countless nervous wrecks, as every patient was obviously going for surgery.

This area wasn't segregated into men and women. Even so I was mildly surprised when a small boy with a shaven head was wheeled into position beside me. At first, he was surrounded by doctors and nurses. But when the area around him cleared, we looked over at each other.

I smiled, I suppose kind of sadly, as I was obviously thinking how brave and well-behaved he was being. He responded with a huge grin.

"How's it going?" came his deep booming voice.

To say I nearly peed down my own leg in shock, is putting it mildly.

I felt the blood rush to my cheeks. I was delighted and grateful that people cannot read each other's thoughts. I had assumed he was a small child, but he was in fact a dwarf.

We made polite small talk, as you do with total strangers, while you all wear the same back-fastened gown and disposable underwear. I would have to vote this place the weirdest place on the planet to meet another person.

Then it was time to go.

58

Emily

Here's One We Made Earlier:
Take one woman with scooped-out breast tissue. Here's one we made earlier! Remove expanders, put in implants. Serve with va-va-voom!

This time when I woke up I found it very hard to keep my eyes open at all.

I do remember trying to focus on the nurse who was standing above me. I knew I was in hospital and quite frankly didn't care about much beyond that.

"How are you feeling, Emily?"

"Oh, I feel great, thanks for asking," I answered, promptly falling asleep again.

Some time later they must have decided I needed to go back to the ward so a green giant, clad in the usual surgeon's green outfit and matching clogs, came to wheel my bed back to the ward.

I heard the nurses ringing Robbie and telling him I was back and would be ready to go home soon. I had my blood pressure taken and they asked me some questions, but I was unbelievably tired. There was no way I could answer. I decided I would think about the questions for a little while and answer then. That was a good plan.

Somewhere in the middle of my dream a dull thudding sensation kept interrupting.

I would manage to ignore it, and then it would come back again. Just as I was trying to drift off to the land of fuzz, it would nag and dig at me. Eventually, I had to use all my strength to open my eyes.

The strip lighting of the hospital ward pierced my eyes. The noises of phones ringing, trolleys clanking and people walking and talking began to flood through my ears.

"Good day, Sleeping Beauty," the nurse greeted me cheerfully.

"Hi," I croaked.

"How are you feeling now?"

"I'm not sure really," I answered, trying to get my bearings and tune into the sensations I was feeling.

"Are you in pain anywhere, Emily?"

"Yes, that's what it is. I'm very sore down both sides and into my back."

"Okay, you stay still. I'm going to go and get you some painkillers. I think from looking at your chart, you were very nauseated and sick the last time, so do you object to an injection rather than tablets?"

"No, I'd love one," I answered smiling.

"Coming up right away!" She saluted with her hand to her forehead and marched away.

The nurse returned promptly with the needle.

"Which side do you think you would be more comfortable leaning towards?" she asked.

"That's a bit like asking which eye I'd like the hot needle stuck into," I answered while trying to laugh.

I mustered up all my strength to roll slightly onto my right hip. All she needed was a small amount of upper thigh to sink the needle into safely. I braced myself and tried to hold the position. I was so weak and unable to move, this proved to be seriously difficult.

Very quickly I felt the stinging liquid flooding the cold, cramping sensation through my muscle.

"All done. That should help with the pain. Try and rest, call me if you need me. I'm leaving the button beside your hand, okay?" She patted my arm and wafted off.

I didn't need to be told twice. Shortly afterwards, I felt my shoulders relax away from my ears, as the pain relief did its job. I promptly conked out and slept.

Robbie arrived mid-afternoon.

"You don't look as green as usual – how are you feeling?"

"Fine surprisingly, just utterly knackered. I feel like I want to sleep for the rest of my life," I answered before falling asleep again.

Mr Green's surgical team surrounded my bed. They assured me the surgery had gone to plan and that I was doing really well.

"So how do you feel about going home now?" one male doctor asked.

"I think I would rather peel my eyeballs and submerse my head in a bucket of acid," I answered.

"Right, so you'd like to be admitted for the night, I take it?" He scribbled on his clipboard. "Bear with me, and we'll try to have you admitted to a ward. This is purely a day ward, so I cannot leave you here. This place shuts down at six."

"Try to?" Robbie said. "She can't come home in this state. She's comatose and we have two small children at home. She doesn't want them to see her like this. She'll have to stay in for a couple of days to regain her strength."

I could hear the panic rising in his voice.

"I understand your predicament, I'll see what I can do." The doctor walked away briskly, shadowed by his team.

Shortly afterwards he returned on his own.

"I'm afraid there are no beds available for admission at the moment," he apologised.

"What do you mean no beds?" Robbie was getting angry. "She's banjaxed – she can't go home in this state. She's just had both breasts reconstructed, not a mole removed! Be realistic here. How the hell can there be no beds in the place? It's a fucking hospital!"

"I know it seems rushed, but the only alternative we can offer right now is to put her on a trolley in casualty and hope that a bed comes up during the night. I must warn you, though, there are six patients on trolleys ahead of her in the queue."

"Hang on a bloody minute!" I tried to sit up, but couldn't move. "How in the name of God am I supposed to go home in this state?" I gestured woodenly with my malfunctioning arm.

"There's nothing I can do, Emily. I have even tried to say that I will stay here with you and monitor you myself. But legally we must shut the day wards down at night. It's a day ward and that's it, literally." He shrugged.

"So essentially there are fifty-odd beds here which will lie idle all night, while ill people lie on trolleys in a hallway?" I said.

"Yep, that's it in a nutshell."

"That sucks. Can we not use Mr Green's visa card and go to the Four Seasons hotel?"

"That sounds like a marvellous plan but unfortunately he has the sense not to allow me access to his bank details," the doctor grinned.

The situation was a total crock of shit. I was in no state to go home. In fact, the thought of having to even sit up was scaring the living daylights out of me at that moment.

Robbie had obviously decided we were leaving because he was hauling my bag out of the locker and unzipping it.

"Right, let's get the hell out of here before I have a row with someone and regret it later. Let's just hope you don't have a convulsion during the night. The health system in this country is a farce. Why the hell are we paying VHI the guts of eight grand a year to be offered a trolley in a hallway?"

He was beyond furious and, while I agreed with him wholeheartedly, I was finding it hard to move, let alone speak or express emotion. All I could do was try and get myself into a sitting position – at least that way I would have some chance of dressing myself.

I had brought a tracksuit with a zip-up front on the top, which I thought would be easy to put on. The bottoms were elasticated so they didn't require buttoning or much manoeuvring. Even so, I was unable to dress myself. In fact, I couldn't even remove the revolting disposable knickers in order to put real ones on.

Deciding I didn't give a toss who saw me, I asked Robbie to put the clothes away and help me put my shoes and socks and coat on. It wasn't as if I was off to a black-tie ball.

With my shoes on, I tried to stand up. Blood rushed to my head and my eyes struggled to remain open.

The room began to spin, faster and faster – the nurse and Robbie were whizzing past, colours, sounds and light rotating past my vision. I felt my stomach lurch. I sat back on the bed and shut my eyes, breathing in and out of my mouth as slowly as I could.

Thankfully the room began to slow down. I could see Robbie's face coming back into focus. I could hear the nurse talking to him.

"I think we'll call for a wheelchair – she's not going to be able to walk to the lift and out to the car park." She sounded very concerned.

"I've parked right outside in the set-down area but even so, I reckon we'll go with the wheelchair idea," he agreed, eyeballing me seriously.

Right at that moment he could have been selling me to an Arab merchant for two camels and I wouldn't have cared. All I wanted was to go to sleep. To lie down in a soft bed, with a warm duvet and comfy pillow. My back was arched in a Quasimodo curve, my head hung forwards off my neck like a baby buzzard's and my arms lay limply at my sides like an ape. Suffice it to say, I was not looking my best.

The orderly arrived with the wheelchair. Robbie and the nurse bundled me into it and we were off. I barely said goodbye to the nurses, I simply couldn't.

We lurched down in the lift and sped towards the car. I kept my eyes shut, willing my stomach not to empty its contents. The cold night air hit me with a smack. It was actually a welcome jolt of freshness. I inhaled the cool air, causing my head to spin again.

"I said, can you stand up?" Robbie was looking at me.

"Oh sorry," I slurred.

I shuffled myself forwards in the chair and tried to stand up. I couldn't use my arms or put any pressure on them, as the incisions were under my armpits. So I tried to steady myself with my thighs.

"I can't do it, Robbie, I'm going to fall!" I wailed.

"This is fucking ridiculous. She should be in a hospital bed," Robbie muttered to no one in particular. "It's okay, the door is open, I'll lift you into the car – are you ready?" He took a deep breath and scooped me from the chair and across into the car seat. He pulled the seat belt around me and clicked it in place.

It dug into me in all the wrong places, so I had to pull it and hold it loosely away from myself.

Robbie drove at about 150 kilometres per hour all the way home. The car seat was completely the wrong shape for my body. I found it impossible to get even remotely comfortable.

We decided I would stay in my parents' house for a couple of nights, at least until the anaesthetic wore off. I didn't want the children to see me in this state. I was not in a position to deal with them either.

When we reached the house, I clawed my way up the stairs and managed to get my coat off. I fell into my old bed. It was strangely comforting to be back in my old familiar surroundings. My parents offered me drinks, food and anything I wanted. But all I wanted was a glass of water, so I could take my next due painkillers.

They retreated with Robbie to the lit fire downstairs. I could hear them open a bottle of wine and chat. Thankfully sleep took over.

I woke some time later, confused by where I was and what was going on. My memory jolted and I realised with satisfaction that I'd made it through the surgery and was finally at home.

It was very difficult to get comfortable that night. I was also incredibly aware of the fact that I was on my own. I know my parents were there but I was psychologically disturbed by the fact that I was not within calling distance of a medically trained nurse.

The pain was different from that after the first operation. The muscle expanders were gone, taking the hateful rigid portholes with them. They were no longer digging mercilessly into my ribcage. Pulling my pyjama top forward I looked down. My breasts looked completely normal. In fact they looked almost the way they were when I was about eighteen or nineteen.

I poked one gently. It was soft and pliable. Unlike the solid, firm, inflexible boobs I'd become accustomed to, they were slightly squishy. I felt the biggest smile taking over my face. My heart leaped and I suddenly felt lighter. My headspace cleared and a sensation of elation and relief took hold. I knew I still had to recover and that the road was not over yet, but I had come a long way, and I had been incredibly lucky so far.

Robbie had gone home to be with the children. Thoughts of the three of them flooded my mind. I couldn't wait to see them.

I was glad when dawn finally broke. Although I was relaxed and fairly comfortable, I was ready to see some other human life. My dad popped his head in the door on the way to work and I was delighted to see him, to have someone familiar to chat to.

We shared hippy tea and toast and chatted about nothing in particular. Robbie phoned to check how I was getting on. He assured me the children were fine. I could hear them arguing in the background.

"No, Maisy, you're a naughty girl, you stop that!" Tia was refusing to put her coat on.

"Please, Dad just let me have a day off. I really need to stay at home and play my Playstation. You never let me do that!"

It all sounded quite normal. I was glad.

I wasn't allowed to have a shower for forty-eight hours, to give the scar a chance to heal. That suited me. I don't think I could have managed to take my clothes off and the thought of water hitting any part of my body didn't appeal to me.

I tried to read a book and after half an hour of going over the same chapter and still not taking it in, I gave up. I flicked through a magazine but couldn't get into that either. I really didn't care at that moment in time what the ultimate autumn/winter coat should look like. I certainly wasn't going to "prune" my wardrobe today.

I looked around my childhood bedroom and it was as if time had stood still. If I closed my mind and blocked out the fact that I was married, I could have been ten years old again.

I had loved roller-skating and crimping my hair. I remembered the hours on end I would spend in this room acting out being a grown-up with Susie.

That afternoon, the children returned from school and landed in on top of me in a flurry of excitement.

"Mummy, you came back!" Louis yelled, launching himself on my bed.

"Of course I did! You knew I was just having an operation and I'd be back very quickly."

Louis climbed onto the bed and wrapped himself around my legs like a puppy. I held Tia's tiny hand and noticed the backs of her hands were still so small they were dimpled.

"Mummy, are you gone back to being a little girl again?" she asked, looking slightly concerned.

"No, Tia, I'm just staying here so Oma and Granddad can mind me for a few days before I come home again." I stroked her hand.

"But will you still be our mummy, even if you're here?" She looked really worried.

"I'll always be your mummy and Louis' too. Even when you're old, I'll be your mummy," I smiled.

"Even if you're a star in the sky and we're a hundred and fifty years old?" Louis asked with wide eyes.

"Even then," I confirmed.

59

Susie

Cooking By Numbers:
Take some ripe eggs, add sperm. Douse with hormones, allow to multiply, produce a miracle.

I spent two days in hospital, making sure the twins were safe. I was a bit like spaghetti without the bolognese. They rigged me up to every machine known to woman. As a result I had two little thump, thump, thump heartbeats going in the room. Over those two days I began to take comfort in their existence. I accepted and grew to love them. Methodically, the tiny heartbeats worked their way into my psyche. I felt myself bonding with the unborn babies nestling in my womb.

I was released and told to be careful and to keep in mind that I was "high risk". Of course I would have to convince myself that I was allowed to live a normal life. In my heart, I felt I should stay in bed and only move when necessary. In my head, I knew that after a couple of days of that kind of behaviour, I'd be ready to act normally again.

Mum was delighted with the idea of twins. It inspired her to open a new section in her shop – christening gowns. She never ceased to amaze me – whatever the occasion, she managed to dress it in white lace. My rapidly increasing bump also got me off the hook on the wedding-dress front.

Mum and I never formally sat down and had a big discussion about our falling out. The pregnancy afforded us the luxury of avoiding that "chat". I don't think it would get us anywhere in the long run. And I had so much happening in my life just then, the row just didn't seem important.

Although we were going ahead with the wedding as planned, my inflating shape meant I would get away with a simple Empire line dress. The veil and tiara and up-style hairdo and over the top make-up wouldn't work with it. So I was going to be left to my own devices. After my hospital visit, Walter gently explained to Mum how I was in a high-risk category and that I needed to be as stress-free as possible. Of course she'd never say so much as "boo" to Walter, so she'd been kind of forced to behave herself.

I told Mum to concentrate on herself for the moment. I knew that meant she might turn up in glass coach with a fleet of footmen and a hooped gown which could be seen for miles. Quite honestly, I didn't care what she did. If it rocked her boat then that was fine with me.

The plan was that both Jim and Mum were to walk me down the isle. But at this rate I might be waddling down on my own. In fact, the way I was expanding, I couldn't see any church having an aisle wide enough. There might only be standing room for one or two people if I kept growing at the current rate.

I was looking forward to marrying, Walter. I was happier than I ever thought I could be. If things continued in this direction, I reckoned I'd be totally unbearable by the time my kids were two. I was going to have to concentrate on not driving a four-by-four and I would make a conscious effort not to buy a Labrador, I promised myself.

60

Emily

The End to a Perfect Meal:
After several courses of surgery, dust with relief and gratitude.
Acknowledge that your cup is half full rather than half empty.

Mum brought me back to the hospital to see Mr Green for a post-surgical check-up.

"How are you, Emily? How's the result? Are you happy or sad? Is the glass half empty or half full?" He sat at his desk and waited for me to reply.

"The result looks great to me. They're so much softer than they were with the muscle expanders in. They feel like a more toned and pert version of my own ones. I'm delighted with how I've turned out."

He examined me and agreed that the result was brilliant. In time the scars would fade and the rest of my breasts didn't look like they'd been tampered with at all. I knew I was very lucky to look so normal. I would be able to change in a communal changing room with no difficulty.

"Come back and see me in six months' time, or before if you are ever worried. From now on, we'll see each other every six months. How's that?"

"Perfect. Once again, thank you. I really think it's time to wear your underpants over your trousers and your "S" on your tummy, so the public know who you are," I added seriously.

"I like to keep my identity to myself," he grinned. "By the way, thanks for the post-it note you left me before your surgery!" He opened the door, smiling. "Take care, Emily, I'll talk to you soon." We shook hands and he retreated back into his room.

As Mum and I walked back down the long, corridor, passing various clinics with patients with an array of appendages and complaints, I took a deep breath and closed my eyes momentarily. I was without doubt one of the lucky ones. I was walking away from this whole experience, in more ways than one.

As the days passed, I felt gradually stronger and less sore. By the second week, I was off all painkillers. My energy levels were returning day by day. I knew I still had a lot of recuperating to do, but the really sore, scary and dangerous part was over. The light was visible at the end of the tunnel. It was six weeks to Christmas. By the time Christmas came, I would be flying. New Year would ring out this past twelve months of ups and downs. Susie's wedding would mark a new beginning for us all.

The past year had been an eventful one for me and my family and friends. But I could say without a shadow of doubt that it had been a positive experience. I knew some of it had been painful and worrying but they were the parts which mattered the least. What was most important was the end result. I was healthy. I got through it all.

EPILOGUE

The Icing on the Cake:
Take two best friends, bake for a lifetime of love and support. Fold in
mutual respect. Add a dollop of surgery and two tiny babies. Ice with
joy and great hope for the future.

As I walked down the shiny floor of the hospital, it wasn't the noxious disinfectant smell that I noticed. My hearing had taken over, for behind the closed doors in all the rooms, I could hear the sounds of babies crying.

My heart skipped a beat as I knocked on door number seven.

"Come in," a tired yet elated voice croaked to me.

I thought I'd be able to keep it together and remain calm when I saw my darling Susie. I'm not sure if it was the look of proud joy or the two tiny bundles, one pink and one blue, nestled together like two fuzzy-headed koalas in the crib beside the bed that caused the floodgates to open. But the second I stepped foot in Susie's room, I began to bawl.

"Stop crying, you muppet, now you've set me off again!" She held out her arms to me and I hugged her so hard she yelped.

"Ohmigod, look what you've grown! Two flavours of baby in one go!

You never could do anything by half measures, could you?" I sniffed.

"Pot and kettle, you're hardly Miss Middle-of-the-road yourself," Susie teased.

As we sat and stared, mesmerised by the two tiny miracles. It was like I felt the whole world shunting sideways. Physically and emotionally, we had come such a long way in a very short time.

"What do you think of Camille for the girl and Reece for the boy?" Susie looked unsure and shy, which I can't say I ever guessed I would see.

"Oh darling, they're beautiful names. They're like two little bunny rabbits in there!" Tears of joy flowed down my cheeks.

We were both brought back to reality with a thump as Camille opened her eyes just to slits and followed by opening her mouth as wide as it could go. An almighty noise came out of the tiny little being. Jumping and jerking, her brother joined in.

"Oh holy God, stereo! They keep doing this. I nearly feel like I should put one of them in the bathroom and the other in the wardrobe to stop them setting each other off. No worries, I have the technology. Watch this for action stations!" Susie took a deep breath and wriggled down the bed slightly. After the caesarean section she was quite incapacitated, but that didn't seem to phase her.

I watched as she scooped the babies up, like little torpedoes, and attached one to each breast. Silence ensued and Susie looked up at me, raised one eyebrow and winked slowly, with her nose slightly in the air.

"Well, I'm so impressed. I've had two kids and I would have pressed the panic button just there. Look at you! All mummied-up and able to feed two at the same time!"

"I hadn't actually intended on breastfeeding, but the nurses encouraged me, even if I only did it a couple of times. I'm topping them up with bottles, but so far I'm really enjoying the closeness." Susie was taking to motherhood like a duck to water.

"What happened to the Kids-don't-like-me Susie?" I asked with a smirk.

"Well, so far these two seem to like me a lot. I know it might be cupboard love, due to the mammaries full of milk and all that, but hey, I'm not going to split hairs."

"So I take it that you've no regrets then? This parenthood thing is not as bad as you previously thought?" I held my head to the side and smiled.

"It's the most amazing thing I've ever done in my life. Why didn't I believe you before now? I should have done this years ago. No wonder the population hasn't ceased growing. This is just wonderful. Em, I was sitting here awake and wired in the middle of the night, staring at my babies and I was thinking that I have you thank for all this." She looked down at the two velvet heads, nuzzled to her.

"How? Am I an unaware sperm donor?"

"No, you big goose! I mean this whole progression thing. If you hadn't found out about your gene, I wouldn't have been inspired to look for Jim. If I hadn't looked for Jim, I wouldn't have been forced to open my heart. Therefore, I wouldn't have fallen in love with Walter and had these pets!" she finished with a happy sigh.

"Your hormones are definitely affecting your head, do you know that?" I laughed. "I like your thinking, but nobody *did* all this but you, honey. What would we have called it as kids? *New You Stew?* Just give me a minute . . ." I closed my eyes the better to concentrate.

She waited, grinning. She knew what was coming next.

"Okay!" I said and then went on slowly and deliberately, looking into her eyes.. "Take one designer gene, add a scalpel and rake up the past. Scratch chin. Wait. Delve into the depths of what you know. Question it further. Open the closed tin of emotion. Mix with new hope and two wonderful men in your life. Serve with newborn twins. Garnish with the happiest expression I've ever seen on your face!"

We both laughed, loving the replaying of our favourite childhood game. The mirth was replaced by quiet comfortable reminiscence as we both got lost in our own thoughts.

"What about you, seeing as we're being so deep? Have you any regrets?" Susie regarded me.

"None. I wouldn't change a thing."

"Really?"

"Yes, really." I stroked Susie's face. "Happy?"

"Definitely. You?" She held my gaze.

"You bet."

I do firmly believe that our lives are mapped out for us by a higher being, that every now and then an angel watching over us decides to intercept. In my case, I was lucky and I'm truly grateful they did.

Next time you see a white feather floating towards you, reach up and catch it. Who knows? Maybe it's sending you a message.

THE END

IN CONVERSATION
WITH EMMA HANNIGAN

1. Have you always written or is it a new discovery?

It's a totally new discovery for me. The closest I've ever come to writing was during a typing course fifteen years ago, where I took up drinking coffee for the first time – purely to keep me awake. I knew that learning the correct way to type would stand to me, as every type of business now involves computers. Little did I know that typing the same mundane sentence over and over again for six weeks would help me on my way to writing a novel. Becoming an author happened quite by accident. I have done a number of other jobs from cooking to beauty therapy to office work, but none of them really floated my boat. Although I enjoyed all my previous jobs and the people I worked with, I never felt I'd found my niche in life. I loved languages in school and adored English class. When we were assigned essays for English homework, most of the class groaned. I loved it. So, although I have no previous experience of writing and have never had anything published before, it's something that feels so comfortable for me already. I just hope that people enjoy reading what I've written.

★ ★ ★ ★

2. Tell us about your writing process. Where do you write? When? Are you a planner or "ride-the-wave" writer?

I have spent quite a lot of time as a patient in various hospitals over the last couple of years. After a short period, magazines and daytime TV began to separate my brain. There was I, the colour of putty, greasy hair stuck to my head and later totally bald, wearing a newly found uniform of surgical gowns or pyjamas if I was lucky, with all these shiny happy people telling me the in-style must-haves. It wasn't relevant to me and made me prone to suicidal tendencies, so eventually I had to make myself a celeb-free zone. Not knowing what else to do, I asked my hubby to bring me a computer laptop. When I began typing I had no preconceived idea that it would turn into a book. I started the exercise as a tool for venting and logging what I was going through. On that first day, I wrote eight thousand words. Once I started writing, (Gaye Shortland, my poor editor, will confirm this) I didn't stop. The characters took on a life of their own – although my fingers were moving on the keys, the story just seemed to evolve of its own accord. Am I a planner or a "ride-the-wave" writer? A bit of both, I think. It's not possible to sit with an empty head and expect to be able to magic a story out of your own arse. You have to have ideas but for me each idea certainly takes on a little life of its own, so the story meanders.

3. There is a lot of humour in *Designer Genes*. Is this a natural style for you or was it difficult to write humour?

No, writing humour is easy for me. I have a rather warped and it has even been suggested by my nearest and dearest, a kind of dark sense of humour, so it's been magical to be allowed to write it down. I am one of those terrible people who end up laughing at the most inopportune moments. I find small children fabulously funny, those times when they say what we're all thinking. I love that. I've had plenty of ups and downs healthwise over the last three years. Although there were hard times and plenty of parts I certainly wouldn't recommend to a friend, I have had some of the best belly laughs imaginable. I see humour in most things in life. I do believe laughter is a magical medicine which goes a long way to helping to heal even the deepest wounds. I would whole-heartedly agree that "a day without laughter is a day without sunshine". My husband used to come into the room when I was writing *Designer Genes*, purely to ask me what was so funny. He has pointed out to me, on numerous occasions, that telling yourself jokes and then laughing at them is a sign of madness. But then again, I'm sure sanity is highly over-rated.

4. In *Designer Genes*, what character & scene was most difficult to write?

Without meaning to sound conceited in any way, I honestly didn't find any of it difficult to write. It was like a dam had burst as soon as I began to type. From the first line to the final full stop, I adored what I was doing. Just to clarify, I am not saying that I think that every word I've written is brilliant or amazing. I have no idea how my book is going to be received. In fact every time I think of people reading it I have to do anti-natal-class type breathing to try and steady my nerves. But as far as the writing part goes, when I turn my computer on I could be in a high-security prison or a five-star hotel and it would all be the same to me. I float away to the land of my own imagination and nothing else matters.

5. Who are your favourite authors and favourite novels and why? And has this influenced your writing style?

My favourite authors have always been the Irish ladies: Cathy Kelly, Marian Keyes, Patricia Scanlon, Melissa Hill. If I see an Irish author, I will buy the book. I suppose I can relate to their stories and sense of humour and I feel comfortable with them. I also love Sophie Kinsella and Helen Fielding. At the moment I am reading a book of short stories by Roald Dahl which is simply brilliant. I loved his books as a child and I am now fortunate enough to be allowed to read them again with my children. His wacky and intensely clever observation of people both enthrals me and makes me laugh out loud. I love books which provoke genuine emotion or leave a lasting impression. I think every book I've ever read from Ladybird to Shakespere has influenced what I've written. I have written from the heart and I just hope that my voice is well received and dare I hope – liked.

6. **Please give us a little teaser of the next book?!**

My next book moves away from all things "medical". It dips into the lives of three very different women.

Angie Breen is approaching forty, her body clock is ticking so loudly she's certain passers-by must be able to hear it. Still single and beginning to despair, she goes to drastic measures to ensure she's not going to end up childless and alone.

Serena Doyle is the ultimate trophy wife. Married to Paul, a dynamic businessman, she is the epitome of poise, glamour and sophistication. A couple of years into their marriage, Paul realises that some cracks are beginning to show. Behind the immaculate exterior, Serena is harbouring a secret of her own. Her struggle to conceive threatens to blow the cover on an issue she's been hiding – even from herself.

Ruby White is sixteen and the very precious only child of a wealthy South Dublin couple. Her parents are in disbelieving shock when she announces her pregnancy. Determined to keep the impending baby a secret from their circle of privileged "it" people, they conjure up a plan to save face and most importantly the family reputation.

With a working title of *Milk and Alcohol*, we meet three very different women and see how the baby bind, and all the issues it brings, affects them.

Laced with fun and tongue-in-cheek humour, it made me laugh while I was writing it, so I hope it will do the same for the people who read it!